Home or Away

Also by Kathleen West

Minor Dramas & Other Catastrophes
Are We There Yet?

Home or Away

Kathleen West

Berkley
New York

BERKLEY
An imprint of Penguin Random House LLC
penguinrandomhouse.com

Copyright © 2022 by Kathleen West
Penguin Random House supports copyright. Copyright fuels creativity, encourages diverse voices, promotes free speech, and creates a vibrant culture. Thank you for buying an authorized edition of this book and for complying with copyright laws by not reproducing, scanning, or distributing any part of it in any form without permission. You are supporting writers and allowing Penguin Random House to continue to publish books for every reader.

BERKLEY and the BERKLEY & B colophon are registered trademarks of Penguin Random House LLC.

Library of Congress Cataloging-in-Publication Data

Names: West, Kathleen, 1978- author.
Title: Home or away / Kathleen West.
Description: New York: Berkley, [2022]
Identifiers: LCCN 2021042008 (print) | LCCN 2021042009 (ebook) | ISBN 9780593335505 (hardcover) | ISBN 9780593335512 (ebook)
Classification: LCC PS3623.E8448 H66 2022 (print) | LCC PS3623.E8448 (ebook) | DDC 813/.6—dc23
LC record available at https://lccn.loc.gov/2021042008
LC ebook record available at https://lccn.loc.gov/2021042009

Printed in the United States of America
1 3 5 7 9 10 8 6 4 2

Title page photograph: Ice Rink © redcarphotography / Shutterstock
Book design by Elke Sigal

To Kevin

Home or Away

CHAPTER ONE

LEIGH MACKENZIE

May 2022

Leigh ran out of the blue house and flung open the back seat of Charlie's station wagon. "You're here!" she shouted. Gus, her nine-year-old, hadn't even had time to undo his seat belt as Leigh dotted his freckled face with kisses. "Welcome home to Minnesota!"

"Mom!" Gus laughed. He tapped the back of her neck half-heartedly, and Leigh remembered those toddler days when he'd dug his fingers into that same spot. Charlie had pried each digit up in order for Leigh to make it out the door for work.

And now, her son was already pushing her away. "Wait until you see the place with paint!" She spun toward Charlie, who enveloped her.

Charlie held his cheek against hers. "Three months is such a long time," he murmured. Their temporary separation had been practical. Leigh had started her new job at Lupine Capital in March as an ill-timed retirement left her boss shorthanded. Meanwhile, Leigh and Charlie both thought Gus would be better off finishing third grade in Tampa.

"It was too long," Leigh agreed as Gus threw an arm around her waist, "but it gave me time to get this place in shape. Come see your room!" She untangled herself from her husband and grabbed his and Gus's hands.

Leigh had been in the blue house for only a week herself after camping in an Airbnb near her parents'. Now, though most of the Mackenzies' belongings were still en route from Florida, they had updated bathrooms, a new kitchen, and fresh paint in every room. Plus, Leigh had just finished the hockey zone in the basement, a surprise she'd manufactured for both her son and her husband.

"I already know where my room is," Gus said. They'd looked at the house on a trip "home," as Leigh still thought of the suburb in which she'd grown up, the previous winter. As they crossed the threshold, Gus dropped her hand and scrambled up the stairs.

"Did you do okay on the last leg of the drive?" Leigh ran her fingers over Charlie's handsome stubble. They'd talked several times in the last few days, and Leigh knew the solo road trip had been taxing.

Charlie rubbed Leigh's biceps, and her skin tingled. "I skipped the Iron Furnace in Illinois, which was clutch," he said. "Turns out that even for me, there's a limit to how many historical markers I'm willing to appreciate."

Leigh laughed. Gus had complained loudly on speakerphone about stops at various roadside attractions. "I'm so happy you're finally here."

"Me too." Charlie kissed her. He tasted familiar, like coffee and peppermint.

"The green is awesome!" Gus bounded down the stairs. "Does Uncle Jamie say it's Lions green?" Gus had been obsessed by Liston

Heights Lions hockey since he was a toddler. Leigh's brother, the boys' varsity coach, kept him well stocked in old practice jerseys.

"He says it's perfect." Leigh raised her eyebrows. "Speaking of perfect, are you two ready for your surprise?"

"Surprise?" Gus balled his hand into a fist and bit a knuckle, clearly excited.

"I did something cool in the basement." Leigh pointed at the door that led to the wide-open furnished space downstairs. Gus sprinted ahead and Leigh pushed Charlie's shoulder. "Go see," she urged.

"You didn't tell me about this." She could smell Charlie's Old Spice wafting behind him and felt overcome by a desire to snuggle in, to let him hold her as they watched something easy on television and sipped drinks. In all their years together, they'd never before spent so much time apart as they had that spring.

"Holy hockey balls!" Gus shrieked from below. She could hear his shoes squeaking on the synthetic ice tiles she'd installed.

"Whoa," Charlie said, catching up. Leigh had transformed the room into a hockey practice facility with a special shooting surface, net, and custom paint job. She'd even ordered decals of several Minnesota Wild players and adhered them to the walls. "When did you have time to do this?" Charlie asked.

Leigh worked a zillion hours a week at Lupine. Between the travel and the research, she had called in a favor from her brother to finish Hockey Zone. "Jamie," she confessed. Her little brother had spent several hours in the Mackenzies' basement, painting the baseboards yellow to simulate a real rink. Leigh had attached a shooting tarp over the net she'd ordered, a picture of a goalie printed on it. When she'd stood back to admire the setup, she had an unexpected desire to shoot on it herself although she hadn't laced up in twenty years.

"My stick is in the car!" Gus ran for the stairs, but Leigh stopped him.

"Jamie left you one of his old ones." She pulled the well-worn Bauer with fresh green tape from its place against the wall. "He also left you these pucks."

"Oh, sick!" Gus overturned the bucket she'd handed him, the pucks scattering in a four-foot radius. "Mom, you can even bend your stick against this stuff!" He grinned at them over his shoulder as he pressed the stick into the tile. Pucks sailed.

"The wall," Charlie whispered, as the third shot missed the net entirely and thunked into the drywall.

"We'll repaint." Leigh shrugged, remembering the myriad holes she'd put in her own parents' basement walls. "It'll be a while before his slapshot is hard enough to do any real damage."

Charlie nuzzled her ear. "I love it when you talk dirty to me."

Leigh giggled and led him up the stairs, leaving Gus to practice. "Let me show you your new office. I said they had to finish the wallpaper before you got here."

"Did you use shark tone?" Charlie tapped her butt cheek as they climbed the second flight. That's what he called her work voice, the one she used for final negotiations.

"Sure did." Leigh pulled him into the empty room they'd decided would be Charlie's study. "I can see you in here, babe," Leigh said, "writing your great American novel."

She hoped Charlie could see it, too, could envision himself glancing up from his manuscript out of the row of south-facing windows at their spacious backyard. Charlie had spent so much time with Gus in the last decade, so much time managing the household and Little Lights Bookstore, where he'd worked for years. He'd hardly done any writing since Gus had been born, though it used to be his passion.

Leigh hoped the move back home would be a fresh start for all of them.

Charlie wandered over to the accent wall and touched the banana-leaf pattern, the same he'd used at Little Lights. The wallpaper had become a mainstay on literary Instagram, with authors posing in front of it whenever they passed through south Florida.

Charlie grinned. "I love it." At forty-two, he was still a ringer for Matthew McConaughey, his double dimples every bit as endearing as her favorite movie star's. Leigh's stomach flipped, and she blushed although they'd been together for more than half their lives. She'd missed him.

"Good spot for your desk?" she asked.

Instead of answering, he pulled her toward him again and put a palm against the back of her head.

Leigh was so relieved that he was finally here that she felt like crying. "Thank you for doing this," she whispered. "For moving back here, for driving Gus all the way. I have a really good feeling about Minnesota, especially now."

"Are you kidding?" Charlie kissed her temple. Leigh melted against him. Months of tension—the stress of starting her new job and coming home to an empty house—dissolved. "You were right about Liston Heights," Charlie said. "It's an amazing opportunity. For all of us."

"Good hockey setup, right?" As she rested her head on Charlie's shoulder, she imagined Gus in his new jersey, celebrating his first goals with his new team.

Sometimes, Leigh still couldn't believe that she had managed to raise a hockey fanatic. When she'd learned she was pregnant, she decided she'd keep her child from skating, an insurance policy against the heartbreak she had experienced at the top of the sport. But her brother had gifted Gus a pair of toddler skates without giving her a heads-up. Her parents had once again installed their backyard rink, and no one could get Gus to come inside on their winter visits home, even with the promise of Santa.

Regardless of her best intentions, by age five, Leigh's son was a superstar in the Tampa Junior Lightning House League. In the most recent season, he'd averaged more than a goal per game.

Gus was clearly talented (a prodigy, his biased uncle said), but Leigh and Charlie balked at the more intense Florida programs that required national travel to find top-level competition for the kindergarten set. In Minnesota, hockey was different. So many kids played the sport that you could find great competition at every park in the Twin Cities metro area.

When an offer of a managing director position at Lupine Capital materialized, Leigh found herself yearning for home. She imagined Gus in a Liston Heights Hockey uniform just like the one she had worn. Though the end of her athletic career had been miserable, the beginning had been magical. Hockey was Minnesota's hometown game, with whole suburbs turning out to cheer on the high school stars. Youth associations like Liston Heights fielded ten teams per age group. There was so much room for Gus to grow here.

As she had described the possibilities to Charlie, he caught her enthusiasm. He'd experienced the culture, too, although from the outside. Leigh had taught him the game when they'd watched her brother's high school team. And after ten years in Florida, Charlie was eager to ditch the unrelenting heat. There were bookstores and coffee shops in Minnesota, too, he said. He could finish his novel anywhere.

"The basement is awesome," Charlie said now, still holding her. "Did you work on finding him a summer team?"

Leigh flinched. This was the hiccup. Moving back had left Leigh with the uncomfortable task of getting in touch with her old teammates and hockey contacts. Leigh was counting on their loyalty, even though she'd left the sport behind on the same day she'd flown home from the Lake Placid Olympic Training Center in 2001. Not six hours after the final cut for the Salt Lake team, she'd catapulted her Minnesota Gophers duffel from the top of her parents' basement stairs onto the concrete below. She'd javelined her stick down there, too, the blade bouncing against the floor. Leigh wished the stick would have at least splintered, if not snapped.

It had been twenty years since Leigh had ghosted everyone after being cut from the team, including Susy Walker, her former best friend, and also their old coach, Jeff. Instagram told her they both lived in Liston Heights. Leigh had thought moving home would be worth it—Lions hockey was the best, and Gus deserved his shot—even though she'd been so careful about keeping her old life separate from the one she built with Charlie and Gus.

Now that she was here, they were all so close to the truth of her past. She had her first moments of doubt as she pulled away from Charlie and led him back to the main floor of their new home.

"Too late for a real summer team," Leigh said over her shoulder. "But Jamie and I got him in with that hotshot coach. First session is next week."

Charlie nodded and walked into the kitchen. From there, they could hear Gus's stick tapping in the basement, the regular thuds of pucks against the shooting tarp. "Last night, I was checking out the Liston Heights Hockey Association page," he said. "You know that your old coach is on the board, right? Jeff Carlson? It says he coached the national team when you were on it, but I didn't really recognize him."

Leigh turned away from her husband and opened the refrigerator. She'd done the same Google search and had read the article about Jeff and Susy coaching together. Jeff had been quoted as saying he "just wanted to pass on the life-changing love of the game to the next generation."

That line had triggered a sudden surge of rage. The game had changed Jeff's life, and he'd so casually ruined hers. If Leigh had known what the end of her hockey career would bring—darkness, self-doubt, a band of regret that she could still feel tightening beneath her diaphragm whenever she stepped inside an ice rink—she wasn't sure she'd ever have started playing. The joy had only just started coming back in the stands, watching her son participate in the sport he loved so much.

Last season, Gus had been obsessed with the spiral notebook that his uncle Jamie had customized for him. In "Gus's Hockey Bible," as the cover read, her son tracked his points, his hours on the ice, and the quotes he'd internalized from coaches. He wanted to be the best. In order to have a legitimate chance, he'd have to adapt to the intensity of Liston Heights, the hotbed of Minnesota hockey.

Although they hadn't talked in years, Leigh knew Susy coached year-round here. She'd seen the Instagram posts. Her old friend and rival stood on the bench, towering over the players, her arms crossed. Leigh had never coached her kid's team. Though she could watch games from the stands, she'd never been able to get back on the ice after the Olympic selections. Jeff and Susy knew exactly why that was.

"Damn," Leigh said as she stared into the fridge. "Charlie, I meant to pick you up some IPAs and I forgot."

"It's no problem—" Leigh spun around and caught her husband's look of disappointment. She had ordered pizza for the three of them to be delivered in forty-five minutes. After the road trip, Charlie certainly deserved a beer alongside his pepperoni.

Leigh cut him off. "It's five minutes away," she said. "And I'm almost out of gin, too. I'll be right back." She pointed at the new sectional she'd ordered for the family room. "Take a load off."

CHAPTER TWO

SUSY WALKER

May 2022

Susy went straight from the handoff with her ex-husband in the high school parking lot to the liquor store closest to her townhome. Since her new place didn't have a cavernous pantry and sleek beverage cooler, she made more frequent trips to the store than when she and Dirk had been married. But it had been easy to downsize after he finally admitted to sleeping with half of the Swedish national hockey team.

Susy studied the six-packs on the usual shelf. She always picked the same Fat Tire. It wasn't as basic as her old go-to Rolling Rock, but it wasn't fussy, either. After she paid, the bell rang over the door, and Susy glanced up. Leigh Mackenzie walked in. Susy dropped her wallet. She'd imagined a million times running into Leigh. After all they'd been through, Leigh evaporated after Lake Placid, as if not making the Olympic team erased all of their years of friendship. This was definitely Leigh now, though—brown curls, straight back, pointy chin. Susy thought of her even more frequently since the flurry of messages had crowded the '02 and '06 Olympic team group chats the previous spring. Someone had finally lodged a formal complaint against Jeff Carlson after years of rumors. Leigh, as she was absent from the Team USA alumni groups, likely had no idea.

Susy reached for her fallen wallet. She lingered at the adjacent door and watched Leigh squint at the gin bottles. Her freckled cheekbones were still reasonably sharp. She'd scooped her shoulder-length hair into a ponytail at the back of her neck. Susy should say something.

"Leigh," Susy croaked.

"Excuse me?" The cashier had finished ringing up the next customer.

"Oh, nothing. Thanks." Susy walked out and then, when she stood even with her car door, turned back to stare at the shop. Her old friend exited a couple of minutes later. Susy could see the extra padding around Leigh's middle, though she was hiding it pretty well beneath a flowy top. Her hips, too, while always strong, were wider. Susy looked down at her own muscular quads in Nike golf shorts. She weighed herself each Saturday morning, a holdover habit from her college days. She'd actually shed weight since her last Olympics in '06. It was natural, as she no longer spent long hours in the weight room beefing up to face the Canadians and the Swedes.

Susy pictured Astrid Nilsson, the defender from the Swedish national team, whose texts were the ones she first found on Dirk's phone. That woman had to be over two bills, quads each larger than a Christmas goose. Leigh looked different from that. Softer. Still beautiful. Leigh meandered into the second row of the lot toward an Audi with Florida plates, a brown bag tucked under her arm and a six-pack in her hand.

"Leigh?" Susy's voice was louder now, despite nerves that rivaled those she tamed in the face-off circle. Certainly, with the Salt Lake City Olympics twenty years in the past, the two former teammates could talk.

Leigh scanned the parking lot before finding her.

"Leigh? Is that you?" Of course it was her. Susy had traveled to thirty or more cities with this woman, slept six feet from her for months at a time. If things had ended differently, Leigh would be like a sister. Instead, Susy felt like she was approaching a ghost.

Leigh reached into her car, and for a second Susy thought she'd just go, ignore her. Instead, Leigh put her bag on the front seat and stood up. She'd plastered a smile on her face in the interval, the same one Susy had seen in Leigh's recent company headshot via Google.

"Hey, Suse." Her tone was casual, as if Leigh had expected to talk to her, as if they'd agreed to meet right there.

"What are you doing here?" Susy pointed at Leigh's license plate. "Did you drive up for vacation?"

Leigh leaned against the open doorjamb, still grinning. "We moved here. My husband and son just got here, actually."

"Charlie?" Susy asked.

"You remember him?" Leigh reached a hand up to smooth a stray curl away from her sunglasses.

"You don't forget Jake Brigance." Susy laughed. The two of them had rented *A Time to Kill* after the house party where Leigh had drunkenly kissed Charlie in the corner. They'd paused on close-ups of Matthew McConaughey's face and analyzed the similarities between him and Leigh's new conquest. The second they'd walked into that party, they'd spotted Charlie. Leigh had swung an arm in front of Susy's chest and growled, "Mine."

"Right." Leigh ground her toe into a pebble. Several black smudges stood out against the white soles of her Vans. Leigh had always loved those sneakers. She'd worn a bright pink pair in the airport en route to Lake Placid all those years ago.

"You moved back? When?" Susy hoped for a moment that the

two of them might have dinner together or a drink, but then she flashed back to the decision room, the way Leigh had jerked her arm away from Susy's hand as Coach Miller skipped on the list from Looney to Merz. There would be no Mackenzie on the Olympic team. After that, friendship had proved impossible.

Leigh looked over Susy's shoulder. There was a crease next to her lips, a deep smile line that hadn't been there when the two had celebrated wins in the season before the Salt Lake Olympics. "I started a new job in March." Leigh tapped the roof of the car. "And my parents are still here, and Jamie. And the truth is, Gus wants to play Minnesota hockey, and I can't stop thinking about him having that experience. He finished third grade in Tampa, and he and Charlie just got here tonight." Leigh smiled. "I came here for Charlie's IPAs."

"That's awesome," Susy said, meaning it. "I coach here, you know. In Liston Heights."

Leigh nodded. "I've seen on Instagram. I bet you're great."

Susy teared up. The emotion surprised her. She had two Olympic medals at home, but still Leigh's opinion mattered. "You know Jeff's here, too, right?" Susy blurted it and then covered her lips with her fingers. This segue hadn't been part of her hasty reunion plan.

"I realize that," Leigh spoke slowly. "But I've left that part of my life completely behind. I don't need anyone to know anything except that I'm a regular hockey mom now."

Susy held her breath for a second. Leigh should know the latest. "Okay. But some people do know some things. There are some updates about Jeff." She wished she could skip over this part. When she imagined seeing Leigh again, it was silly stuff she thought of first: the USA chants, their stupid joke about Zoolander's Blue Steel, all the nights they stayed up late talking until one of them—usually Susy—fell asleep.

Leigh's face flushed in a millisecond, in exactly the same way Susy remembered, bright red from her collarbone to her temples.

"Yeah." Leigh sat down on her driver's seat and left both feet flat on the parking lot's yellow spray paint. "I was worried about that. More people know what happened in Lake Placid?"

Susy didn't mention Leigh's name in the '02 group text last spring when the team speculated about who might sign on to the complaint against Jeff. Leigh had always been private. "There's an official complaint against him now," Susy said. "You weren't the only one—"

Leigh raised a hand to cut her off. "It was a huge mistake." She kept her eyes on the ground. "My biggest."

Susy felt a little nauseous having landed in such fraught territory right off the bat, but she still didn't want Leigh to leave. "Are you playing summer hockey?"

Leigh pulled her feet into the car, but she didn't shut the door. "Me or Gus?"

"I meant Gus," Susy said. *Gus.* Leigh had named her son after her father, the soft-eyed man that Susy had seen on so many sidelines, even in tiny towns when the women's national team had played high school boys for practice. They'd had no bigger fan.

"What kind of hockey does Gus have to play this summer to be competitive? I was going to ask you that, actually, once I worked up the courage to message you." Leigh cracked the knuckles on her index fingers, the same way she always had before she put on her gloves.

Leigh was nervous, too. Susy felt better about her own jitters. "He wants to make Liston Heights Squirt A this fall? There's a spot on my triple-A team." Susy pulled out her phone.

Leigh bit her lip. "I don't think he's quite ready? We're going to spend the summer doing catch-up, so he has a shot in the fall. He's been playing house league in Tampa." She put her hand on the door handle, ready to close it.

"They're nine." Susy shrugged. "Lots of time. Can I give you my number? You can ask me whatever you want."

"Text me," Leigh said, and recited the digits as Susy entered them into a message. She searched Slim Shady GIFs on a whim and smiled as she sent a blinking Eminem. They'd listened to him nonstop in their final summer together.

"You've got my number now," Susy said. "Again."

Leigh turned her key in the ignition. "Thanks." She half smiled. "See you soon, I guess."

Susy waved as Leigh closed her door and wished she'd thought to ask for a spontaneous drink. Although, twenty years was quite a large chasm to bridge in one chance meeting.

CHAPTER THREE

LEIGH MACKENZIE

May 2022

Leigh felt so flustered after the parking lot encounter with Susy that muscle memory took her back "home" to her parents' street before she realized she hadn't routed herself to the new house.

She pulled her car over at the end of her parents' block, the toxic memories gripping her. Susy's fingers had snaked over Leigh's knuckles in Lake Placid. "Looney," Coach Miller had said, reading the roster in alphabetical order. Leigh had held her breath; she remembered a silent *Please.*

But Coach said, "Merz." He said, "Mleczko." And then Leigh had swatted Susy's hand away. There was no Mackenzie on the Olympic team.

For the rest of their lives, people would introduce Susy as a medalist. And Leigh had nothing to show for every sacrifice and every early-morning practice and every slam into the boards. All of it, all seventeen years in the sport, had been for nothing. After Leigh pushed her friend's hand away, only pride kept her from slamming her forehead into the table in front of her.

Everything had been over in that half second, and the pain of the moment had impaled Leigh. She had spent twenty years trying to breathe again. She'd chased an adrenaline rush in finance, but even though the stakes in her career were millions of dollars, nothing was the same as scoring a winning goal. And she hadn't been able to face anyone in hockey, especially not Susy, who'd had her dreams realized just seconds after Leigh's were decimated.

Leigh blinked at her parents' house and turned on her signal, ready to make her way back to her adorable family. The phone rang, and the console showed it was Charlie.

"Sorry!" Leigh could hear the emotion in her voice as she answered.

"You okay?" he asked. "I got worried."

In her mind, Leigh still sat for the moment in the Lake Placid decision room. Her whole body convulsed the way it had when Coach Miller had excised her. Only Charlie had been able to make that heartache dissipate even a little. And she'd kept such terrible secrets from him anyway, secrets whose keepers were right there in Liston Heights.

Leigh hadn't anticipated the complications of the move, and seeing Susy again brought back flashes of the two weeks of selection camp, memories she'd managed to escape for longer and longer periods of time as she aged.

"I'm okay," Leigh said, willing it. "I just ran into Susy at the store." Leigh wiped a stray tear from her cheek. "Weird, right? On Gus's first night here when we're trying to get him on her team?"

"That seems like a good omen." Charlie laughed. "He's still in the basement, Leigh. I just checked on him. He's shooting like twenty pucks a minute. You were right about him deserving a chance in Minnesota hockey. He's excited. *I'm* excited."

"Let's make it happen, then." Leigh forced herself to relax her shoulders, pushing Lake Placid back down with them. She stared at her parents' second-floor window, the one that used to be hers. All of her ambition had been cultivated in that house, and all her failure lived there, too. Leigh didn't want Gus to associate any negativity with their new home. She didn't want him to have any regrets. "It'll be intense," she said, "but if he's willing to work for it, I'll do whatever it takes to make this move worthwhile."

CHAPTER FOUR

EMAIL FROM HEAD MANAGER CATHY KELLIHER

June 2022

Dear Liston Heights Hockey FAM!!!

It's me, your plucky head manager, sending out the first email of the new hockey year.

The peonies are blooming and the temps are rising, but let's remember: there's no such thing as an off-season for the world's greatest game. This message (YES, I expect you to READ THE WHOLE THING) details hockey training opportunities for your soon-to-be Squirts, but before I get into them, permit me to reiterate some of the Liston Heights Hockey Association core principles.

We list RESPECT and INTEGRITY first for a reason. If we're not good people, then it hardly matters if we're good players. Let's embark on our summer training with our priorities in line. In fact, please click the link below to order your SUMMER OF SPORTSMANSHIP T-shirt. In doing so, you'll support the association's scholarship fund, always a worthy cause.

While it's tempting to hang up your skates for the summer months, those players with their eyes on the top levels need to use this time to sharpen their skills along with their blades. Muscle memory will carry us only so far, parents. But, lucky for our LIONS SQUIRTS, we're offering myriad opportunities for every level. (And let me tell you, you don't want to wish you'd trained just a tiny bit harder come tryouts. This group of Squirts is highly skilled, and the kids had better be ready.)

Click the link at the close of this message to review open spots on summer teams, extra clinics, dryland training, shooting sessions, pond hockey leagues, private coaching, and more. As the legendary coach Bob Johnson reminds us, "It's a great day for hockey."

He meant every day, folks.

I am yours on the rink and off (but let's be real, mostly ON!)

Cathy

P.S. Go Lions!

CHAPTER FIVE

CHARLIE MACKENZIE

June 2022

The Mackenzie family had been in Minnesota together for just four days, not even enough time for Charlie to hit the nearby park for a run, when he drove Gus to his first session with Rob Greystone, the hockey coach he and Jamie had enlisted. According to Jamie, who'd already warned Charlie that Gus was "Florida good," this coach could transform him ahead of fall tryouts.

"And I practice with him alone?" Gus asked as they arrived.

Charlie pointed at the door to Greystone's Greytness Hockey Training, a storefront buried in an industrial complex. "Yeah, it's just you and him," he said. "Big opportunity."

Gus pursed his lips and nodded. Charlie himself would have killed for a training opportunity like this as a kid. Hockey, with its cost and time commitment, had been impossible. As it was, Charlie made his own way in distance running. While the pinnacle of his organized sports career was a runner-up T-shirt from an intramural basketball tournament at Macalester College, he had compiled a growing list of ultramarathon finishes, including a 50K in stifling humidity the previous spring. He felt the same waves of adrenaline watching Gus play hockey as he did in his own races.

Inside Greytness, they walked toward a small ice rink with three training areas separated by floor-to-ceiling netting. A kid and a coach worked in each stall. Though Charlie couldn't discern their words through the glass, he could hear the coaches' whoops as the skaters finished their stick-handling challenges.

"How old are those kids?" Gus asked. Charlie squinted. One was definitely a few years older than Gus, but the other two looked about his size. Their agility seemed more developed, their reflexes faster. Jamie was right about the talent pool in Minnesota.

"I'm not sure." Charlie felt jittery and regretted his second cup of coffee.

"They're good." Gus reached for Charlie's hand, a gesture that had become more and more infrequent as third grade passed.

"Don't be nervous, okay?" Charlie bent to whisper in his son's ear. "It's just the first lesson. Plenty of time to get things down." He kissed his temple, which smelled of coconut shampoo.

Gus swatted at Charlie's face. "Dad," he said. "Stop!"

"Welcome!" A young guy in a Wild cap appeared. "Is this Gus?"

Gus kicked the carpet, eyes down. His reddish hair—the same shade as Charlie's—flopped over his forehead.

"Hi." Charlie stepped toward the desk. "I'm Charlie Mackenzie, and this is Gus."

The guy clicked the mouse. "Ah! Florida, right? I know your uncle Jamie. I'm Joe." He grinned, revealing a gold cap on the lower half of a canine tooth. An errant puck had likely been responsible, the metal a badge of hockey honor. "You good, Gus? Excited?"

"My uncle Jamie says I'm 'Florida good' at hockey, not 'Minnesota good,'" Gus said.

Charlie gasped. He hadn't realized Gus had heard that particular conversation. Joe rested his forearms on the counter. "Does that mean you think you're behind?"

Gus shrugged. "I guess." He looked up at Charlie. "Dad, isn't that why we came here? For like, tutoring?"

"We're just here for—" Charlie started, but Joe interrupted.

"Tons of top-level kids come here. How old are you? Eight?"

"My birthday was May fifteenth."

"Right, nine." Joe nodded. "Did you know that the youngest player in the NHL is nineteen?"

"Quinton Byfield," Gus said. "The Ontario Reign."

"Good one!" Joe gave Gus a fist bump across the counter. "So, if my math is right, that means you've got at least ten years. Probably more."

Gus shrugged, and Joe pointed at the locker room on the other side of the lobby. "Change in there, okay? Super important to bring your A game. You ready, Florida?" Joe pointed two finger guns at Gus.

"Yep." Gus offered a finger gun of his own. "I'll come out when I need help with my skates." Gus grabbed his bag from Charlie's shoulder and dragged it away.

"Thanks," Charlie said to Joe.

"No worries. Hey, once you're done tying the skates, head up to the viewing room, stairs to the left of the ice. We don't want parents watching from down here. Keeps the focus on the work, you know?"

"Okay." Charlie backed away. He glanced at a sign above the rink. "No excuses," it said. Another affixed next to it read, "No regrets."

"He's in," Charlie texted Leigh. "And we're not in Kansas anymore."

As soon as Charlie had tied Gus's skates, Rob Greystone appeared. Charlie recognized his square jaw from his headshot on the website.

Greystone tucked his right hockey glove under his arm and offered his hand. Charlie hadn't re-embraced handshakes post-pandemic, but Greystone was doing Gus a favor. Charlie grabbed his sweaty palm and pumped. "I've heard good things about you Mackenzies!" Rob turned to Gus and offered the same hand.

Charlie and Leigh had drilled Gus on unnecessary touching, as well. Gus eyed Greystone's outstretched fingers and lightly touched his palm against the coach's in a horizontal high five.

"Good enough." Greystone laughed. "Okay, so. What are we after today?" He tapped his stick against Gus's shin pads.

Gus spoke before Charlie could answer. "I want to make the A-team."

Rob cocked an eyebrow. "Ambition! You're already on the right track. So it's June now." Greystone pointed at the calendar mounted over the desk where they'd checked in. "That gives us, what? Four months before tryouts? And seven months until the Nova Tournament?"

The Mackenzies had talked about Nova over the years, seen pictures of Jamie playing there as a fourth grader. "I guess so." Charlie noticed Gus's square shoulders and strong eye contact. He looked like Leigh on the morning of a big negotiation. Even his freckles seemed earnest. "Can I do it?"

Greystone shrugged. "Honestly? I have no idea, but you're here and willing to work, right?"

Gus grabbed his stick from the rack against the locker room wall. "I'm a super hard worker." He lumbered toward the ice. "Everyone says so." His freckles weren't the only thing he'd inherited from Leigh.

"Well, then." Rob followed him. "Let's get started." Charlie's chest swelled as he jogged up the steps toward the viewing area. He watched Greystone lead Gus through a set of one-footed turns. The contrast between Gus and the kid in the adjacent stall glared. Charlie's heart fluttered. Gus looked slow and wobbly, especially on his left foot.

Forty-five minutes later, Charlie met Gus in the lobby, his grin as wide as it had been when Charlie had announced they'd skip the stop at the Iron Furnace Historical Site on their recent pass through Illinois.

"Dad, did you see?" Gus blurted. "My soft touches got so much smoother, and I didn't even move my right elbow on that last set!"

"Florida's a natural." Greystone knocked the top of Gus's helmet. "Go change. I'll talk with your dad about what's next. We'll have you dangling in no time."

Gus's gait had become a swagger. When Charlie looked back at Greystone, though, his face had gone grave.

"Level with you?" The coach towered over Charlie in his skates. "I'm iffy on the October tryouts."

"Oh." Charlie's cheeks flushed. He'd been convinced by Greystone's pep talk, which had been meant for Gus.

"Look, the kid *is* a natural. I don't bullshit. But he'll need a ton of training to have a shot in Liston Heights." He walked toward the computer. "So . . ." Greystone clicked decisively. The printer whirred on the far side of the counter. "Here's what I'm proposing." Rob slid the paper in front of Charlie. "I think we should start with two or three times per week. We'll alternate between stick handling, skating, and shooting. The skating sessions, we'll do earlier in the mornings, so we don't have to share the ice."

Charlie's eyes roamed over the prescribed appointments, looking for some indication of price. Rob's thick finger, his cuticle raw, finally directed Charlie to the bottom line. "I'm thinking we can bill this as a package. I'm estimating sixty-four hundred dollars for the summer, with maybe a little extra just before tryout clinics begin."

Charlie hesitated, but he knew what Leigh and Jamie would say. Anything to increase the likelihood of Gus's dreams coming true. "Okay. Let's go for it. There's only one chance to catch up, right?"

"You're at a critical juncture," Greystone said. "Time to capitalize."

The locker room door squeaked open behind them. Charlie looked over his shoulder at Gus. "Okay?" Gus asked.

"We charge monthly," Greystone said.

Charlie presented his credit card. "We'll be back the day after tomorrow."

CHAPTER SIX

GUS MACKENZIE

June 2022

Monday, June 6, 2022
Event: 1st Session at Rob Greystone's Greytness
 Hockey Training
Hockey Minutes This Week: 45
Lifetime Hours: 307
Quote from Coach Greystone: "Keep your head up."

"So, was it good?" his dad asked as they drove out of the parking lot.

"Yeah." Gus reached for the notebook he kept in the car, a journal Uncle Jamie had sent him at the beginning of the previous season to keep track of his hockey minutes. "Gus's Hockey Bible" was printed below an outline of a skater. Uncle Jamie said on their

FaceTime calls that more time on the ice was the key to Gus "fulfilling his potential." He said it would take 10,000 hours to become the best hockey player he could be.

Gus wrote his stats with the pen he kept clipped in the journal's spiral. Today was a good fresh start. Coach Greystone had said he was "a natural." His minutes with him would add up. Besides actual skating, the only other things that counted toward the 10,000 hours were stick-handling drills and shooting. With the basement hockey zone, Gus would be able to add those faster, too.

It was a good thing because 10,000 hours—600,000 minutes—was too many. He'd asked his teacher to help him with the math and together they'd figured out that at his current rate, Gus wouldn't get to 10,000 hours until he was seventy-seven or seventy-eight years old. That was too late for the NHL. Gus had asked his mom how old her parents were. Gram was seventy-two, and Big Gus was seventy-one. Even when Gus was little, they'd said they were too old to ice-skate. Stamkos, the center on the Tampa Bay Lightning, was only thirty-one, and people already wondered when he would retire. Gus had to get to 10,000 hours before he was thirty.

He finished adding his forty-five minutes to the journal and pictured Coach Greystone crouched in a ready stance, passing pucks to Gus over and over as he skated back and forth on the tiny rink. He replayed everything Greystone had said about focus and vision. "Keep your head up," Gus wrote.

"Can we stop by and see Big Gus and Gram?" Gus asked as he finished.

Gus knew this would be a "yes." His parents had told him that one of the big benefits of moving "home," as they called it, was seeing his grandparents. He'd been to their house twice already in only his first four days in Liston Heights. Gram kept gumdrops in a crystal dish. She had miniature cans of ginger ale in a little refrigerator next to the dishwasher. Maybe now, in Minnesota, he'd spend afternoons with his grandparents. In Tampa, he used to go to his dad's bookstore after school. Since his dad was the assistant manager, Gus sometimes got a free cookie from the café or an early copy of the latest *Stick Dog*. Gus had camped in the back room or in the children's section of Little Lights Bookstore for at least as much time each week as he spent in the rink. If they hadn't moved to Minnesota, Gus might have become a 10,000-hour expert in bookstores before he became a professional hockey player. That wouldn't be as "prestigious"—his mother had taught him that word—but at least there were the cookies.

Kiddo!" Big Gus air-fived him in the driveway of their yellow house. Gus's grandpa held a leaf blower and wore a Minnesota Gophers cap.

"Hi, Big Gus! I had hockey!" His grandfather loved hockey as much as Uncle Jamie did. Big Gus had already told him he'd watch every single game Gus played in a Liston Heights uniform, home or away.

"You're all sweaty," Big Gus said. "How many minutes you get today?"

"Forty-five." Gus ran from the car to the front door and peered in the window. The candy dish with the heavy lid sat on a table just inside.

"Total lifetime hours?"

"Not quite three hundred and eight," Gus called after him as Big Gus walked away into the garage.

"Ah."

Gus looked in the window again at the candy. His mouth started to water.

"I think someone's after your gumdrops." Gus's dad stood in the driveway.

"Yeah," Gus admitted, "but I also want to see the pictures again in Mom's room." He'd been up there the day before. He'd seen the photos of his mom playing hockey lots of times, but it was different now that he was joining the exact same team she'd been on.

"He asked for you guys," Gus's dad said.

"We'll keep him for a bit." Big Gus winked. "I bet you have some house errands to do, right? Leave the kid here."

"It's okay?" Gus's dad asked.

"You kidding?" Big Gus put both of his arms around Gus's shoulders. "I've been waiting to be neighbors with this hockey champion for nine years."

Gus opened the door and headed straight for the gumdrops. There were six green ones right on top. He tried to accumulate all of them in his palm while holding the lid in his other hand.

"Very ambitious!" Gram, wearing a Liston Heights Hockey T-shirt, appeared from the kitchen. "Ambitious" was another word Gus had heard from his mother. He had a mental list of them he sometimes repeated to himself in warm-ups.

Prestigious, ambitious, tenacious, relentless.

"Let me hold the top for you." Gram grabbed the lid. Gus shoved the first two gumdrops straight into his mouth.

"So you had a hockey lesson?" Big Gus asked while he chewed.

Gus shifted the candy into his cheek so he could speak. "It was just me and the coach. Power turns and stick handling." A drop of spit projected from Gus's mouth on "stick" and landed on the table.

Big Gus swiped it away with his thumb and rubbed Gus's sweaty head with the same hand. "Atta boy," he said. "Getting after it."

Gus swallowed. "Gram," he said, grinning, "I'm up to three hundred and seven lifetime hours."

"Whoa." Gram counted on her fingers. "How many days is that?"

"Almost thirteen," Gus told her, "which isn't really enough for the NHL. It's less than a half of a percent of all my days alive." His teacher had helped with that math, too.

Gram shrugged. "Well, maybe there's more to life than hockey."

Gus shook his head. "Nope," he told her. She was clueless. "Not if you're a Mackenzie."

Big Gus pulled him into a hard side hug. "Sure enough." He chuckled. "Now, bring that candy with you while I dig up those pictures of your mom." Gus followed him up the stairs. "I wish I'd tallied *her* lifetime hours," Big Gus said. "You might be even more tenacious than she was."

"Tenacious," Gus repeated.

"You know what it means?" They turned into his mom's old bedroom. Gus stared at the plaque in the middle of her bookshelf. It had a picture of his mom on one side and "National Champions" engraved on the other.

Gus knew this one by heart. "It means you don't give up no matter what."

Big Gus walked over to the plaque and touched an empty spot next to it. "This was where your mom always planned to put her Olympic medal."

Gus rested his head against Big Gus's rib cage. "But she never went to the Olympics," he said.

"Right again." He could feel Big Gus's sigh. "She almost made it, but not quite."

CHAPTER SEVEN

LEIGH MACKENZIE

August 2001

Twenty-one-year-old Leigh saw four players she knew in the Minneapolis–Saint Paul gate area, but she didn't pause her mix CD to say hello. The song "I'm Blue" began just as Leigh approached the window overlooking the plane. She put her hand against it and felt the radiant heat of the August morning despite the concourse's aggressive air-conditioning. On the ground below, squat trolleys rolled up, and guys in fluorescent vests attached a ramp to the belly of the airplane. A University of Minnesota Duluth duffel slid onto the conveyor, and Leigh's heart skipped.

The bag was definitely Susy Walker's. Though they talked at least weekly, Leigh hadn't seen her in person since the team had lost the World Championship final to Canada the previous April. Leigh missed Susy. Something felt different between them as the weeks before the selection camp dwindled. It wasn't as if they could crash basement parties together or fill Solo cups with Rolling Rock. So intense was their training that they didn't even have any news to report to each other beyond ice time.

The Olympics required singular focus. The longest break Leigh had taken from her skating-and-strength-training regimen had been the day she'd crewed for Charlie at the Headwaters fifty-mile race. Leigh had worried that helping him would be too exhausting, but it turned out that running the final miles with Charlie had been the most inspiring hour of the summer. He stumbled toward the finish line, where her entire family rioted. She thought of Olympic medals as Charlie collapsed across the finish line. Leigh's father had hoisted him up, all back slaps and bear hugs.

At the World Championships just three months before, Susy had stood against the boards as the clock ticked down on the one-goal game. Leigh had gone out as the sixth attacker when the US had pulled their goalie. The score had been 3–2. In the last twenty seconds, Granato took a hard slap shot from the point, which was deflected off the Canadian goaltender's paddle. It skittered past Ruggiero on the blue line. Seven seconds to go and the puck was in no-man's-land. It would've taken a miracle.

Leigh had fallen to her knees at the buzzer and clunked her helmet against the ice as the Canadians dogpiled on the other end. The picture of Leigh with her face on the rink—she could still feel the frost against her chin—had made the paper. And the privilege of that soul-crushing disappointment, of being on the ice as the game ended, made Leigh even more hopeful that she would make the Olympic team. She had been among the best prospects the previous season. Still, anything could happen. Susy could have overtaken her in the months since that loss.

Susy's bag disappeared into the airplane along with a pair of taped-together sticks. Leigh's only certain advantage over Susy and everyone else was Jeff Carlson, their assistant coach.

"Let's stay in touch." Jeff had grabbed Leigh's forearm as she'd prepared to leave the arena after the World Champs. His fingers had been hot against her clammy skin. "I can help you prepare for the Olympic selection camp, you know?" He'd leaned in, his breath smelling of corn chips. The following week, Leigh had gotten a letter from Jeff. He'd torn it from a spiral notebook with the fringes still attached and filled it entirely with his compact printing. The first paragraph was a recap of her game versus Russia, the rush he'd felt in his belly when she'd connected with Looney and the shot had gone in.

Leigh's hands had shaken with nerves and something else—pride?—as she read the letter. Though they'd been friendly, Jeff, the youngest and hottest of the assistants, had never singled her out. In the second paragraph, Coach had said he imagined burying his face in her hair. He wondered what it would feel like to be alone with her. Her eyes were the deepest brown, the most complicated he'd ever seen.

After she'd read that part, Leigh had dropped the letter on her bed. She'd covered her eyes with open fingers as she picked up the paper and read the rest. When she was finished, she looked up at the bulletin board she'd packed with overlapping pictures of her and Charlie. Her latest favorite was one from last summer when Leigh had visited the Ward family in Michigan for a week. Charlie had snuck into the guest bedroom every night. Leigh remembered blushing over coffee in the mornings, certain his family knew what they'd been up to.

And now here was Jeff writing about her complicated eyes. Leigh belonged on the Olympic team, he said. She imagined herself walking in the opening ceremonies, saw the blue line on the ice beneath her skates as officials ringed her neck with a gold medal.

At the gate, Leigh watched her Gophers bag launch onto the conveyor belt. Jeff's letter had extended onto the back side of the paper. Coach Miller trusted him, Jeff wrote. Both men thought she could be a goal scorer, a game changer. Would Leigh write him back? Would she use the enclosed phone card to call him? They could strategize. Strategize and get to know each other even better. "I'm drawn to you," Jeff had written.

Leigh had tipped over on the bed at that line, just as she had collapsed on the ice two months before. And then she'd dialed. When Jeff picked up, Leigh's nerves evaporated. They settled into easy banter, exactly the type she'd thought nothing of in practice. The two of them had been friends, kind of. Or at least friendly.

And Leigh would do anything to make the Olympic team. That's what everyone, including her parents and Charlie, always said about her. It had been a compliment. Her ambition, her tenacity, her maximum effort when other people settled for just enough. All of these things had been celebrated since she was a little girl.

In the months since Jeff's letter had arrived, Leigh had frequented the weight room. She'd played men's league with a couple of the other Minnesota women. She'd shown up for conditioning and eschewed alcohol save for the beer she'd clinked against Charlie's after the Headwaters finish. And Leigh had talked to Jeff a couple of times per week, using the phone cards he continued to send. Mostly they talked about the game, but sometimes he mentioned her beauty, her humor.

Leigh had almost convinced herself there was nothing wrong with what was going on between them, except that she hadn't told Charlie or her parents about it. It would be worth the secret-keeping when she made the team, when she made them all proud.

CHAPTER EIGHT

LEIGH MACKENZIE

September 2022

On your way out?" Leigh's boss, the managing partner of Lupine Capital, poked his head into her office. It had been six months now since she'd started, and Fred had been getting more chatty as she racked up deals.

Leigh closed her laptop. The pad of her thumb hit the edge of her RBG sticker. "Women belong in all places where decisions are being made." Gus had read it to her proudly the previous Christmas.

"You need something?" Leigh asked Fred. She planned to meet her brother for a quick dinner while Charlie took Gus to Greystone's. Then, Charlie had promised Gus drive-thru as a prize for crossing the 400-lifetime-hockey-hour mark. Jamie had created a monster with that hockey bible. Leigh had started several texts to Susy about it and deleted all but one. Susy would love it. She'd love Gus! She'd even said so in her friendly reply. And yet, every time Leigh felt drawn back to that friendship, she remembered the Lake Placid decision room, the calm sound of Coach Miller's voice humiliating her. Susy had seen how confident Leigh had been beforehand. Leigh had told her she was 99.9 percent sure the Olympics were a done deal. And then Susy had won silver without her.

Fred leaned against the door and glanced at the painting Leigh had hung across from her desk. "I don't need anything specific." He pointed at the art. "That's nice."

"Thanks." Leigh loved the abstract pink and red piece. She glanced at the familiar brushstrokes, the subtle rusty tones she hadn't seen until she'd really looked at it. Leigh had told Jamie she'd meet him by six. She zipped her tote and hoped her boss would take the hint.

"So . . ." He knocked the doorjamb. "This might be awkward."

Leigh mentally flipped through the events of the last week. She hadn't had any questionable interactions with Fred or anyone else. Her fact-finding trip to Kansas City had gone well, as had her strategy session with a new partner. Leigh ran her tongue over her teeth, checking for embarrassing lunch remnants that Fred might feel compelled to point out. Nothing.

"Hit me." She smiled. The men for whom she worked generally liked Leigh's straightforward demeanor, her ease with sports metaphors, and taste for gin.

Fred closed the office door behind him. "Your brother is the varsity coach for the Liston Heights boys' hockey team. Is that right? His name is Mackenzie, too?"

"That's right." Leigh relaxed. Whatever Fred wanted, it wasn't about her job performance. "We're all Mackenzies. Even convinced my husband to take the name."

"That's a confident man."

Leigh shrugged. People acted like Charlie was a hero, but the truth was he liked her three-syllable name better than Ward. Fred hesitated. "So?" Leigh prompted.

"So, I know this is delicate." Fred chewed the edge of his thumbnail. Leigh's initial apprehension dissolved into full-on amusement. Her boss was unflappable, a hard-ass who dismantled companies like he was pouring flat soda out on hot asphalt, and here he was off-balance about something related to high school hockey. "Obviously, I recruited you because you're the best in the consumer sector. But my son Lincoln also plays hockey at Liston Heights. He's a junior. He's been working his butt off in the off-season, and I think he'll be on the bubble at this fall's tryouts. He played JV last year."

"Listen," Leigh said, "I don't have much of anything to do with Jamie's coaching decisions."

"Sure, yeah. I just thought—" Leigh recognized the desperate look in Fred's eyes. She remembered the truth she'd discovered in Lake Placid years before: someone else's snap coaching decision could change everything, forever.

"I'll mention it to him." Leigh smiled. "Put in a good word. I know a little something about being on the bubble."

"Thank you. I know you do." Fred's eyes morphed from desperate to guilty. "I googled. I'm . . ." He turned and opened the door. "I'm sorry about '02."

At the pub, Leigh's brother had already ordered her usual gin and ginger.

"I could get used to drinking with my sister." Leigh still thought of Jamie as a kid. She'd schooled Charlie in hockey as they'd watched Jamie's games. Her husband had known nothing—not icing, not offsides, not shifts. They'd made out after the games, Leigh doling out kisses for correct answers about strategy. Now Charlie talked about hockey more than he did about anything else.

"Something so funny happened on my way out of the office," Leigh said. "You know Fred Page? My boss?"

"Page. Like Lincoln Page?" Jamie sipped his beer. "The kid in my program?"

"I didn't realize you had a connection. Fred assured me he hired me for my mad skills and not for an in with my baby brother."

Jamie grinned. "Well, I'm very influential and important."

"Right." Leigh rolled her eyes. "Fred wants you to know that Lincoln has worked his butt off in the off-season. He wants the bubble to break in his favor at tryouts."

"Don't they all."

Leigh's cocktail tasted a little light on the gin. She'd have two. "Well, will it?"

"Will what?"

Leigh opened her mouth to clarify that she meant the bubble breaking for Lincoln, but was interrupted by a man in an overcoat and slicked-back hair. "Hey, Coach."

Jamie lifted his chin. "Hi, John." Leigh could see the beginnings of her brother's first real wrinkles, midway between his ears and the corners of his mouth, exactly where her smile lines had appeared.

The man shifted his weight. "Gearing up for tryouts? How's Trent looking?"

"Wow, John. Straight to the point. This is my sister." Jamie indicated Leigh.

"The Ms. Hockey! Nice to meet you." John grabbed her hand for a shake. "You got kids?"

"Yep." Leigh thought of the hand sanitizer she kept in her purse.

"They play hockey?"

"First-year Squirt."

"That's a thirteen, then."

"That's right," Jamie said. "Thirteen." Leigh realized they meant Gus's birth year.

"Tough," John said. "This crop of Liston Heights thirteens is really strong. They had three on the Brick Team. Unheard of. Ashberry, Matzke, Magnussen—" He paused. "I'm sure you know Georgie Magnussen because of her mother, Susy Walker. Was she disappointed that Ashberry got the head coaching slot?"

Leigh blinked at her brother. She knew Liston Heights was a hockey town, but she wasn't prepared to discuss Gus's prospects with strangers.

"Hey, John, can I call you tomorrow?" Jamie said, his eyes back on his menu. "Trent looks good. We've got six weeks till tryouts."

"Thirty-two days. It's go time." John rubbed Leigh's shoulder and walked away.

"Whoa, intense." Leigh looked at the place John's hand had been. "And very little regard for personal space."

"Shit like that happens all the time." Jamie lowered his voice. "These coaching decisions, they're huge for the kids, right? I don't really like that guy, but if Trent Stevens doesn't make the top line this year, his recruiting prospects are sort of fucked." He pointed at Leigh. "And if your guy Lincoln Page doesn't make varsity this year as a junior, I'm much less likely to invest in him as a senior, when there's an almost-as-good sophomore I can develop for a couple of seasons."

Leigh's shoulder twinged, an old injury from her playing days. She rubbed the same spot John Stevens had touched and then leaned over to grab her hand sanitizer. "But for Gus, though." She squeezed the bottle, and the gel felt cool in her palm. "It's just Squirts, right? Plenty of time to not be so fucking stressed?"

"Come on, Leigh-Leigh." She loved it when he called her by the old nickname. "You've gotta know it's so different now from when you played. It's even different than it was for me."

Leigh squirmed in her seat, anxious to release the familiar tension, an uncomfortable ache she associated with the Lake Placid selection camp. She both wanted Gus's tryouts to be over, and also to delay them.

"Can I be honest?" Jamie didn't wait for her answer. "It wouldn't hurt for you to do what Fred Page and John Stevens are doing."

Leigh raised an eyebrow. "What do you mean? You like it when high-intensity parents interrupt your dinner date with your favorite sister?"

Jamie chuckled. "No, but they're showing me they care, right? They're all in. If I schedule a last-minute practice at nine thirty on a Friday night, Stevens and Page can't complain about their kids having other plans."

Leigh drained half of her weak drink and scanned the restaurant for their server.

Jamie looked suddenly pensive. "Lately, though, I've realized that there's something important these intense parents don't understand. They don't get how important it is to lose. Not making that top line? It could be exactly what Trent needs. He'd then spend months hustling his butt off, learning to make plays he never had to when he was alongside the best."

Leigh remembered the game-winner she'd scored with thirty seconds left in the NCAA final in 1999, the dogpile she'd been on the bottom of. It had been one of the best moments of her life. The very next weekend Charlie had appeared before her at that house party, as if he were attached to the trophy. Leigh wouldn't have been at the party at all—wouldn't be the same person she was today—if she hadn't been top line. "But you need the wins," she said.

"Leigh-Leigh, duh." Jamie glugged a third of his own drink and flashed his handsome grin at the server. "But you don't learn if you don't lose."

Leigh frowned. "Are you for real right now?"

"I mean, yeah. I'm for real." Jamie knocked the table. "But let's pick our moments. Let's not let Gus lose right this second."

"What should I do?"

"I told you Jeff Carlson is on the board of the Liston Heights Hockey Association. Call him. Tell him you're all in for Gus." He turned toward the server, who'd basically sprinted over as soon as Jamie had smiled at her. "Can we have another round? Plus a burger for me with cheddar and fries?"

"Double that," Leigh said, hoping Jamie hadn't noticed her flinch when he'd mentioned Jeff. She'd perfected her imperviousness over the years, skipping past former teammates' old photos on Insta. When Gus asked for details about the national team, Leigh told him about the World Championships and the European tour the year before. She never mentioned the coaches at all. She never said, "Lake Placid." Thinking about calling Jeff now made her limbs heavy.

For Gus, she thought. *To give him his own chance.*

CHAPTER NINE

SUSY WALKER

September 2022

Susy waited outside the girls' locker room, giggles and hollers filtering through the door, and thought of Leigh. While Leigh had been judicious and businesslike in virtually every other area of her hockey existence, she was typically the last one in the locker room, chatting with anyone who'd lollygag with her.

Maybe that was why it stung so much that Leigh had disappeared after '02. It seemed she had enjoyed being with Susy. Susy hadn't thought their connection had been just about medals and accolades. There were also the moments when Leigh had slipped Swedish Fish into everyone's bags before they'd left the rink, the times she'd blasted "Tubthumping" and "Mustang Sally" during warm-ups.

Now Susy could hear Georgie's trademark low singing voice.

Even when hockey got busier—when Georgie started playing with the boys full-time—Susy tried to keep these Sunday-night girls' skates on the calendar. The girls played all levels, some brand-new to the sport, and if Susy managed to keep it light, they had so much fun together. She led them through silly drills in addition to real shooting and face-off practice, incorporating handball and relay races that appealed to everyone and highlighted nontraditional strengths.

It was a shame that girls had to wait until their high school years to find a sisterhood in hockey if they wanted to compete at the highest level. Hockey was changing, but not fast enough to grow a talent pool of elite fifth graders like you'd find on the boys' side. It wasn't evolving fast enough to field a whole international Brick Tournament just for girls.

Susy and Leigh's generation had been raised to think that playing with boys made them tougher and more impressive, but now that Susy spent her days working with middle schoolers, now that she saw the ways they could support one another if they had decent role models, she questioned that message.

The first bars of Olivia Rodrigo's latest hit sprang forth and Susy leaned her head against the cinder block. Now that the players had moved on to their dance party, it would be several more minutes until they came out. She wouldn't rush them.

Instead, Susy opened the text thread she had going with Leigh. Their messages were sterile and spare, save for the photo Leigh had sent of Gus's training journal. Susy had sent a few videos of stick-handling drills for Gus. Leigh had thanked her, but nothing had sparked a back-and-forth.

"Waiting outside the girls' locker room at the rink and having flashbacks to 'Jessie's Girl,'" she wrote now. It had been another of the songs the team had loved. Susy hovered her thumb over the send button, but got distracted when a message from Dirk came in.

"Can you take Georgie this weekend?" her ex asked. "I'll trade you for one of yours."

"No problem," Susy wrote. She never said no to more Georgie. Maybe when the hockey season ended, Susy would take Dirk up on his offer and ask a few of her pals to the North Shore of Lake Superior for a cabin overnight. Maybe Leigh could come with them.

She rejected the idea as soon as it materialized. Leigh had made it clear that she wasn't interested in going back.

Susy scrolled Twitter for the duration of another song before the music stopped and the locker room door swung open. All eleven girls who'd skated that night filed out en masse. They'd waited for one another as usual, rather than just leaving one by one.

"Thanks, Coach!" Tricia yelled as she spotted her mom's car outside.

"Next week?" Susy asked her.

"Wouldn't miss it!" Tricia said.

Georgie was at her elbow then. Susy leaned down and kissed her head, ignoring the ubiquitous helmet smell. It was a myth that only boys carried the pervasive mustiness.

"That was so fun, Mom." Georgie said it every weekend after the girls' skate.

"Yeah. Best part of my week, too." Susy and Georgie stood in the carpool circle, waiting for each of the girls to disappear into their vans and SUVs. Two of the stragglers kicked at each other's shoes, engaged in some kind of game as they waited for their parents. Their laughter echoed against the concrete building. "Your shot was on fire," Susy said.

Georgie nodded. "Yeah, but did you see the way Tricia bent her stick?"

Tricia had played C-level hockey the year before, taking the sport up on a whim when she'd become close with Georgie.

"I did." Susy threw an arm around her daughter's shoulder. "Awesome, right?" Georgie's shot was a million times stronger than Tricia's, but she'd noticed that the gap between them had closed a tiny bit. "That's what's so great about you," Susy said. "You're all about team."

"You're still friends with your old teammates, right?"

Susy bit her lip as another of the girls waved over her shoulder and climbed into her car. She thought about her unsent text message to Leigh.

"Lots of them," she said. Georgie had met many of the women with whom Susy had played over the years. Holiday cards from the team and their families always dominated their gallery wall.

"But not all?"

"You know." Susy started to walk toward their hatchback as the last of the Sunday Skate parents pulled into the circle. "There are always ones you're closer to, but in the end you're still part of the same sisterhood."

Susy thought about Leigh, the way they'd stood next to each other to receive silver medals at the World Championships, the photo she kept of that moment.

"Is this your way of telling me I have to be nice to Shayla?"

Susy hit the trunk button on her fob, and Georgie hoisted her bag in. Shayla was a puck hog, for sure. She'd attempted several solo plays that night during which she should have passed. After the most egregious, Georgie had slammed her stick on the ice and let out an audible groan.

Still, they'd piled out of the locker room as part of the same group. "Just a suggestion," Susy said. "You know, for the sisterhood."

"Fine." Georgie shuffled into the back seat and Susy selected the "Locker Room" playlist she'd made from her Spotify menu.

CHAPTER TEN

GUS MACKENZIE

September 2022

September 10, 2022
Hockey Minutes This Week: 120
Lifetime Hours: 416
Days until Tryouts: 32
Quote from Greystone: "Not half-bad."
Quote from Uncle Jamie: "Hands coming along."
Quote from Mom: "Holy s-h-i-t."

"You ready for your session?" Gus rolled his eyes at his cereal before looking up at his mom. She was doing that fake smile, the same one she put on when Gus and his dad chose something from the Marvel Universe for family movie night. Gus didn't get why his mom didn't like superhero movies. She should love the Black Widow, who was smart and had insane fighting skills. But if his mom got to choose, it was always some boring movie with "spontaneous singing," as his dad liked to say.

"Why are you rolling your eyes?" She walked to the sink to dump her coffee.

"Mom, I go to Greytness like three times a week. It's just *your* first time." His lessons with Greystone that summer had all been during her workdays, but now that school had started, Gus was up early on Saturday to meet his coach. There were only thirty-two days until tryouts started. Gus had begun a countdown in the hockey bible.

"Well, I'm excited to see it. Jamie and Dad say you look great."

"Greystone says I'm relentless." His mom would like that, his giving 100 percent.

"What sets Mackenzies apart," Big Gus had told him last week, "was that we don't 'lallygag.'" That word of theirs made Gus laugh.

"Where's Dad?" Gus asked. "Running?" His dad was always up early. If he'd finished his miles, he was reading in the living room. Plus, his dad had never missed a single Greystone session. Gus could see him, and sometimes Uncle Jamie, too, from the ice as they watched him through the windows. After the lessons, Jamie rubbed Gus's sweaty head and handed him a piece of Bubblegum Extra. "Getting better," he'd say. "Hands coming along."

It was always "getting better," Gus had realized a couple of weeks ago. It was never, "already great."

Gus wondered what his mom would think of his stick handling now. It had been a long time since she'd first taught him those drills. "Dad's meeting us after practice," his mom said.

"But where is he?"

She did the fake Marvel smile again. "He and Uncle Jamie went to watch some other kids play hockey."

"Which other kids?"

"Kids your age in a tournament. I guess some of them play for Liston Heights during the winter."

"So . . ." Gus lifted an overflowing spoonful toward his mouth. A few Cheerios plunked into the milk before they made it past his lips. "They're scouting the competition?" he asked as he chewed.

His mom shook her head. "These kids would be playing for Liston Heights, too. Like, they'd be your teammates."

"I mean competition for making the team." Gus swallowed. "Dad and Uncle Jamie are seeing how good I have to be?"

"I guess that's right." Her fake smile stayed. "They're seeing how hard you have to crush." She reached over and ruffled his hair as Gus scooped another mound of Cheerios from the bottom of the bowl.

Gus considered this news. "Did you scout the competition when you were on Team USA?" he asked. His mom barely talked about being on the national team, but Big Gus had recapped pretty much every single one of her games that summer. At his grandparents' house there were pictures of his mom cut from the newspaper. Whenever he and Big Gus looked through those, his grandfather told him he could be just like her.

Gus's mom looked out the kitchen window. "I guess I did scout the competition. I always knew who I'd have to beat at my position," she said. "You're getting pretty smart."

Gus knew that was true. Things that his parents used to keep secret from him seemed more obvious now. "Like," he said, "it's better to know where I really stand than to go into tryouts blind. That's what Coach Greystone says. No use blowing sunshine . . ." Gus paused, not sure if he should repeat the rest of the phrase that Coach Greystone used when Gus missed a drill. Gus laughed thinking about the swear word. His breath rippled the milk in his Cheerios bowl.

When he looked up, his mom's eyes sparkled, and she was laughing, too. "Blowing sunshine where?" she asked.

Gus shook his head. "It's not a good word."

His mom threw her head back and laughed harder. He wondered how she knew.

*V*isualize success, Gus told himself as he watched Greystone demonstrate the complicated course of stick-handling obstacles. At the end of the line of cones, Greystone "passed" the puck to a tire on the right side of the rink. If he hit the tire square, the puck would bounce back to his stick, and he'd shoot it. If not, the puck would ricochet sideways and all of that work on the course was for nothing. He'd have to start over. No goal.

As Greystone's pass bounced back perfectly from the tire, he buried it in the unmanned net. Gus looked up at his mom. She held a fist in front of her mouth.

She doesn't think I can do it.

He skated to the beginning of the course and lifted his chin. He imagined his mom holding her breath in the viewing area.

Go. Gus made it past the first obstacle and between the first and second cones. He turned sideways and thought about looking up to see her reaction, but for sure he'd bobble the puck. Instead he pushed it under the second obstacle and picked it up on the other side. Two cones to go until he hit the tire. In Tampa, his dad had been the big cheerer in the family. His mom, when she was there, stayed calm. She hardly ever reacted when Gus scored a goal or connected a pass. He'd heard his dad ask her about it once when they didn't know he was listening. She'd said something about "normalizing success."

Gus skidded to a stop in front of the tire. Stick back, pressure on the ice. He sent it directly into the middle. It rebounded, and he one-timed it into the net.

"Yeehaw!" Greystone raised his stick. Gus laughed and the two of them fist-bumped. "I'll tell you what," Coach said. "On your first day here back in June, I wouldn't have imagined you could do that. You've worked your ass off."

Gus laughed harder. "Ass" again.

In the lobby afterward, his mom's smile wasn't that fake Marvel one anymore. She grabbed him in a bear hug and bounced him up and down. "You're a completely different player, kid," she said, laughing. "Holy shit."

CHAPTER ELEVEN

LEIGH MACKENZIE

October 2022

You're doing what tonight?" Charlie asked as he shoveled taco meat onto a tortilla for her.

Leigh didn't want to make a big deal out of her plans. She whispered, "I'm meeting Jeff Carlson for a drink."

"Why are you whispering?" Charlie whispered back. Gus had eaten already and now knelt next to the family room coffee table engrossed in a YouTube origami tutorial. He paused the video and held his paper up, twisting it to check his most recent fold. He didn't appear to be paying any attention to his parents.

"Gus," she mouthed. "Anyway," she continued quietly, "Jamie said it's smart, right? To rekindle my old alliances? Or whatever."

Charlie had reiterated Jamie's advice after they'd scouted that top-level team. Even Leigh's exclamations over Gus's performance at Greytness hadn't diffused Charlie's stress after seeing what they were up against in Minnesota. Apparently, Susy's daughter and a couple of others could really skate.

Leigh had messaged Jeff on Facebook that morning. He'd written back within minutes. "Can't wait to catch up. Lions Tap at 8." It had all been horribly easy.

Charlie beamed at her as he handed over a bottle of chipotle seasoning. "Are you kidding? Of course it's smart! Your connections are one of the perks of moving back here, right? The State of Hockey? I'm proud of you. I know you don't like to think about . . ." He hesitated. "Those days."

Leigh tried not to wince. "Anything for Gus," she said.

"Wouldn't it have been easier to start your lobbying effort with Susy?" Leigh shrugged and took her time assembling her burrito, avoiding Charlie's eye contact. She couldn't tell him that she'd tried at least weekly over the summer to send a meaningful message. But she wasn't sure how to act around Susy after having abandoned their friendship.

Charlie grabbed an open can of sparkling water from the counter and sat across from her. "Do you think you'd coach? Do you have time? Jamie said that would help, too, with Gus's chances. Maybe Jeff will ask you?"

Leigh heard Jeff's voice in her ear, a hoarse whisper in the dark of the referees' locker room. "How bad do you want it?"

She squeezed her tortilla and held her breath, banishing Jeff from the dinner table. When she looked up, Charlie's hopeful smile made her feel like crying. Her husband still looked like a movie star. His smile still mesmerized her.

How would he look at her if he knew the truth?

Every time she'd opened her mouth to tell Charlie about Jeff and Lake Placid, she imagined his smile dissipating. He'd never look at her—or think of her and their engagement and their wedding day and their life as parents to the most wonderful nine-year-old on the planet—in the same way. And the more time that passed, the more she couldn't tell him. The best way to keep him from knowing, to keep everything as good as she was so lucky to have it, would be to ask Jeff, face-to-face, to keep the past in the past.

"Look at this thing!" Gus called. He held up his finished product, an origami jumping frog with a pentagonal head.

"Really cool, kiddo!" Leigh put her hand out, and he delivered it to her. She held it by one of its triangular legs and inspected all of its angles. Gus put his head on her shoulder, and she inhaled his coconut shampoo. If Charlie divorced her, he'd almost certainly get custody of Gus. He'd have to. She traveled at least a couple days a week. Leigh didn't pick Gus up from school or supervise his homework. She'd even missed dinner that night.

"I'm going to try an elephant next!" Gus was on his knees in front of his iPad, a square piece of gray paper ready.

"Maybe I'd coach." Leigh tried to imagine putting skates on, making practice plans with Susy Walker. "But I don't know how it would work with the travel."

"It could work if you were an assistant!" Charlie looked at their backup kitchen light fixture above Leigh's head. They'd settled for that one—little shells hanging in a sort of triangular shape—instead of waiting for their first-choice pendant to clear back order. Leigh had convinced Charlie to go for the compromise—that a finished kitchen was better than a perfect one—just as she'd convinced him to marry her after Lake Placid.

At seven forty-five when Leigh was still snuggled next to Charlie on the couch, he jostled her lightly. "You have to leave," he said. Gus was already reading in bed, halfway to sleep. She wanted desperately to text Jeff and tell him she couldn't make it, but there was no viable excuse. Home was peaceful, work handled. Charlie was dying for her to go. Plus, tryouts were in nine days, and Jamie said the Squirt A decisions relied on favorites and favors. If Leigh didn't show up for Jeff, she'd be failing Gus.

Leigh cut her engine and sat for a moment in the car, steeling herself. She grabbed a tinted lip balm, and just as she'd recapped it, smacking her lips together, someone pulled in beside her. She glanced over, and there was Jeff, grinning. She swallowed hard and waved. Then she forced herself out of the car.

"Leigh-Leigh." Jeff held his arms wide on the sidewalk. He wore a Liston Heights Hockey pom hat.

Leigh dropped her key fob in her pocket and kept her hand there. "Jeff," she said. "It's good to see you." She delayed her approach, hoping she'd be able to avoid a hug. He didn't move, though, didn't lower his arms.

She patted his back with one arm as he embraced her. Leigh had wondered whether any of her old attraction would resurface, but as her face landed just next to Jeff's neck, she nearly gagged as she recognized his same smell from twenty years ago, like Speed Stick but stronger, as if it were baked into his coat.

"I was wondering when we'd get to catch up." Jeff let her go, but held her biceps, inspecting her like a new shirt. "I've been keeping tabs on Gus during clinics. I had no idea you'd let your better half take care of all the hockey stuff." Jeff opened the door to the restaurant. "Seems like a nice guy, your husband. But he doesn't know hockey, does he? I would have thought you'd want to supervise."

"You've talked to Charlie?" Charlie would have mentioned meeting Jeff. Leigh's shoulder twinged, and she rubbed it.

Jeff put his hand on her lower back and steered her toward the hostess stand. Leigh's fingers tightened into a fist. "Not yet," Jeff said. "Don't worry. I'm not moving in on your husband."

Leigh stepped sideways, out of Jeff's reach, smiled at the teenage hostess, and raised two fingers to indicate their party size.

"High-top or booth?" The girl grabbed menus.

"High-top," Leigh said at the same time Jeff said, "Booth.

"That one in the back corner?" Jeff pointed at a table far from the rest of the clientele.

The hostess frowned. "We're not seating that section just now—"

"We'll get drinks from the bar and sit there, okay?" Jeff winked at her. "You can even give me a bar mop, and I'll clean it myself when we're done."

Jeff breezed past the hostess. Leigh let him get a few paces ahead.

"Still like champagne?" Jeff asked over his shoulder.

"Gin and ginger." Leigh had retired champagne at the same time she dumped her hockey gear in her parents' basement. Its sourness, whenever she'd tried it again after Jeff, made her queasy. Even at her wedding, she'd abandoned her flute seconds after the requisite toast.

"You sit." Jeff pointed at the table. He winked at the hostess again. "It won't get too dirty." He walked toward the bar. The hostess frowned at Leigh, undoubtedly judging her for hanging out with such an asshole.

"So," Jeff said when he sat down. He slid a lowball across the table at her, and she sipped.

"So." She remembered the opening line she'd practiced. "Youth hockey is a lot different than it was when I was growing up."

Jeff put his forearms on the table. Wiry hairs poked out of the cuffs of his flannel. "It's a whole new world," he said. "Kids start training earlier and earlier."

"Is Gus behind?" Leigh had practiced this part, too, but now that Jeff was right in front of her, every word felt like a battle. She tried to hold his eye contact, but he diverted his gaze to his own drink, a hazy beer with a thick foam cap.

"Are you sure you want to know?" Jeff took a sip.

She needed to. "Just give it to me, Jeff," she said.

His eyes glinted as he grinned. "You used to say the same thing back in the day, as I recall."

She dropped her hands into her lap and dug the nail of her index finger into the pad of her thumb. "Ancient history," she managed.

Jeff smiled even more broadly. Leigh could see all the way back to his molars, a strand of saliva connecting the tops and bottoms on the left side. "Doesn't seem that long ago now, looking at you. The years have been good for you, Leigh-Leigh." His eyes dipped to her chest and she rounded her shoulders forward.

Leigh thought of her career, the nameplate outside her sizable office. "Managing Director." And then she pictured her son, his origami animals lined up on the coffee table as she'd forced herself out the door. "Can we talk about Gus?"

"Does your husband know about us?" Jeff wiped his mouth with the back of his thick hand.

"He knows you were my coach." Leigh tried to banish the mental flashes of the referees' locker room at Lake Placid, the blue-and-white-checked tile in the shower.

"Listen. I have good—hell, fucking great—memories of that time." Jeff pointed at Leigh. "You were electric."

"Stop." Leigh closed her eyes for a second. "It was a mistake, Jeff. For both of us."

"You never told him." Leigh opened her mouth, but Jeff kept talking. "Look, I get it. And it's your life, your husband, right? I figured you would have ditched that guy after college."

Leigh remembered the full skirt of her sleeveless wedding gown, the bumper toes of her Vans peeking out beneath it at their reception. Charlie had bear hugged Leigh's father after his toast, the one in which Big Gus had teared up as he recollected Charlie finishing the ultramarathon and collapsing into his arms. "I knew I was celebrating another son, the kind of person who could get through anything." Leigh remembered how Big Gus had looked at the medal afterward, too, the hand-carved wooden circle with a leather strap attached. About two hundred and fifty people started Headwaters every year, and fewer than half finished. Charlie kept the medal at the bottom of his sock drawer.

"Can you just tell me about Gus's prospects?" Leigh asked Jeff. She picked at a rip in the booth's pleather upholstery.

"I'll level with you," Jeff said. "I've watched the clinics. I know the evaluators. Gus's raw scores will put him on the B-team."

Leigh nodded. She'd expected this.

"But there's coaches' discretion." Jeff smiled again. "And there's you."

"So, what does that mean?" Leigh pressed.

"What do you want?"

More than anything Leigh wanted out of the bar, away from Jeff. She wanted to curl around Gus in his bedroom in their new house. She wanted to breathe in his shampoo and then fall asleep beside Charlie. She wanted Jeff, again and forever, out of her life. But she also wanted Gus to make it. She wanted him to know she believed in him, that he could achieve his dreams. It was why she'd uprooted her family and moved here.

"I want him on the team," Leigh said.

"I can do that." Jeff rotated his pint glass.

"That's it?" She thought about Jeff's letters, their calls, his throaty promises that hadn't come to fruition in '02. She thought about the way her dad always looked at the place in her bookshelf she'd planned to put her own Olympic medal.

"Can we be friends?" Jeff asked.

Leigh startled. "Friends?"

"You disappeared off the face of the earth. I thought we had something special."

Leigh took a long drink and let the ice clink against her front teeth. "I was twenty-one. I'm married now. I'm a mom." Leigh wanted to add that Jeff disgusted her, that what she had done with him was, in fact, disgusting.

"I'm not talking about the referees' locker room." Leigh's mouth dropped open as she remembered the feel of the tile against her kneecaps, the red marks she'd had on them when she stood. "I'm talking about drinks. Friendliness. A smile here and there." Leigh squeezed her thighs together, flexing every muscle in her legs. "I don't want to be strangers." Jeff chuckled. "I mean, we're not strangers."

"Friends." Leigh hoped it could be a theoretical attachment.

Jeff glanced toward the bar and then back at her. "And I need something else from you in order to put Gus on the roster."

Damn it. "What?"

"You're not looped in with the USA Hockey alumni, so you might not know about the controversy." For the first time all night, Jeff looked hesitant, just the tiniest bit uncertain. Leigh waited. "There's a complaint."

Susy had tried to tell her this in the liquor store parking lot, but beyond a cursory and fruitless Google search, Leigh had never followed up. "It was a misunderstanding." Jeff grabbed his pom hat off the bench next to him and then dropped it again. "Sydney Kirkpatrick from the 2014 team in Sochi says I took advantage of her."

Leigh blanched.

"But you know that's bullshit, right, Leigh? Because you and I—" He smiled. That smile had made her feel important, special, when she'd gotten to the Olympic Training Center in '01. "Anyway," Jeff said, "I need you to make a statement and send it to my lawyer."

"A statement?"

"Yeah." Jeff looked relaxed again. He drank his beer. "Just a letter that tells the truth about what happened between us, that we were two consensual adults having a normal relationship."

Leigh remembered the heavy gray door of the referees' locker room, the dead bolt, the smell of Jeff's Speed Stick mixed with disinfectant, the damp skin of his thigh against her cheek.

And then she forced her attention back to Gus. He was asleep with his hockey bible under his pillow. He'd worked so hard. She also remembered Charlie's tweed couch from college, the one she'd collapsed on when the selection camp had been finally, miserably over.

"If you do the letter, I'll make sure Gus's scores put him over the bubble. And, of course, I'll keep our history private. You obviously don't want Charlie to know."

Leigh thought about telling Charlie now that she'd betrayed him—him and all of her ideals. She'd spent so much time making up for the miscalculation she'd made with Jeff. She left the sport, she committed to building the best, most comfortable life for her husband and son. And all of it had been done in the shadow of a series of lies.

What was just one more?

"Yeah." She grabbed her jacket from the seat next to her. "Yeah, I'll write it. I'll be in touch." She tried not to run for the door.

CHAPTER TWELVE

EMAIL FROM HEAD MANAGER, CATHY KELLIHER

October 2022

Hey-Hey, Lions and Lions Fans!

You all know what time it is! Leaves are falling and nerves are rising, which means it's Squirt Tryouts. I'm popping into your email to provide just a few reminders and guidelines. First of all, before I info dump (as head managers are wont to do), I want you to actually say this phrase aloud to yourself right now:

It's. Just. Youth. Hockey.

What's that?! What's that, you say? Can you repeat it?

One more time? That's right! IT'S JUST YOUTH HOCKEY!

Okay, phew! We've got that covered, and we're going to keep it forefront in our minds, right, Lions?

The next thing you need to know is that tryouts are completely closed to parents. As I write this, board members and parent volunteers are papering over the glass in the rink lobby. No peeking, no prodding, no finagling, no exceptions. Team placement decisions are for the coaches and the evaluators and NOT for parents or private coaches. RESPECT. THESE. BOUNDARIES!

Third, here's how our system works: our team of outside evaluators (highly respected coaches from other associations and area schools) will score the kids on a number of criteria. (A full list is available in the tryout packet you'll receive at check-in tomorrow. Score sheets are shredded at the close of evaluation period.) Five (5) A-team spots at each level are determined expressly by evaluator scores. The remaining skater spots are coach's discretion. Here's a quote from the association's bylaws: "The A-team coach may consider temperament, needs at a given position, hockey IQ, and other intangibles" to choose the remaining skaters. Goalies are scored by a different team of evaluators, but coaches have discretion there, too.

Parents: we'll all do better if we can just trust that the coaches have our kids' best interests at heart. Player development is the top priority, and that doesn't happen if a kid is playing at the wrong level. As Lions, we commit to creating a world-class experience for every kid at every level. We can't do that if we don't have your cooperation and support. THANK YOU.

Cuts for the A-team will be posted by midnight on Wednesday. Check the website. You'll need to have the kids' pinny numbers memorized because we won't post names. Privacy and dignity are paramount in our process. Within ten days, all skaters will be placed on a team. YOUR KID WILL HAVE FUN AND DEVELOP ON ANY TEAM.

Let's hope we don't have any challenges or disputes this year, but just in case: If you're not happy with your team placement, my first advice is to take a deep breath and think about the children. This is for THEM. If that doesn't help, you need to email the Squirt coordinator, Craig

Rathmann at icecoldhockeydad@hotmail.com. That'll trigger the appeal process, which you can read about in the packet you'll receive at check-in.

And, finally, a word about check-in.

BE ON TIME. There are no makeup skates for kids who come late. Arrive fifteen minutes before your assigned skate, come only to your assigned skate, and come prepared to give your best.

No excuses, No regrets, and GO LIONS.

Questions? Reply to me or reread this message.

Your head manager,

Cathy Kelliher

CHAPTER THIRTEEN

CHARLIE MACKENZIE

October 2022

A stern volunteer with a tight ponytail and a Lions sweatshirt handed Charlie a stapled packet. The words "LISTON HEIGHTS HOCKEY ASSOCIATION TRYOUT POLICIES" in bold caps filled the cover.

"Very important," she barked, and then turned to Gus. "Got your practice jersey?"

Gus squirmed, his mouth twisting. "It's in here," Charlie said. He patted the bag he'd slung over his shoulder.

The worker frowned. "Squirts carry their own bags." She licked her finger and paged through her spreadsheet. "What did you say your last name was?"

Gus yanked at the straps of the bag and hissed, "Dad."

Charlie dropped it. "Mackenzie," Charlie said. As he spoke, a girl a full head taller than Gus marched up to the table.

"Hey, Cathy." The girl smiled. One of her incisors appeared freshly missing.

"Aw. Sunshine." Cathy reached a finger out to chuck the girl's chin. "Just a second, sweet pea. I've gotta get this new kid situated."

The girl appraised Gus, scanning the length of him. It had to be Georgie Magnussen. Charlie had seen her only in full pads on the ice, and though it always took a few weeks for him to recognize the kids without their helmets on, there hadn't been more than four girls in the clinics and none as tall as Georgie. Gus looked at his shoes. His reddish hair poked out under a Tampa Bay Junior Lightning cap.

"You like the Lightning?" Georgie asked him. "You a bandwagon? They were second in their division last year."

"Uh." Charlie could feel Gus's anxiety, the way he typically froze up in new situations.

Charlie swiveled his head, looking for Georgie's mom. There hadn't been an opportunity during the clinics to reintroduce himself to Susy.

"Mr. Mackenzie, could we focus?"

"Sorry." Charlie turned back to the volunteer. She shoved a pen at him and pointed at a waiver, which he signed without reading. "Are you Cathy Kelliher? From the emails?" He tried for his most charming smile. "Thanks for all the helpful information."

"Practice jerseys only," Cathy said. "Pinny over that. Locker Room B. Kids only." She licked a finger and flipped to a different page of her sign-in sheet. "And you're welcome for the emails."

His charm had failed. Charlie repeated the directions back to himself in his head. *Kids only in the locker room?* "Oh, but I usually tie his skate—"

"Kids only." Cathy smiled at Georgie, dismissing them.

Gus struggled under the weight of the duffel as they walked

away. Charlie noticed several other kids hauling their equipment in bags with wheels. Gus pinched the side of Charlie's jacket. "Dad." His face had gone pink with embarrassment.

"It's okay, buddy." Charlie scanned the crowded lobby for a quiet corner where he could talk Gus into the right headspace. Even with Jeff's help—Leigh had said he could make the difference if Gus were in the ballpark—if he didn't skate well in this session, Gus wouldn't make the cut.

Charlie made a move toward the vending machine, took a knee, and looked Gus in the eye.

"Hey," he said. "Shake it off. That lady"—he nodded at the registration table—"she wasn't the nicest, but she's not a coach, and she doesn't make the rules."

Gus dropped the bag. He took a long shaky breath and hung his head. The brim of his cap shielded his face. "Can you shake it off?" Charlie tried to sound neutral, calm.

"Dad." Gus sniffed. Two tears streaked toward his jaw, and Gus wiped them with open palms. "Dad," he said again, "you're embarrassing me. I've got this." He grabbed the bag by both straps and nearly fell over as he jimmied it onto his shoulder. He shuffled off toward the locker rooms.

"What about tying your skates?" Charlie called after him. Gus had never once tied his own skates. The whole thing was a process with eyelet-by-eyelet tightening. Leigh had shown him way back in the beginning. If it wasn't done correctly, Gus's ankles would collapse, and he'd lose the benefit of the extra edge work he'd done with Greystone.

Charlie surveyed the lobby of fit-looking parents in Lions caps and beanies. His stomach rolled. In Florida, Charlie's running set him apart from most other dads at the rink. Here, it seemed like any one of them could knock out a ten-miler after tryouts with no problem. Once Gus had made his way haltingly down the stairs toward the locker rooms, Charlie followed. He'd intercept him regardless of Cathy's crabby directives. Certainly, Gus couldn't be the only nine-year-old who didn't always tie his own skates.

When Charlie made it to Locker Room B, he was relieved to find several other parents outside. A too-thin woman chewed her nails and squinted up at the evaluators' tables, where several men paged through what Charlie assumed was the same spreadsheet Cathy had consulted at check-in, but supposedly with the kids' names removed.

"Damn it," the woman said. "Talon Seizkin again. I thought he was banned after last year."

Charlie looked at the other parents, none of whom responded to this woman.

He stood slightly apart from them and watched the Zamboni as it left a thick wet trail around the perimeter of the ice.

"You new here?" The guy who'd spoken slapped his free palm with a rolled-up copy of the tryout guidelines.

Charlie smiled. "Yeah. That obvious? This isn't like what we're used to."

"Where'd your kid skate last year?"

The Zamboni wheeled around for its next swath. "We're from Tampa."

"No kidding." The guy gave an exaggerated nod. "The Junior Lightning."

"You familiar with Florida youth hockey?" Charlie knew that Minnesota was a different world, but this was beyond even what he expected. Minnesota hockey parents kept tabs on youth associations around the country?

"I just happen to know the Tampa Bay scene. Lots of retired NHL guys there. Some of my pals have their kids in that league."

The retired pros mostly had their kids on the national travel teams. "We did house league," Charlie said. "Not the national stuff. Wait—you're pals with ex-NHLers?"

"I played one season with the Stars out of college. Arnie Senko." He offered his fist, and Charlie bumped it.

"You have a Squirt now?" Charlie racked his memory, but he didn't think Jamie had mentioned any Senko.

"Yeah, and the kid can't for the life of him tie his own skates. We've got to put in some practice time there, but until we do, I'll be stopping him before he gets on the ice."

Charlie relaxed. If the ex-pro needed to help his kid, then Gus was fine.

The too-thin woman kicked at the boards and both Charlie and Arnie looked over at her. "Fuckin' Seizkin," she muttered.

"Let's tie their skates," Arnie said conspiratorially, "and then maybe we can get into what's up with that."

When both of their kids were on the ice—Gus had swatted Charlie's hand away as he attempted to pull him in for a last-minute hug—Arnie jerked his head toward the other side of the rink and beckoned that Charlie should follow. Tryouts were closed to parents, so this felt illicit, like he was on his way to a drug deal or a dead drop, things Charlie had seen only in movies.

"Where are we . . . ?" Charlie started to ask, but Arnie held a finger to his lips. Charlie lagged a half step behind as they marched through a dimly lit hallway under the bleachers on the visitors' side. After a minute or so, Arnie stopped and pointed at the concrete floor next to him to indicate where Charlie should stand. From that spot, a good two feet back from the lights of the arena, Charlie looked head-on at the left corner of the ice.

"You've done this before?" Charlie asked.

Arnie nodded. "They haven't always closed tryouts, but I like to watch in private. There's too much drama in the stands."

Gus breezed by the boards then, and Charlie stepped forward. Arnie grabbed the sleeve of his jacket and pulled him back.

"Uh-uh," he said. "Too much light closer to the rink. We gotta stay back or else we'll get caught. You can't quite see the opposite corner, but it's the trade-off." Arnie pointed at the far-side net. The swath of ice parallel to them was out of their sight line.

"Fair enough." Adrenaline shot through Charlie's limbs now that Gus's moment was finally here, and he shifted his weight. The coach, Ashberry, had just whistled the kids to a knee in front of him. Susy Walker and another assistant set cones for the first drill. "Ugh," Charlie said. "My kid is definitely not a standout on stick handling."

"But he's also one of only four or five that has any idea how to pass." Arnie's tone was matter-of-fact. "Keeps his head up on the rush."

Charlie's mouth gaped.

Arnie laughed. "This is Liston Heights, man. People are watching."

The kids broke into several groups. "That's Abe." Arnie pointed. His kid was among the fastest in the drill, tapping his stick on either side of the puck while also keeping his eyes on the net and his shoulders square. At least half of the players had their chins glued to their chests. Now that he knew who he was, Charlie realized he had noticed Abe during the clinics. Arnie muttered under his breath as he watched, clearly nervous despite Abe's skill.

They both turned away from the kids when they heard footsteps behind them. "Well, Senko?" A guy in a Lions jacket and cap turned the corner. Charlie felt his cheeks flood. There was no getting around the fact that they weren't supposed to be here. Charlie touched the folded-up rules packet that stuck out of the back pocket of his jeans.

Arnie, though, smiled. "Carlson, I thought the whole reason you joined the board is that you wouldn't have to watch tryouts in hiding."

"I figured you'd be here." Charlie exhaled as the two men bumped fists.

"Jeff, this is Charlie."

Jeff offered his fist. "Jeff Carlson." Charlie cocked his head. He recognized Jeff from the website.

"Charlie Mackenzie."

"So you're the Mackenzie husband," Jeff said. "Leigh still running the show, eh? Her name so great that you decided to take it?"

Charlie was used to a certain kind of guy making a big deal about his decision to become a Mackenzie. "I didn't have the best last name, anyway." This was his standard response, easier to explain than Leigh's compelling arguments about both his complicity in the patriarchy and the appeal of her Scottish heritage.

"So happy you guys are back." Jeff stepped toward the rink, not worried about being spotted. He folded his arms, surveying. The kids in Gus's group lined up near center ice and headed toward the face-off circle on the far side. "These one-legged turns really weed out the kids with weaker balance," Jeff said. "Arnie, you see O'Malley?" He pointed at number eleven.

"Simon?" Arnie nodded. "He's definitely done some work in the off-season."

"I think he trained with Jamie," Charlie offered.

"That where your kid got his sea legs?" Jeff asked. "Number twelve?" He raised his chin at Gus as he started toward the cone.

"Jamie recommended Greystone." Charlie held his breath as Gus wheeled around and headed back to the line. Nik Ashberry, who'd started at the same time, beat him by at least a second and a half.

"Don't worry about that," Arnie said. "That other kid is Nik Ashberry. You heard of him?"

"His dad's the coach." Charlie didn't want to admit that he and Jamie had scouted the summer team.

"Yep," Arnie said. "And Nik is one of the top two or three Squirts in the state."

"So, how is Leigh?" Charlie snuck a look at Jeff as the next pair of kids started the drill. Number forty-two was clearly slower than Gus, and so was sixteen.

"She's fine," Charlie said. "Good. You talked to her when? Two weeks ago?" Charlie knew it had been nine days. Gus had the whole family counting down.

"She seems happy enough to be back in the State of Hockey?"

Charlie squinted. While Arnie appeared genuinely friendly, Jeff's questions seemed double-edged. "She has a ton of hockey memories, obviously, but she wants Gus to have his own thing. She doesn't talk much about Team USA."

Jeff chuckled, though nothing Charlie had said was funny. "That makes sense."

Charlie frowned. *What made sense?* He was about to ask when Arnie pointed at the next pairing. "Georgie's obviously a no-brainer." Susy's daughter looked almost as sharp navigating the turn as Nik had.

"Yeah," said Jeff. "But I don't know, Mackenzie, your boy might have a shot. These skating drills aren't going to be where he gets his marks, though, right? It's going to be the three-lane shooting drill and the one-on-one, from what Greystone says."

Charlie's jaw dropped again. Greystone made reports to board members?

"Don't look so shocked." Jeff patted Charlie on the shoulder, in the same spot he'd punched before. "The hockey community's small. I'm surprised Leigh didn't warn you about that. People know all kinds of things about each other."

She had, in fact, warned Charlie about that. It had been the one "con" on their moving-to-Minnesota list besides "unbearable wind-chills." Charlie followed Jeff's gaze back to the ice. The group skated forward this time, turning right instead of left. Ashberry beat Gus again, but by less.

Jeff kept talking. "It might take a couple of sessions for the evaluators to see what they're dealing with in terms of Gus. But hey"—he turned toward the hallway—"I'm rooting for you, okay? I'm always rooting for Leigh."

"Dude's a little weird," Arnie said when Jeff had left. "But wow, Leigh Mackenzie! I think she was one of the first Ms. Hockeys, yeah?

Those women were pioneers. Girls' hockey didn't even become a varsity sport until they were in high school."

"Yeah." Charlie grinned. He'd caught Gus bragging about his mom at Greytness. It was nice having a little clout.

"What happened after '02?" Arnie asked. "She didn't play for the team that year. Did she retire that young?"

The kids were setting up for a passing drill. "She was done after that. Lost the passion for it. We got married, went to grad school." It had all happened after that selection camp.

"You guys got other kids?"

Charlie kept his eyes on the ice, not wanting to give away that this was a sore spot. "Just the one," he said. "You?"

"Abe's the caboose. The other two are in college." They watched Gus complete a sweet pass to another kid in front of the net. "Nice play there. Just got to hope the evaluators catch those moments."

"Did your older two play hockey?" Charlie asked.

Arnie nodded. "Ronan made it to D Three," he said. "Both played for the Lions' high school team. They're just a couple of years younger than Jamie Mackenzie. They idolized him for sure."

It was true what Carlson said. Everyone knew everyone else in Minnesota hockey.

On the ice, the coaches had called the kids to the center and began dividing them into four teams. "Three-on-three," Arnie said. "I wasn't expecting this right out of the gate, but Ashberry usually goes big. It's hard to see it all from here, but we'll get the gist."

Abe started at right wing. When Gus began his shift, he passed to number seven, who bobbled in front of the net. No goal, but that wasn't Gus's fault.

Arnie muttered as play continued. "Nice pass," he said at one point. "Bury that!" he urged Abe. Sure enough, the puck whizzed between the goalie's head and glove.

"Nice one." Charlie offered a fist bump. Gus took the ice with the next line.

"Now watch how your kid keeps his head up," Arnie said. "The other ones? They only see their feet." Gus slid the puck to number seven again, but the kid turned it over, his attention so focused on the ice in front of him that he didn't see the defender's impending poke-check. "The team's going to need someone who can make the play," Arnie said. Charlie hoped Gus could be that one.

CHAPTER FOURTEEN

LEIGH MACKENZIE

October 2022

I'm flying home early." Leigh's fingers shook as she sent the text to Charlie. Her elation bubbled out of her. Fred Page had met with the owners of Heritage Cutlery three separate times before she'd come on staff, and they'd never agreed to sell.

Now they'd signed, and the addition of a custom knife maker to their enamel cookware company would send its value through the roof. Leigh had called to alert Lupine's kick-ass attorney and Fred's assistant of the pending deal. If she prayed to the airport gods, she might just make it to the second half of Gus's final scrimmage, the only portion of the Squirt Tryouts that were open to parents.

"Huzzah!" Charlie sent an *Arrested Development* GIF along with his message. "Game starts at 7."

"Don't tell Gus, just in case." Leigh didn't want him expecting her, only to disappoint.

"I won't. Can't wait to see you."

Leigh couldn't wait to see Charlie, either, especially after her first major win at Lupine. "Xoxo," she typed.

In the gate area with thirty minutes to takeoff, Leigh answered the callback from Fred. "You fucking did it!" She beamed as he spoke. "I've been trying to get Doug to sell for a year. He kept talking about the family history of bladesmithing and the mechanical type-writer in the original production office. How the heck did you do it?"

"I don't know!" But Leigh did know. She'd listened to Doug talk about the company's history for several hours, and then she'd mentioned a couple of other family business acquisitions she'd handled. She promised he could stay on as a consultant and choose his successor. And then, she'd listened for another six or seven hours about his troubled grandson and his angling for the company.

"Did you get him to spill about the grandson?" she asked Fred. "That revelation came at about hour six." Leigh had promised Doug that she would run the business better than that kid. Heritage Cutlery would grow.

After all of it, Doug had hugged her hard. They'd both been teary. And now it was all Leigh could do to stay in her seat. This was closer to the thrill of national championships than anything she'd done at her last job.

"I didn't get to the grandson," Fred said. "But you're a genius. You're the new era of Lupine."

Leigh pumped her fist, not caring who saw her celebrating. "I'm lucky to be part of it," she said.

"Are you kidding? Cristal on me when you get home."

"Not a champagne girl." Leigh wrinkled her nose. "But you can get me a case of really nice gin."

"Deal."

After touchdown Leigh raced to the car she'd left in the long-term lot and straight to the ice rink.

As soon as she pulled the arena door open, Leigh felt the high of the Heritage acquisition start to fizzle. She had to see again the photo of herself in the rink's entryway, part of a display of locals who'd gone on to collegiate success. And then, as she pivoted toward Rink 2, she encountered a volunteer at a check-in table.

"Yes?" the woman asked as Leigh peeked over her shoulder toward the ice where kids were playing, their green and yellow pinnies distinguishing the teams.

"Oh." Leigh pointed at the rink. "I'm just here to watch the final scrimmage. My son is playing."

"It's two spectators per child." The woman held a Sharpie over a printed list.

"No problem." Leigh tried for her most winning smile, the one she'd so recently used on Doug at Heritage. "I'm number two." She laughed. "So to speak."

The woman didn't smile. "Child's name?"

"Mackenzie. Gus."

The woman looked up from her list. "I was wondering when you'd make an appearance! I'm surprised we haven't seen you here in person."

"Here I am!" Leigh fought to maintain her cheer. She found Charlie through the glass in the stands, back row, forearms on his knees. "Can I?" She gestured toward the door.

"I'm Cathy Kelliher." The woman puffed her chest out, her mouth a thin line.

"From the emails! Thank you so much for all of the helpful information." Leigh took a step toward the door, but Cathy still hadn't dismissed her.

"There are volunteer positions open, you know. Many of the moms like to donate their time, especially those with hockey knowledge."

"I'll consider it," Leigh said. It was a final vestige of the patriarchy, this type of conversation. Everyone—the doctor's office, the school, the hockey volunteer coordinator—assumed that Leigh, not Charlie, would be the one to do the kid's stuff.

"There's a manager slot open on the B1 team. I'll call you." Cathy finally checked off Leigh on her paper, and Leigh raised an eyebrow. Only the parent of a B player would be the manager. Who was Cathy to relegate Gus to the B-team?

Leigh had bolstered Gus's chances with that letter to Jeff's attorney. There were three paragraphs outlining their affair. She'd spent a late night in her office remembering the details she'd tried so diligently to forget—the carpeting in the Lake Placid dorms, the slightly musty smell of Jeff's car, and though she hadn't written about it, the void she'd tumbled into when she realized it all had been for nothing.

The last thing Leigh needed was an email writer with an inflated sense of self-importance harshing her vibe on what was a crowning day in Leigh's finance career, and perhaps the most consequential skate of Gus's young life. "I'm not sure I have time for managing, but it's nice to meet you." She walked inside.

Leigh tried to shake off her discomfort as she hurdled the top row of bleachers and slid in next to her husband. She squeezed Charlie's thigh and kissed his cheek. "You made it." He put an arm around her shoulder. "I'm so glad you're here. Gus looked great on his last shift."

"Where's your tryout buddy?" Charlie had mentioned a new friend, a guy who'd shown him a secret spot where he could watch the closed sessions.

Charlie pointed across the rink at two men huddled together. Leigh pulled her hand from Charlie's leg and wrapped both arms around her middle as she recognized one of the two as Jeff.

"Here he comes," Charlie said.

Leigh watched Gus glide out on the ice, his strides stronger by far than they had been the previous season. He was playing left wing and immediately got himself in position. Leigh could feel her heartrate accelerate. In Tampa, she'd never been nervous. Gus had been the best! But here, people like Cathy thought he belonged on the B-team. He was new, and he had a target on his back, perhaps because of her own banner in the lobby. The expectations would be higher for the kid of an All-American.

Leigh's attention shifted to the center on Gus's line, a girl with a ribboned ponytail spread over the back of her yellow pinny. Leigh's spine straightened. The girl's edgework was the best of anyone's on the ice. The kids skated into the corner after the puck, and the girl came out with it. Her stick seemed like a magnet for it. She kept her head up as she flew into the neutral zone. Leigh barely noticed Gus a few strides behind her, in position and ready for a lateral pass. There was no way this girl would need it.

As she changed directions in front of the net, dekeing the goalie, she slid the puck in behind his left skate. Brilliant. "That's Georgie," Leigh said mostly to herself. Her eyes scanned the bench. Susy was there, her own ponytail swinging. As Georgie skated over, Susy tapped the top of her helmet. Leigh's hand went to her head. Susy had tapped Leigh's helmet lots of times when they'd been on Team USA together. She did it only when she was legitimately impressed.

The memory of their old closeness overwhelmed her, and Leigh thought of the texts she'd never sent to Susy. She swallowed hard as Gus lined up again on the center red line.

"She's amazing," Charlie said.

"She's incredible." Leigh heard the thickness in her voice. Charlie turned to her as the ref dropped the puck.

"Whoa," he said. "You okay?"

Leigh took a deep breath and looked at Susy again, her arms folded as she stood at the end of the line of players. She looked happy and confident, smiling beneath the brim of her Lions cap. Although Leigh had killed at work, she wouldn't be able to share that joy of the Heritage deal with Gus the way Susy could bond over hockey with Georgie.

At the end of the scrimmage, Gus stayed on the ice with Susy and Georgie for an extra moment, his little face gazing up at Leigh's old teammate. Although Leigh had left hockey behind of her own free will, she couldn't help feeling jealous of the obvious connection it garnered between her old friend and Gus. It was one thing to study photographs of Leigh playing, and a totally different one to actually share ice time. Leigh had been so adamant about keeping the game at arm's length.

Gus and Georgie exited the locker room together fifteen minutes later, their bags dwarfing them as they shuffled across the rink lobby.

"Mom!" Gus dropped his bag and grabbed her middle. "I thought you couldn't come."

"I made it! Just in time for the last half." She smiled at Georgie over Gus's head. "You looked great, too."

"It was his best showing yet, I think." Georgie grinned. "I'm Georgie Magnussen. I know you. My mom played with you when she was younger."

Leigh smiled at Georgie's adultlike assessment of Gus's performance. "Yes," she said.

"I think there are some pictures of you in one of Mom's albums. Silver medals? I think you're crying in the pictures, though."

"That was the World Champs. Came down to the last few seconds." Leigh looked around for Susy and found her blond ponytail in front of the vending machine. *Dr Pepper*, she thought to herself, remembering her old roommate's penchant for it. She always had a warm one in her bag on the bus.

"Those losses are the toughest," Georgie said, "but there's always the next game, right? That's what my mom says."

"Sure," Leigh said, but that game had been her last on Team USA. Susy looked over her shoulder, a bottle of Dr Pepper in her hand. She waved and jogged toward them.

"All right, you two?" she said to the kids.

Leigh clenched her jaw, and to her horror, she felt for a moment like she might cry again, thinking of the bond Susy had already forged with Gus. "Wow," Leigh managed. "Suse, Georgie looked amazing out there."

"Told you," Gus said to Georgie. "I knew she'd think that."

Susy reached out and touched Leigh's elbow. "It's so fun to see you here. Thanks. Georgie, you watching for Dad?"

"It'll be Mormor." Georgie looked at Gus. "That's 'grandma' in Swedish. And yes, Mom, I'm watching." She rolled her eyes.

"I've gotta get upstairs," Susy said. "We've got some decisions to make. Good game, you two. Leigh—" They made eye contact. Leigh wanted to grab on to her, to steal a sip of her soda as she had so many times even though she herself preferred Diet Coke. Susy smiled. "It's really good to see you."

CHAPTER FIFTEEN

SUSY WALKER

October 2022

Susy sipped her Dr Pepper as she waited for Ashberry and the others to make it into the conference room. She had lingered on the ice with the last few players, including Gus Mackenzie. He didn't seem to want to leave. His pass had connected with Georgie in the final minutes of the scrimmage, and she'd buried it over Chris Mc-Millan's blocker. When Ashberry called the kids together to end the session, Gus had twice glanced over his shoulder at the spot on the ice where he'd made the play a few minutes before. Georgie had tapped for it, but he'd already begun the pass. Gus didn't rely on her cue. He knew where to send it.

And still, Susy didn't need to see the evaluators' notes to know that Gus's scores would be lower than at least thirteen other kids'. On paper, they shouldn't take him. They'd kept him through two cuts because of his IQ. And, if Susy was being honest with herself, they kept him because his mother was Leigh Mackenzie. Her heart had jolted when she'd seen Leigh arrive midway through the second period of the scrimmage. Susy had been embarrassed to recognize that she cared so much about being in the same space as Leigh, how much it had meant for her to compliment Georgie's play.

Anyway, Ashberry wouldn't want to treat the season as an opportunity for Gus's development. Colin Kelliher was almost as good at passing and could stick handle and skate as well as O'Malley and Rathmann. She ran through the argument she could make for Gus. And then she remembered all the times Leigh hadn't answered her calls after the Games in Salt Lake, the friend request on Facebook Leigh had ignored for a few months after the kids had been born. Leigh hadn't reached out when news of Susy's divorce hit ESPN.com. She hadn't even suggested they get together over the previous summer, after Susy had approached her and answered a few of her questions via text. Still, Susy wanted Gus.

"Hey." Ashberry walked in, the brim of his cap slightly off-center. "Any surprises for you out there?"

Right to business, then. Susy thought back on the previous hour, the twenty-five kids they'd had on the ice. She went with the most obvious choice first. "Well, clearly we'll take McMillan in the net. Are we going to carry more than one goalie?"

Ashberry shook his head. "I don't want to. It can be nice at this age to have two in case a kid gets rattled, but I know Mac." He scrolled his phone as he spoke. "Played with him last summer at a couple of tourneys. He keeps his head."

"Okay." Susy reached into her bag and pulled out a small, fat spiral-bound notebook. She'd torn out a few of the perforated pages to leave notes in Georgie's lunch bag over the last month or so during clinics and tryouts, inspirational quotes from Ruth Bader Ginsburg and Malala Yousafzai. Susy flipped the notebook over and opened it to the last page.

She numbered one to fifteen and wrote McMillan on the first line. "How many skaters are we taking? Fourteen?"

"I like thirteen." Ashberry peered over his reading glasses at her empty list.

Susy drew a slash through her number fifteen. Thirteen skaters would give them three lines of forwards and two sets of defenders. Fourteen was a better number. It would allow them some wiggle room for absences, but she wouldn't argue the point. She wrote Nik at number two and Georgie at three. They wouldn't be sitting here if their own kids weren't on the team.

"First five picks are by score." Ashberry leaned toward her, collapsing his chest against his thumbs. "Carlson will have those, but we know who it is."

Susy straightened her index finger, counting. "Matzke," she said.

Ashberry nodded. "And Senko."

That would've been Susy's pick, too. She wrote him down. And just as she'd extended her ring finger and prepared to declare O'Malley as the last automatic, Jeff Carlson arrived in the conference room with two other guys, the Squirt director whose kid would make their list, and the parent coach of the B1 team. Jeff dropped evaluations in the middle of the table, five stapled packets.

"I'm assuming I can add O'Malley to my list," she said as the men got settled.

Craig Rathmann, the age-group coordinator, nodded. The packets were organized by score, and Simon O'Malley's was sixth, but he'd be on their list regardless. Georgie had the fourth-highest total. Ashberry was first. Susy bit her lip. She'd argued for the head coaching spot over Ashberry. Both Jeff and Craig had told her they "were going in a different direction." Nik's raw score underlined their preference.

"Who else you got on there?" Jeff pointed at Susy's notebook.

"Matzke," she said. "Senko."

"And your kids," the director added. "I assume they're on the list." He chuckled, but Susy felt suddenly uneasy, though Georgie was clearly top five.

Ashberry had picked up his phone again, and Susy felt anger piling on top of her unease. Ashberry didn't seem invested enough to put his phone down to roster the team. Maybe the only thing that mattered to him was Nik's spot, front and center on the first line. Susy held the opinion that games were won and lost on the third line, with that last push. She'd been third line in Salt Lake City, and again in Torino.

With Ashberry quiet, Jeff took charge. They went through the packets in order and added three more. Rathmann, Teeterow, Dellinger.

It was on the next highest score—number nine in the pool—that they got stuck. "I coached Kelliher on my summer team a year ago." Ashberry dropped the sheets as he spoke. "I don't want him."

Jeff rubbed his stubble. "You don't want Kelliher? He's blazing fast."

The B1 coach squared his shoulders. "I can have Kelliher? We might be able to beat Maple Grove if I get Kelliher. Can I also have that kid who can pass? The new one?"

He meant Gus Mackenzie. Susy looked at Jeff, who'd flipped to Gus's scoresheet. He'd finished seventeenth by the numbers, out of the running for the A-team if they went numerically.

Jeff's voice was calm, but Susy saw the glint in his eye. "You know he doesn't skate all that well yet." He put his finger on the page where an evaluator had noted the deficiency.

"But he keeps his head up," the B1 coach said.

Ashberry pushed his chair way back and set his heels on the table. "I like that one. Good listener. Works hard. And isn't he Leigh Mackenzie's kid?" Susy nodded. They hadn't talked about it, but Ashberry would have heard from Arnie or Jeff about Leigh's return. "What's Leigh like?" Ashberry asked the table.

"Incredibly competitive," Susy said. "One of the most intense players I've met."

"Leigh will make sure her kid can skate." Jeff bumped his fist on the laminate. "I say you take him. We'll give Kelliher to B1."

"If you say so," Ashberry agreed, though he hadn't really needed Jeff's encouragement. Susy wrote "Mackenzie" on the list. She grabbed her phone and typed "Congratulations" in her text thread to Leigh, and then deleted it.

CHAPTER SIXTEEN

LEIGH MACKENZIE

August 2001

Leigh clicked new batteries into her Discman as she sat on the bus at the Albany airport. The players from her flight had shuffled into separate rows, even though Susy and Leigh usually sat together. Leigh counted seats from the front. There would be forty women arriving, forty women for twenty-three spots on the preliminary Olympic team roster. Almost no one would have to double up in these bus seats, not now and especially not when the camp was all over.

Leigh put her backpack on the seat next to her. Blink-182 blasted and she closed her eyes. Leigh attempted to visualize the opening conditioning test—her high-knee drive and deliberate arm swings on the treadmill—but Jeff kept popping into her consciousness. She saw the shadowy stubble on each of his cheeks, his dark eyes so different from Charlie's greenish ones. She saw his crooked smile, the way he'd looked at her after the semifinal in the World Championships, his fist pump after the assist she'd had in the team's routing of the Russians.

Leigh kept her eyes closed through "All the Small Things" and into Destiny's Child and Dave Matthews Band. Finally, the bus rolled out of the airport toward the Olympic Training Center. In an hour, Leigh would be able to see the foothills of the Adirondacks. The trees would thicken as her muscles bunched in anticipation of the two weeks to come. Over her music, Leigh could hear Susy talking to Cammi a couple of rows back. She said something about dead-lifting. Something else about speed drills.

When they arrived at Lake Placid, Leigh dropped her bags and went straight to the testing room. A trainer pointed at one of the five or six treadmills. "Mackenzie?" she asked. Leigh nodded. Susy hit the machine next to her. When Leigh's elapsed time was eight minutes and her heart felt like it might actually explode, she flicked her eyes toward her friend without jostling the mask she wore to measure her CO_2 output.

Susy's fingers stretched from her palms as she ran. Her shoulders were relaxed and her neck long. Leigh couldn't help it, she kept her inspection going. She looked down at Susy's quads, her knees driving almost as high as the front bar on the treadmill with each stride. She looked like Marion Jones, who'd won so many Olympic medals in Sydney.

"Mackenzie!" Her head whipped back to the trainer who had just reached over to increase her incline. "Eyes on your own paper!"

Leigh could feel Susy's gaze then. Already, the camp seemed more cutthroat than all the others.

"You got more in you." The trainer hit the pace button. Leigh imagined pulling a rope in front of herself with each stride, attempting to stay upright. *Get on your toes.* She pictured the biggest

Russian defender in that semifinal game, the way Leigh had beaten her to the puck nearly every time.

"Now we're getting there," the evaluator said. "Feeling like you're hitting max?" Leigh allowed herself a sidelong glance at Susy. "Don't look at her," the woman said. "This is about you."

Leigh jabbed a thumb at the ceiling, indicating that she wanted more, wanted faster.

"You sure?" The trainer looked at her screen. "Your heart rate is pushing one-ninety."

Leigh let her vision blur. She stretched her fingers like Susy had. She drove her knees. Even if she'd wanted to at this point, she couldn't look over. Every ounce of her was focused on maxing out.

Finally, after ten seconds or sixty, Leigh couldn't be sure, her toe clipped the front of the treadmill and she stumbled. She grabbed the railings and without thinking that it meant quitting, put her feet on the side runners, safely away from the conveyor belt.

"Good choice." The trainer hit the emergency stop button. "I was about to remind you that if you kill yourself on the treadmill, you can't actually score goals in the Olympics." She smiled, but Leigh was too tired to laugh. She ripped the mask from her face. A metallic taste materialized at the base of her tongue and for a moment, she wondered whether she would faint. All the while, Susy's feet pounded the machine next to her, her cadence increasing.

"We've got a ways to go with Walker," Susy's trainer said. "Not even close to max."

Leigh wobbled away toward the door. She had talked to Jeff the previous night, right before she'd finally fallen asleep. "I can't wait to see you. You're ready," he'd said. But as Susy pushed further and faster on her treadmill than Leigh had, she felt like she'd failed the first test.

"We're on the bus to the rink in forty minutes," someone said. She'd have just enough time to bring her bag to her room, splash water on her face, and then head to the lobby. But when she reached the hallway, Jeff was there. He grabbed her wrist, and she startled, her exhaustion overcome by adrenaline.

"That was a good start." He pulled her away. "Come on." Leigh let herself be led into a dark office, her whole body shaking from the effort of the test and now from the surprise of seeing Jeff.

He closed the door behind them and held his hand over the switch, so she couldn't flip it on. Leigh could see his smile in the light that filtered through the tempered glass window. "On the bus in forty minutes," Leigh mumbled. She didn't want to be late, but she realized she'd been waiting for this moment, too.

"I just need one of those forty minutes." Jeff's hand was on Leigh's hot cheek, his chest touching hers. It had seemed different on the phone. She hadn't been sure they'd kiss, though she'd definitely imagined it. Their conversations had started about hockey, and then Leigh had begun to tell Jeff about the biostatistics class she took that summer, about Jamie's triple-A games, about her dad's obsession with *The Mighty Ducks* movies. She never mentioned Charlie. On some level, she had definitely wanted this closeness with Jeff. As he touched her, though, all Leigh could see was Charlie's red hair and green eyes. She blinked and smelled Charlie's Irish Spring soap even as Jeff backed her against the wall, enveloping her in his own muskiness.

"I have a boyfriend." Leigh said it as she put a hand against his shoulder. It wasn't a push away, exactly, but a pause.

Jeff laughed and Leigh could feel his breath in her ear. "I don't want to be your boyfriend," he said. She shivered, her sweat cooling her skin. He put his thumb and forefinger on either side of her chin and tipped up her face. His lips were against hers in a split second. Leigh's heart rebounded to the rate where it had been on the treadmill, and she wondered whether this kiss would mess with her recovery. Leigh stood completely still. She stretched her fingers out as she had in the run and then balled them into fists as Jeff's tongue touched hers. It felt thicker than Charlie's. As he moved his hand to her chest, Leigh had the impulse to apologize for her sports bra.

"Mmm," Jeff sighed as he ended the kiss. He slid his arms around her back and hugged her to him.

"I'm so sweaty." It was all she could think to say.

He squeezed her and then let go. "I'll see you after the ice session." He smiled. "I'll find you." He left the room and Leigh leaned her head against the wall. She needed a minute to make sure her legs still worked.

CHAPTER SEVENTEEN

EMAIL FROM CATHY KELLIHER, HEAD MANAGER

October 2022

Dear Hockey Family,

The moment of decision has arrived, and I've been asked by the board of directors to send some reminders before lists are posted online under the tryout tab tomorrow night.

First of all: The evaluators were all experienced and caring adults from other associations. They're highly skilled and trustworthy.

That said, in order for our kids to learn appropriate behavior, it's important for us to MODEL IT. Please consider just accepting the team placements. Help your children process any negative emotions and then turn your attention to preparing for a GREAT SEASON. Remember: fun knows no level, and every child in the association will have competitive away tournaments.

Also, know your child's placement is IN THEIR BEST INTEREST. Kids develop best on teams that match their ability levels. Parents, time on the ice is more important than label on the team. Can I get an "Amen"?

And for those of you who resist the suggestions above, let me review the appeal policy in the parent handbook, a document you all affirmed when you completed your online registration. If you choose to appeal, your online application must include a $60 credit card payment to the association. If your appeal is successful (let me tell you, it's RARE), then we'll refund your sixty. If it's denied, we keep the fee.

Questions? Let me just remind you that my position is the head manager, not the decision-maker. I'm the messenger. If you're upset, take some deep breaths, and then if you can't take the high road and help your child do the same, call or email the coordinator for your age group.

GO LIONS!

Cathy

CHAPTER EIGHTEEN

LEIGH MACKENZIE

October 2022

That night Gus grabbed Leigh's hand after she finished reading a chapter of *Percy Jackson*. "I might not make the team," he said.

"It's true." She rubbed his thumb. Leigh had hoped Susy might have texted her a heads-up either way, but she'd been radio silent all the way through the tryouts. "There's a chance you might not make the A-team. But you know what else?" Gus waited. "You just might. Isn't that so exciting?"

Gus nodded, though his smile looked tentative.

"Whichever team you make," Leigh said, "you're going to have a great season. Minnesota hockey is a whole new deal."

"Greystone said I have a chance." Gus dropped her hand and flipped over to his back. He put both hands behind his head and his elbows out wide, a startlingly adult posture.

"You definitely have a chance," Leigh confirmed. "Did you leave it all on the ice in the last scrimmage?"

"What do you mean?"

"Did you try absolutely as hard as you could? Nothing else you could have done?"

Gus's chin bobbed fast. "I was so tired at the end I thought I was going to puke."

Leigh leaned over him for one last hug. "Then that's all you can do. You've gotta be satisfied with your effort."

In her head, Leigh heard again the thud of her duffel bag, the way it bounced on the concrete steps when it was all over. She forced another smile for Gus. "Night, sweetie."

"Are you guys going to wake me up when the results come in?"

Leigh flicked off the overhead light. Gus's bedside lamp shined over his little face, the shadows highlighting the dimple in his left cheek she'd first noticed minutes after he'd been born. It matched his father's exactly. "Want to just find out in the morning?"

"Dad said you could wake me up."

Leigh wouldn't rouse him just to deliver bad news. If it was a "yes," she'd think about it.

I'm going to bed," Leigh said an hour later as Charlie refreshed the tryouts page for the thousandth time.

"But it should be here any second. Don't you want to know?" He looked so cute on their couch with his laptop on his thighs and his finger hovered over the refresh button. He sat like this on election nights or on lottery notification days for the trail runs he entered with limited participants. Charlie had become a hockey fiend in the five months they'd been in Minnesota. There'd been no question that he'd shell out for extra Greystone sessions in the week before the tryouts. He'd started listening to podcasts about the youth scene on his runs.

Leigh put her hand on Charlie's shoulder for leverage as she stood up. "The results will be the same if I see them in the morning." Leigh could feel adrenaline prickling down the length of her arms. She did want to know what team he'd made. She wanted desperately to know, especially after she'd sent that letter to Jeff Carlson's lawyer. She'd written it like a memo reporting on the viability of an acquisition: the facts, with snippets of confident analysis. "Adult," she'd written. "Informed" and "consensual."

Jeff had hired a woman to defend him. Leigh had been surprised to discover that. The lawyer looked like a normal fiftysomething, nice, even, with a short haircut and gentle eyes. If Kate Thompson, attorney-at-law, could be on Jeff's side, then so could Leigh. Leigh had chosen to get involved with Jeff, after all. It had been her mistake. No one made her dial his number; he didn't force her to follow him into the empty dorm rooms or the referees' shower. He didn't make her betray Charlie. She was the one who thought the transgression would be worth it.

Charlie flipped his Buccaneers cap backward. A curl stuck endearingly to his forehead in the open space between the top of the hat and the adjustable strap. He clicked refresh again. "I know you did this a million times, but I still don't get how you can be so calm."

Leigh thought back to her high school tryouts and then to her final youth hockey days as a thirteen-year-old. "It wasn't really a thing." She'd been the best, anyway, of all the girls she played with. In high school, she would have made most boys' varsity squads.

In fact, the only team in her entire career that Leigh hadn't made was the one she'd wanted to be on most of all. She rolled her tricky shoulder and kissed the top of Charlie's head.

"I'm dying." Charlie moaned. "And this is Squirts. I can't even imagine the pressure of playing at the higher levels."

"Anyway." Leigh didn't want him to imagine too much of that pressure. She put her palm on the top of his head and pushed it back and forth jokingly. "I'm going to sleep. How long are you going to stay here?"

Charlie stretched his arms in front of him, linking his fingers and flipping his palms out as if warming up for a sprint. "I'm dedicated," he said.

Leigh laughed. "Well, I'm sure you'll let me know what happens." She headed up the stairs toward their bedroom and peeked in at Gus on her way. He turned in his sleep as she cracked the door, his mouth gaping and his breathing heavy. *Let him make it.* A roster spot would be a validation of his hard work, of his shooting in the driveway and the one-on-one sessions. Leigh couldn't imagine too many nine-year-olds exhibiting more dedication. Gus deserved a chance, Leigh thought, even though she didn't believe in "deserving it" as a justification for anything anymore, not after '02.

After Leigh had brushed her teeth and changed into sweatpants and Charlie's ancient finisher shirt from the Headwaters Ultramarathon, she heard a shout from the family room. The results. Despite her attempts at calm, she sat up straight, drew in a big breath, and held it as Charlie jogged up the stairs and down the hallway.

Their door flew open. "Leigh-Leigh!" His eyes shone, and his smile looked as gleeful as it had when he'd shown Gus the first *Star Wars* movie. His dimples looked handsome and boyish. "He did it."

"He did it," she repeated. She flopped back on the bed and smiled at the ceiling. "Thank God." And *she* had done it, too. She'd reached back into that hard and horrible time and made it into something good.

"Let's tell him." Charlie was halfway out the door, but Leigh didn't want to miss it. She vaulted from the bed and raced Charlie down the hall. They were both laughing as they skidded outside Gus's bedroom. By the time they'd opened the door, they'd made so much noise that their son was awake and rubbing his eyes.

"Why are you being so loud?"

Leigh looked at Charlie and grinned. Then she threw her arms wide and had the celebration she'd wanted for herself all those years ago. "You made it!" she and Charlie screamed together. And then she was jumping and hugging and dancing.

"Mom," Gus said after a minute. "Okay, I get you're excited. But you're being a little extra."

Leigh threw herself down on his twin bed and pretended to sleep. "You're right." She laughed. "No worries, I'm over it now."

"But I made it?" Gus was waking up now, processing the news.

"You did. You really did it, kid. And we're so proud." Leigh tackled him again, rubbing her nose into his neck as he giggled.

CHAPTER NINETEEN

LEIGH MACKENZIE

October 2022

Leigh considered pouring a shot of Tanqueray before they got in the car and headed to the rink for the first practice and concurrent parents' meeting, but Gus was in the kitchen and could potentially see her. The older he got, the more he tracked her behaviors. She didn't want to send the message that if she got nervous about something, she could fix it with alcohol.

She also didn't want to admit to having nerves about a stupid meeting. Gus was the one who was actually going to have to play hockey.

"Mom," Gus mumbled as he folded the last of his grilled cheese into his mouth. "I'm nervous."

You and me both, kid. Leigh had avoided attending everything related to Gus's hockey unless she could sneak in the back—too much residual anxiety, too many comparisons, too much stress. But in the case of the kickoff parents' meeting, Charlie had pleaded. Things were different in the State of Hockey. Leigh had connections that could help Gus. People knew who she was, and she should make an appearance. Charlie was right. Leigh had already used her influence to get Gus on the team. Now she should at least show up as a thank-you.

Since Leigh decided against the alcohol, she opened the pantry to search for some stomach-settling carbs. She grabbed a handful of pretzels and then turned around to face her son. "How nervous are you?"

Gus looked so earnest. He'd combed his hair neatly across his forehead. As a former elite athlete and current cutthroat dealmaker, Leigh was basically the world's expert on handling nerves. Dealing with Gus's might distract her from her own.

Gus swallowed. "It's like, I'm even more nervous than I was for tryouts. I—" He shook his head at her, his eyes comically wide, and she fought a smile. "I never thought I would, like, make it. Jamie and Greystone? They said it was a long shot."

"It's a testament to your talent, kiddo." Leigh grabbed his plate and shook the crumbs into the compost bin.

"That's what Dad told me," Gus said. "Raw talent."

"What about it?" Charlie appeared on the landing in his Buccaneers cap and a hoodie from his Tampa bookshop. Full Florida. Leigh considered asking him to change, since the whole point of the evening was to display their commitment to Liston Heights Hockey, but no one would recognize the Little Lights logo as a relic of the Sunshine State.

"Gus says he's feeling a little nervous about the first skate."

"Oh, buddy." Charlie walked to the back door and slid into his Salomon sneakers. Leigh made a mental note not to wear hers. Her mom had bought them matching pairs when they'd closed on the house. "The best," Leigh's mom had told them. "Like regular sneakers, but with tread for the packed snow." Leigh hadn't yet organized her shoes in her new closet. Only the high-rotation work pumps and two pairs of Vans had made it out of the box that Charlie had labeled, "Imelda Marcos Lite." He'd given all of the boxes whimsical titles and written poems on the underside flaps. The box of shoes said, "Wiggle your toes in my favorite pink socks." Leigh had taken pictures of her husband's poems as she opened each of the boxes. Someday, maybe she'd be organized enough to print a book of them, a keepsake from their epic move.

Charlie bent over to tighten his shoelaces. "You made the team because you deserve it!" he said.

She pushed the thought of the letter she'd written to Jeff's attorney away as Gus opened the coat closet. His hockey bag took up almost all of the space inside. "It was a long shot," Gus said again, his smile impish and expanding.

"A long shot doesn't mean impossible," Leigh said. "It just means everything has to line up exactly right and you have to take advantage of all of your opportunities. And, honey, you did." Leigh blinked away the photo she'd googled of Sydney Kirkpatrick, the member of the '14 national team who'd filed the complaint against Jeff. Sydney had dark hair, too, like Leigh's. In her headshot, a few strands of it stuck to her necklace, which appeared to be a St. Christopher medal. Leigh had zoomed in 300 percent on her computer screen to see that necklace. Sydney's bio indicated she'd been twenty-three years old when she'd played in Sochi. Jeff would have been thirty-nine or forty by then.

Although Leigh hadn't lied in her email to Jeff's attorney, Sydney's accusations did make her feel queasy. Leigh's letter, though, wasn't a denial of Sydney's claims. It's just that her own situation was different. Leigh was only five years younger than Jeff. She'd chosen to engage with him, to capitalize on his interest in her. Her gamble just hadn't paid off.

Leigh rubbed Gus's back. "Dad and I watched that final scrimmage, and you were in position one hundred percent of the time. I don't think any of the other kids could say that."

"But I didn't score any goals." Gus dragged his bag to the door and zipped his coat. "Mom, let's go," he said. "I don't want to be late for the very first practice."

Leigh looked at her watch. Gus took after Charlie in terms of punctuality. For them, "on time" meant ten minutes early. "Okay," Leigh said, "but first, raise your right hand."

"Mom!" Gus stomped his foot, a babyish impulse that made her laugh. "You don't have to do this."

"Apparently I do. I've been hearing a ton of self-doubt from you, young Padawan." She flashed on Sydney Kirkpatrick. Leigh was good at motivational speeches. Who had been there to give Sydney a pep talk when she'd filed that complaint?

Gus picked up his bag. "You don't even like *Star Wars*."

"Nope," Leigh admitted, "but I understand it, which is all that matters. Raise that hand." She could see Charlie tapping his watch in her peripheral vision, but she ignored him. They could spare a minute for a little confidence boost.

Gus gave Leigh a hard eye roll, but acquiesced, hunching under the ridiculous weight of the bag.

"I," said Leigh, "state your name."

"I, Gus," he said.

"Gus what?" She tipped her head toward him. He knew this drill.

"I, Gus Ward Mackenzie." Gus stomped again. "Dad!" He tried to recruit Charlie to his side, but Charlie shrugged. He and Leigh had agreed in the beginning not to contradict each other in front of Gus. Charlie was better at following the rule than Leigh was.

"The faster you do it"—Charlie zipped his new black parka—"the faster it'll be done."

Leigh soldiered on. "Have earned my place on the Lions' Squirt A-team." She pointed at her son. Gus stumbled a bit on his echo, but she decided to let it pass. "And will comport myself with confidence."

"What's 'comport'?" Gus lowered his hand and frowned at her.

"Hand up!" Leigh pointed at him. "It means 'behave.'"

He sighed and repeated.

"And will remember always"—Leigh hadn't preplanned a suitable ending for this particular oath and fell back on an old standby from the 1990s, a silly mantra from *SNL* that she'd said to herself from time to time in her playing days—"that I am good enough, fast enough, and that gosh darn it, people will like and appreciate me."

Charlie coughed, masking a laugh. Leigh glared at him as Gus repeated the finale. "Mom," he said when he finished, "you're really embarrassing."

"That's how moms are supposed to be." Leigh pulled his pom hat over his combed hair. "Now let's go."

Leigh tried to ignore her thumping heart and mild nausea as Charlie pulled into the packed Braemar Ice Arena parking lot. "I'm good enough," she told herself, just like she'd said to Gus. And besides, Gus had already made the team. Jeff couldn't very well take that away now. Leigh had already acted, too. She couldn't very well retract her letter in support of Jeff without raising flags. Gus should take advantage of this amazing opportunity—the one for which they'd moved here.

As he shifted the SUV into park, Charlie tapped Leigh's thigh. "Thanks," he said quietly. "I know you don't want to do this."

Leigh rolled her neck, releasing some of the tension that had built on the six-minute drive. Jeff's face appeared as she blinked. He'd be here tonight. He'd texted her after she'd mailed her letter and suggested another round of drinks soon. "To discuss Gus's progress," Jeff had written, "and make sure things are going well."

She'd tried to demur, but Jeff had pressed her for a date. "I helped you displace three sure things for Gus's spot on the team," Jeff wrote. "We gotta connect."

"You were right," Leigh said to Charlie. She put her hand on top of his. "It's better if I show I'm invested. We're invested."

Gus knocked on Charlie's window and shouted, "Pop the trunk, Dad! I see Nik going in." Gus pointed at Coach Ashberry and his kid at the entrance. "It's time."

Leigh sucked in her belly when she saw her reflection in the rink door. Charlie held it open. Gus disappeared toward the locker room.

Leigh didn't see Jeff approach and startled at his voice. "I was wondering if you'd show your face around here, Mackenzie!" He bumped a hip against hers. Leigh's stomach rolled. "Squirt As!" Jeff offered a thick hand to Charlie. Leigh stared at the black hairs on the back of Jeff's knuckles. "Good to see you again, man."

"Jeff," Leigh said. "You remember Charlie." Leigh took a half step away from them both.

"Of course." Jeff grinned. "My tryout companion." Charlie had mentioned meeting Jeff under the bleachers where he'd hidden with the ex-NHL guy. Leigh hadn't thought it seemed like a particularly smart move, breaking the association rules right out of the gate. But she guessed it had paid off well enough, just like her compromise letter had.

Jeff winked. "It's nice to see you out in the open this time."

"Yeah." Charlie laughed. "Arnie gave me quite an initiation."

"You Mackenzies have good instincts about new friends."

Leigh cringed. Jeff was an inch or two shorter than Charlie was. She was sure Jeff hated that. He'd told her once that he'd preferred coaching women because he didn't like it when the players towered over him.

"It's nice to have the tryouts behind us, and what do you know?" Charlie grinned. "The kid made it!"

Leigh tried to hide her wince, then made a show of looking at her watch. "Jeff, uh, we've got a meeting. Someone's got to tie Gus's skates, and then the parents—"

"Oh, I know." Jeff pointed up the stairs. "Squirt As. I always make an appearance there. Hey, quite a coup that little Gus made the team, eh?"

Leigh narrowed her eyes. Jeff had promised he wouldn't tell Charlie anything about their past.

Charlie said, "He's been working his butt off. We're very proud."

"He aced out a couple of kids who really paid their dues," Jeff said. "But as Leigh knows"—he looked back at her and winked—"sometimes things don't work out, even if you do everything right. Wild cards and all that."

Leigh shivered. "See you up there, okay, Jeff?" She linked her arm through Charlie's and led him toward the stairs. "That fucking guy." Charlie swiveled his head around to discern whether anyone had heard her cursing. "Sorry," she said. "I know we're trying to make a good impression."

CHAPTER TWENTY

SUSY WALKER

October 2022

At the previous week's Sunday Skate, the girls had compared notes about the teams they'd made for the upcoming season. A few of them would play on the girls' A-team for Liston Heights. Another played park league, which didn't even hold tryouts. Everyone else had been B or C.

"My goal was B," Tricia told Susy as they walked into the rink together. "And I made it!"

"I'm not surprised," Georgie said. "The way you've been doing drills lately, I think you'll be A next year."

"It's because of Sunday Skate," Tricia said. "Even my mom agrees. Without this extra practice, I wouldn't be able to reach my full potential."

Susy smiled down at the tops of the girls' heads. An hour later, she sat outside the locker room as usual, overhearing the weekly dance party. Georgie would have fun in the boys' locker room, too, Susy knew. The year before, "Sweet Caroline" had inexplicably become the hype song, blasted on repeat after each victory. But when she came out of the girls' locker room, Georgie always looked a little more wild, happily reckless in her release. She kept herself reined in with the boys. In just a couple of years, she'd be kicked out of their space for good.

Now, as Susy surveyed the crowd of parents in the conference room for the team meeting, Georgie was already ensconced in the locker room. Leigh and Charlie Mackenzie sat alone at the table closest to the door, the same one Susy and Jeff had sat at when they'd rostered Gus.

After Lake Placid, Susy had figured Leigh and Charlie would have broken up. Instead, they'd gotten married. She hadn't heard about it until at least a year later when someone from the team had run into Leigh's dad.

"We're very lucky in Liston Heights to have both a long legacy of hockey excellence and also some of the very best parent volunteers you could ask for," Jeff Carlson said in his welcome.

Susy knew almost every parent in the room. She had coached half the kids the year before or the year before that. Heck, she'd been there the first time Nik Ashberry made a backhanded goal in the Mite Jamboree. She'd even taught him the dangle that got the job done, but that fact hadn't given Halden Ashberry any pause when he'd fought Susy for the head coaching position.

Susy would be leaving the meeting soon, thank God, before the best (and most overzealous) parent volunteers launched into their spiels about required shifts in the rink's concession stand and enamel pins for trading at the Nova Tournament in January. After her formal introduction, Susy would start practice, and she couldn't wait. She was here to play, not for this get-to-know-you bullshit. Some of the families were nice—she knew this—but she'd realized at the beginning of her coaching career that being friends with other parents was complicated when she controlled their kids' positions and playing time.

Leigh, Susy knew, wasn't one for bullshit, either. Her eyes were on her phone as Jeff finished his speech. She wondered if they might communicate more regularly now that the season was under way, if she might see Leigh before and after the games or text with her about the skills she wanted Gus to work on outside of practice. Maybe they could revisit some of their glory days, the happy ones before Lake Placid. Not many people in Susy's life could relate to the thrill and the pressure of playing in a Team USA jersey. Of course, maybe hockey was the last thing Leigh wanted to discuss. Susy had drafted texts to her that summer, but deleted them. If they didn't share hockey, would they have anything else in common?

And Leigh had been among the best hockey players Susy had seen, despite her failure to make the Olympic team. Leigh had stolen that puck from Susy on the blue line during the '99 NCAA Nationals the weekend before they'd met Charlie. Then, Leigh had outskated nearly everyone at the Four Nations Cup in 2000 and at the World Champs in '01. If the Olympics had been a year earlier, Leigh would not only have been on the team, but they might have all won gold medals.

Susy had run her fingers over her silver medal a million times—the figure with the torch, the engraved message, "Light the fire within." But no amount of replaying or wishing could change its color. Two of her teammates at the University of Minnesota Duluth had played for the Canadians that year. Back at school after the Olympics, Susy had been the best on her own team, but two other girls in the locker room had been best in the world.

Knowing Leigh's pedigree, Susy was thrilled to have Gus on Squirt A. When Susy watched him skate, she recognized Leigh's fire, the little something extra it took to stick with a play when everything fell apart. Gus had exuberant tenacity. And, yes, his skating was sloppy. His stride went wide and ended short, but he understood the game. Faster and stronger kids were repeatedly offsides and carrying the puck when they should pass. Gus had the instincts the team needed. And Susy hadn't even had to fight for him. Jeff had done that for her. He'd smoothly traded Kelliher away for Gus's spot.

And now, at the front of the room, Jeff had passed the speaking baton to Ashberry. It was time for Susy's introduction.

"I know she's dying to get on the ice with the kids." Ashberry pointed at her. "So let me introduce our illustrious assistant coach, Susy Walker." Susy flinched at "illustrious," but when she searched Ashberry's face, she couldn't detect sarcasm. Although he hadn't wanted to be *her* assistant, he liked her.

Susy walked to the front and smiled first at Leigh, who looked up. "I'm thrilled to be here." Susy channeled the same energy she brought to back-to-school night, spine straight. "Hockey is my first love. I've had the pleasure of working with many of you before. I've played and coached hockey for basically my whole life."

"I should have said," Ashberry broke in, "Susy was among the first girl standouts in Minnesota. A pioneer. She's a multiseason All-American and has two Olympic medals, a silver from Salt Lake City and a bronze from Torino."

"The silver is my favorite of the two." The assembled parents laughed. The Olympics were perennially part of her bio. At back-to-school night, parents' mouths made comical O's when she got to that part of her speech. She supposed not many Olympic medalists ended up chairing the PE departments at suburban middle schools. But she liked both the job and its stability.

"That was a long time ago, and actually"—Susy glanced at Leigh, who'd gone back to Instagram or whatever she was scrolling—"there's another former member of Team USA in our midst tonight." Leigh laid her phone flat and bit her lip. Her husband grabbed her hand. "Leigh Mackenzie has recently returned to the motherland from Florida." She pointed at the back table and the twenty-five or so heads in the room swiveled. "Leigh and I were teammates in the early aughts, and she's a former Ms. Hockey. One of the first ones, isn't that right?" Susy knew it was. Their senior year was only the third of the Ms. Hockey contest. Susy had worn a Laura Ashley dress to the ceremony and pushed her toes into the tops of her velvet flats as the local newscaster had announced Leigh as the winner.

"A long time ago." Leigh pulled at her ponytail. Susy remembered she'd worn a pink tweed skirt with a matching blazer to the awards banquet, her brown shoes with a blocky heel.

"So far, I haven't gotten Leigh to agree to help out on the ice, but . . ." Susy raised her eyebrows. Parents' gazes ping-ponged between them. Charlie's dimples deepened as he beamed at his wife.

Leigh waved. "We'll see," she said.

"Anyway." Susy let her old friend off the hook. "I'm over the moon to be on the staff with the Squirts this year. My daughter, Georgie, is on the team. She's played with the boys since she was little, and I appreciate how welcoming families have been over the years." Susy glanced meaningfully at Scott Holtz, who had complained to the board about girls' participation at the Squirt level. Jeff Carlson had told her about it, and Susy had suggested that Jeff send Scott the raw data from the tryouts that showed Georgie with 92 total points of 100 and Liam Holtz with 74, the second-lowest evaluation score of any skater on the team.

"Before I head to practice, I'd like to share my goals for the kids this year." Susy had made notes for this part. She brushed her hand against the pocket of her joggers and felt the folded piece of Liston Heights Middle School stationery there, but realized she didn't need it. "First and foremost, Squirts is about skill development. We're going to play positions, we're going to execute passes, we're going to put the puck on the net." She smiled. "It's easier said than done, right?" Most parents smiled back or nodded. Scott Holtz folded his arms and looked at Ashberry. Susy checked on Leigh again and inadvertently made eye contact. She winked at her, and then immediately regretted it. *Were they five years old?*

Susy felt her face heating as she continued. "Wins will come if we focus on skills first. I'm for equal playing time at this level, and I want the kids to have fun. Happy kids are good players, and I want—Coach Ashberry and I want"—she glanced over and caught Halden in a side conversation with Jeff—"the kids to stick with hockey for a long, long time."

Susy looked back at Leigh, who still stared at her. Her eyes looked friendly enough. There had been so many times they'd laughed together, playing stupid road-trip games as the team bus traversed New England, and "ding-dong ditching" other players' hotel rooms. Suddenly, Leigh grinned and then looked down at the table in front of her. Susy wondered if she could still hear the national team's off-key caterwauling. They'd usually belted "Fallin'" by Alicia Keys before an extra intense workout.

"Anyway," Susy said, grateful to be finished, "I get to kick off practice tonight, so I'm going to take advantage of my twenty minutes without Coach Ashberry. Who knows what I can accomplish alone." She tapped her fingers together in a mad-scientist move, and several parents laughed again.

She walked to the back of the room and as she passed Leigh, she tugged her ponytail. Susy had her Olympic medals. Things had ended better for her than they had for Leigh, which had been the reason all those years ago that she'd stopped trying. She'd assumed Leigh would despise her for taking her spot.

But the women were in their forties now. They'd been passing in and out of each other's circles for months. Susy could be the one to rekindle their friendship. She jogged toward the locker room. Their ice time started in about ninety seconds.

CHAPTER TWENTY-ONE

GUS MACKENZIE

October 2022

October 25, 2022
First Practice
Performance Rating: 3/5, Worse than Kelliher
Minutes This Week: 57
Lifetime Hours: 435
Quote from Coach Ashberry: "It's a long game."

"Where's Kelliher?" one of the A-team kids said as he sat on the bench next to Gus.

"Didn't make the team," someone said from across the room. "Didn't you see the list?"

"Didn't make it?" the first guy echoed. "Colin? Whoa. He scored like four times in the scrimmages."

Gus snuck a look at the kid next to him. He'd been pinny number seven in tryouts. His name started with *L*, Gus was pretty sure. Liam or Lucas.

The kid stared back. "Who are you?"

"Pinny eleven." Gus shoved his foot into his skate. His white tube sock bunched near his ankle and he tugged it up under the Velcro of his shin pad.

"Of course!" It was Georgie talking now. She sat across the room, directly opposite Gus. He hadn't realized that everyone else was listening. "That's Gus from Florida."

"Florida!" a kid Gus knew as Owen yelled. "Oh, man, you took Colin Kelliher's spot!"

Before Gus could reply, one of the moms walked in and grabbed her kid's skate laces. The players went quiet. Gus's hands shook as he held the sides of his left skate. His toe hit the tongue as he tried to put it on, and the skate fell on its side. Gus tucked his chin to his chest and blinked back tears, shaky from nerves. He breathed in through his nose and held it. Crying now would be a disaster. He grabbed his boot and tried again. "Resilience." He heard his mom's voice in his head. "Persistence."

His foot slid into the skate. Gus wiggled his toes against the inside and then ran his hand over the green *L* in the middle of the new practice jersey. He kept his eyes on the floor. In his peripheral vision, he could see the goalie collapsed on his stomach while his dad wrenched the leather strap of his leg pad tight against his skate blade. Not very many parents had come into the locker room. Gus hoped his dad wouldn't forget him. When he tied his own skates, his ankles wobbled, and these kids were already faster.

Maybe it would have been better if Gus had made the B-team. Then Colin Kelliher could be here like everyone seemed to expect. Greystone had prepared him to be a B-team player. He'd told him at his final session before the last tryout that it was "possible, but a long shot" for Gus to make A. There had been no tears then, even though Gus's lungs had been burning from his last set of sprints. Gus liked that Greystone and Jamie told him the truth. Greystone said being a good hockey player was a "long game." Gus knew that already. He hadn't even clocked 500 hours of the necessary 10,000.

Though he hadn't told his parents or Big Gus (they were 110 percent people, 100 percent of the time), Gus had decided after the first cut in tryouts that making the B-team would be just fine. Even the C-team kids at Floyd Elementary wore their hockey sweatshirts to school and talked about their team's stats. It wasn't like in Tampa, where only a couple of kids in the whole school played hockey. In just the fourth grade at Floyd, there were twelve players across the three classes. Sure, Nik Ashberry and Simon O'Malley acted like they were kings of the entire grade. But Cyril Franklin also knew every single NHL team and had told Gus at recess that his goal was to make B2, the second-to-lowest level.

It wouldn't be that bad to play hockey with Cyril. That kid at least hung out with him at recess. Nik and Simon, meanwhile, spent each day building a stick structure at the edge of the playground. When Gus asked to join, they said they had "too many people already" working on it, even though it was just the two of them.

"Sorry!" Gus's dad hopped over duffel bags to get to him in the locker room. "They just got finished telling us that there are no parents in here after tonight." Gus's dad dropped to his knees and pulled a skate up to rest on one of his thighs. "So, we'll practice tying these at home, okay?"

Gus nodded. His dad looked at the kid on his left whose skate laces were limp, the boots loose.

"Do you need help with yours?" Gus's dad asked. "You're William, yeah?" Gus's dad and Jamie seemed to know all of the kids already.

"Yeah," William said. "Thanks. My parents probably got super into the meeting. They love these things." He rolled his eyes.

Gus's dad finished with his skates in a minute and then shuffled over on his knees to where William was sitting. "Want me to redo this one?" He touched the skate William had tied himself.

"Yes, please," William said. "I suck at this."

Gus silently pleaded with his dad not to correct William's use of "suck."

"Imprecise," his dad always said about that word. "Say what you really mean. Something that 'sucks' frustrates you, it disappoints you. You're not dealing with a lollipop."

Gus's dad winked at him. "No problem," he said. Gus and William smiled at each other. Other kids always liked Gus's dad. He drove all the carpools and took kids out for pizza. In Florida, most of his friends had moms who did that kind of stuff, but in Gus's house, it was always the dad.

Just as his dad finished with William's second skate, a red-faced guy wearing a Lions hockey jacket burst in. "I forgot about your skates!" he said to William.

"The Florida kid's dad helped me," William said.

"I'm Charlie."

"Kevin," William's dad said. "Thank you. I got really into Jeff Carlson's speech about sportsmanship, and I forgot to slip out." Gus's dad wiped his hands on his pants and stood up. All around them, kids grabbed their sticks and streamed out.

"Okay, Dad?" William pointed at the door. "I think it's time."

"Go get 'em," Kevin said. "First day, so good impression. Have fun." He slapped William's breezers. "Work hard!"

Gus looked up at his dad, wondering if he'd get a similar pep talk. "It's exciting," Charlie said. "One hundred and ten percent."

Gus couldn't get a full breath in as he lined up with the kids outside the rink door. Suddenly it was open, and they all sprinted toward the bench where Coach Walker had dumped a large bucket of pucks.

"Hey, Florida!" He turned to see Nik Ashberry next to him. "Race ya!" Nik was already flying by the time Gus took off. Nik hockey-stopped a couple of seconds ahead of him. "You're going to have to get faster." Gus reached his stick out to swipe a puck from the pile. "My dad says some of your scores were lower than Kelliher's."

Lower than Kelliher's? What was he even doing here? "Florida hockey is different," Gus mumbled. What was it his mom had made him say before they'd left the house? That he was good enough and people liked him? What a joke.

Gus skated away from Ashberry toward the net as the goalie scuffed the ice in front of it. The goalie wasn't ready for shots, but that didn't stop O'Malley from burying one top shelf.

"Hey, Florida," the goalie said. "I'm Mac."

"Hi." Gus stood still next to the goal, and Georgie Magnussen skated up to them.

"Mac's the best," she said. She rubbed the top of his helmet with her glove. "Mac, Gus's mom used to play on Team USA with mine."

She skated off toward the face-off circle, looped around, and saucered her shot over Mac's paddle.

"Still warming up here, Georgie," Mac said.

Gus tapped his stick against the goalpost. Other kids skated around him like the water bugs he'd seen on his family's airboat tour in the Everglades.

"You gonna shoot or what?" Georgie asked.

It felt like something was stuck in Gus's throat. He looked toward the locker room and wished he could start tomorrow instead of right now.

Georgie took off again, throwing in some backward crossovers as she waited for William and O'Malley to shoot. When she got back to Gus after putting another one past Mac, she said, "My mom says a lot of these kids are cone jockeys." Gus had never heard that phrase. "It means kids who know how to do the drills, but don't have good instincts in the game," Georgie explained. "You're not a cone jockey. That's what my mom told me."

She skated away again. Gus took the puck back around the net and then out to the red face-off circle. He shot toward Mac's blocker side, and the puck snuck in off a bad bounce.

"Nice," Mac said, not looking. His eyes were on Nik on the other side of the zone. Ashberry lifted the puck easily toward the upper-right corner. It winged in just below the bar.

There was no doubt Ashberry had the better shot, but maybe Gus could keep getting lucky. It didn't have to be perfect, Uncle Jamie said, as long as it got the job done. Gus had no choice but to start his job right now.

CHAPTER TWENTY-TWO

CHARLIE MACKENZIE

November 2022

In Gus's first-week practices, Charlie tried to pull his focus from nine-year-old hockey. He'd spent their first four months in Minnesota with the singular goal of getting Gus on the right team. In between sessions at Greytness and scouting excursions with Jamie, Charlie unpacked their lives into the new house. Along with that task, there'd been a spate of trips to Goodwill, where Charlie finally let go of at least half of the items in the box he'd labeled "Hold on tight." His poem inside the flap had been just three lines long.

> If I had known for sure you'd be solo,
> I would have spent every nap time with my nose in your fuzzy head.

When he'd opened and emptied that box in the bright morning light of Gus's east-facing room, Charlie could see clearly the dinginess of the old fuchsia security blanket, the corners rusty-looking. Gus's life in their new house would be more hockey trophies and music posters, and less magnetic blocks and corded stuffed rabbits, even if Charlie had been in denial when he'd packed all that stuff.

With school started and settled, Charlie could start making the rounds of the metro area's independent bookstores to see if one might be a good fit for his employment. And he could get serious about training for that summer's Headwaters Ultra. He'd entered the lottery the night Gus had made the A-team, coat-tailing on that auspicious athletic news. He'd find out in January if he was one of the lucky 250 runners. If he was, Charlie would need a solid base of mileage by then as a foundation on which to build his fitness.

In addition to getting back into ultra shape, Charlie could unearth the manuscript. He'd buried it in a box labeled "Dead Dreams." Morbid, yes, but he'd laughed when he'd written it. Inside, his Sharpie lettering ran over both box flaps.

"Someday," you told yourself. "Later, when Gus is older."
You didn't realize you'd be ancient then, too.
Oxidized. Over the hill.

On the day of Gus's fourth hockey practice, Charlie stood in the office with his hands on his hips, inspired by the banana-leaf wallpaper Leigh had remembered. Charlie eyed the box in the back of the room. He got as far as opening "Dead Dreams" and rereading his packing poem, before he tasted the familiar sourness at the back of his throat. He'd been an A student in his creative writing program, but then again, hadn't everyone?

Charlie pulled his printed pages out from beneath the stapler he was pretty sure Leigh had lifted from her old office. An unopened pack of his favorite ballpoints flopped to the floor as he excised the novel. He thumbed through the manuscript and checked the page numbers. He'd made it to 132 before he'd put the book away for good. He'd petered out just as his main character had stepped off the bus at the Olympic Training Center in Lake Placid, New York.

The problem with going back to it at this point was that Charlie knew what happened next. His character—Lavinia, he'd named her—abandoned her dreams and settled for Cormac. And Cormac had, apparently, suffered a crisis of imagination. He wouldn't finish his novel. He'd drive across town with bottles of Lavinia's freshly pumped breast milk and keep the dates for dentist appointments in his head. His life stalled. His love for Lavinia, their easy companionship, and his admiration for her ambition weren't enough to spur him along.

Charlie, Cormac's alter ego, hadn't finished *his* novel, either.

Instead of reading the pages as he thought he might, Charlie put them in the top-right drawer of his desk, and his pencils in the long, thin middle one. Then, because he couldn't face the fictional hockey world he'd invented based on Leigh's collegiate life, he opened his laptop and navigated to the Liston Heights Hockey Association website. With each click, his jaw loosened. He wouldn't dive back into the novel today. He scooted his computer farther to the left side of his desk until his forearm lined up with its edge, as far away as possible from the drawer that held the book. He was sure the story needed reworking, and besides, there was the hurdle of having to tell his wife that he'd written a novel based on her biggest failure. Not that he thought of it that way. In his mind, even being on the cusp of making an Olympic team vaulted her into a separate stratosphere. Leigh had no idea the impression she made on people, exuding an effortless competence that others couldn't access.

Charlie burned an hour looking through the team's prior results and researching their opponents on Youth Hockey Hub, a site Jamie had shown him that compiled stats and analyzed the strength of each team's schedule. After he'd picked up Gus, helped him with homework, and assembled Vietnamese-style meatballs with ginger and fish sauce, he poured Leigh a glass of rosé as she walked in the back door.

"Hey." He kissed her forehead.

"No practice tonight?" She surveyed the family room, looking for Gus. Their son had retreated to the basement for more shooting.

"Nope!" Charlie tucked his hands into his pockets. "And he even finished his homework. We're free."

Leigh grunted. "Maybe *you* are." Her eyes looked flat as she collapsed into a kitchen chair and plunked the wine on the driftwood table. They planned to replace it at some point, the material more suited to Florida than the tundra. "I've got a million financial statements to read before my trip next week."

"Shoot." Charlie thought of his own ignored pages upstairs. Maybe it would spark his motivation if he actually had crunch times like Leigh did, if someone was counting on him to bring in millions of dollars per chapter written.

Of course, both Gus and Leigh counted on Charlie to handle the hockey and everything else. He grabbed his water glass and sat across from her. "I did some research about last year's Squirt As," Charlie said, trying to think of something light, given her mood. Leigh stared at the floor and chewed her bottom lip. Charlie followed her gaze down and watched her foot slide back and forth on the wood. "That's what you did with your day?" she asked. "You researched last year's Liston Heights Squirt A-team?"

Charlie cocked his head. "Well, not the whole day." He'd also gone on a run and folded two loads of laundry. Still, Leigh never criticized the way he spent time. He handled the household. That had been their deal from the beginning.

"I'll keep you from being a starving artist," she'd said as they both entered their graduate programs in the fall of 2002. They both knew her MBA was the one that would pay the bills. Charlie had wondered whether her parents would disapprove of the unconventional roles they'd adopted in their relationship; but Helen and Gus had seemed thrilled to have him, hugging him as fiercely after his MFA defense as they had at his Headwaters finish. Charlie's wedding to Leigh had been the victory lap, everyone cheering as the minister pronounced them "the spouses Mackenzie."

"I've been thinking," Leigh said. "I wonder if this was the wrong play, putting Gus on A. We shouldn't act like hockey is his only skill, or like, the only important thing. I got a text from Susy with dryland drills for him to practice. He's behind."

"Obviously, it's not Gus's only important thing." Charlie tried to squash his annoyance. He'd made everything nice for Leigh, the house unpacked, dinner ready, Gus happy and on the best hockey team. The kid was already downstairs working drills. He'd catch up.

But Leigh got like this sometimes, overly melancholy when things piled up at work. And her statement didn't make sense. They'd decided together to put everything into getting Gus on the team. That was what they all had wanted, Gus most of all. And watching Gus play Minnesota hockey had been Leigh's dream since the first time she'd laced up his toddler skates. She'd been the one to point out that Minnesota hockey would be a million times more stimulating than Tampa House League.

Leigh kept her eyes on her socks. "Gus needs to know that we'll love him and respect him even if he's never good at hockey."

"What?"

"I mean, if he never catches up to Georgie and those other kids."

"But Gus *is* good at hockey. He made the team." And for the next four and a half months, it was going to be his major thing. Later, in the spring or the summer or a year after that, Charlie could focus with Gus on math or poetry or film editing, or whatever else he wanted to do. Leigh's impetuous overanalysis was what he didn't like about their arrangement. Charlie did the primary parenting as requested, and then she second-guessed when she felt like it.

Leigh leaned her head all the way back, so she stared up at the chandelier they both had decided they didn't like. "We have to accept him no matter what."

"Obviously, Leigh." Gus was the person Charlie loved and knew best in the world, even including his wife. Gus fascinated Charlie, had endless dimensions. "Obviously, I know hockey isn't everything, but look—"

Leigh couldn't very well disparage him for taking an interest. What did she think he'd been doing this summer while she made a name for herself sixty hours per week at her new office? "I left my job to come here. So, yeah, I'm thinking about hockey. I thought it was important to you."

He hadn't felt angry when he'd started telling her all this, but as he finished, a fury sparked. She never seemed to see his sacrifices. His job in Tampa hadn't been a moneymaker. They'd called his checks their "vacation fund." But he'd been important to Little Lights. The store had become a regional destination for touring authors under his watch. Their social media had national reach. And there'd been the proximity to words when he'd worked there. He'd felt closer to his own future as a writer. He knew the spot on the fiction shelf where his novel would appear. Charlie had already decided he'd publish under his original name, Ward. His book, *Ice Time*, would be shelved not far from David Foster Wallace's *Infinite Jest*. Charlie curled his toes under and squinted at the meatballs he'd made. He'd planned to reheat them while Leigh changed her clothes.

"There are other things I could have done besides just accommodate you," Charlie muttered.

"Sure. Because I'm stopping you from writing your novel. *I'm* keeping you from greatness." She wheeled her arm around the room, the white cabinets, the farmhouse sink, the second-place light fixture. "I can see it's been a real sacrifice for you to be here."

Every time Leigh went for the jugular of Charlie's unwritten novel, and with each discrete apology after the fact, Charlie thought it would be the last one. But just like Leigh couldn't get over the Olympics, she also couldn't take this particular weapon out of her arsenal. In fact, she sharpened it while Charlie wasn't looking.

"God," Charlie whispered. "Don't be ugly, Leigh."

She ignored him. "What happened to your own dreams, Charlie? Have you written any new chapters while I keep paying those grad school loans? I saw the last alumni magazine. People publish their books all the goddamned time. Even people with kids."

CHAPTER TWENTY-THREE

LEIGH MACKENZIE

August 2001

L eigh dialed Charlie after the film session that afternoon. When he answered, she could hear his roommates in the background. She looked at her watch to verify the day. They all bled together with her to-do list limited to hockey. It was Sunday night. The boys would be watching *The Simpsons*. She felt guilty for interrupting until she remembered it would be a rerun. The "Men of Ashford Avenue," as Charlie and his roommates called themselves, never missed an episode, so they'd doubtless already seen whichever exploit of Bart they were watching.

Leigh drove the conversation with details about her workouts, the conditioning runs, the film sessions in which they had watched the final excruciating seconds of the team's World Championship loss. She left very few holes in her narrative where he might ask her anything, especially not whom she was hanging out with or which coaches had felt her up near the training room.

Leigh asked Charlie about his summer job in the writing center at the university. As he told stories about that week's tutoring clients, she remembered Jeff's hand over her sweaty T-shirt. As she thought of it, Leigh slipped a hand inside her bra and pressed on the soft flesh next to her armpit.

Twenty minutes later when she and Charlie were just professing their final "I love yous," Susy came back in. She was quiet and kept her eyes down. When she hung up, Leigh felt itchy, less calm than she had when she'd made the call. Usually, Charlie made her feel Zen.

"You okay?" Susy picked up her book, the Lance Armstrong autobiography, *It's Not About the Bike.*

"You get to the part about quitting yet?" Leigh had read and reread it that summer. If Lance could win the Tour de France three straight times after beating cancer, then surely Leigh could keep her spot on the national team.

Susy flipped back a few pages. "I underlined that part. 'Pain is temporary'?"

"Yeah." Leigh opened the door and took a step into the hallway. She'd copied Lance's quote about quitting and tacked it to the bulletin board above her bed at home. "Even the smallest act of giving up stays with me," Lance had written. "If I quit, it lasts forever." Leigh tried to smile, but her cheeks felt heavy. "I'm going to get a snack and maybe go for a little walk." She didn't wait for Susy's reply before she let the door click shut behind her.

Leigh tugged on the strings of her hoodie as she walked into their floor's snack room. She ran her fingers over packets of instant oatmeal and sleeves of cheese and crackers. Susy had a case of Luna Bars in her suitcase, which were undoubtedly healthier than these options, but Leigh just needed something to keep her stomach full. It would help her fall asleep. Plus, she didn't want to ask Susy for another bar. That box had been just one more piece of evidence that Susy was intricately prepared for this camp. She seemed like a veteran this time, and even though Leigh was, too, she felt new.

"If I quit, it lasts forever," she whispered as she surveyed the snacks. She'd say it to herself in the gym the next morning. The women would max out on their squats and dead lifts. Leigh poured a packet of apple cinnamon oatmeal into one of the cardboard bowls stacked below the sink and eyeballed the water. As the microwave whirred, Leigh raised her arms above her head and stretched her back and obliques. Everything hurt. As much as she'd tried to simulate the stress of training for six hours per day before she got to the selection camp, it was impossible. Playing against the boys' high school teams wasn't the same as matching up against the best women in the world, hour after hour.

As Leigh tipped her head to the left, she heard footsteps behind her and then let out a little yelp as Jeff's arms snaked around her waist. "Shhhhh," he said in her ear. She gasped as Jeff's fingers pressed the underside of her breasts. The microwave dinged, and she giggled.

"Shhhh," Jeff said again.

Leigh turned toward him, her heart pounding. She'd just told Charlie, her boyfriend of almost two years, that she loved him, and now here she was with Jeff, his hands firm against her rib cage, his breath hot in her ear.

"I want to be alone with you," he said. The microwave dinged again.

"That's my oatmeal." She pushed one of his arms down in order to step back. The cinnamon smell mingled with his Speed Stick. Jeff let her go and leaned against the half-size refrigerator. She peeked at him as she stirred the oatmeal with a plastic spoon. She dripped cold water in from the sink. When she looked up, Jeff's eyes glinted.

"Satisfied?" he asked.

Leigh had been with Charlie forever. She knew everything

about him, every shirt—including the race-finisher one he'd lent her for good luck at the camp—every book in his bookshelf, every stain on his threadbare sheets. Jeff was five years older than them both. He had a new Toyota Camry and the ear of Head Coach Miller. Still, a warning light seemed to flash in front of her eyes. She wasn't single, and certainly flirting with a coach to increase her chances of making the Olympic team was technically wrong.

Another Lance quote popped into her head. "If you worried about falling off the bike, you'd never get on." Wouldn't it all be worth it once she'd won?

Leigh put her oatmeal on the counter. "It takes more than a cup of Quaker to satisfy me." She giggled again. She imagined what she'd look like on-camera, sweatpants and wet splotches on both shoulders of her hoodie from her damp hair. No makeup. Is this what an Olympic hockey player looked like? Is this what Jeff wanted?

"Oh yeah?" Jeff grabbed her again, laughter in his voice, too. His palm landed just below the band of her bra. "What does it take to satisfy you?"

Her fingers flitted around his waist. Holding him there crossed another line. She pictured gripping the weight-lifting bar in the morning, gritting her teeth and pushing herself further than she ever had before. She let her fingers slip just beneath the waistband of Jeff's jeans where his back hollowed. "I want to make the team." Leigh moved her hand again, reached for her oatmeal despite Jeff's proximity.

With his free hand, Jeff pinched the bowl and put it back on the counter. "You know who has something to do with you making the team?" He put both arms around her, his biceps over hers. "I do."

Leigh tipped her chin up and held her breath. Her lips were centimeters from Jeff's again. Charlie was on his falling-apart tweed couch back in Saint Paul. He and his roommates had likely cracked Rolling Rocks. Charlie might go to the library after *The Simpsons* was over, even with a beer in his system. He might write a poem and save it for her on a piece of notebook paper, like the one on which Jeff had written his first letter.

Leigh let herself tip toward her coach, let him hold some of her weight. She felt her lips hit his at the corner. "Someone might see," she whispered.

"I brought my keycard." Jeff grabbed her wrist and pulled her into the hallway. She looked back over her shoulder at the oatmeal but resisted the urge to ask him to wait. There would be food available after they'd finished whatever this was. Jeff beeped them into an empty dorm room just two doors down from the kitchen. He didn't bother with the overhead light and led her to the unmade bed. The plastic coating on the mattress crackled as she sat down on it, and Jeff pulled one of the extra blankets from the tiny closet.

"You're unbelievable," he said. He put the blanket down next to her and shrugged out of his Team USA jacket. He let it fall to the floor and then pulled off his white T-shirt. A swirl of hair sprouted between his pecs. Leigh reached out to touch it. Charlie's chest was smooth, no thick hair. Jeff put his hot hand over hers and then guided it down over his stomach. With his other hand, he undid the button on his jeans and tugged the zipper down.

"You're going to look so good with that medal around your neck," he whispered. And Leigh closed her eyes and let herself see it.

CHAPTER TWENTY-FOUR

LEIGH MACKENZIE

November 2022

The morning after her fight with Charlie, Leigh dug her favorite cross-body purse from the moving box her husband had labeled, "Frilly Adornments." She'd already memorized the one-line poem inside, so often had she retrieved accessories without putting any of them permanently away: "My wife. Too glittering for parametric amplification." He'd learned the term as they'd considered chandeliers for their remodel. No one else Leigh knew would write poetry on moving boxes. It was both adorable and genius. And still, she'd disparaged Charlie's creativity just the night before.

Unpredictable bitchiness had been her biggest character flaw since high school. Leigh knew this. It was the same trait that made it hard for her to start fresh with Susy. How could they move past the way Leigh had ghosted her after Lake Placid? Leigh hadn't even reached out when the team had lost, even though she knew that Susy would have been devastated. She'd read about her divorce on the Internet and hadn't even sent a Facebook message. But then again, Susy hadn't reached out, either. There'd been the one call, and then silence, even though surely Susy could have imagined the pain of leaving Lake Placid without an Olympic berth.

By the time Leigh made it to the kitchen, she was desperately sorry for bringing up Charlie's novel. "I don't know why I do that," she said when she saw him at the table with his newspaper. "You're brilliant, and I know it. And I'm awful."

He didn't look up from the *Star Tribune* as she apologized. "You have to stop going for the kill." He licked his thumb and flipped to the box scores. She'd been here before: she'd have to pay a little longer for losing her temper, but if she brought home a craft IPA and offered to go with him on a jog, he'd probably be ready to forgive her.

She left for work before Gus was up and without a goodbye kiss, but two hours later, she swiped open a text from Charlie. He wondered if Leigh could handle dropping Gus at hockey practice the following Tuesday. The owner of Little Lights Bookstore back in Tampa had asked him to moderate an online panel of adventure writers after the new assistant manager realized he had a conflict. Leigh couldn't very well say "no" to a literary event after she'd shit-canned her husband's whole career. She double-checked her travel schedule and then acquiesced.

It was only after she said "yes" that Charlie revealed that the practice was at Mariucci Arena, the University of Minnesota's home ice. The coaches had said at the information meeting that the kids practiced there sometimes. Other parents had seemed excited about access to an NCAA facility, but Leigh thought it sounded atrocious. Not only would parking be a total pain on campus, but Leigh would have to revisit the place where she'd won and lost so many times.

"Got it," Leigh texted back, anxious for the tension between her and Charlie to dissolve. She tried for a joke: "Two can drive carpool, hotshot."

She looked up at her office painting, at the impasto brushstrokes that reached between the larger pink color-block on top and the red beneath. She hoped her husband's reply would be lighthearted.

"Speaking of potential for actual carpools," he wrote, "I'm making friends. Arnie asked me to go out for drinks and a hockey game next Thursday. Twice in a week, but, you good for bedtime that night?"

"Deal." Leigh typed, both agreeing to spend Thursday night with Gus and also, she hoped, to putting their argument behind them.

The same afternoon, Leigh opened an email from Amelia Matzke, one of the moms on the A-team, titled, "Feature in the *Liston Heights Magazine*." She'd been at the parents' meeting the other night, heard about Leigh's and Susy's history on Team USA, and wanted to run a story in the local glossy for which she was a freelancer. She would engage a photographer to do a shoot with the former players along with their kids. She'd copied Susy on the message.

Leigh frowned. Her erstwhile teammates had done plenty of where-are-they-now pieces, but Leigh had mostly avoided them, even turning down a hall-of-fame offer from her high school. She didn't need to remind anyone that her athletic career had screeched to a humiliating halt.

But then again, Susy had smiled at her at the team meeting. She'd tugged her ponytail as if they were both still nineteen. Leigh closed the email.

She'd reentered this world for Gus. She imagined his face when she told him he'd be in a magazine. Leigh would consider the piece, but only if Susy responded first.

Neither of them had responded thirty-six hours later, when it came time for Leigh to drive carpool. She shifted into park and activated her hazards in the fire lane outside Mariucci. "Ready?" she asked Gus. He undid his seat belt and held the door handle. Leigh reached back and stopped him with a light touch on his forearm.

"Go out on the curb side," she said.

Cars careened around the corner on slushy Washington Avenue, speeding too close to Leigh's door. It was always like this in Minneapolis. They'd had their first two inches of snow that day, and even lifelong Minnesotans forgot how to adjust to the conditions. Once Gus stood safely on the curb, Leigh waited for a break in the traffic and then hustled around to the hatch. She handed Gus his bag and stick.

"It's that door." Leigh pointed at the building.

Gus squinted. "How do you know?" Two students parted around him on the sidewalk.

"I've been here before." Leigh pushed Gus lightly between his shoulder blades toward the door. "Lots of times." She'd practiced inside that same building every day for years, but had entered just once since being cut from the Olympic team, to announce she was finished with the game. Leigh could still remember the feeling of Coach Maggie's desktop against the tip of her nose as she'd dropped her head in her arms and cried as she'd quit.

Gus disappeared inside, and Leigh parked in the closest ramp, stuffed her hands in her pockets, and tucked her chin into the extended collar of her parka. She trudged back along the sidewalk to Mariucci. As she passed Ridder, the women's arena they'd built long after Leigh's tenure, she stopped to stare at a life-size poster of the team's defensive star, Madeline Wethington, outside. Leigh had seen a feature on the top-ranked Gophers in Charlie's *Star Tribune* just that week.

"Excuse me." Someone jostled her shoulder.

Leigh realized she was blocking pedestrian traffic. "Sorry." She migrated toward the new arena. While the main entrance was locked when she tried it, the smaller door a few steps to the left gave way. Leigh could hear the sounds of another youth practice in session. She opened the rink's inner door. Two clusters of kids did a horseshoe passing drill with a coach on either side of the rink. A goalie stood in each net, working through a series of T-pushes, and Leigh pictured her own goalie, Ilse Thurgood, there. Ilse had held off the Bulldogs' six-on-five for seventy-five seconds, securing the Gophers' second national championship in '99.

Leigh strolled the concourse, scanning memorabilia and photographs of the women's players, which had apparently been moved over from Mariucci. She clenched her jaw as she approached the wall of All-Americans near the west-side concession stand. Her own plaque featured an action photo etched in black and white. "Leigh Mackenzie, Forward," the plaque read. "Class of '02, All-American Honors '99, '00, and '01." Anyone looking at it would wonder what had happened her senior year. She reached up and touched the edge of her skate in the photo and then moved her finger left to Ilse Thurgood's. Ilse hadn't been selected for the final Olympic team camp. She'd finished her career with the Gophers and had earned All-American honors all four years.

A guy on his cell phone walked up behind her, and Leigh startled. She dropped her hand from the plaque. Her fingers grazed the weatherproof shell of her jacket.

The man frowned at her, suspicious, and she walked away from him toward the exit. What was she even doing in here? Back outside, Leigh turned toward the men's arena, where Gus would begin practice in fifteen minutes. A woman jogged up on her right.

"Oh!" The woman stopped short, and Leigh realized it was Susy. Her boots slid a bit in the slush. "Leigh! It's you."

"Hey!" Leigh forced a smile. She grabbed her ponytail and smoothed it over her shoulder, remembering the tug Susy had given it at the parents' meeting, as if no time at all had passed. The gesture had proven that the distance between them was indeed Leigh's fault.

Now, Susy touched Leigh's arm. "It's a trip to be on campus, right?" Susy asked. The two started walking again. "It was wild for me when Georgie started practicing here last year. I remember so clearly all the games I played—all the games *we* played. I lost the national championship in there." She pointed at Mariucci, and Leigh remembered Susy behind the Bulldogs' net, slamming into the boards after Leigh scored the game winner in '98. Though Duluth had lost, Susy had been an All-American, too. "Were you checking out Ridder? Isn't it gorgeous?"

Leigh's instinct was to deny having been inside, but Susy had probably seen her walk out.

"Yeah." Leigh kicked slush. "I can't believe women's hockey has come so far. Could you have imagined? Our own arenas?"

"No." Susy laughed. She seemed so happy and relaxed, even as they remembered Duluth's defeats. Leigh, on the other hand, couldn't think of Lake Placid without a hollow opening in her chest. "It's so cool," Susy said. "Georgie and I go to a bunch of games every season. Hey—" She swiveled her head toward Leigh. "We should all go! You and Charlie and Gus. We could meet you there."

Leigh blinked. She took in a breath of chilly air and held it. She imagined Charlie smiling at Susy. She wondered if they remembered 2Pac's "California Love" playing in the basement the night they'd first met.

"Or not." Susy waved her mitten in front of her face after several awkward seconds had passed. "That was a bad idea." She picked up her pace and started jogging.

"It's just—" Leigh held her shoulders up near her ears.

"No, it's okay," Susy shouted as she ran away from Leigh. "I'll talk to you later."

Leigh felt like crap by the time she stomped her shoes on the mat inside Mariucci and slunk down the stairs. She and Susy hadn't faced off against each other in more than fifteen years. And Susy was going out of her way for Gus. Certainly, her extra attention had been out of deference to their shared past.

When Leigh reached the bottom of the stairs, Susy was seated on a bench in front of her, bent over her skates. Leigh forced herself forward. "Hey," she said. "Should we do that photo shoot?" She wanted absolution, irritated with herself for offending both Charlie and Susy in the same week. "That feature for the *Liston Heights Magazine*?"

Susy snapped her head up. "Oh. I assumed you wouldn't want to."

"Well, I don't really." Leigh shook her head. This wasn't the peace offering she was aiming for. "But it might be fun for the kids, right? To have their pictures in the magazine?"

Susy shrugged. "They do like each other, you know."

"I know," Leigh said, though she didn't. Gus hadn't said too much about Georgie either way, except that she was "totally sick" at hockey, an assessment that sent an embarrassing wave of jealousy through Leigh. "Look." Leigh's stomach roiled. Twenty-five years ago, she'd been standing in the same hallway when she'd thrown up in the garbage can before the first game of the Frozen Four in her freshman season. "I don't know why I acted so stupidly out there. Of course I'd like to go to a Gopher game with you. Of course *we* would." She thought she might actually mean it. They'd watched countless games together in film sessions and rinks all around the country. "And I want to do the magazine story. Is that journalist mom here? Amelia?" She pointed at the stands, wondering if she could accept the woman's offer right then and there.

"I walked in with you, so I haven't yet taken attendance." Leigh could hear Susy's sarcasm, but it was mild. "She's short. Long brown hair."

Leigh nodded. She could find her, even if it meant asking Arnie Senko for a heads-up on who was who. "I'm on it."

Susy bent back over to tie her other skate. "Cool."

Leigh made her way to the stands. She could do this. She'd invited Susy back into her life after all, by moving home to the same place she coached. A new kind of friendship could start at the photo shoot, something to make everyone happy.

CHAPTER TWENTY-FIVE

CHARLIE MACKENZIE

November 2022

Charlie gave Leigh very few details about his plans for the evening, partly because he still resented her comments about his writing, but mostly because he didn't want her to know that a major portion of the big night out with his new friends would include watching other people's middle schoolers play hockey. It seemed like a weird way to have fun, but he was new to the group, and just felt lucky to be included.

Charlie had made it through forty minutes of rapid-fire commentary from Susy and Arnie about the prowess of various thirteen-year-old forwards before they'd decided to skip the third period. Charlie found himself grinning as the trio clinked their pints at the brewery closest to the rink.

"So," Susy said after the first sip of IPA went down, "what do you do, Charlie? I mean besides ferrying Gus to hockey and home again." She rolled her eyes. "With Minnesota hockey, I know that's more than a full-time job all on its own."

Charlie felt relieved that Susy didn't seem to expect him to report a fancy office position like Leigh's. Susy's cheeks were pink in the humid taproom. Besides beer, the place smelled like wet wool and garlic. Charlie's mouth watered as he watched a server deliver an olive and goat cheese pizza, the same type he'd ordered, to an adjacent table. He thought about Little Lights, the café at the bookstore where he'd perfected his latte art, and his half-full Moleskine on his home-office desk. He'd filled six pages with ballpoint scribble that morning. And of course, there was the unfinished manuscript in the right-hand drawer.

"Well, really I'm a writer." He blurted it, then coughed and looked away. Twentysomethings on a date tipped their heads together at a high-top in the back corner, and Charlie regretted the confession. "Stay-at-home dad" would have been good enough. "Writer" seemed overly pretentious and borderline dishonest given his lack of productivity.

"What?" Susy thunked her drink onto the table, recapturing Charlie's eye contact. "That's so exciting! Do you write fiction?" Her eyes—a golden brown—flashed in the low light. Charlie suddenly remembered the pink ribbed tank top she'd worn beneath an open flannel shirt at that basement keg party all those years ago. Susy had linked arms with Leigh as they revealed they were members of the US Women's National Hockey Team. Her eyes had sparkled then, too.

Charlie ran his hand down the side of his cool glass. "I mean, yeah." He felt himself smile. "I've been working on a novel forever. I managed a bookstore in Florida." *Assistant managed.*

Susy leaned forward. "I'm a huge reader. I'd love to write a book someday. How'd you get started? And"—she put her palm flat against the table, millimeters from his coaster—"is there someplace I can read your stuff?"

Charlie glanced at Arnie, who was scrolling his phone. "We're down 2–1," Arnie muttered, reporting the score from the game they'd just left.

"There's time." Susy waved a hand, brushing his comment away. She kept her eyes on Charlie.

"I placed a few stories in online journals, but . . ." He trailed off. He hoped Susy wouldn't google him. Charlie's website was out-of-date, his headshot a picture Leigh had taken of him on the beach just before Gus had been born. "I recently picked up my novel again." The statement was technically true. He'd touched the pages.

"Good for you." Susy sat back. "There's a teacher at school who's writing a novel. It takes such discipline. Like being an athlete in so many ways, right? That's why I hope I might be able to do it someday. I have, you know"—she chuckled—"work ethic."

Charlie thought about his runs, the GPS maps he'd been collecting on Strava, the app he used to track his progress. He wondered if Susy had a profile on the site. "I imagine your work ethic is well above average," he said.

Susy smiled. "Tell me about your novel."

Everyone had given up asking Charlie about *Ice Time*. Ten years was an awfully long time to expect people to sustain interest in a creative project.

"Well." Charlie rubbed his forehead. "It's actually about a would-be Olympian, on the cusp of making the women's hockey team—"

"We scored!" Arnie banged the table with a closed fist. "2–2, seven minutes left in the third."

Susy cocked an eyebrow, sharing her exasperation with Charlie. "That's great, champ." The server arrived then with their pizzas.

Susy and Charlie chewed as Arnie updated them on scores from around the metro. When he'd finished his litany, Susy looked up at Charlie over her half-eaten slice. "So, does Leigh know you're writing a book about her?"

"It's not . . ." He closed his eyes for a beat and then smiled at his plate. He couldn't really claim *Ice Time* wasn't about his wife. Susy knew too much. Instead he said, "We haven't really discussed it."

Susy smirked, her eyes gleeful. "Well, that's fascinating," she said. "Writing a secret book about your wife. Don't you think?"

CHAPTER TWENTY-SIX

GUS MACKENZIE

November 2022

November 15, 2022
Performance: 1/5, failed when it counted
Minutes This Week: 201
Lifetime Hours: 447
Quote from Mom: "There's more to hockey than scoring goals."
Quote from Greystone: "Next right thought, next right action."

Gus's mom was out of town for his first game with the Lions, but she FaceTimed before they left for the rink.

"You ready?"

"Are you sitting in your hotel room?" Gus knew she was. There was a strip of brown wood against the wall behind her and a lamp attached to it not far from her ear.

"Yeah."

"Is it nice?" he asked. "Is there a TV?" Gus wished he were there with her, wished he could have taken the airplane and asked the flight attendant for the whole can of Sprite. His dad might get him a Sprite after the game if it went well.

"It's a nice hotel, yeah. But, kiddo, I'm calling about the game. Your first one!"

Gus scrunched his shoulders. It was like tryouts all over again, his grilled cheese stuck at the base of his throat. If he thought too hard about the game starting in an hour, he might cry.

"Oh, buddy." He tried not to look at her, but he couldn't help it. Her eyes were big, like when he fell off his bike or bonked his head. His mom felt sorry for him. Maybe she knew he wasn't going to play well, that he wasn't ready for this new level of competition. Maybe she knew his scores in evaluations had actually been lower than Colin Kelliher's.

Gus swallowed hard. His dad had hung up a new Jared Spurgeon poster next to the Stamkos one he'd brought from their old house. He still thought of that old house as "home." He missed Tyler from his Junior Lightning team, missed the knee hockey set in the garage.

"Nerves are hard," Gus's mom said, "but you've played a hundred games at least, right? You probably know exactly how many games you've played." She laughed. "I've seen you with that hockey bible."

"I don't know how many games," he said. Maybe a better hockey player would know that statistic, but Gus had started tracking only when Uncle Jamie had given him the bible last season. In the past year, Gus had played twenty-seven games. He probably hadn't played a total of one hundred even since the very beginning. "I think maybe only eighty," he said.

"Okay, and this is just one more. Hey." His mom tapped her finger against the screen as if she could reach out and touch him. "New team colors on your back, that's all. Same game play. Same drill."

Gus leaned closer to his iPad. "What if I don't score any goals this season?" Nik Ashberry would score at least fifty in their thirty-five games. Georgie, too.

"There's more to hockey than scoring goals." Maybe she was right, but all of the pictures Big Gus showed him of his mom were of her setting up to shoot, shooting, or celebrating a goal. Uncle Jamie had asked him on every single FaceTime last season what his point total was. When he was up to 55 assists-plus-goals, the highest total on his team, Jamie had sent him a five-dollar bill in a card that said, "World's Greatest Nephew."

Gus's dad knocked on the door. "Time to go, kiddo." He put his arm around Gus's shoulder and smiled at his mom on the iPad. "I'll text you updates," he told her.

"Constant updates!" She blew him a kiss. "Oh!" Her eyes went wide. "Need an oath? Good enough, fast enough?"

Gus shook his head. "No time, Mom. Gotta go." He pressed the hang-up button before she could insist.

Gus had been nervous before in Tampa, his heart pounding during the anthem at a playoff game or in overtime, but usually when he was skating, he didn't have time to be nervous. Instead it was "next right thought, next right action," as Greystone put it. But during this game against Wayzata, he had the itchy feeling of being worried all the time. On the bench, he shifted his weight from skate to skate. On the ice, he wondered what the other kids were thinking of him.

But after his third shift in the second period, Gus finally started feeling better. The score was tied at 1. He hadn't been on the ice when the "bad guys," as Big Gus always called the opponents, scored. Big Gus was there, standing against the boards in Wayzata's zone. Gus had seen him bang the Plexiglas when William had scored the team's first goal on a sick no-look pass from Nik. Gus hadn't been on the ice for that one, either. When it was his turn, Coach Walker held the door open for him. "Connect," she yelled as he picked the puck up from behind the Lions' net where the second line had dumped it. She meant for him to focus on his passing. Coach Walker had drawn the plays on the whiteboard between the first and second periods. The arrows had shown where he was supposed to skate and where his line mates, Owen and Liam, were supposed to be.

And on that third shift, Gus did it exactly like he was supposed to on their first try. He skated the puck to the boards where he beat the forward from Wayzata and nudged it up to Owen. As Owen zipped through the neutral zone, Gus hustled down on the right side. Liam was almost offsides, but not. Gus could see the ref's wide-spread arms, the sign that they were good. The Wayzata defender tipped the puck away from Owen, but Gus was there. He picked it back up in the right corner and centered it. The likelihood of Owen being there was about fifty percent, but this was a lucky time. Owen got his stick on it and fired at the Wayzata goalie.

The kid blocked it with his leg pad, but Big Gus banged on the Plexiglas anyway. Gus could hear it as he tried again, digging the puck out of the corner where it had been deflected. The Wayzata player tried to pin him against the boards right next to where Big Gus was standing, but Gus managed to knock the puck out and pass it back into the slot. This time Liam found it, but his shot went wide. The Wayzata forward beat him, and they all hustled back.

The line hadn't scored, but as Gus slid off the ice at the end of the shift, he knew something for sure: maybe his evaluation scores had been the lowest of any kid on the team, but in those two minutes, he'd done his job. Coach Walker knocked his helmet, and Coach Ashberry swatted his shoulder. It was the equivalent of a gold star.

In the third period, Gus felt good, not restless or out of breath. He imagined what he'd write in his bible. He'd rank his performance at least a 4 out of 5. He'd watched Nik and William on the first line, and Gus's passes were as "generative" as theirs. That was one of Coach Walker's words. It meant the offense made something happen. With ninety seconds left on the clock, the third line was set to take the ice again with the game still tied at 1. This was it. Winning the first district game would set the team up for an awesome season.

Gus did everything right on his first try. He lifted the stick of the Wayzata defender, and Liam connected with Owen from high in the slot. The goalie froze Owen's one-timer, and they headed for a face-off. While Liam won face-offs a lot in practice, he lost this one and the puck skittered out of their zone. Rocco, the best defender, beat it to the net and skated it back in. Gus was right where Coach Walker had drawn the X. He clapped his stick against the ice just once, and Rocco passed it to him.

Gus took two strides toward the middle and saw the piece of open net between the goalie's leg pad and blocker. He shot. If Georgie or Nik had shot it, it would have slid in beneath the goalie's elbow. Instead, Gus's puck flew at least three feet wide to the left of the goal, slammed off the boards, and right into the stick of a bad guy. That kid had a full second all alone to find a forward, who then beat Simon into the Lions' zone. Mac didn't stand a chance against the kid's blocker-side snipe.

Gus watched his grandfather tip his head back and raise his palms to his forehead as the puck went into the Lions' net. 2–1 with only seven seconds left. Gus's dad put his phone back into his pocket. He must have been filming.

As he skated to the bench, Gus had a flash of what his mom would have looked like if his shot had gone in. She would have been so happy, her hands high in the air.

Instead, she would see Gus choking, losing the game for the whole team.

As the buzzer sounded, the kids clustered in their zone before lining up for handshakes. "Should have taken that last shot yourself, man," Simon said to Owen.

He was right. Gus was the wrong person for the job.

CHAPTER TWENTY-SEVEN

LEIGH MACKENZIE

November 2022

Leigh watched Charlie's footage of the errant shot in her hotel room and promised she would console Gus the next day when she got home. "He's despondent," Charlie told her. "He keeps saying he choked."

"Well—" Leigh hedged.

"Are you saying he did choke?" Charlie sounded annoyed. He didn't like her to be hard on Gus, didn't like it if she asked how many problems he got wrong on a math test.

"Everyone chokes sometimes." Charlie should know. His ESPN viewing hours rivaled Gus's hockey practice totals. And there was nothing Leigh could say that would put the shot *in* the net. Or even on the net. It hadn't been close. Her dad hadn't sugarcoated it when he'd called to report. Being honest about the bad play didn't take away the great shift he'd had earlier in the game.

Still, Leigh didn't want to get into it with Charlie. She pumped Gus up as soon as she walked into the house. She focused on the positive. He'd been in the right place to receive the pass. He hadn't hesitated with his shot. With more practice and more repetitions, he would get there.

"But we lost because of me." Leigh knew Gus's feeling. Every player eventually had the experience of being on the ice when the last-ditch effort in the third period hadn't been enough. For Leigh, the last time had been in her final game with Team USA.

She'd believed there would be a miracle all the way until the buzzer. That's the way Leigh had always played—counting on victory. She had been certain she would make the Olympic team until the instant she hadn't.

In less than twenty-four hours, Gus would be back at practice, prepping for the team's next matchup. Athletes had to move forward quickly. They couldn't dwell. "There were a lot of missed opportunities in the game before yours, kiddo," she told Gus. "You'll get 'em next time."

Leigh was too busy at work the next day to give any more thought to Gus's wild shot. The light outside her office window had long since faded, and still Leigh picked through her to-do list. Her office phone rang, and caller ID said it was Nicole, a senior partner at the law firm Lupine retained. Leigh clenched her stomach for bad news—why else would Nicole call at six thirty?—and then almost laughed when Nicole forwent any pleasantries and said, "Wanna grab a drink? Or dinner? I'm hungry, and it's late, and you're new in town and seem cool, so . . ."

"That sounds lovely. Let me just see." Leigh grabbed her cell phone to check for texts from Charlie. Gus had practice, she knew.

"No pressure," Nicole said. Leigh had been in a meeting with her earlier that day. Nicole had scooped her reddish curly hair into a ponytail and she'd stood up in the second hour of negotiations to untuck her button-down from her pencil skirt, a move that had made Leigh smile. "I just thought if you were still in the office, I'm right across the skyway."

Leigh glanced at the redlined memo she'd been editing about potential losses on a resin production company. She quickly counted the number of months it had been since she'd been out with a friend with taps of her fingers on her desktop. When she got to her second hand, she decided. "Yes! Thank you!"

Nicole laughed at her enthusiasm. "Maybe your day has been as long as mine?"

"I guess so, and"—Leigh closed all the tabs on her browser and hit save on her document—"I was just remembering that the last time I actually went out with a friend, I was in Tampa. I've lived here now for more than six months. It seems I've lost all ability to connect with people—" She paused. Nicole would change her mind about having drinks with someone with so few social skills.

"You need a night out." Nicole saved her. "Let's go to Kieran's down the block."

"Only if you don't judge me for eating the pub pretzels for dinner."

"I wouldn't dream of it. Ten minutes. I'll meet you in the lobby of your building."

"Yes!" Leigh veritably shouted. *Calm down,* she chastised herself. *You're acting like you've never had a friend in your life.* Leigh got a flash of Susy then, remembered her tangled bedhead when they'd woken up in Prague, two hours before the team had to report for warm-ups.

"Let's explore," Susy had whispered that day. They'd spent the morning in the Old Town Square together, taking turns exclaiming over the ancient buildings, the dramatic castle spires. In the end, they'd been among the last players to line up for the bus, earning a dour look from Jeff Carlson, which Leigh had tried to diffuse with an airy smile. Later, Leigh had dug deep to shake off her fatigue during that Prague game. Her line mates had spent the morning in the recovery room with the massage therapist and the ice bath. They'd undoubtedly be fresher, but, Leigh told herself, she was the better player anyway.

At the bar, Nicole led her to a two-top in the sticky corner opposite the pool tables. "This place is kind of a dive, but the bacon Tater Tots are divine." She gave a chef's kiss.

"Honestly," Leigh said, "I'm so grateful. I only wish I asked you to do something similar eons ago. I haven't reconnected with friends much since I've been back in Minnesota. It's been so busy with the new gig and with my son, Gus, starting a new school and new hockey." She was babbling. *Shut up.* "Sorry," she added, unable to heed her own advice. "I'm babbling."

"No, I hear you."

A server approached, and the two women ordered cocktails. Leigh's stomach rumbled as she added the pretzels, too. "And a side salad." She laughed. "For good measure, I guess."

"It's easy to get totally wrapped up in work," Nicole said. "I mean, it's private equity. The field isn't exactly known for work-life balance."

"Yeah, and I keep deleting the daily Goop email about meditation."

Nicole snorted. "The law firm's wellness emails! Straight to the trash. Tell me about your family. Everyone adjusting okay?"

Leigh considered Charlie, who'd become obsessed with snow tires and winter running gear in addition to his focus on hockey, and Gus, who had few social engagements beyond the hockey rink. "It's hard to be new, I guess. My husband, though, he has a more flexible schedule. He's started to hang out with some of the hockey parents, and he's training for an ultramarathon." Charlie had been thrilled about the outing with Arnie and Susy. He'd come home completely devoid of any residual anger about her meanness.

"No ultramarathons for you? Do you run?" The server dropped off their drinks and Leigh offered Nicole a toast. The two women clinked glasses.

"I can jog a ten-minute mile, but, you know, Lupine Capital doesn't leave a lot of time for workouts."

"And no hockey mom friends yet?" Leigh couldn't remember if Nicole had kids, and she wasn't sure how to talk about hockey with someone new. Although Leigh's connections to the sport had gotten the attention of the headhunters, she'd talked about it at work only with Fred Page, whose son Lincoln had indeed made the Liston Heights varsity team. Both Fred and Jamie had texted her with the good news.

"You hate hockey?" Nicole tried filling in the blanks.

"No, but"—she took a gulp of her gin and ginger—"I used to play pretty seriously."

"Really? Did you play in high school?"

Leigh nodded. "And in college."

"Where'd you go?" Nicole asked.

"The U." The server arrived with her pub pretzels. Leigh grabbed one and dunked it into the beer cheese sauce.

"Minnesota? But that's like D1 national championship hockey." Nicole peered at her. Leigh bobbed her head in acknowledgment. "Is it, like, hard for you to watch regular youth hockey? To see the mere mortals? Do you coach?"

Leigh thought of Susy, her lithe body and narrow waist. Leigh looked down at her own rumpled middle. She thought about dodging the line of inquiry with another topic, but there was something about Nicole—her slightly messy hair, her genuine smile—and Leigh hadn't been out with anyone in so long. "I was all in with hockey until I was twenty-one." She looked over Nicole's shoulder at the mural painted across from the bar. A bird in the lower-left corner took flight over the heads of three little girls in matching yellow dresses. They looked like a team. Leigh continued, "And then I had a big disappointment and just left the sport behind entirely."

Nicole sipped her drink, as if Leigh were supposed to go on.

"Actually," Leigh said, surprising herself again, "I kind of gave up athletics altogether. I never expected to be forty and so out of shape." She gestured at her body with her free hand. "And"—she leaned forward—"I've been rounding down, but you seem nice, and I don't want to start our friendship with a lie: I'm actually forty-two."

Nicole threw her head back and laughed again. The dimple on her left cheek matched Gus's and Charlie's. Leigh replayed her last comment. It had been only a little funny. Nicole was generous with her mirth. "Well, thanks for your honesty. And I get the burnout, totally. I ran cross-country at a Division Three school." She shrugged. "I know that's not the same as playing a major sport at a land-grant university. But I was pretty burnt out after my last race senior year. I took a full two years off. And actually now—" Nicole's face flushed. "Well, it's kind of dumb, but I've been training for a turkey trot."

"That's not dumb." Leigh pushed her salad to the side and stabbed one of Nicole's bacon Tater Tots, which she'd moved to the center of the table.

"My sister plays hockey in a women's league," Nicole said. "Do you want her cell phone number? You're probably way too good for these ladies, but it could be fun."

"I think I'm happy just watching," Leigh said. She wasn't, actually. Even spectating basically gave her hives. "I don't even have equipment anymore."

"Well, it's probably not too late."

Salty cheese from the Tater Tots coated the inside of Leigh's mouth. She thought about the phone calls she hadn't returned to her former teammates after Lake Placid. She heard the thud of her bag as she took the stairs down to the lobby in the Olympic Training Center. She remembered the smell of Charlie's flannel shirt as she'd buried her face in it after she'd flown home.

No matter what Nicole said, it was indeed too late to play actual hockey with a bunch of grown women. She'd end up in the emergency room instead of back in her glory days, and there were so many unfortunate memories.

CHAPTER TWENTY-EIGHT

SUSY WALKER

November 2022

It didn't surprise Susy that Leigh and Gus were fifteen minutes late for the *Liston Heights Magazine* photo shoot. She herself had raced out of school, whisked Georgie from the neighboring elementary, and arrived at the rink two minutes early. She regretted her hustle now and glanced intermittently at the door. She'd given Georgie a couple of bucks for the vending machine to keep her busy.

"What do you remember about Leigh from back then?" Amelia asked, finally starting the interview without her second subject. "You must have been through a lot together."

Amelia flipped open a steno pad, and Susy stared at the banners above the rink door, Leigh's picture among those of the other Liston Heights youth players who'd gone on to compete in college and beyond. "Well, she's incredibly driven," Susy said. "A supremely talented athlete."

"When did you first meet?"

"High school. We played against each other, and then in the first year of college—she went to the U and I went to Duluth—we both made the national team selection camp for the first time. We were roommates."

"Nice." Amelia smiled. "And there she is!"

Susy peeked over her shoulder. "Sorry!" Leigh called, Gus at her side. She hurried to the table where Susy and Amelia sat, tension in her smile. "I'm still late all the time, Suse," Leigh said. "It's a terrible flaw. Gus, there's Georgie." She pointed at the vending machines, and Gus jogged away.

Amelia jumped in. "It's okay! Since the kids are occupied, I'm going to turn on my recorder, okay? I'm thinking the format for the piece will be a transcript with a short introduction. The photo of you and the kids will run above it. My photographer will be here in about fifteen minutes to shoot you on the ice. Did you bring the jerseys?"

"I've got ours," Susy said. She'd retrieved a Team USA jersey from the storage trunk in her garage for the occasion.

Leigh looked nervous as she slid into one of the attached benches of the picnic-style table. "I had to go over to my parents' house to get this from my old closet." She grabbed her Gophers jersey from her tote. "I didn't save any from Team USA. I have Gus's Lions jersey, too, though it hasn't been washed. Good thing the photo won't be scratch-and-sniff."

Amelia laughed. "This'll be a fun piece. The readers will love catching up with the local elite."

Susy glanced at Leigh, who bit her lip. "Hardly elite," Leigh said. "Anymore."

Amelia waved her hand, dismissing Leigh's self-effacement. "I already asked Susy this, Leigh, but what do you remember about your old friend from back in the day?"

"You got a head start!" Leigh rolled her shoulders back, and though she smiled, she pulled nervously at her fingers.

"Can I have this?" Gus held up one of Georgie's peanut butter cups to Leigh from across the lobby, his thumb in the center of the candy.

"Um?" Leigh looked at Susy as if for permission. Georgie grinned, chocolate already at the corners of her mouth. Susy would have to clean her up before the photo.

"Fine with me," Susy said. "They won't have crashed yet before we take our glamour shot."

Leigh smiled. "Back in the day we couldn't even be bothered to comb our hair for our official headshots."

"Really?" Amelia pressed. "Not too concerned with appearances?"

Susy glanced over. Leigh hadn't been too concerned with appearances in Lake Placid. People besides Susy had started to notice the special attention Jeff paid her, for sure. Susy always assumed that Leigh just thought the rumors would be worth it, that they wouldn't matter if she made the team.

"It was always more about the play," Leigh said. "More about wins than what other people thought." Was it still that way for Leigh? And what did she imagine Susy thought about her?

"And what do you remember most about Susy?" If Amelia detected any tension between them, she didn't show it. Susy grabbed the edge of the plastic-coated bench, digging her fingers into the underside.

Leigh wouldn't say anything less than complimentary about her to Amelia, but what did she remember?

Leigh gazed at the ceiling for a beat and then over at the kids, who'd pressed their hands against the glass above the rink, watching a goalie practice in progress. "Susy played the game with so much integrity." Leigh looked back at the table and then smiled. "I know I never told you this, Suse, but I admired you so much."

"Stop," Susy said automatically, her breath shallow. Before that last camp, Leigh had been a step ahead. She'd spent most of their time on the ice together trying to beat her, in every drill, in every skate.

"It's true, though. Always," Leigh continued. Her brown eyes looked wet. "Your love for hockey was so pure. You showed it in every practice. When you made mistakes, you got back so fast."

Susy opened her mouth to interrupt, to remind Leigh that she was the one who'd capitalized on one of Susy's mistakes to win the NCAA championship.

"No," Leigh persisted. "You made your own opportunities. You deserve every success you've accomplished."

Susy thought about the silver medal, the one that she still wished were gold. Was Leigh happy that at least there was an asterisk on Susy's career? That the gold medal was missing?

Amelia interrupted then, leading them through a series of innocuous questions about their favorite pump-up songs—"Tubthumping" had been both of their favorites—and postgame snacks. Susy had liked fruit leather and Dr Pepper. Leigh went with beef jerky.

After Susy mentioned that trip to Prague, the photographer arrived. "Rink A," Amelia called to him, and the guy gave a thumbs-up. "I know time is limited for you two superstars, so we'll finish this up and let you get dressed. I know this last question might be sensitive—" She paused and looked at the kids. They'd found a puck and were rolling it to each other across the empty viewing area. Susy could see the fingerprints they'd left on the rink glass. "How did it feel, Leigh, when Susy made the Olympic team and you didn't?"

Susy snapped her head up. "Maybe we should focus on the time we were together—" she said. Leigh had slipped her fingers into the mesh of the table, her knuckles white as she gripped the steel.

"It's okay." Leigh gave Susy a closed-mouth smile. "Not making the team was the biggest disappointment of my life." Leigh's voice sounded clear. "There's no doubt about that." She looked over her shoulder at her picture above the rink doors. Susy bit her lip, nervous. "In a lot of ways, it's plagued me. But when I imagined giving Gus the best shot he could have in hockey, I knew it had to be here. With Susy."

Leigh let go of the table and stood. Her skirt was creased from a day at her desk. "Should we change?" she asked. "Gus!" she called without waiting for an answer. "It's time for the picture."

Georgie kicked the puck they'd been playing with into a corner and ran over. Her shoes squeaked against the floor as she arrived a step ahead of Gus.

That was nice," Susy said as the two of them donned jeans and their jerseys in the bathroom. The kids were already dressed and mugging for the photographer.

Leigh blinked at her, uncomprehending.

"What you said about me to Amelia," she said. "About what it was like."

"Oh." Leigh jutted her chin toward the mirror and then dipped down to grab a cosmetic bag.

"I thought you didn't like me anymore," Susy said. "I thought you were probably happy that we lost the gold."

Susy felt a lump in her throat as Leigh dabbed concealer under her eyes and then swiped on another coat of mascara. She felt like she was a teenager again, desperate for acceptance. Susy and Leigh had stood together like this in hotel rooms. Leigh used to say they should just try to be "a tiny bit pretty." While not traditionally gorgeous, Leigh had an allure—a girl-next-door appeal that Susy had never pulled off. Charlie's choice all those years ago seemed to prove the difference between them.

"My life—" Leigh started and then stopped. She capped her

mascara and fluffed her hair. "It just felt like everything ended that day. I can't explain it." Leigh didn't make eye contact as she zipped her bag again and headed toward the door. "Let's get out there."

Susy had a flashback of leaving the locker room together. Outside, the kids were standing back to back in their Lions jerseys on the ice. Georgie stood an inch or so taller than Gus, who couldn't stop giggling.

"I think he's having a good time," Susy said.

"Yeah." Leigh slowed, letting Susy come up alongside her. "Maybe we shouldn't ruin the picture with our baggage."

Susy couldn't tell if she was serious, but Amelia shuttled them into the shot anyway. "Go ahead and put on your medals," the photographer said.

"Oh no." No one had told Susy to bring those. And, of course, Leigh didn't have one.

"No medals," Leigh said, her voice flat. Susy looked over and caught Gus gazing up at her, concern in his little face. "Just jerseys." She gazed forward with her hand placed firmly on Gus's shoulder.

CHAPTER TWENTY-NINE

LEIGH MACKENZIE

August 2001

There'd been her high school boyfriend in the summer before she'd started at the U, and then there'd been Charlie, and now, Leigh realized as she flopped over on the blanket he'd laid out for them, there was Jeff.

He propped himself up on an elbow, leaned over her, and pushed the sweaty hairs away from her forehead. He pressed his lips against the bridge of her nose. "I have been thinking about that for, I don't know—"

Leigh put her forearm over her eyes, embarrassed by the scrutiny. They hadn't pulled the flimsy shade, and light from the parking lot streamed into the empty room.

"Honestly, Mackenzie. You've been killing me." Leigh hadn't tried to do any killing, at least not before she'd gotten Jeff's letter that summer. She'd done only her usual things: outworking everyone in practice, never giving up on a drill. She'd followed all of the coaches' suggestions and directions from the beginning from her very first national team selection camp three years before.

Leigh's dad constantly reminded her that making the Olympic team would require nothing short of singular focus. "Relentless," she'd heard him call her when he was on the phone with his brother. "Just dogged."

Jeff ran his finger down Leigh's sternum, stopping when his hand was even with her breasts. "Can you even believe that in six months, you'll have a gold medal here?" He traced a wide circle, dragging his finger over her chest.

She spread her fingers over his back and pulled him toward her. He tasted different than Charlie, no hint of peppermint, no coffee. "I can't believe I'm doing this," she whispered as he moved his hand again to her forehead. "I don't do stuff like this."

Her stomach rumbled, and she suddenly remembered the oatmeal she'd left in the snack room, a trail of breadcrumbs for Susy or anyone else who wondered where she'd disappeared to. She'd told Susy she might go for a walk, Leigh remembered. Susy had been lying on her bed underlining passages in *It's Not About the Bike*. Leigh thought about Lance Armstrong, his eyes focused up-mountain and his seat out of the saddle. Her dad had watched the Tour in the weeks just before she'd left for Lake Placid. "Allez!" her dad had shouted at Armstrong from the family room couch as he rode away from the competition into the Pyrenees on the thirteenth stage. He'd taken the yellow jersey that day and held it all the way until the Champs-Élysées. "Just like that, Leigh-Leigh," her dad had said to her as Lance lifted his arms across the finish line. "Never say die!"

Jeff ran his fingers along her arm and then over her obliques. Her whole body was sore from the gym. She rested her hand below her belly button, and her stomach grumbled again. She laughed. "I should eat."

"That oatmeal is going to be congealed," Jeff said.

Leigh whipped her head toward the hallway. She heard another door slam shut. Footfalls grew louder until they passed. Jeff bit Leigh's earlobe. His hot breath tickled her cooling skin.

"Stop." Leigh smiled as she ducked away and pushed herself to sitting. She wasn't used to being so exposed. She usually pulled her underwear on under the covers after sex, grabbed one of Charlie's T-shirts from the floor while the sheet was still wedged under her armpits. But she felt different this time. This whole thing had been a bold, audacious play.

She thought about Charlie as she grabbed her clothes and started dressing, aware of Jeff's gaze. She should have told Charlie, maybe, before she'd left, about Jeff and his letter. Maybe they could have taken a break, like Ross and Rachel had in *Friends*. Everyone knew the TV characters would end up together in the end, when the timing was exactly right.

But now, since she hadn't told Charlie, she could just keep the two men completely separate. She'd just said "I love you" to Charlie on the phone in her dorm room, and the truth was, she did love him. Charlie could finish a *New York Times* Friday puzzle in under fifteen minutes, and he wrote her poetry on sticky notes. Jeff had told her flat out that he didn't want to be her boyfriend.

Leigh pulled her hoodie over her Frozen Four T-shirt. "Um," she said. Jeff hadn't moved. "So, I'm going to go?" She jerked her thumb toward the door.

"Wait," Jeff said. "Who was out there?"

"I don't know." Leigh shrugged. "Is this, like, not allowed?" She gestured at the air between them.

"Better if people don't know, right?" Jeff winked at her. "But now *I* know a little more about your potential strengths as a member of the team."

Leigh smiled. Jeff was awkward, for sure, but definitely handsome. He spent time in the gym—Leigh could see his well-defined pecs and biceps. Charlie had a runner's body, an impossibly lean waist, defined quads, and over-sharp collarbones.

"You think I have a shot at the team?" That was why Leigh was here, after all, at the training center. She stepped toward Jeff and tipped her head to the side.

He grabbed her again around the waist and slipped his hands once more beneath her shirt.

"You're number one on my list." He kissed her on the nose.

"And you're in the room, right? When Miller decides?" Leigh pictured the coaches throwing chips on the table, bidding on certain players.

"The coaching staff and the director, Leigh-Leigh. I'm on your team." Leigh flinched. Only her family and Charlie called her that.

"Just Leigh," she said. "Okay?" She walked to the door and cracked it open, listening. The hallway sounded empty. "Bye," she whispered.

She flexed her fingers as she walked back into the snack room.

"Hey." Leigh gasped and both of her hands flew to that same spot on her sternum that Jeff had traced. Susy stood there, her eyebrow cocked. "Sorry," she said.

"You scared me!" Leigh retrieved the oatmeal bowl. She dropped it, cold and solid now, into the trash can.

Susy pulled the hot water lever on the coffeemaker and held a white ceramic mug beneath it. "You didn't eat your snack?"

"I got distracted." Leigh touched her sweaty temple and knew she looked flushed. Her face burned even hotter.

A door clicked shut in the hallway, and Leigh heard Jeff clear his throat. In a second he passed the snack room. He didn't look inside.

Leigh grabbed a replacement bowl and started over with the oatmeal. She didn't look at Susy as she splashed the water in, but she could feel her stare. Susy backed away from the counter as Leigh put her bowl in the microwave.

"Oh my God, Leigh," Susy said finally. "What about Charlie?"

Leigh put her hands against her chest again. "It's nothing." She glanced over her shoulder at the empty hallway. "Nothing. Okay? Don't tell?" She imagined Susy telling a captain or maybe the trainer. Word would get out, and then when Leigh made the team, her status would be compromised.

Susy shrugged. "It's your business. You know I'm not a gossip." She walked out and Leigh waited with both hands on the counter for the microwave to ding.

CHAPTER THIRTY

CHARLIE MACKENZIE

November 2022

Charlie gripped his shitty vending-machine coffee. Though he wore the heavy-duty mittens Jamie had bought him, each of his fingers felt like icicles. A few drops of liquid sputtered out the hole in the cheap plastic lid of his cup, and Charlie watched them seep into the yellow leather.

"Told you it was a cold rink," Arnie said.

Charlie shivered as he swallowed a gritty sip. "Fucking freezing."

He'd skipped his run that morning. As the temperatures dropped, it became harder and harder to get himself out the door, especially in the dark. The only thing that had propelled Charlie along the marsh path for his run the day before had been the promise of "kudos" from Susy on Strava, the fitness app. They'd friended each other after their first outing at the brewery and Charlie now checked twice daily for her workout updates, usually when he was in the carpool line at Gus's school. Susy ran farther and lifted more weights than Charlie did. He consoled himself by remembering that she was an Olympian. Even so, Charlie had a ways to go if he was going to come close to his ultramarathon finishing time from '01. And the discrepancy between Charlie's runs and Susy's reminded him uncomfortably of the gap between Gus's play and Georgie's, though the two had become friends after the photo shoot. Gus had invited her over for a session in the Mackenzies' Hockey Zone basement.

Charlie looked up at the stands, taking in the small crowd of other die-hard Lions' parents. Both Matzkes sat there. Amelia had a fleece blanket over her lap and a Starbucks cup in her hand. Charlie thought about offering her ten bucks to trade beverages. Her husband, Kevin, chewed his bottom lip and stuffed his hands in his jacket. The Liston Heights families had all driven forty minutes to get to this miserable rink, and despite the ungodly game time, Ashberry had required them to be an hour early as usual for warm-ups. "Come on," Charlie had texted the group chat he had with Susy and Arnie about the start time. Susy had sent back the shrug and wink emojis. "Stamina," she'd typed. "Work ethic."

Charlie had been surprised to hear from Leigh that even Big Gus planned to make an appearance that morning, albeit in the second period, making good on his promise to watch every game Gus played in a Lions uniform. His father-in-law was giving Charlie a clearer picture of the intensity Leigh and Jamie had marinated in as kids.

Arnie whacked Charlie's arm. "It's starting." The first line crouched in position, and the teenage ref lazily dropped the puck.

"I saw on Youth Hockey Hub that this team is ranked ninth in state." Charlie knew Arnie would be impressed by his research.

Arnie grinned. "You check our ranking, too?"

"Naturally." Charlie nodded. "We're thirty-two, up from forty-one last week."

"Pretty good." Arnie raised his cup in a faux toast to the team. "But not as good as nine."

On the ice, Nik Ashberry rocketed the puck to William Matzke, who skated past one Elk River defender before sliding it center to Abe Senko.

Arnie rocked back on his heels as Abe's shot went wide. Charlie snuck a look at his friend's placid face and then scanned for Gus on the bench. He was at the end of the line of forwards. Susy leaned over his shoulder, pointing at William. Both boys played right wing, and clearly Gus needed extra tutoring. On the ice, William passed the puck back to Hank Teeterow, but the defender bobbled it, and the offense raced back to cover the Elk River rush.

"Okay," Arnie said. "These guys are ranked nine, but did you look at their schedule? Winning big over Rogers and Sauk River isn't all that impressive. Wait till they play some tournament games against real teams. The Hub claims to correct for strength of schedule, but they don't always get it right."

The second line took the ice with Georgie Magnussen at center. She rushed into Elk River's zone, stole the puck from a defender behind the net, and passed it to Lucas Dellinger, whose one-timer bonked off the post and then under the goalie's leg pad. 1–0, Lions. Dellinger slid on a knee and pumped his elbow. Gus lined up for fist bumps with the rest of the kids on the bench.

"Nice." Arnie slapped his palm against the Plexiglas to cheer the goal. "Beautiful pass from Georgie." The second line skated back to the center. "She's gotta be leading in assists," Arnie said. "I'm surprised Ashberry has her on the second line. Although she's a fantastic center, and of course, so is Nik."

They were quiet for a minute or two, and then Charlie held his breath as Gus's line finally took the ice. Gus raced to pick up the puck the other team had dumped behind the Lions' net. Chris McMillan, the goalie, yelled something at Gus as he slapped his stick against the ice, but Charlie couldn't hear. Charlie tried to keep his body relaxed, but even as he raised his cup to choke down more coffee, he could feel his jaw tense. His throat closed against the liquid, and he coughed.

"You can see how he's watching the play develop." Arnie pointed at Gus, who hesitated near the blue line. An Elk River forward charged in from the left. Gus fired it to Axel Rathmann, who then sent it back to the defender as Gus lifted the stick of the player who dogged him. "Kid's got great instincts," Arnie said.

Charlie tried again with his coffee. These were the phrases he kept hearing from Arnie and Susy about Gus: "great instincts," "high IQ," "on the cusp." They were like sorry pats on the back, indicators that Gus wasn't yet contributing to the success of the team. The Lions' number thirty-two ranking had everything to do with the first two lines. Gus languished on the third.

After an okay sequence in which the kids kept it in the Elk River zone for a good twenty or so seconds, the puck came back to Gus, but Owen's pass was slightly wide. The Elk River kid took two quick steps past Gus, and the whole fleet of players sped toward the Lions' net. Lucky for Gus, Susy had put the team's best two defenders out with the third offensive line, and after briefly getting tied up behind his own net, Rocco skated it out of the zone.

Charlie relaxed as Gus stumbled through the door to the bench, replaced on the ice by Nik's superior crew.

"That was his best shift yet," Arnie said. "He was in position the whole time. He anticipated the play." Arnie pointed at the ice where a few moments ago, Gus had failed to pick up the pass. "He was on his man the whole time." Arnie clapped Charlie's shoulder. "Kid's got a shit ton of potential. That's why they put him on the team."

Charlie cocked his head, wondering what details Arnie knew about what had gone down in the decision room after evaluations, whether Leigh's intervention with Jeff Carlson had been a factor when it came to rostering Gus. The period ticked away without any goals. Despite their discrepant rankings, the teams played even.

Charlie looked back at the stands. Amelia had spun in her seat to talk to Cathy Kelliher who'd appeared behind her sometime after the puck drop. She had a notebook resting in her lap. A kid, Colin probably, leaned his head against her biceps.

"What's Cathy doing here?" Charlie poked Arnie's shoulder and pointed toward the stands.

"Oh shit." Arnie let out a low laugh. He rested his forearms on the thin gap between the boards and the Plexiglas. "She's serious."

Charlie blinked. "Serious about what?" His inbox had been flooded with missives from Cathy, reminders of volunteer obligations, threats about rule-breaking. Charlie had broken the tryout rules, aided by Arnie. Charlie glanced back at Cathy, careful not to stare.

"Real inflated sense of importance, that one," Arnie said. "I can't believe she's here."

"Why is she here?" Cathy pointed something out to her kid on the ice and made a note on her pad. Amelia had turned back around and caught Charlie looking. She rolled her eyes.

"She's pissed," Arnie said. "Thinks junior there should have made the A-team." Charlie's stomach flipped. "To be fair, he was definitely on the bubble. But . . ." Arnie lifted an open palm toward the ice. Gus clapped his stick in front of the net, but Owen turned the puck over. "The coaches wanted Gus."

The buzzer blasted, signaling the end of the first period. "Who gets the final say on the roster?" Charlie asked. The ref skidded toward the scoring table as the kids huddled around Ashberry and his whiteboard.

"Ashberry. Walker. Carlson. Rathmann." Arnie tipped his cup again toward the bench. Susy's blond ponytail flipped over her shoulder as she whispered to Axel. "For what it's worth, I think they were right to take Gus. If I didn't think he were good enough, I probably wouldn't have shown you my secret tryout spot."

Charlie looked back up at Cathy, and this time, he caught her eye. He started to raise his hand in recognition, but she frowned and turned back to her kid. Cathy's pen stabbed something on the notebook page.

"Better not to even try to be nice to her." Arnie cleared his throat.

Charlie's stomach started to hurt. He contemplated the granola bar he'd seen in the vending machine adjacent to the one that had dispensed his coffee. "Who comes to a seven thirty Saturday game in Elk River to watch other people's kids?"

Arnie sighed. "She's making an appeal to the committee, is what I heard. Thinks she can get little Colin instated."

Charlie gaped. "That's a thing? A month into the season?" Cathy Kelliher's own emails had said quite clearly that tryout results were final.

"Not really. Don't worry about it. But the board members get a little, you know . . ." Arnie shifted his head from side to side. "Territorial."

The same nerves that Charlie had fought during tryout week kindled again. He took a big breath in and held it.

"We're catching another game tonight if you want to come," Arnie said. Charlie exhaled. "Come," he urged. "Little Miss Sunshine isn't invited." He jacked his thumb toward the stands where Cathy sat. "We'll watch the top-ranked Squirt team and then Susy wants a stout afterward. We were thinking we'd just go for a period or two and then try out the Steel Toe Brewery. You free?"

"Let me text Leigh." Charlie held his glove in his mouth as he messaged her. "Plans tonight?" he wrote. "I'm finally in with the hockey crowd." He added a GIF of Michael Scott sprinting out of the Dunder Mifflin office building. He knew it would make her laugh. She wouldn't care about him going out. If anything, it would be the notification of his text making noise before eight a.m. on Saturday that would bug her. While he had his phone out, he opened Strava and clicked on Susy's profile. Her run the prior afternoon had been six miles at 8:02 pace. He'd better take advantage of this afternoon's forty-degree high and get his butt out the door for his 9:15s. "What time are we going?" Charlie asked.

"Game's at seven." The buzzer sounded again, and the top line started the second period. On the first play, Abe caught the pass from Nik and scored on a snipe from just outside the crease. Arnie and Charlie pounded the glass. "I can't believe we're up 2–0 already," Arnie said. "Elk River should be roaring back." Charlie hoped not. "Anyway," Arnie said, "the game's a half-hour drive from Steel Toe. We'll be there by eight thirty, latest."

Elk River scored on a breakaway after Simon missed a play near the blue line, and Charlie's heart jumped.

"Told ya," Arnie said, unfazed. "Roaring back."

Charlie dumped the dregs of his coffee in the nearby garbage can and braced himself for Gus's next shift. By some miracle, his kid's first pass connected to Owen, who got a shot off within thirty seconds. It'd be nice to have something to talk about with Arnie and Susy besides how good Gus might be at some distant date in the future. Colin Kelliher might be ready for the big time right now.

CHAPTER THIRTY-ONE

GUS MACKENZIE

November 2022

November 19, 2022
Game vs. Elk River: 3–2. L
Record: 0–2
Performance Rating: 4/5
Minutes This Week: 260
Lifetime Hours: 451
Quote from Jamie: "Haters gonna hate."
Quote from Ashberry: "Our team is in the room."

Gus saw Colin Kelliher in the stands at the Elk River game. His mom, the manager lady, had been sitting next to him, scribbling in a notebook, and Colin looked pissed. Colin had blocked Gus's shot during the final scrimmage minutes in tryouts and whispered "loser" at him as the two of them skated to the face-off circle when the play went dead. Gus might have cried about being called "loser," except Uncle Jamie had taught him a new phrase. "Haters gonna hate." Gus had just told him about the recess stick situation with Nik and Simon when he said it.

"Haters?" Gus had asked.

"People who don't get what you're about." Uncle Jamie had patted him on the back. "You just keep your head down and keep doin' what you're doin'."

"Haters gonna hate," Gus said to himself when, after the Saturday game in Elk River, Colin Kelliher stood by the boards as the team skated off the ice. They'd lost 3–2, but Colin still fist-bumped Nik and William and lots of other kids as they stepped past him. Gus hadn't been sure what to do with his hand when he approached Colin. He held it sort of halfway up, so that if Colin decided to bump him, it would look like he was ready for it. At the same time, if he didn't, then "Haters gonna hate."

In the end, Colin hadn't even looked at Gus as he'd walked by. Gus turned back to watch over his shoulder, and he wasn't the only one Colin hadn't acknowledged. Neither Georgie nor Rocco got fist bumps, either.

"You getting on the team?" Gus heard Mac ask Colin.

"I think so," Colin said. Mac was last off the ice, and Colin walked next to him toward the locker room. "It's bogus. My mom has a meeting with the board. Anyway. See you at the sleepover?"

"Yeah."

Sleepover. Gus had been invited to only two kids' houses since they'd moved to Liston Heights. Cyril, first, and then Gus shot pucks in William's driveway. William's mom had taken them to Dairy Queen. Gus had ordered a Peanut Butter Cup Blizzard, the ice cream melting faster than he could eat it. Then Georgie had come over to shoot. But there'd been no sleepover.

Gus replayed what Colin had said about getting on the team as he loosened his skates. Coach Ashberry was talking about hustling in the third period. He said their lack of stamina was why they'd "come up short." Gus stared at the rubber floor, now spotted with wet marks from the skates.

"Can I get everyone to freeze?" Ashberry said, annoyed. They weren't supposed to get undressed while he was talking. Mac was allowed, but only because he was a goalie and had to wear so much stuff.

Gus folded his hands in his lap. Behind Coach's back, Nik unrolled his socks and kicked his left skate off. Meanwhile, William had literally frozen with his jersey half off, his face covered. A few kids laughed.

"Guys!" Ashberry threw his arms out. "What do we say about respect?"

Gus pointed at William as the coach zoomed his stare around the room.

"Can I unfreeze?" William called from under his shirt.

"Matzke," Ashberry said, "don't be an idiot."

William pulled the rest of the jersey off, and Gus grinned at him. His hair had gone all staticky and stuck out in spurts over his ears. Coach thunked William's head with his whiteboard marker. Gus's teachers could never get away with stuff like that—calling kids idiots and hitting them with markers. But that was one thing Gus liked about hockey. Adults just said stuff straight out.

"All right, so." Ashberry whacked his free palm with his marker in a regular rhythm. "Coach Walker and I talked about it on the way in, and we've decided to give the game puck to someone who *did* hustle all the way through the third period. This person deserves it, even though we lost."

Gus thought back to his last several shifts. He had hustled, hadn't he? He'd focused on the back check? Ashberry had yelled at Owen from the bench about energy, but never at Gus.

"This person never gave up on the play," Coach said. "He's

willing to do the grunt work, to clear the puck from the zone, even when there aren't going to be many scoring chances." Gus had been behind the net a few times. He'd passed it out of the zone, reminding himself about what Coach Walker said about not "reverting to dump and chase."

"This is someone who truly knows that defense is the best offense," Ashberry said.

Gus exhaled. It wasn't him. It'd be a defender. Coach Walker pulled her silver Sharpie out of her pocket and uncapped it. She'd already written "Game Puck" in bubble letters in the middle of the one she was holding. Now she'd add the name of the player on the textured rim. She'd write the date. Gus had watched carefully last time she performed this task. William had gotten the first one. He had held the puck out to his parents as the team left the locker room. Gus knew his mom's eyes would sparkle if he ever held up a game puck to her.

"Rocco," Coach Ashberry said. Rocco jumped over his bag on the floor and stood in his socks in front of the coaches. Coach Walker bit her lip as she formed the letters on the rim and then slapped the puck into Rocco's hand. Gus clapped. Everyone did. Rocco had played hard. He'd saved Gus's butt on a turnover at the end of the second. Rocco was a great choice.

"Okay," Coach Ashberry went on. "So, we're going to double down on our skating. We're going to get stronger and faster, so we can match teams like this all the way to the final minutes. Sound good?"

Gus nodded. A few other kids called out their yeses.

"Any questions?" Coach asked.

Owen piped up. "Is it possible to get added to the A-team?" he asked. "Like, after the season already starts?"

Coach Ashberry squinted at the door, on the other side of which stood Colin Kelliher. Coach looked like he might be ready to say, "idiot" again like he had to Matzke. Instead, Coach Walker interrupted. "That would be highly unusual." She winked at Owen. "We're happy with the team we have here." She looked around the room. "But if someone joins us," she added, "then that'll be fine, too."

Gus grabbed his mouthguard case and spit his into it. When she said "someone," Coach Walker meant Colin Kelliher, the ultimate hater. He might join the team. Gus flicked the tab on the mouthguard case a few times, wishing Coach Walker had said "impossible," instead of "unusual."

Gus could feel Owen staring at him. "If someone got added," Owen asked, "would it mean that someone else would get cut?"

Gus dropped the mouthguard case and pulled off his left elbow pad even though he wasn't supposed to undress. He thought of the way his mom had handed him the whole container of ice cream the night after he'd made the team. She'd tossed him a spoon, no dish. Just last night, she'd shown him the picture that was going to be in the local magazine, Gus standing just in front of his mom and next to Georgie. The picture was about playing for the A-team, not being a loser. Gus wondered if it could still get published if he got kicked off.

"Our team is in the room," Coach Ashberry said. Gus looked up. Ashberry looked mad, his cheeks red like when Lucas had gone offsides for the third time in a single period.

"Our team is in the room." Gus repeated the line to himself, letting his lips move. Despite hockey usually being so easy to understand, he wasn't sure exactly what Ashberry meant.

CHAPTER THIRTY-TWO

LEIGH MACKENZIE

November 2022

What are you hearing about this special meeting of the Liston Heights Hockey board?" Jamie's text came in just as Leigh had finished her weekly meeting with Fred Page. She opened her digital to-do list, so long it required extensive scrolling. She felt like she was finally getting a handle on the midwestern consumer sector and her current slate of acquisitions, but the fast pace of Lupine Capital and the need to lobby lenders made her jittery.

She liked the fast pace, she reminded herself. Private equity had been the perfect outlet after her athletic career ended—the high stakes, thrilling last-minute deals, and even the betrayals and failures spurred her on, just as hockey had.

Leigh flicked open the message from Jamie. Charlie had mentioned a board meeting, something about a kid wanting to be added to the A-team, but she'd been half paying attention when he'd told her, distracted by the flurry of texts from Nicole about representation periods and warrantees.

"Why in the world would I be up to date on the Liston Heights Hockey board meetings?" she typed back to her little brother. Her brain was filled with a full slate of pending deals and inquiries. Leigh had a little extra bandwidth for Gus's progress, the drills and YouTube videos Susy sent for her to go over with him. But for general board politics? She'd let Charlie handle that stuff.

Jamie wrote, "The schedule and minutes are published on the board tab of the website." Leigh rolled her eyes. Jamie coached high school, not youth, and he still checked the website nearly daily for updates. Her phone rang in her hand. Jamie.

"It's too much to text," he said when she answered.

"What's too much?"

"Okay." Jamie sounded out of breath. "I got this from a kid on my team, a ninth grader who has a fifth-grade brother in Squirts. Apparently, the Kellihers have raised a huge stink about Colin's placement on B1, and they're demanding a whole inquiry into the evaluation procedure."

"So?" Who cared that some random kid on a different team was unhappy?

"I made some calls after I heard, and apparently my player was right. This woman—this Kelliher woman—is particularly upset about Gus making A." Leigh squinted at the painting opposite her desk, her eyes locked on the division between the pink and red color blocks, the smudgy white line.

"But tryouts are long since passed." Leigh felt pressure at the back of her throat. In her mind's eye, Jeff Carlson tugged his collar and looked at the floor in the conference room in Lake Placid. "It's youth hockey," she added, mostly to reassure herself, to distinguish her Olympic-selection memory from the reality at hand.

"It would be completely unprecedented for them to move Gus,"

Jamie said. She waited a beat and squinted back at the pink. "I can't imagine they'd do it," he finally continued, "but I'd work your board contacts just in case. You've rekindled things with Jeff?"

Rekindled? Leigh held her breath, processing his choice of words. Jamie didn't know anything about her affair. He'd been eleven years old when she'd stared at Jeff in that decision room, his neck red where he'd scratched it during his introductory remarks. Leigh should have known the second she walked into the room that she hadn't made it. Jeff hadn't looked up from the carpet.

"We had drinks," she told Jamie. "And Charlie's made friends with Susy Walker. They've been out a couple of times with Arnie Senko, watching different games."

"Good," Jamie said. "Friends in high places. You're a former national team member. You're not the kind of parent the hockey association wants to upset. Plus, Gus already made the team, fair and square."

Leigh cracked a knuckle. "Was it?" She moved her focus to the top left of her painting where hints of burnt orange invaded the dominant blush.

"Was what?"

"Was it fair and square?" Leigh brought her knee up against the front of her desk and leaned back, shifting her gaze to the recessed lights in the ceiling. "I called in that favor with Jeff."

Jamie was quieter than she'd like. A whine came from the back of his throat before he formed his words. "Whatever strings you pulled, it still had to be close."

"We both know he was on the bubble," Leigh said. She hadn't made it to every game, but she'd seen enough minutes to know Gus was the weakest skater of the forwards. B would have been an appropriate placement, too.

"Still, he had to be in the ballpark," Jamie said.

Leigh held the bottom edge of the phone away from her cheek. Her letter to Jeff's lawyer had probably been the ticket into that ballpark. Leigh felt her cheeks flush. Her lunch—a cafeteria tuna melt and a side of baked jalapeño chips—roiled her stomach. "Okay," Leigh said. "I'll call Jeff." Gus already had a Squirt A jacket and hat. What would they do with those if Gus were demoted?

"Yeah," Jamie said. "Call Jeff. Maybe you could, like, volunteer to coach or be on some committee?"

Leigh put her foot back on the floor. "One thing at a time, junior."

She opened a text thread with Jeff before she could talk herself out of it. Her stomach flipped again. "I'm hearing some buzz about a special board meeting," she wrote. "I'm going straight to the source I know I can trust." *Barf.* But she knew Jeff would respond to flattery. "What can you tell me about Colin Kelliher and Gus's solidity as a member of the A-team?" She sent it.

Leigh had hoped her interactions with Jeff could end after that first meeting, after she'd sent the letter to his attorney. She should have realized that moving to Liston Heights would bring more than a little discomfort back into her life. Susy provided a constant reminder of everything Leigh had tried for and failed to achieve. And Susy's daughter, too, seemed destined for a greatness that Leigh couldn't imagine for Gus. Watching her in that scrimmage and afterward had been the first thing since 2002 that had actually made Leigh feel like skating again. Georgie clearly had a string of triumphant moments just waiting in her future. And there was Leigh's dad on the sidelines watching her son, just as he'd done for her and Jamie. What were his expectations of the next generation?

And, finally, there was Jeff, someone she'd never wanted to see again after he'd presided over the worst day of her life. Jeff and Susy knew exactly what she'd been willing to do for a chance at the Olympics. They knew, and Charlie didn't.

Leigh was still holding her phone and staring at her to-do list when Jeff's reply came in. "Meet me for a drink tonight, and I'll make sure the scoresheets from evaluations get permanently misplaced. I don't know how Cathy Kelliher got wind of it anyway. Besides, Ashberry didn't want Colin."

Leigh remembered the sticky vinyl in the booth at Lions Tap. She had to go, both for Gus and for herself. She couldn't get on Jeff's bad side at this point, not with both Gus's hockey future and her own marriage at stake, her secret uncomfortably close.

"Fine." Leigh would get Charlie up to speed and tell him she was taking care of it. He'd be grateful. "I'll be there at eight." If she hurried, she could get home for dinner with Gus and a little snuggle time before she had to go back out. She tapped the compose button and started to tell Charlie when a text from Susy came in.

"Important: Have you heard of Sydney Kirkpatrick? Her complaint has gone public."

Leigh dropped her phone in her lap. She touched her collarbone in the spot where Sydney wore that St. Christopher necklace. Leigh let her vision blur over the pink and red color blocks in her painting. Leigh had danced in Gus's room the night he'd made the A-team. The price of that happiness had been taking Jeff's side over Sydney's.

Leigh grabbed her phone. "I don't think so," she typed back. It wasn't until she'd pressed send that she realized she'd sent the text to Charlie instead of Susy. She had to write back to clarify her mistake.

CHAPTER THIRTY-THREE

SUSY WALKER

November 2022

Susy and Arnie had just finished quizzing Charlie about the exceptional defensive play in the Liston Heights High School game they'd watched when Leigh walked into the brewery. It was the first time she'd agreed to join them for post-hockey drinks, and Susy was slightly embarrassed to find herself sweating with nerves.

"Leigh's here." Susy tried to keep her tone light. She waved at Leigh, who looked stiff and uncomfortable even from twenty feet away. Their friendship had been easy during those years on Team USA. Susy had been grateful the captains had decided they'd be good roommates. Knowing she'd be falling asleep next to Leigh always made Susy feel less nervous about leaving home. The truth was, she'd never connected that well with other girls. Leigh had been the first.

Leigh strode to the table, her hair pulled back. She wore the same dark-rinse jeans she'd chosen for the photo shoot. Amelia Matzke had told Susy the magazine was set to hit the local grocery stores and city mailboxes the following week. The photo of the four of them would run on the cover.

"Join us for a beer." Susy pulled out the chair next to her. She had sent Leigh that text about Sydney the other day in the hopes that it might lead to conversation like the ones they'd had in the old days, after dark in dorm and hotel rooms. But Leigh hadn't said anything except that she hadn't heard of Sydney Kirkpatrick, that she wasn't comfortable discussing the allegations. It was odd, Susy thought. Leigh's Twitter feed was filled with feminist sentiments and retweets. A sexual harassment claim would be a cause she'd latch on to. And there had been her own devastating experience with Jeff.

"Just one beer." Leigh exchanged a look with Charlie, who shrugged affably and handed her his pint glass.

"Sit," Charlie said. "You'll like this IPA. Try it, and I'll order you one." He stood up. Susy watched him run his hand along Leigh's upper back as he walked past her, and Susy felt a frisson of jealousy. Her husband had been a total dick, but it had been nice to have someone to rub her shoulders and order her drinks.

"I told my mom we'd be home by nine," Leigh called to Charlie.

"Nine thirty won't really be a problem." Charlie gave a thumbs-up. "I'll text her. Do you want one of those?" He pointed at his beer. She grabbed the pint and sipped gingerly. She flinched against its bitterness, but Leigh said, "It's nice."

Susy cocked her head. Leigh had been nothing if not brutally honest as a young woman. She was the first to call someone out, to offer a critique. Honesty, and of course snipes to the upper-right corner, had been Leigh's hallmarks. At least until that last camp. Susy remembered standing in the snack room at Lake Placid. Jeff Carlson had just sauntered down the hallway. Leigh had lobbed her cold oatmeal into the trash.

"I'm dying to know how it feels," Susy said, determined to scratch the surface with her old friend.

"How what feels?"

"To be back! After all these years, and back in the hockey scene? It's gotta be wild."

"Oh." Leigh pulled on her ponytail. "I guess I hadn't considered that I was back in the hockey scene."

Arnie chuckled then, snapping the tenuous thread that Susy felt growing between them. She remembered Leigh's moodiness, her occasional bitchiness. "Leaving the hockey parenting to Charlie, eh?" Arnie asked. "I would have thought someone of your caliber would want to have more oversight. Shouldn't you be staring over Coach Walker's shoulder?" He smirked. "We've been trying to give Charlie an education, but Padawan has a long way to go."

"It's just youth hockey," said Leigh. Susy raised her eyebrows. *Just?* If Leigh noticed, she ignored her. "Plus, Charlie runs everything in our house." Charlie arrived at the table and slid a full pint over to her. "Even more since we moved back."

"It's tough in a new position." Susy was guessing, trying to be sympathetic. She herself hadn't changed jobs since Georgie had been born. She'd thought a couple of times about new gigs. There'd been the offer from St. Lucia's University in Wisconsin. They'd needed a coach for their D3 women's hockey team. But that would have required travel. Dirk traveled incessantly. Susy didn't want Georgie shuttling between babysitters when she already had to deal with the headache of joint custody. And as her hockey coach, Susy got to see Georgie on Dirk's days, too.

Charlie kissed Leigh's cheek. Susy looked down, embarrassed by another swell of envy. She hadn't dated much since her divorce. Maybe she should try again on one of the new apps. She could crop the photo they'd just taken for the magazine, leave the USA showing in the picture.

"Is gym teaching busy?" Leigh asked.

Susy swallowed. She hated it when people called it "gym." "PE is draining sometimes." She tried to keep her voice light. No need to subject Leigh to her speech about "gym being a place, and 'physical education' being the content."

"That's how she stays so fit," Arnie piped in, and rubbed a hand over his own swollen belly. "Gets to exercise all day at work."

"I don't know about that." Susy snuck a look back at Leigh. Leigh ran a hedge fund or something, light-years from supervising trench ball. Susy rubbed her thumb and forefinger together, thinking of the etching on her Olympic medal. This was her go-to fix for moments of insecurity. Though Leigh was some kind of money shark, she was missing that medal.

Arnie belched lightly. "Have I mentioned lately how lucky we are to have you, Suse? Seriously," he said, "to have a two-time Olympic medalist committed to *youth* hockey. And doubly lucky our kids are the same age as Georgie. We've got you locked in." Arnie's expression grew more serious. "Well, at least until you switch her to girls'."

Susy looked at Leigh, whose beer was already a third of the way empty. "When did you start playing with girls, Leigh?" she asked. "Not until high school, right? Of course, we didn't really have options."

"Ninth grade," Leigh agreed. "Arnie's right, you know. The team is super lucky to have you. It's such a time commitment." It was a compliment, and yet Leigh's eyes looked flat, as if she were playing the part of a friendly person, the feeling not penetrating her facade.

"I suppose the nights and weekends aren't ideal," Susy said. "But I find myself searching for extra ice even when the Squirts aren't practicing. I've been meaning to tell you about my Sunday Skate, Leigh."

Charlie popped in, excited. "Sunday Skate?" Leigh took another sip of her beer and drummed her fingers against the table.

"It's only for girls," Susy said. "Mixed ability, minimal structure, parties in the locker room—would you ever . . . ?" Susy pushed her coaster back and forth. "I thought of you while I was sitting outside the locker room last week. Remember 'Mustang Sally'?"

"Yeah." Susy expected her to smile, but Leigh looked over her shoulder at the door. "Well? How was the high school game tonight?"

Charlie jumped in. "Before you got here, they were quizzing me, testing to see if I noticed all the things I should have about the play."

"Speaking of." Susy pushed away her disappointment. Leigh had been clear about her feelings since 2002. "Liston Heights shorted the bench at the end. Did you notice the third line stopped playing?"

"Right!" Arnie chimed in. "We didn't talk about that."

"But why would they do that?" Charlie asked. "They were already good for the win, right? Not really in danger?"

"Point differential," Leigh, Arnie, and Susy said together.

Charlie laughed, startled by the stereo.

"It can be important for league standings." Leigh shrugged.

"See?" Arnie pointed at her. "She might say she's retired, but she's still got it."

Susy sipped her beer and glanced furtively at Leigh, irked by her dismissal of the Sunday Skate. "I could talk to Jeff about getting you a coaching spot," Susy said. "He'd likely be inclined to help you, given your history together." She snuck another glance at Charlie. Susy could see hope in his smile, but no suspicion. He put his arm around Leigh. Charlie never reacted to hearing Jeff's name, but Leigh had recoiled against the back of her chair. Susy thought again about the cold oatmeal in Lake Placid, about Leigh's flushed cheeks.

She'd never told him, Susy guessed, about what she'd done to up her chances for Olympic hardware.

"I keep asking her," Charlie said. "Now that we're back here, there's so much opportunity to reconnect with the sport—with old friends." He rubbed Leigh's shoulder again. "The word will be out when the magazine debuts next week, right?"

Leigh's lashes obscured her eyes as she drained her beer. "No coaching this season," she said. "Too much work, too many new things." Leigh turned to Susy, her eyes flashing. She could never hide her anger, and clearly Susy's comment about Jeff riled her. "But speaking of reconnecting, maybe we could get a coffee sometime? Just the two of us? I've been meaning to suggest that."

Susy felt a surge of excitement, and then it faded. She'd missed Leigh so much over the years, but now Leigh wanted to connect only because she needed something. Susy was pretty sure it was her silence.

CHAPTER THIRTY-FOUR

LEIGH MACKENZIE

August 2001

My bangs are growing out funny, and they look so stupid in a headband," Susy said to Leigh in their dorm room. The light outside their window had turned pinkish. Dinner would start in thirty minutes. Susy pulled her blond hair down over her eyes and scrunched her nose in displeasure.

Leigh looked up from the *InStyle* she'd been paging through. The outfit she'd just inspected featured a knee-length cobalt dress with peep-toe ankle boots. As if Leigh or any of the other hockey players would have an occasion to wear such an ensemble. Once they made the team, they'd be in two-a-days, alternately lifting increasingly heavy barbells in USA gym shorts and throwing on sweaty dry-fit tights beneath their breezers to take the ice.

"Come here." Leigh closed the magazine, sat on the edge of her twin bed, and pointed at the floor next to her. "Let's try braiding them."

Susy frowned. "I didn't wash my hair after the afternoon skate."

"Who cares?" Leigh said. "I've touched sweaty hair a million times."

Susy flipped her wrist and looked at her Timex. Leigh could see a tan line at the edge of the band as it slipped. She'd been running a lot that summer, for sure. Susy's stamina never flagged, whereas in the final minutes of the toughest skates, Leigh found herself wheezing. "Do we have time before dinner?" Susy asked.

"It'll take two minutes." Leigh combed out the left side of Susy's hair with her fingers. Susy hadn't said anything about the oatmeal the night before. She hadn't asked about Leigh's phone call with Charlie or about Jeff's appearance in the training room that day after lunch.

Jeff had coughed as he leaned against the doorway, staring at Leigh as she swung her legs out of the ice bath. Leigh's thighs had been pink and splotchy from the cold water as she hop-skipped after Jeff toward an empty locker room off the pool deck.

Leigh pulled Susy's growing-out bangs to the left and began a tight French braid, trapping the shorter pieces in the plait.

"So," Susy said as Leigh brought the braid toward the crown of her head, "are you going to tell me what's going on with Jeff?"

Leigh tugged Susy's hair tight, and her head jerked back. "Sorry. I just want these shorter strands to stay put." She held all three pieces of hair with one hand and smoothed the fledgling braid with the other.

"Did you and Charlie break up?" Susy asked.

Leigh knew Susy had liked Charlie, too. How could she not? Charlie was the nicest person in the universe and also looked like a literal movie star. But Leigh had won the national championship the week before they'd met him. There was that thing about the victor and the spoils. And Charlie was devoted to Leigh. He and the guys from his dorm floor had painted GO LEIGH USA on their skinny chests in red, white, and blue for the World Championship final. Leigh still had the photo of them all together in her nightstand. Charlie's cap was backward, as usual. He'd flexed both stringy biceps for the picture and looked adorable.

"No," Leigh said. "We're not broken up."

"Oh."

Leigh grabbed a bobby pin from the corner of the desk next to her bed. "Hang on." She pinned the braid to the back of Susy's head and stood up to grab some more bobbies from her toiletry bag. They didn't make eye contact as she walked back with three pins in the corner of her mouth. "Suse." Leigh added another pin in a crisscross and lightly tugged the tangles out of the rest of her hair. "I've never wanted anything more than I want to make this team. It's the Olympics. We're so close. It's everything I've dreamed about since my dad showed me the Miracle game." Leigh had been just a month old when Team USA beat the Soviets in Lake Placid in 1980. Her dad still quoted Al Michaels at least monthly. "Do you believe in miracles?"

And Leigh did believe in them. She'd been Ms. Hockey and she'd won the national college championship twice. But she'd also lost to Canada in the World Champs. She'd felt the ice against her face as the Canadians whooped all around her.

Leigh believed in miracles, but she also believed in padding her stats. She gathered Susy's soft hair in a ponytail, low enough that it wouldn't impede her hockey helmet.

"So, that's what you're doing with Jeff?" Susy asked. "Like, you think if you're—" She tried to turn around. Leigh didn't want to look at her, so she pulled the ponytail out and resmoothed it.

"I'm just checking every box, okay?" she said. "It'll be worth it when I'm on the team." Leigh reread the Muhammad Ali quote Susy had written out in red Sharpie and taped to her bed frame. "Don't quit. Suffer now and live the rest of your life as a champion."

"Are you going to tell Charlie?" Susy asked.

Leigh remembered the first camp she and Susy had been at three years before when they'd both been freshmen. By the time they'd finished the first excruciating on-ice conditioning test side by side over the red line, Susy had yanked off her helmet and spat vomit onto the ice. Leigh had tasted blood and her vision blurred. She'd reflexively grabbed for Susy as they shuffled toward the locker room. Jeff had knocked on each of their helmets as they walked, indicating a job well done.

Charlie could understand that level of suffering. Leigh had seen him at mile 45 of his first ultramarathon, after all. She'd seen the wild look in his eyes when they turned back into the woods after the final aid stop, his stride nothing more than a shuffle. Although he wasn't suffering to become the best in the world, that run had taught him about pushing his limits. It would mean something to him, too, if she made it to the Olympics. He could understand her sacrifices.

"I'm not going to tell him if I don't have to," Leigh said. "It doesn't really have anything to do with him. Can we keep this between us?" Leigh patted Susy's shoulders and lay back on her bed, finished with her hair.

"It's your business," Susy said. "But you don't have to do it. You're going to make the team anyway."

"We're both going to make it." Leigh rolled over the knot of her ponytail to finally look at her friend. "I don't think either of us has ever wanted anything more in our entire lives. Wouldn't you do anything?" Leigh asked. She thought about her parents waiting by the phone for her call at the camp's conclusion in just two days. If she failed, everyone's efforts—her parents' early mornings and equipment expenses, not to mention the anxiety they felt as they cheered her on—it all would be for nothing.

Leigh didn't wait for Susy to answer. "It'll all be worth it when it's over."

CHAPTER THIRTY-FIVE

CHARLIE MACKENZIE

November 2022

Leigh fishtailed on the fresh snow as she merged onto the highway, and Charlie wondered whether he should have insisted on driving home from the brewery. He rolled his neck, discerning the effects of his two IPAs. Not enough to inhibit him.

"I can't believe you've become, like, best friends with my old roommate from Team USA." Leigh sounded pissed.

"I should have asked if you wanted me to drive," Charlie said lightly.

Leigh scoffed. "You think I'm drunk? Like after one beer?"

Charlie remembered how she'd sucked it down after Susy had mentioned coaching. Leigh had definitely flinched when Susy had said Jeff Carlson's name. That reaction had to be related to something more than just the sourness of the hops.

"You never talk about Jeff," Charlie blurted, "or about your time on Team USA at all."

Leigh shot into the left lane and accelerated around a rusty minivan. Charlie grabbed the handle above his window and gritted his teeth.

"That's because Jeff is a goddamn fucking asshole."

Charlie stared. In twenty years, she'd talked about Team USA only when Gus asked about it, usually after spending time with Leigh's parents, who remained enormously proud. When Leigh did drop a story, the plot of it all took place on the ice—power plays, turnovers, celebrations. She had never once mentioned any conflicts with her coaches. Charlie replayed Susy's seemingly casual reference to Jeff's interest in Leigh coaching, the way Susy's smile had curled up on the left side. Had she looked mischievous?

Charlie considered how hard he should push now. There was no denying Leigh's sudden anger, her restlessness. He softened his tone. "Why are you upset right now?"

The tops of Leigh's knuckles whitened as she held ten and two. Charlie snuck a glance at the speedometer, which hovered just under 70 in the 55 zone. "I didn't know I was going to have to talk about it tonight. Look," she said, "it's nothing. It's been a long day. I wanted to see Gus before he had to go to bed, and now—" She snapped her mouth closed and her cheeks hollowed as she clenched her jaw again.

Charlie felt his pulse slow as it often did in response to Leigh's agitation. He'd always countered her peaks with his own valleys. "It's Friday night. You knew we were going to have a drink with my new friends." Charlie kept his voice low and slow. "It's not unreasonable to make an effort now that we're here." Despite his vocal dispassion, his own anger had begun to swell. He moved his free hand to his belly, quelling it. "I thought when we moved to Liston Heights, it would be an opportunity to reconnect." In Florida, Leigh had had a couple of friends at work. There were some pals from business school before that. But, Charlie realized, there was no one Leigh kept in touch with through multiple life stages.

"I don't have any friends," Leigh admitted.

Charlie studied her, watched the waves of anger pulse in her jaw. "Why didn't you invite Susy to our wedding?" he asked. "Weren't you like, best friends?"

Leigh's right eye twitched. "Seriously, Charlie?" Her voice rose to a shout. "It's just fucking weird, okay? It's frankly bizarre that she's glommed on to you."

"Glommed on to me? I'm the new one. Arnie invited me."

"Whatever." Leigh whipped her head to the right, checking the blind spot over Charlie's shoulder. She pulled even with a Kia Soul driving too slow in the fast lane.

"Are you mad at me for having friends?" Charlie glanced at the driver of the Kia. It was a kid, a baseball cap low on his brow as he rocked his body in time with music, the bass of which Charlie could just barely hear.

"There are what? Like, more than fifty thousand people in Liston Heights," Leigh said, "and you become best friends with the woman who watched me crash and burn?" Charlie grimaced as Leigh wove back into the fast lane.

"You're going to crash and burn right fucking now." Charlie tensed his abs and cowered away from the median. One patch of ice, and they'd be spinning. "Could you quit this craziness before we orphan our son?" Charlie snuck a look in the mirror on his side, checking for police and traffic.

"I don't need help with my driving," Leigh snapped, though she did slow down. Charlie thought back to the bar, to Susy's and Arnie's cheerful welcome, their invitation for Leigh to stay. "Susy's nice, right?" Charlie said once the speedometer was back under 65. "You'll go to coffee with her?"

"You don't know her. You don't know what she's really like."

Her voice had quieted, but still sounded steely. It was the same tone Leigh had used when their plumbing mainline had burst in Tampa and the insurance agent broke the news that it wasn't covered. Two hours later, she'd secured them a partial payment. That voice, its edge like a skate blade, was the reason Charlie usually left tricky negotiations to her.

Charlie knew he should drop it, but he thought of Jamie's players winning in the final minutes that night. The Lions' victory had come because of persistence. "Really?" he asked. "There's something salacious to know about a mild-mannered PE teacher? Susy is, like, a secret maniac who shoves razor blades in the school's volleyballs, or what?" Leigh zoomed over two lanes toward their exit. Charlie gripped the "Oh shit" handle again. "Because I feel like Susy's pretty transparent."

Leigh snorted. "Oh right." She flipped the turn signal on, her arm flailing up toward the ceiling as it clicked. "Your divorced friend who's always been into you is so nice and transparent." Leigh glanced at him for a split second and then veered off the highway. Their tires crunched over the refrozen slush.

"'Always'? You mean at that one college party twenty years ago?" Charlie deflated. He wasn't looking for anything with Susy. He'd thought he had everything he needed at home. He pictured his manuscript in the drawer, the middle of the novel where he'd gotten stuck.

"Aren't you even going to say anything?" Leigh spat. "You're not even going to deny this"—she lifted her hand from the wheel and put it down again—"flirtation or whatever it is?"

"Leigh." Charlie kept his gaze focused ahead as Leigh pulled into her parents' driveway. He remembered being here as a college kid, remembered Leigh announcing to Big Gus and Helen that the two of them were engaged. Charlie had seen trepidation in Gus Mackenzie's eyes when Leigh had made her feverish announcement. She'd been only twenty-one years old. Gus's fingers had shaken as he'd unwrapped the foil on a dusty bottle of champagne and dropped an ice cube in each of their flutes. While Leigh's parents had been nervous about their commitment, Charlie hadn't. "That accusation is too stupid for me to respond to and you know it." He shifted the car into park for her. "I'll wait here."

Leigh slammed her door. Maybe a different sort of person would have stopped to apologize right then, but this was Leigh. Tenacious and unflinching. It would be a full day before she said she was sorry, and then only if she felt she had to.

Charlie would be entitled to insist on an apology. They both knew he'd never be unfaithful to her. His own parents had spent his growing-up years hugging and kissing in the kitchen. Their ease with each other was all Charlie imagined when he agreed to marry Leigh. He hadn't been looking for some kind of roller coaster thrill ride. The Wards, Charlie's parents, still read side by side on the couch now in the evenings. It seemed comfortable, if a little quiet.

And Leigh did dazzle Charlie, though perhaps the thrills had faded in twenty years. The byproduct of Leigh's passion was the occasional outburst. She'd be over it by tomorrow, and he hoped he would be, too.

Suddenly warm despite the outdoor temperature, Charlie punched a finger at the console, redirecting the dry heat toward the sunroof. A minute later, Leigh appeared at the front door, holding Gus's hand. He looked sleepy under his Lions stocking cap.

Charlie waved at Helen on the step and smiled for Gus's benefit. Leigh opened the back door, and Gus slid in. "I already know," he said. "The Lions won 4–2. Uncle Jamie called."

Charlie winked at him and reached a hand back to squeeze his knee. "It was a good game."

"Did you see it, Mom? How were the forwards?"

Leigh shook her head and avoided eye contact with Charlie. "I was working," she said. "If I'm going to watch hockey, I'll do it when you're playing."

"But you missed my game on Sunday," Gus said. Charlie felt vindicated. Gus was disappointed in Leigh, too.

CHAPTER THIRTY-SIX

LEIGH MACKENZIE

December 2022

Leigh felt guilty as soon as she woke up the next morning. Charlie wasn't the type to stray, and Susy wasn't some kind of evil seductress. They'd both been trying to be nice to her at the brewery, to include her in their hockey club, a place she still didn't feel she belonged.

All those years ago, Susy had backed off immediately when Leigh had claimed Charlie at that party. She'd never expressed any jealousy or resentment about that, even when she'd discovered what was going on with Jeff.

Leigh had to admit her behavior at the brewery had been a direct response to her forced meeting with him. That's what she'd been doing the night before she met Charlie and his friends. Jeff had agreed at the Lions Tap to keep Gus's roster spot safe—he agreed that removing Gus from the team would prompt more questions than any of them wanted to answer—but he also broke the news that they'd probably have to add Colin Kelliher to the A-team. "His mother has seen the evaluations," Jeff said. "Colin had the ninth-highest raw score. I blame the Squirt coordinator for telling her. Loose lips."

"Won't adding Colin raise people's, I don't know"—Leigh had stared wistfully at the hostess stand, wishing she could leave the bar and erase Jeff for another twenty years—"suspicions?"

Jeff gulped his gin and ginger. He'd copied her order. "Mostly people will just think Cathy Kelliher is a pushy pain in the ass." He shrugged. "Which she is."

"Okay." Leigh drank down her cocktail and drummed her fingers on the table. "I was hoping to get home to kiss Gus good night."

Jeff had reached across and grabbed her wrist. She startled and noticed the beads of sweat near his hairline. "One more thing," he'd said. "I might need you to answer some questions for my lawyer."

Leigh blanched. Susy had texted about Sydney Kirkpatrick. Leigh had googled images of Sydney again. She'd looked at them with her eyes half-open, not wanting to see Sydney as a real person. There had been one picture of the younger woman in shorts and a Team USA T-shirt. In the photo, Sydney bent next to a little boy who'd tried on her silver medal. The kid's smile redefined "megawatt."

"What kind of questions?" Leigh asked.

"About our relationship." Jeff tapped his empty glass on the table. "About how it was genuine and not tied to any"—he coughed—"promises I made about the team."

Leigh held her stomach in. She remembered standing naked in the gray light of the dorm room at Lake Placid. She hugged her arms across her chest.

"Okay?" Jeff had said. "And then I'll make sure Cathy Kelliher never knows that Gus's raw score was only seventeenth."

Leigh didn't want to talk to any lawyers. "I thought you said the last time we came here that the evaluations would be destroyed."

How would Leigh explain meetings with Jeff's lawyer to Charlie? She'd proposed marriage to him right after she'd gotten off the plane from Albany. Leigh hadn't mentioned to Charlie then, or ever, that she'd given her assistant coach a blow job in the referees' locker room just twenty-four hours before. Leigh squeezed her elbows, digging her nails into the skin beneath her rolled-up sleeves.

"Listen, I don't want to force you." Jeff had leaned across the table toward her, and she smashed her back against the cracked pleather booth. "But Gus has a long future in the association. I'll owe you guys for a long, long time."

Although she'd lashed out at Charlie and not at Susy, Leigh still felt uneasy as she arrived for coffee with her old friend. Susy pulled her Infiniti SUV, a nicer car than Leigh expected of a junior high PE teacher, into the row behind her. Of course, Susy had been married to Dirk Magnussen. There had to be some spousal support involved in their split.

"Hey." Susy smiled as they met at the door. Leigh could see a twitch in her jaw, the same tell she'd had in college when she was nervous.

They both ordered, paid separately, and when they were seated, Susy launched in. "First, I just want to tell you how happy I am to be coaching Gus. The kid is amazing and, Leigh-Leigh, he has boundless potential. You can see it, right?" Susy's cheeks pinked as she slid her arms out of her parka. "In fact," Susy said, "I've already started thinking about summer. Does he have a team?"

"I'm not sure about summer. Have you asked Charlie?" Undoubtedly, he and Jamie had already started to make plans.

Susy smiled. "I will. And Leigh, Charlie's so nice! Aren't you so glad you ended up with a guy like that? You're so lucky. Dirk is—"

She made a face like she'd tasted rancid meat. "A total cheating jackass." As soon as she said it, Susy's eyes flew wide open and her face flushed.

Leigh sucked in her breath. They both knew Leigh had been a cheater, too. With Jeff.

"Sorry!" Susy blurted. "That's not . . . I didn't mean—"

"Whatever." Leigh managed a closed-mouth smile. "It was a long time ago, but as I mentioned to you on that first day we ran into each other . . ." Leigh remembered the humid summer night in the liquor store parking lot, Susy's presence there a reminder that she'd walked right back into her old life. "Charlie doesn't know the details of what happened then. It's been so long. I don't know how I'd . . ." She blinked.

Susy sighed and pulled her phone out of her pocket. "I get that, Leigh, but also you were a kid then. What happened wasn't really your fault."

"What are you talking about?" Leigh remembered Jeff's letter, the phone card he'd sent, the stubble on his cheeks where Charlie's were smooth. She remembered telling Susy that everything with Jeff would be worth it if she made the team. She'd have one or two medals herself, just like her friend did. Big Gus wouldn't always look at her with that smidgen of disappointment.

But now she knew everything she'd actually risked. She might never have had Gus. The sacrifices looked different.

"You didn't tell me every single detail, but isn't it fair to say that Jeff—I don't know." Susy sipped her coffee and frowned. She lowered her voice. "He pressured you, right?"

Leigh rubbed the center of her forehead. "Susy, I have so much regret about that time." Leigh thought about the first call she ever made to Jeff, the way she'd fallen for his compliments about her strength and speed. "But Jeff never made me do anything."

Susy tipped her chin down and peered at Leigh as if she were a librarian looking at a noisy patron. "That's what you're going with?"

"What do you mean?"

"Can I just tell you what I know about Sydney Kirkpatrick?"

"How do you know about her?" Leigh asked. She'd often worried about some kind of whisper network, a text chain of women who knew Leigh back then, who knew about what had happened with Jeff.

"There's a WhatsApp group for both teams, the Salt Lake team and the Torino team," Susy said. "Some of the girls are in broadcasting, you know? They keep in touch with the younger players."

Leigh imagined her old friends texting without her, the community they'd forged after she'd been cut.

"So here's Sydney's story, the short version." Susy cleared her throat. "You remember she made the team in '14?"

Leigh nodded. She didn't remember, but she'd googled.

"Okay, so after that, she played the next two years through World Champs in '16. She was in the pool for Four Nations the following fall, but didn't make the travel squad."

Leigh pushed her shoulders forward and rounded her back. She felt like putting her head on the table, collapsing like she had after losing to the Canadians. Instead she flexed her abs and tried to stay totally still. "In the summer before the Olympic selection camp, Jeff contacted Sydney. They started texting. He told her he could influence Coach Stewart." Stewart had been the head coach for Pyeong-Chang. "He said Sydney still had potential, and that Jeff had missed her at the Four Nations Cup."

Leigh closed her eyes. If Susy stopped there, Leigh had a feeling she could tell the rest of the story herself. But Susy's tone became feverish.

"At the training camp, Leigh, he ramped it up." Susy looked both excited and teary. "He cornered her after training sessions and treatments. He told her she was special, that she deserved to be there, and that because of their relationship, he could put her back on the team. If only she would—"

"Okay, stop." Leigh pulled her ponytail out and shook her hair over her jacket. She slid her arms out of her sleeves, suddenly hot.

"It's familiar, right?" pressed Susy. "This is what happened to you. He targeted you. He knew you were on the bubble—"

"I wasn't good enough." Leigh looked at the ceiling, feeling close to tears herself.

Susy reached across the table, almost touching Leigh. "Listen to me," she said. "Who knows what you could have done at that camp if you weren't running around with Jeff Carlson? He stole your focus. And he promised you something he couldn't deliver."

Leigh blinked again. She remembered the scrimmages, remembered shooting wide in the final minute of the last one, just as Gus had done in that game versus Wayzata. She'd looked over at Jeff on the bench right after she'd missed.

"He saw your vulnerability, and he took advantage. And he did it to Sydney, too."

Leigh had found the details. Sydney Kirkpatrick hadn't made the 2018 roster and had to settle for just the one medal in Sochi. *But at least she had that.* "Even if you're right about the situations being similar, what does this have to do with me now?" Leigh asked. "It was another lifetime."

Susy raised her eyebrows. "We only get one life. And do you want Jeff Carlson coaching other girls? Promising them things in exchange for who knows what?"

"But you've coached with him in Liston Heights." She'd read about that online, too. "You don't think he's a good guy?"

"This thing from Sydney—" Susy shook her head. "It's so similar to what happened to you, Leigh. It changed how I thought about that camp. It changes how I remember you. You were a victim. I care about you."

Leigh shook her head. She didn't want to hear about Susy's concern, not with Jeff's request to vouch for him on her mind, and not as Susy pursued a friendship with Leigh's husband. "Look," she said as she put her jacket back on, "I appreciate your sentiment, but my situation was different. I made a bad choice. Something I never told Charlie. I know you're friends with him, but . . ."

"Don't go yet," Susy said. Leigh remembered the way she'd swatted Susy's hand away in the Lake Placid decision room, the calls she hadn't answered afterward.

As she felt tears threatening, she stood up and grabbed her coffee. "I want to be friends, Suse, but the past has to stay in the past. That's where it belongs."

CHAPTER THIRTY-SEVEN

SUSY WALKER

December 2022

The phone rang, and Susy glanced at the console. Jeff Carlson. She clutched her gearshift as snowflakes landed and melted on her windshield. After the WhatsApp thread about Sydney Kirkpatrick, Susy had started to rewrite the past. Leigh had been a completely different person, an infinitely more confident player at the World Championships in April of '01 than she had been at Olympic selection camp the following August.

It could have been, as Susy had thought back then, that Leigh hadn't worked hard enough over the summer. Or maybe Jeff distracted and manipulated her in the two most important weeks of her life. Susy remembered Leigh tiptoeing into their room after midnight the morning of the final scrimmage. She'd heard Jeff's murmurs from the hallway as Leigh had opened the door.

Susy had hoped to convince Leigh at their coffee to add her voice to Sydney's, to make an official complaint to USA Hockey. There were a few news stories emerging about Jeff in which he was called an "unnamed coach." Players had spoken up to support Sydney. Susy wasn't sure if the fact that there were others would make Leigh feel better or worse about what had happened to her.

But in any case, now Jeff was calling. He'd report the board's decision about Colin Kelliher. Susy could send him to voice mail, but then she'd have to call him back later, either him or Ashberry. Better to deal with it now. Susy jabbed the button on her steering wheel as she pulled into the parking lot of the brew pub she, Arnie, and Charlie had agreed on.

"Yeah," she said.

"Walker." Jeff was all business, too. "I wanted to give you an update on your roster."

Susy held her breath. Certainly, they couldn't cut Gus five weeks into the season. It'd be a terrible precedent, and one they'd have to explain to a whole slew of parents. Jeff and the hockey board would want to keep their machinations more private. "Yep," she said.

"Short version, okay? I just got off the phone with Ashberry. You guys are getting Kelliher. It's politics. His mother has been head manager for eons, and they sponsor a couple of teams. But you remember him from tryouts. He's good enough."

Susy imagined another kid on the bench, how the lines would shift. She'd wanted an extra skater on decision day, a flex person who would help them cover absences. Kelliher would be fine. "I know he's fast," she agreed.

"And," Jeff said, "the family had inside information on his tryout scores. Didn't come from me."

"But no cuts?" Susy confirmed.

"No. Gus Mackenzie is safe."

"Got it." Susy hovered her finger over the button to hang up. "Good."

"Isn't it great to have Leigh back?" Jeff blurted. Susy watched a group of three laughing women pile into the pub, one hanging on to the elbow of another. It could have been great to have Leigh back. But she wasn't the same Leigh Susy had known in the '90s. She was guarded and secretive and had barely lasted ten minutes at their coffee date. Even when Leigh came to Gus's games, she stood in the shadows, as far away as possible from the rink.

"Yeah," Susy said. "The Mackenzies are a great family, for sure."

"Right," Jeff said. "Family. Okay. You good, Walker?"

Susy sniffed. "I'll look forward to seeing Kelliher at practice tomorrow."

"Bye." He hung up before she had time to hit end.

Susy glanced at her Garmin as she walked into St. Isidore's, a newish place in the warehouse district across the highway from Braemar Ice Arena. If she'd parked on the opposite end of the complex, she could have stopped into Rob Greystone's facility and checked out which Squirt A players were on his agenda for the afternoon and evening. Rob had been honing Gus Mackenzie's instincts, for sure. Susy could see an easier wrist flick on Gus's shot. He might start being a goal scorer for them as the season went on. At the moment, he looked for the pass nine times out of ten, shooting only when he couldn't not.

Neither Arnie nor Charlie had arrived at the pub yet. Susy ordered a stout at the counter and sat at a high-top. Just as she hung her jacket on the back of her chair, her wrist buzzed. "I'm out." The text from Arnie lit up her watch. "Sorry so last minute. Angela got a flat tire at 62 and France, and I have to be her roadside assistant."

Susy picked up her pint and swallowed. That left just Charlie. If Arnie's text had come ten minutes earlier, they probably would have canceled. Instead Charlie walked through the front door, frowning at his phone, a dusting of snow in his reddish hair. She already had her hand up in a wave when Charlie saw her. His frown lingered slightly longer than it should have. Would he want to drink with

Susy alone? Would it bother Leigh? "Arnie bailed." Charlie slid out of a new-looking Carhartt jacket, the tips on the collar still crisp. He was trying pretty hard to fit in with the hockey crew.

"I know. Sorry. You're stuck with me. Unless—" Susy would give him an out. "You know, it's okay if you'd rather head home. Maybe the flat tire is a sign." The three of them had planned to watch the Wild game.

"Nah." Charlie looked at the bar. The beanied server slouched against the back counter, looking tired. "I gotta give that guy something to do." He pointed at Susy's full glass. "Need anything? Pretzels?"

Susy shrugged. "If you ordered some, I'd definitely help you out."

"The beer cheese sauce is good here. They make it themselves." Charlie put a hand up to his mouth and leaned toward her, as if confiding a secret. "I may have stopped in once or twice with Jamie and Gus after sessions at Greystone's."

He walked away, and Susy was embarrassed to feel her stomach flip, as if this were a date. She and Leigh had met Charlie when they'd barely been out of high school. Charlie had been king of the fraying flannel and baggy jeans. She watched him now as he chatted up the bartender and recognized the same easy vibe they got from him at that basement party. He was so approachable. How had Leigh, the most intense and competitive person she knew, landed the most easygoing husband? The bartender chuckled in response to whatever witticism Charlie delivered. He slid his card across the bar, leaving the tab open. Susy looked away from him before he turned back.

"Anything on the Hub?" he asked.

Susy grabbed her phone and hit refresh on the browser tab she had open for hockey scores. "Nothing earth-shattering."

"Did you check the YHH Twitter? Isn't Orono playing Delano tonight?" Charlie started clicking, checking for an update from the district matchup. "Not yet," he said after a second. "And no brackets for the Nova Tournament. We wait." He held his pint up, and Susy clinked it with hers. She dabbed her mouth after taking a sizable swig.

"What're Leigh and Gus up to tonight?" she asked.

"I have no idea." Charlie rolled his eyes. "I left her some dinner on the stove, and we passed in the mudroom. No time to check in."

"Leigh was running late, right? She always cut it close." Susy smiled as she remembered knocking fervently on a hotel bathroom door, just a minute to spare until the team was supposed to meet in the lobby for a dinner in Prague.

"Oh my God, it drives me crazy!" Charlie laughed. "She doesn't care about time. She's always been like that." He drank again. The light went out of his eyes as he deflated against the back of the chair. Susy wondered what memory had occurred to him. "Maybe it's not that she doesn't care about time," he said, "but that she doesn't care about *other people's* time."

"That's not it." Susy remembered Leigh's baffled expression as they jogged toward the hotel elevator that night in Prague. "It's not like the bus will leave," Leigh had said. And, of course, she'd been right. "Leigh just knows people will wait for her."

Charlie's eyes flew open. "Yes!" He nodded, amazed. "That's it. I've been waiting for that woman for twenty years." A pause extended between them, and Charlie craned his neck toward the television where the Wild were two minutes from the end of the first period. "It's weird to talk to someone else who knows her. Leigh keeps her circle really small."

"Well, I used to know her." Susy looked at the door as if Arnie were about to show up after all. The three women who'd come in before them cackled in a booth near the window. Susy hadn't been expecting to discuss the Mackenzies' marriage, though she was definitely curious.

"I don't think she's changed much," Charlie said. "Still intense. Still competitive. You know she dropped hockey and went straight into investment banking, right? Private equity is basically its own Olympic sport." He pulled at his collar. "She's fierce. Believe me, I know that firsthand."

Susy shrugged. "What is she fierce about at home?" She wasn't sure if the question was too personal.

"Ah." Charlie glanced at the Liston Heights insignia on the down vest Susy had layered under her coat. Suddenly she wished she'd tried harder with her outfit. There was a pink sweater in her closet that flattered her skin tone.

"Are you okay?" Susy asked.

"Yeah." They watched Toews wing one past the Wild's Stalock. "Damn it." Charlie drank. "The Wild really know how to lose."

"It's early." Susy let him watch for a few seconds while she refreshed her browser again and thrilled a little when she saw that the Nova brackets were up. The Squirt As would head to the iconic tournament in January. "We're in business," she said, and Charlie leaned across the table toward her. She flipped the phone to the side, so they could both see.

Charlie tipped his head even closer to Susy's. If she moved her face three inches to the left, their cheeks would be touching. She held her breath, waiting for him to realize, but before he could move or not, the bartender arrived. "Pretzels and beer cheese."

Charlie straightened up and rubbed his palms together. "Thank you. I didn't realize how hungry I was." His eyes twinkled again as he grabbed a nugget of pretzel and submerged it in the sauce. He pushed the plate toward her, the edge of it clinking against her pint. "Mmmm," he said.

She grabbed one. "No double-dipping though, right?" She froze, her pretzel poised above the cheese.

"No promises." Charlie reached across and pushed her hand down, sinking the pretzel into the ramekin. Susy sucked her breath in, surprised at his touch. She popped the bite into her mouth. "Good, right?" He reached for a second.

"Pretty damn good," she said.

Charlie frowned as he chewed, his mood darker again.

"What?" Susy asked. "Thinking about Nova? I really don't think that first game against Cloquet will be a problem. Nine times out of ten, we beat that team."

Charlie shook his head. "No, I think we've got Cloquet. There was a game of theirs on Live Barn last week, and the third line is especially sloppy."

"Live Barn?" Susy laughed. "Wow, Arnie has made a bigger dent with you than I knew. It's one thing to drink with us and quite another to drink alone while you stream nine-year-old hockey on the Internet."

Charlie shrugged. "You sound like Leigh. I'm just trying to take an interest."

"Well, Leigh was pretty intense about hockey, too. You kind of had to be."

Charlie stared into his glass. "Things have changed. She hates talking about it now."

Susy hesitated and then went for it. "But things are okay with Leigh." She grabbed another pretzel. "I mean, right?"

Charlie craned his neck toward the television. They watched as Kulikov dealt one to Spurgeon from the blue line for a one-timer off the left post. "Damn it," Charlie said.

"The Wild sure know how to lose," Susy repeated. Maybe Charlie would ignore the comment about Leigh. Just when the silence had extended—as the Blackhawks gained control and Suter escaped the zone while defending the rush—he spoke.

"Have you ever done an ultramarathon?" Charlie slid the coaster from beneath his glass. He folded it in half and started to tear at the edges. Leigh used to do this, too. She picked at menus and coasters and sometimes pulled napkins apart. She never just sat still. "I entered the Headwaters lottery," Charlie said, "but I'm not as fit as I used to be."

"I've thought about an ultra." Susy had run a couple of regular marathons with friends. She hadn't done anything crazy fast, just covered the distance. But she knew from reading Charlie's Strava captions that he was aiming for the popular Northern Minnesota race the following summer.

"Would you consider entering the lottery, too? I'm looking for a training partner." Charlie shoved another pretzel in his mouth and stared at her.

Training for an ultra together would mean a lot of time. Alone, just the two of them. "Leigh wouldn't mind?" Susy hadn't meant to ask it like that, to insinuate that there was anything weird or wrong about them being alone together. Charlie did, though, have the smile of a movie star. If Leigh wasn't worried, maybe she should be.

"Leigh's a confident woman, and we've been together forever." Charlie pushed his chair back and grabbed his empty glass. "And it's not like she tracks my ultra training. Want another?" He pointed at her half-full glass. "Might as well save us a trip?"

"Okay." She drank her beer down and then handed him her glass. As she did, their fingers grazed. It was inadvertent, for sure, but she could tell by the way Charlie's shoulders shot up that they'd both noticed.

CHAPTER THIRTY-EIGHT

EMAIL FROM HEAD MANAGER CATHY KELLIHER

December 2022

HOCKEY FAM!

I know you're sick of seeing me in your inbox, but I'll let you in on a secret: the sooner I can get 100% of families to order their trading pins for Nova, the sooner I can stop spamming.

Can we be a TEAM and get this done?!

Those of you who haven't played at the Squirt A level before might not realize that the $150 you'll spend on pins will be the MOST FUN investment of the year. At Nova, kids from all over the country gather to trade their team's custom pins. When my older son Brody did it, I found myself tearing up watching because of the special connections he was making.

Plus, in the past, our "roaring lion" pin has become one of the most sought-after souvenirs of the tournament. Parents from other associations have begged me for extras afterward. The pin money is WORTH IT. And, if you can't swing it, send me a private message and I'll cover you from the scholarship fund. We have more than enough from the SUMMER OF SPORTSMANSHIP T-shirt sale. (Btw, those have become iconic, amirite?)

Get your money in, so I can get our order in. Venmo is easiest @danglesnipecelly1.

And one more thing: it's not fair to rely on the same families every time for score book and clock duties. If you haven't been signing up for these volunteer shifts, I SEE you. Let's be a TEAM!!!!

GO LIONS!!!!

Cathy

CHAPTER THIRTY-NINE

LEIGH MACKENZIE

December 2022

Y ou said you run, right?"

Leigh snapped her head up and stashed her half-eaten box of Mike and Ikes in front of her monitor. Nicole leaned into Leigh's office. They'd finished their meeting together ten minutes before, but Fred had sidelined Nicole to consult on another project. Her reddish hair hung over her shoulder and she seemed awfully cheerful for a Monday morning. Between her pink-striped shirt, beaded necklace, and loose curls, she looked like she could be headed to a garden party rather than settling in for a week of mergers and acquisitions.

Before she could consider an answer to Nicole's question about running, Leigh glanced down at her own outfit, a flowy white blouse over navy pinstripe pants. "Um. I mean, I sort of run?"

Nicole hopped into the room. Her hot pink flats flashed from under her high-waisted white trousers. "Sort of? Can I sit?" Nicole plopped into the only other chair in the office, and Leigh minimized the statement she'd been annotating. "I was just thinking since you're basically a world-class athlete," Nicole said.

"Hardly." Physical fitness was no longer among Leigh's attributes.

"Well, an athlete, then. I've been looking for a training partner."

"I don't know." Leigh flexed her toes in her pointy shoes. "I think my sporting days are over."

"I'm not talking hard-core competition." Nicole shook a fist to signify a fight. How did this woman have so much energy? "Just, like, a couple of miles once or twice a week over lunch."

Leigh glanced down at her blouse and imagined taking it off in the company bathroom, replacing it with a sports bra. She wrinkled her nose. "I'm not sure about sweating in the middle of the workday." In college, she'd sprinted straight to her Hellenistic religions seminar across campus after practice. She viewed that four-minute tear as an extension of whatever conditioning Coach Maggie had mandated. She'd never minded the sweat at her temples or along the band of her sports bra as she sat down for discussion of ritual sacrifices and mysterious cults. But she was twenty-some years older now than she had been then. And she wasn't even sure if she could break a 10:30 mile.

"That's not a great excuse," Nicole said. "We live in a beautiful running city. We're steps from the Stone Arch Bridge. And I thought you were going to be cool. I need some work friends besides Fred." She whispered the boss's name, and Leigh chuckled.

An alert popped up on Leigh's screen then, an email from Cathy Kelliher entitled "Enamel Trading Pins—ACTION REQUIRED." She rolled her eyes. There had been six or seven emails per week in the two since Cathy had taken over for their former team manager. Leigh left most of them unread.

"What?" Nicole asked.

"Youth hockey," Leigh said. "Time to pay for our team trading pins."

Nicole grimaced. "Is that a euphemism for something?"

"No." Leigh laughed. "The kids are going to this tournament where they exchange pins with other teams. We have to pay a couple hundred bucks for our share."

"Okay, but I feel like you're stalling on my running question."

"I'm just not sure that I'm a run-during-the-workday kind of gal," Leigh said again.

Nicole shook her head, unconvinced. "I'm hearing you, but I also think we're gonna give it a try."

Leigh snorted. Ordinarily, this kind of insistence would annoy her, but Nicole's upbeat smile made her feel like giggling. "Well, what would this look like? Once again, I'm telling you I'm not in good shape."

"I'm not concerned about that," Nicole said. "You're a former world-class athlete in the prime of her adulthood. You'll be back in shape within two weeks. Can you bring your stuff tomorrow? It's not supposed to be all that cold."

"Oh my God." Leigh turned around and peered out her window at the salt-encrusted street. Light snowflakes drifted onto the cars, collecting on their headlights. "I forgot about the freezing cold." Charlie had been running five or six mornings per week, using a headlamp as the sun rose later. He'd started logging his workouts in some kind of app that he checked at least a couple of times per night. He had special winter running clothes, and she'd caught him inspecting his abs in their full-length mirror.

"Nope!" Nicole said, standing. "No excuses. You've already agreed."

"I haven't!" Leigh replayed the conversation and verified her ambivalence.

"Do you need to borrow some tights?"

Leigh pictured the box in her closet stuffed with hardly worn capris and dry-fit tops. "Aerobics Barbie," Charlie had labeled it. There weren't any full-length leggings in there suitable for Minnesota winter running.

Leigh stared at Nicole's white pants—a bold choice for the slush—which were, Leigh thought, at maximum a size 6. She couldn't stretch out this woman's workout gear on their second friend-date. "No, I'm good." She wasn't good, but there was an Athleta at 50th and France. A winter running outfit would just have to be one of their essential moving-home purchases.

The next afternoon, Leigh's new tights and jacket sat in a duffel bag beneath her desk. Although their run was scheduled for eleven thirty, she'd been sweating since her nine o'clock check-in with Fred. She'd left the meeting with a list of eight or ten "action items."

With the copious number of to-dos, Leigh didn't actually have time for a midday run, but Nicole texted her ten minutes before their arranged meeting time. "Go change, lady!"

Leigh felt like she might throw up, but she ducked under her desk and grabbed her bag.

The cold air froze Leigh's lungs as Nicole led her toward the path along the Mississippi River. She'd looked at the temperature on her watch before they'd set out, and it had been a mere twenty-two degrees. As a native Minnesotan, Leigh knew that plenty of people ran outside in conditions like these, but she couldn't help thinking it was foolhardy.

"You're an athlete." Leigh couldn't tell if Nicole was asking or stating a fact. She knew for certain that she didn't at all resemble an athlete at the present moment. Her legs felt unsteady beneath her, her thighs jiggly.

"I mean"—Leigh took a giant breath—"theoretically."

"Quit being modest," Nicole said. "After we had drinks, I googled you, so I know all about your hockey stats, Miss Team US Friggin' A."

Leigh glanced over at Nicole and almost laughed aloud at her earnest half frown. "Well, it's been a long time. Speaking of," she huffed, "cool it, Speed Racer. I didn't agree to a sprint."

Nicole giggled and commenced a shuffle. "No problem. I got a little excited there."

"That's okay." They turned onto the bike path, which had been recently plowed after their aggressive December snow. A ridge of icy residue lined each side. "Now, tell me a story to distract me from my abject misery." Leigh hadn't spoken so forcefully to anyone, she realized, since arriving in Minnesota. She used to be completely forthright with her hockey teammates and with her Florida work friends, but somehow since her homecoming, she'd closed in on herself. She'd been looking over her shoulder, feeling nervous most of the time, wondering how many people knew about the deal she'd made with Jeff or suspected her history with him.

"Hmmmm." Leigh snuck another glance at Nicole, who chewed on her bottom lip as she thought. "Okay. I'll tell you something totally crazy."

Leigh's heart skipped a beat. She hadn't meant to elicit any sort of sordid confession from her new friend; she certainly wasn't ready to offer her own in return. "Don't feel like you have to."

"Oh no. You're getting the full story." Nicole jabbed Leigh's upper arm with an outstretched index finger, and Leigh almost veered off course. "This is the epic tale of how I ended up attending my junior prom with one guy and then leaving with another. Get ready."

Leigh tried to laugh, but sucked wind. She focused on taking one breath at a time. She couldn't very well ask Nicole to slow down again. Instead she'd have to dig deep and keep lifting her knees. "Thumbs to hips," she said to herself, cueing her arm swings as Nicole launched into a story about a strawberry-colored minidress, a guy with a matching cummerbund, and then something about a gold lamé bow tie.

Twenty minutes later, they were finished with the loop around the bridge, and Leigh put her hands on her knees, willing her heart rate to slow. "So," Nicole said in a final flourish, "I bet you had no idea that your nice new work friend was actually a two-timing floozy in a too-short dress."

Saliva collected in Leigh's mouth, and for a split second she worried she would vomit. She swallowed hard and squeezed her eyes shut.

"Leigh?" She felt Nicole's hand land between her shoulder blades and rub. "Are you okay? Let's walk it off." She grabbed her elbow and pulled her toward the building. "Just move a little. You'll feel better soon."

"I might be a two-timing floozy in a too-short dress," Leigh said, her head swimming.

"Don't be ridiculous," said Nicole. "You're wearing chic Athleta leggings with the size sticker still attached." With her free hand, she reached down and plucked the "L" from the outside of Leigh's knee.

"Ugh." Leigh put a palm to her face. "You let me run in those for a full twenty minutes without saying anything."

"I didn't want to embarrass you." Nicole pulled her forward. "But are you really a two-timing floozy like me? That makes me feel a little better."

Leigh scuffed her feet on the packed snow. "Something happened in college, yeah." She had no idea why she was confessing it. Her defenses must have crumbled as her heart rate raced, but Nicole jostled her arm and bumped against her shoulder.

"That was eons ago," Nicole said, "but I want to hear about it next run."

CHAPTER FORTY

LEIGH MACKENZIE

August 2001

On the last night, Jeff took Leigh for a drive. They parked someplace between the village of Lake Placid and the Olympic Training Center, and Jeff popped a bottle of champagne he had in the back seat.

"Isn't this, like, tempting fate?" Leigh asked as Jeff handed her a paper cup.

"It's a done deal. I've got your back." Jeff leaned over and kissed her cheek. Leigh shivered.

As they tapped their glasses together, Leigh felt energy swirling in her chest. If she had been outside of the car, she would have started twirling or dancing at Jeff's assertion that she'd made the Olympic team. When the Gophers had won the NCAA championship that first time, the newspaper had run a picture of Leigh screaming, her arms at her sides and her face pointed at the arena's rafters. She hadn't even remembered the moment; her body had been snatched by joy.

This milestone—the Olympics—was even more mind-blowing. It had started when Leigh was five, when her dad first put her on a team with the boys in her kindergarten class and she'd beaten them all in full-rink Ships Across the Ocean.

"The Olympics." Leigh felt as if she were choking as she fought to keep her voice at a reasonable volume. The sour champagne seemed stuck in her throat.

Jeff put his drink in the cup holder and wrapped his arms around her, kissing her neck. His touch felt stifling as the thrill of making it swelled, but she tried to stay still. The success was due to Jeff, after all. He'd believed in her and guided her through.

When she walked in the opening ceremonies in Salt Lake City, when she waved to her parents watching on TV, no one would have to know about Jeff. They could just remember all of the wins she'd had before and all the ones that were still coming her way.

In the morning, Leigh shook Susy out of bed and asked to borrow her tinted lip balm. Did they take a team photo right after the announcement? Leigh wanted to be ready. "Do you want me to braid your hair?" she asked Susy.

Susy sat on the edge of her bed, her thumbnail in her mouth. "How can you be so calm?" she asked. "I actually think I'm going to puke."

"Uh-uh." Leigh sat down next to Susy and patted her thigh. "I've got a good feeling. We're going to get it."

Susy pushed her bedhead out of her face and squinted at Leigh. "Do you know something I don't? Does your good mood have something to do with you disappearing after dinner last night?"

Leigh grinned. "That's nothing. Let's go!" She pulled her to standing and dragged Susy across the room toward the sink. "Brush your teeth. We gotta get down there to become Olympians!"

Susy rubbed Leigh's biceps and then her own. "What are you doing, weirdo?" Leigh asked.

"Borrowing some of your confidence." Susy spun around and turned on the tap.

As Leigh walked into the decision room, she felt the same pleasant tingling that she let herself enjoy for twenty-four hours after every big victory before getting back to work. A few shoo-ins, the captains mainly, had been cracking jokes before Jeff Carlson raised a hand for attention. Leigh tried to catch his eye, but he seemed to be looking everywhere but at her.

Her stomach flipped as she remembered the night before in his car, and the days before that, secret moments in the referees' locker room, an empty dorm, a dark office across the hallway from the lab. He'd said on the first day that he didn't want to be her boyfriend. Somehow that had made what they'd done okay, that caveat and also the promise of an Olympic medal.

Leigh flashed on Charlie's face as she sat there waiting for the announcement, his deep dimples, his easy way with her parents and younger brother. They could still be together after this. Jeff was a temporary thing, just another sacrifice she had to make. He had nothing to do with Charlie and nothing to do with Leigh's future as his wife.

Leigh searched Jeff's face again as Coach Miller signaled for him to begin. She let herself stare at him, her body completely still, looking for the tiniest acknowledgment. Jeff was saying something about the quality of the pool of players, the difficulty of the cuts. It was the same bullshit they said every time to make the losers feel better. Leigh had heard the speech three times already, each time she'd made the national team for another tournament.

And then Coach Miller started reading the roster. Jeff looked at his feet, the brim of his USA hat shielding his face. Leigh pressed her middle finger and thumb together, tempted to snap at him, to make him look at her. Miller read alphabetically. He got to "Darwitz" and then "Dunn." No one spoke or reacted. Some of the women in the room had been cut already, but Leigh kept her eyes on Jeff, not wanting to witness anyone else's anguish. He kicked the carpet as Miller read "Kennedy" and "King."

And then, when Jeff still wouldn't look at her, Leigh realized the truth. Her inhale burned her chest. She replayed the pass she'd bobbled in yesterday's scrimmage. The sour taste of champagne stung the back of her throat. Every joint in her hands stiffened.

The crash had been instant and bleak.

Afterward, the day passed in a blur of furious packing and sobbing. She had three missed calls on her phone when she landed in Minneapolis, all from Susy, but there was no time to think about calling her back before her parents enveloped her in baggage claim, the same way Jeff had in his car. Their embraces were just as claustrophobic, but this time it was her despair that overwhelmed her. Leigh wanted to leave her luggage next to the carousel and sprint out the airport door, to run until every muscle in her body hurt as much as her heart did.

And after she'd made it back home, the only person Leigh wanted to see was Charlie. She called him the minute she'd thrown her duffel down the stairs in her parents' house. On her way across town in her Honda hatchback, she rehearsed the story about Jeff in her head. "I didn't think I had an option," she'd tell Charlie. "I was so scared of not making it." She thought about saying, "It didn't mean anything," but it felt like too much of a lie. Jeff didn't mean anything to her, but their affair had meant that Leigh was willing to do anything for her dream. She'd been certain his support would make the difference. And she'd been flattered by his special attention. God, she felt so stupid.

And when Leigh saw Charlie, her commitment to honesty faltered. He opened the door to his apartment and flashed his adorable crooked grin. She crumpled as she walked in, collapsing against him. They were nearly the same size, Leigh solid from the years of dedicated weight lifting in addition to her hours on the ice. He backed up into the couch, and they both fell down on it. Leigh's tears soaked his T-shirt.

"Whoa," Charlie had said after several minutes. "Whoa. Are you okay?"

"No," she snuffed. She'd never be okay again. "I'm a complete failure. I'm over."

"How can you even say that?" Leigh felt Charlie's hand on her damp forehead, his smooth cheek on her temple. He lightly untangled the curls she'd hidden beneath her Gophers hat that had fallen to the floor.

"The Olympics was the point of everything." Leigh cried harder. She'd never imagined falling off the peak just steps from the summit. She wouldn't play hockey again. For a few seconds with her face pressed against Charlie's chest, Leigh wondered if she might just as well die. She'd lost hockey, and she might lose Charlie, the best, most genuine person she knew. Charlie never would have betrayed her for his own gain.

She convulsed in Charlie's arms as she thought of the hair that grew in a swirl on Jeff's chest. Leigh had made Charlie wait six months for sex, not wanting to lead him on or distract herself from hockey. And then with Jeff, she'd just been willing. It had been just another hoop to jump through, and she'd been flattered by his attention. There were forty girls there, and she had been the one he'd picked.

She was supposed to make the team. Leigh and Jeff had sipped champagne not even twenty-four hours before.

"Leigh-Leigh," Charlie whispered, "you're amazing. How old are the other women on the team?"

"Angela was only eighteen when she made it in '98. She won a gold medal as a teenager! Who cares about Ms. Fucking Hockey?" Leigh had always been jealous of Angela Ruggiero. She started coughing then, choking on her tears.

"I'm going to get you a drink," Charlie said.

"No." Drinking twice in a day. This was why Leigh hadn't been good enough. She didn't pay enough attention to the little things. As a rule, Leigh never drank alcohol when she was training. As a high schooler, she'd been paranoid about getting busted and losing eligibility. In college, she'd made a pact with her teammates. They would be the fittest, most well-conditioned, healthiest players in the country. If they lost, it wouldn't be because they'd gotten seduced by a stupid frat party. As far as her team knew, Leigh would be playing with them again the next season. She could close out her eligibility, win another title, maybe contend for the Patty Kazmaier Award given to the top collegiate player in the country, especially now that the real winners were on the Olympic team.

Although she could—should—play, she knew as she lay there, trying to hold Charlie in place, that she was done. She wouldn't skate anymore. If she didn't deserve a spot on the Olympic team, she didn't deserve a spot on the ice at all. Her performances had never been about "the love of the game," though she'd had that, too. It had been about being the best, scoring the goal when the team needed it most. She'd been climbing the national ranks, and now she'd been bested by two dozen other women.

"You're having a drink now. All I have is Rolling Rock anyway. It's basically water." Charlie gently repositioned her so her head was on the armrest, and walked away. Leigh closed her eyes. The sticky utility drawer squeaked in Charlie's kitchen, and Leigh knew he was retrieving the mermaid-shaped bottle opener that the guys had found in the place when they'd moved in.

She blinked her eyes open when she heard him stop in front of the couch. He held two bottles and had a giant wet spot on his

T-shirt. "Oh God," Leigh said, pointing. "I'm so sorry." She forced herself to sit and wiped her nose on the hem of her own T-shirt. It came away damp and slick with snot. "Gross," she said. "I'm disgusting."

"You're pret-sgusting." Charlie smiled and handed her a paper towel. Leigh tried to smile back, but her cheeks felt too tired. "Pretsgusting," a hybrid of pretty and disgusting, had been born on a happier night when Leigh had dumped a bottle of hot sauce on her white jeans in the middle of one of their dinners. Now, she blew her nose noisily into the paper towel. When she pulled it away from her face, a strand of mucus stuck to her lip.

"God." She wiped again. "I'm sorry."

"Drink." Charlie sat beside her, handed her a bottle, and clinked it even though there was nothing to toast. She joined him in a long swallow. She flopped back on the couch and stared at the ceiling. "Okay?" Charlie asked. "Better?"

Leigh shrugged. "I'm probably not going to kill myself." She imagined a free-fall from a snowy mountain.

She could feel Charlie's head turn toward her, but she didn't look back. "Don't joke about that." There was gravel in his voice. "Not funny."

"Sorry." She wouldn't jump. She couldn't do that to Jamie. Her little brother had stood in a Wayne Gretzky jersey in the front hall when she'd arrived home from the Albany airport.

"I wish you'd made it, Leigh-Leigh," Jamie had said.

Although she'd wanted to collapse right there, she'd forced herself forward and ruffled his hair. "Me too, buddy." Her mom had shuttled him into the kitchen as Leigh had hauled her equipment to the back staircase.

"I'm not going anywhere," Leigh told Charlie then. "You're stuck with me." He drank again and threw an arm around her. She put her head on his shoulder and a new wave of tears came as she thought about the plastic-coated mattress in the empty dorm room where Jeff had taken her, her skin cool in the air-conditioning.

"Thank God for being stuck," he said. "You hungry?"

She looked down at his wet shirt and then at her own snotty one and dingy jeans. "I'm not dressed to go out."

"I'm gonna call for pizza," Charlie said. "We'll live it up."

"Where are your roommates?" Leigh asked. Charlie rattled off their locations—the library, a party across campus, an hour south visiting a girlfriend at another school.

"It's just us at least for a little while," he said. Leigh drank again and felt her arms getting heavier with the alcohol, its quick effect an argument for periodic sobriety. "Sausage and mushrooms?" Charlie asked.

Charlie hated mushrooms. "We can just do sausage."

"No," Charlie said. "We're celebrating. You need mushrooms."

"Celebrating?" Leigh's voice broke again.

"Oh God." Charlie put his beer on the coffee table and put both arms around her. "That was the wrong word, but, Leigh-Leigh." She could feel his breath against the top of her head, and she hoped he'd hold on to her forever. She tilted her chin down, resting it in the hollow next to his collarbone. She scrunched her nose into his T-shirt, inhaling the Tide smell and trying to push away the memories of Jeff's Speed Stick. "You have so much to be proud of. You've done so much."

As she kept her head there, she remembered the feeling of Jeff's biceps against her own. Charlie's arms felt lithe and light compared to the pressure Jeff exerted. Charlie held her loosely. She cried harder, knowing that she might have wrecked everything. "I have to tell you something," she said.

"Anything." He let her go and leaned back against the couch. "But should I order first? How hungry are you?"

Pretty hungry, she realized. "I could eat."

Charlie patted her knee. "Let me just call, and then you can tell me everything." He walked to the kitchen, hitching up his too-big jeans. She heard him lift the phone and place the order at the Italian Pie Shoppe, the best and most expensive place.

"Deep dish?" he called to her.

"That would be amazing." Her voice wavered. In the forty minutes before the pizza arrived, she'd have to tell Charlie about Jeff. The whole thing felt despicable, the summer of phone calls, the way she'd smiled at him during the camp's orientation, the shower in the officials' locker room. By the time Charlie had come back, Leigh had her hands in her hair at her temples. Nausea gripped her, and she ran for the bathroom.

"Leigh!" Charlie called after her. She slammed the door and collapsed on her knees in front of the scuzzy toilet. The urine splatter was enough to make her feel sick. She heaved a couple of times, but nothing came up.

"Leigh?" Charlie called again from the door. "Do you need some water?"

"I'm okay." She gripped the vanity and clawed her way to standing. In the mirror, her eyes looked red and puffy, her cheeks hollow. *I'm ugly.* She turned on the tap to splash her face and Charlie opened the door.

"How can I make this better?" he asked. She pulled her shirt up to dry her face and peered at him. He looked as devastated as she felt. "I hate seeing you like this."

"I love you," she blurted, crying again. It was true. They'd said it a million times already, the words coming easily from the first month they'd spent together.

"I know." Charlie grabbed her hand and led her from the bathroom back toward the couch. "I love you, too."

Leigh met his eyes and searched them. He was completely clueless, no inkling about Jeff. "This is going to sound crazy." Leigh's arms tingled. She saw Charlie in a new light now, understood his goodness. "And I know we're really young, but Charlie, I'm absolutely sure." She collapsed onto the couch. Leigh had to be with him forever.

"What are you talking about?" He looked so worried all of a sudden that Leigh started to laugh. She looked down at her wrecked outfit and laughed harder.

"I'm such a mess, but, Charlie." She looked him square in the face and put her hands on his smooth cheeks. "I want to get married. I know it's crazy. But next June after we graduate, let's get married. I love you so much." The Olympic dream was dead, but maybe this one—a dream of a future with the best person she knew—could thrive.

He blinked at her and his mouth hung open. She threw herself toward him, buried her face in his chest, and squeezed his rib cage. "It's crazy, but I just—"

"Leigh." He pushed her back and she noticed the tears in his eyes now, too. "Leigh, yes. Of course I want to marry you. I've been planning it since Y2K."

She sputtered, laughing again. They'd spent that past New Year's Eve playing Trivial Pursuit with her roommates. Leigh had failed to answer any questions right except for the ones about the NHL. "Why then? I got, like, last place in that game."

"I don't care if you ever win anything again in your life. I just want to sit next to you, to laugh at your unfunny jokes and listen to you spout obscure hockey stats." Leigh's breath caught. Charlie didn't need her to be the best. "I'd marry you today, but I guess we should, like, get a venue. We should tell our families. You need a dress—"

Leigh sprang from the couch, suddenly invigorated again. She ran to the kitchen, threw open the refrigerator, and grabbed the loaf of cottage-style white bread she knew would be there. She undid the twist tie and ran with it to the living room. In a flash, she wound it around Charlie's ring finger and then kissed it.

"Aren't you supposed to be the one with an engagement ring? Of course, I have no money and about forty thousand dollars in student loan debt." She fell against him again. "Full disclosure for our future." He hugged her harder.

"I don't give a shit about any of the details," she said.

"Should we tell our parents?" Charlie glanced at his flip phone on the table.

"Tomorrow." Leigh pulled Charlie to his feet. "Let's celebrate first." She led him into his dark bedroom, the boy smell permeating the space. Her damp T-shirt was off before he'd closed the door, and her jeans in a puddle next to Charlie's overcrowded nightstand.

"We probably have thirty minutes until the pizza gets here."

Leigh laughed again, this time at Charlie's practicality. "I don't think we're going to need that long," she said.

Between the bedroom and then the pizza followed by the sleepy snuggling while watching reruns of *Friends*, Charlie never asked what she'd planned to tell him before she'd launched into her teary proposal.

Still, that night and a million times afterward, she'd imagined the right words to explain what had happened at Lake Placid. She'd have described the pressure she felt, the stress, the blind ambition, the expectation. She could have said Jeff hadn't meant anything, which was almost 100 percent true.

Leigh could have told Charlie and then still executed the same proposal, presented the same twist-tie ring. Instead, she'd kept the affair with Jeff a secret from everyone.

Except from Susy Walker. If she kept that friendship going, the truth about Jeff would always be too close.

CHAPTER FORTY-ONE

CHARLIE MACKENZIE

December 2022

So, you're in." Charlie pulled his skull cap lower over his forehead, and he and Susy jogged out of the Mackenzie driveway toward the marsh loop. It had been a week since Arnie had ditched them at the brewery.

"I paid the fee and hit Enter Lottery." Susy's arms swung in an easy cadence beside him. "I can't believe I did it. You're very persuasive. I realized after I forked over my hundred bucks that if we're *lucky*, we get to run fifty miles."

Charlie grinned. Leigh had slept in his old Headwaters finisher shirt the previous night, as she did multiple times per week. She'd claimed it right after they'd gotten engaged. The name of the race had been printed in a font that looked like trees. "It's a suffer-fest for sure," he said. "But you won medals in the Olympics. You like that kind of thing."

"Is it the hardest ultra you've run?" Susy's knees started to drive higher as they reached the end of the block. Charlie hoped he wouldn't have to tell her to slow down, at least not until his watch indicated they'd made it a full mile.

"Hard to say." Charlie remembered the hairpin turns on the trail, the roots that jutted up from sandy soil, the downed trees he'd had to hurdle on the second loop, even when he was nearly blind with fatigue. "It was my first ultra, so I had absolutely no idea what I was getting into." He laughed. Preparing to run fifty miles on a technical single-track trail had been complete guesswork. "I was twenty-one. It's probably good I was so clueless. If I had known there'd be that part around thirty-seven miles when I cried next to a peeling birch—"

"Oh my God, stop." Susy took a few quick steps ahead, outrunning his horror story.

"I'm just kidding!" Charlie caught up. "I mean, I did cry, but it won't be as bad this time. Leigh can maybe crew again." He wished she would, but Charlie wasn't sure she'd make the time to prepare.

"Tell me about that," Susy said. "I'm kind of surprised Leigh agreed to run around in the woods with you just weeks ahead of the Olympic selection camp."

"Really?" A half step behind Susy, Charlie could see their breath in little puffs of white before they charged through them. "I guess that's true—she was pretty focused on hockey that summer. But to be honest, it never occurred to me that she wouldn't be there. I trained for months." He laughed again. "Although, I guess not on the same level as you two train. Or *did* train."

Susy was quiet for a beat. She looked like she was about to speak a couple of times, but didn't.

"What?" Charlie prompted.

"This way?" Susy pointed at the turn. Charlie now looped the marsh more than once each morning, his fitness returning quickly after he'd decided to go for Headwaters again.

"Yep. And don't think you're off the hook. What were you going to say?" Charlie had never had access like this to one of Leigh's friends. He'd known his wife for so long; there weren't many people who could tell stories about her that he didn't already know.

"Don't take this the wrong way?" Susy kept her eyes on the trail, avoiding the small patches of snow-dusted ice without seeming to alter her gait. Charlie felt clumsy next to her and remembered again that she was a two-time Olympian. He shouldn't feel bad about her superior agility.

"Okay," he said.

"Leigh was never the type to, like, help or mentor, you know?" Susy said. "Don't get me wrong, she's a balls-out player—excuse my French—with a killer instinct, but she never, like, reached down the ladder." Charlie thought about Leigh, about her first job as an analyst at Bonham Royal. The entire two years she was there, she plotted her way out, stalking director positions at national banks, measuring her status against the others in her hiring class.

Charlie increased his turnover, just slightly pushing the pace. He'd never really considered the extent to which Leigh's focus was unusually inward. Would he consider her self-centered? His mother had described her that way once. Charlie had brushed it off as typical in-law tension, but it was true—she had so few genuine connections. "Do you, like, not like Leigh?" Charlie didn't glance over at Susy as he asked. He breathed harder.

"Oh no! That's not what I meant at all." Charlie could feel Susy looking at him but didn't turn his head. He couldn't invest too much in a friendship with someone who actively disliked his wife, could he? "I don't want you to think I don't like her. It's only—" She stopped speaking abruptly again. Charlie looked over his shoulder toward the squealing tires he heard on the road behind them. He could see the fishtailing pickup truck through the leafless trees. It straightened out after it skittered around the curve.

"What did you mean, then?" He heard the flatness in his tone. He glanced at his watch and saw that they were on pace for an 8:47 first mile, a good forty-five seconds faster than his usual warm-up. Charlie's fists balled, and his arms felt jumpy, as if he wanted to pick it up even more.

"Well, it's just that Leigh would do anything to be the best, you know? She wanted to make it so badly." Susy's ponytail ticktocked in a perfect pendulum.

They were quiet then, and Charlie thought about his top-drawer manuscript, about how Lavinia—Leigh—hadn't actually made that Olympic team in the end. The character he'd modeled after Susy had made it instead. In the book, the Susy character worked harder, lifted more weight, and ran more miles in the lead-up to the Olympic trials.

But that hadn't been real life. Charlie remembered Leigh in the summer of '01. When he'd met up with her in the evenings, she'd usually done two workouts already and sometimes had plans to jump into a men's hockey league or play against a high school boys' team at night. Her work ethic had been just fine.

"Why didn't Leigh make the team?" Charlie's question came out in a quick burst between his increasingly labored breaths.

They made it another fifty yards or so before Susy answered. He could hear her exhales coming harder now, too. "I don't know." The answer was anticlimactic. Susy pulled her shoulders back as they turned left around the frozen pond, reeds sticking out of the ice's surface.

Charlie backed off the pace, which had continued to ramp up. There was no way they'd make it the whole five miles. "Slower, okay?" He didn't wait for her to answer. "Also, you must have an idea of what went wrong. I mean, you were there in Lake Placid. You saw her in every workout." He wasn't sure why he was pushing. He could read people well—all novelists could, a professor had told him once in grad school—and Susy clearly didn't want to elaborate.

Even though his watch said they'd corrected to a 9:10, Charlie's heart seemed to pound harder as he waited for Susy to speak. Whatever had happened between her and Leigh at that camp had triggered a twenty-year silence. Could it really have been just as simple as Leigh's jealousy?

Susy finally spoke. "She was distracted at Lake Placid, I guess. It's a fine line, right? You have to be so sharp, so ready. You have to be right at the pinnacle of your fitness and potential." Susy held up her thumb and forefinger to signify the precision required. "And if you end up just a tiny bit on one side of that razor's edge or the other, there are four or five girls ready to take your spot."

Charlie tried to imagine Leigh getting distracted and couldn't. His wife was single-minded and strategic. He'd talked to her when she'd been at the camp, and she'd seemed as dialed in as ever. "What was she distracted by?" As he asked, the ball of Charlie's foot skimmed one of the ice patches on the path and he took three reeling steps to right himself, his arms windmilling.

"Whoa." Susy reached an arm out to his shoulder as they stopped. Charlie hit his watch, pausing. "Winter running," Susy said. "Not for the faint of heart. You okay?"

Charlie looked over Susy's head at the sun rising bright orange, trees on either side of the pond casting blue shadows over the marsh as the darkness evaporated. "What aren't you telling me?" Charlie asked. "There's something I should know, right?" Leigh had pushed hockey so far out of their lives until Gus had started playing. And she'd been withdrawn—her laugh harder to elicit—since they'd moved right back into the middle of it. He glanced at Susy, who bit her lip, and then he looked back at the sun, a hand at his forehead to stop the glare.

"I'm not sure I can answer your questions." Susy stepped away from him and braced herself for a quad stretch.

"Is there some kind of girl code?" Charlie smiled, despite the discomfort he felt. If Leigh had a girl code—some kind of friendship bible—she'd long abandoned it. In the decades since she'd left women's hockey, she'd never again had a group of girlfriends.

Susy stretched her arms over her head, and Charlie could see the jut of her top rib through the nylon of her jacket. He looked away. "Oh, you've seen that girl code in action, big-time." Susy put her finger on her watch. "Ready?" They started again.

"What do you mean, I've seen it in action?"

"That night at the basement party? The night we first met you?" The cement walls in that falling-down college rental had been damp with humidity.

"Yeah?"

"Well, let's just say I saw you first." Charlie blinked. He remembered watching the two of them come down the stairs. Susy's blond ponytail had swung over her shoulders just as it was doing now. Her skin had been fresh-looking, her cheeks pink.

"Really?" His arms tingled.

Susy nodded just once, and Charlie felt them accelerate again. "But Leigh is not one to leave anything to chance. She homed right in on those dimples." Susy pointed at Charlie's face.

He veered around another ice patch, his shoes crunching against the crust at the side of the asphalt. "Well," he said, "since we're being honest, can I just say, I remember you're the one I looked at first that night, too?"

"Really?" She giggled. "Am I like, your Angelica?"

"*Hamilton*? I guess that's about right. If Leigh hadn't been there, who knows what would have happened."

He changed the subject then, pulling back from whatever drop-off they skirted with memories of that night. Instead, they talked about the race topography, Susy's first marathon in Chicago ten years before, and, of course, Gus's prospects for the remainder of the Squirt season. But when Susy waved as she got into her car, Charlie couldn't help but feel like something had changed, both between him and Susy and also between him and Leigh.

CHAPTER FORTY-TWO

LEIGH MACKENZIE

December 2022

W e're running on Wednesday this week." Nicole had stopped asking, and now just told Leigh when to bring her gear to work. In the weeks since their first outing, Leigh had added a second pair of leggings to her rotation, this time making sure to remove the tags.

And in the last couple of three-mile jaunts, up from two at Nicole's quick pace, Leigh had gotten to the point where she could speak in phrases as they ran.

As long as she was in town, Leigh always agreed to Nicole's timing. Part of her couldn't believe she was letting herself get bossed around by a new friend. Really, just the fact of making any new friend was remarkable.

"Today, though," Nicole texted, "come have lunch. I doubt you've eaten yet with both McIntosh and Heritage Cutlery closing soon."

Leigh checked the clock. "You're right," she wrote back. "As usual." She grabbed her blazer from the back of her chair and slid on the flats she had folded into her handbag, an easy switch for the snow boots she'd purchased back in November. Leigh remembered the slush she'd slopped through in front of Mariucci Arena before the boots had been delivered. It seemed like a million years ago. Back then, seeing Susy still felt jarring. Now, Leigh regularly waved to her from across the rink.

Charlie was the one who exchanged daily texts with Susy, and they ran together on the weekends. He'd convinced Susy to do Headwaters, provided they both got in. Leigh might be jealous except that he'd always had a cadre of female friends. Susy was the latest in a long line of platonic connections. And Leigh had absolutely no desire to run fifty miles.

After Leigh had paid for the chopped salad and a bag of Baked Lay's, Nicole popped the top of her ginger ale. "Remember on our first run when I told you about my floozy-dom?"

Leigh thought about it nearly daily, actually. She'd promised Nicole her own confession, but she'd avoided ever giving it.

"You made it seem like you had a two-timing story of your own. Something from your youth?"

"Why is this coming up now?" Leigh asked.

"Because I was reading ESPN.com and came across an article that made me think of you."

Leigh used her teeth to rip open a pouch of salad dressing. "You read ESPN.com?"

"Duh," Nicole deadpanned. "So, this article. Have you heard of someone named Sydney Kirkpatrick?"

Leigh felt her brows furrow as she tossed her greens. She had submitted to a forty-minute phone call with Jeff Carlson's attorney the week before. She'd locked her office door and crouched in her chair as she recounted details she hadn't ever admitted to anyone else about their relationship. She'd popped a whole container of Tic Tacs as she spoke, as if the mint could somehow overpower the truth of her past.

"Did Jeff specifically tell you that if you engaged in an affair with him, you'd have a greater chance of making the Olympic team?" the attorney had asked.

"No." Leigh knew she had drawn that conclusion on her own. All Jeff had really said was that he'd be in the decision room, that Coach Miller trusted him.

"Did Jeff threaten your position in the player pool if you refused to engage in sexual contact with him?" The woman sounded dispassionate, as if she were asking Leigh about how many fruits and vegetables she'd put on her grocery list that week.

Leigh's answer to that one had been "No," as well. As was her answer to, "Did Jeff force you to engage in any type of sexual contact?"

Leigh closed her eyes when the attorney asked whether she'd been sexually attracted to Jeff. Her answer then was "Yes." At least, she had been attracted to his power. And there in itself was one of Leigh's biggest failings. Charlie had driven her to the airport before Lake Placid and had handed her the sweetest good luck card she'd ever read. And Leigh had been thinking about seeing Jeff in person, replaying their clandestine phone calls.

Nicole sipped her soda. "Apparently, there's some complaint against USA Hockey."

Leigh dug a crouton out of the corner of the salad container and stabbed it with her fork, bending its plastic tine. "Wow," she managed.

"You haven't heard about it? I just skimmed, but it reminded me of that gymnastics scandal from a few years ago."

"No, I haven't heard about it." Leigh asked next about Nicole's daughter's spelling bee, and then moved on to their favorite *SNL* sketches from last week's show.

Back in her office, Leigh googled Sydney again and found the article on ESPN. "Questions of Propriety Dog US Olympic Women's Hockey Program." Sydney Kirkpatrick was quoted, telling the same story Leigh had heard from Susy, and then there were two other names, women also claiming that "an unnamed coach" had promised them spots on the Olympic teams in 2006 and 2018, respectively, in exchange for who knows what.

Jeff's attorney had told Leigh she might be called upon to give a deposition. With coverage like this popping up, that would be more likely. What would happen if Leigh refused? And could she keep a deposition secret from Charlie? When Leigh got home that night, she could still taste the garlicky salad dressing from lunch. She poured an overlarge glass of pinot grigio, both to erase the taste and to distract herself from Sydney Kirkpatrick.

Leigh stared at the calendar her husband kept on the fridge. He and Gus were at hockey practice and wouldn't be home for at least an hour. She pulled open the oven—it was off, but still warm—and sure enough, Charlie had left her a pork chop and some roasted broccoli on one of their white ceramic plates.

Charlie had always been insanely thoughtful. Even as a teenager, he'd brought her Gatorade and protein bars after big games. He'd stood in full Gophers gear in baggage claim when she arrived home from college road trips. And now, he cooked her dinner. He cleaned their bathroom. He was the one who knew when Gus was about to grow out of his shoes or needed a dentist appointment. She hadn't meant for their move home to put distance between them.

Leigh undid the button on her pants and pushed up the sleeves of her cardigan, the lightweight wool suddenly itchy on her forearms. On her way to the bedroom to change into sweatpants, she wandered into Charlie's office. He still had boxes in the corner. Maybe she could do something for him, unload a few of his books or write her own attempt at a poem on one of his sticky notes.

Leigh set her wine on the desk and looked at the boxes. "Tomes that Make Me Feel Smarter," Charlie had labeled the top one. She pushed it aside to see the one beneath. "Books I Wish I'd Written." Leigh glanced at the windows overlooking the backyard. She could see her reflection. Charlie had put a row of succulents on the windowsill. Flowers had sprouted from the one in the center, spines protruding beneath them. She wandered around to the desk chair.

Leigh pulled open the center drawer and ran a hand over a pack of Charlie's favorite ballpoint pens in bubblegum colors. Charlie was a pretty "regular" guy. He didn't have tattoos or piercings, but he did love a good fuchsia ink. Leigh opened the upper-right-hand drawer and was surprised by a large stack of loose paper. She lifted it out and ran her index finger across the title. *Ice Time*.

It was the same title as his master's thesis. That book had been about a hockey player, a kid based on Jamie, as she remembered it, who shattered his femur in the run-up to the state championships. She flipped the first page over. Charlie had written notes, his handwriting a hybrid between printing and cursive that Leigh knew well. The main character didn't seem to be the kid she remembered, but "Lavinia," a twenty-one-year-old Olympic hopeful.

Leigh glugged her wine. With her free hand, she turned pages. "The only thing more important than her own success," Charlie had written about Lavinia, "was other people's adoration of her." He'd written a scene about her taking credit for her team's national championship. Leigh skimmed to another chapter in which Lavinia lost her temper in a passing drill. Her coach, a facsimile of Maggie from the U complete with a blond ponytail, pulled her aside and told her that no matter how sharp her passes, she wouldn't play in the next game if she couldn't put team first.

Leigh's eyes bugged. On another page, Lavinia refused to go to a family dinner with "Cormac," citing her strength session in the gym even though meeting his parents had been so important to him. Leigh remembered that night. The Wards had come to town on the same evening the Minnesota-based Olympic hopefuls were consulting with Team USA's lifting coach. Charlie said it was fine at the time. But in the book, Cormac called Lavinia selfish. Charlie's Lavinia was a success-obsessed, hypercompetitive bitch.

This was how her husband saw her? Leigh flipped to the end of the manuscript. On page 132, Lavinia arrived home from Lake Placid and threw her duffel bag down her parents' basement stairs, "her failure too big of a black hole to see head-on."

Jesus Christ.

Leigh dropped the pages, put her wineglass down, and stretched the skin above her eyebrows, smoothing out the wrinkles that had become more prominent the second she'd entered her forties.

These chapters—this book—deflated everything. Suddenly, Charlie wasn't her unconditional cheerleader who left warm dinner in the oven. Now she could see he understood the extent of her failures. He attached them to her personality flaws. Charlie knew Leigh was, at her core, deficient.

Why had Charlie agreed to marry her if he felt she had so many undesirable traits? And was he planning to publish his version of her downfall? She paged back through the middle of the book, looking for Charlie's reasoning. In his imagination, why had she failed? She licked her finger and pushed through the pages, but she couldn't find anything definitive.

"Hubris," "weakness," "overconfidence," "delusion." All of those words stuck out as she skimmed. Maybe this was her real secret: that she actually, despite every effort then and since, just plain sucked.

Leigh left the pages on the desk and went back to the kitchen. Twenty minutes and a second glass of wine later, Charlie dropped his keys on the counter and stretched both arms overhead. Leigh banished "Lavinia" from her thoughts and swooped Gus up. Although she'd failed at so many things, she'd always been great at compartmentalizing.

"You smell like hockey." Leigh rubbed her nose against Gus's neck.

"Mom!" Gus dropped his arms and let his weight go, forcing her to put him down.

"How was practice?"

Charlie piped in. "He looked fantastic! That last passing drill, especially, huh?"

"Coach Ashberry said I'm going to become a goal scorer at some point." Gus sprayed his water bottle into his mouth and swallowed. "I hope 'some point' is this season and not ten years from now."

Leigh thought of the manuscript. How many years had passed since Charlie had decided she was a failure? "Go shower." She swatted Gus's backside as he trotted toward the stairs. "And then I think it's my turn to do the bedtime story."

As soon as he was gone, Leigh turned to Charlie. Her anger ballooned as she took in his disheveled appearance, the casual way he washed his hands in their farmhouse sink.

"You been working on your book lately?" She'd made that crack about it, had accused him of laziness. Maybe Leigh had inadvertently prompted him to hone his criticisms of her.

Charlie cocked his head. "I have taken a look at it, actually. I've been adding chapters." He filled a glass of water.

"I thought it was about a kid with a broken leg." Leigh could hear the edge in her voice. *"Delusion,"* she thought. *"Weakness."*

Charlie sipped his water and put a hand on the granite countertop behind him. "Did you read it?" He swallowed and pushed his shoulders back, nervous.

"You think I'm a failure who hasn't worked hard." As Leigh said it, her fury exploded. The characterization was so unfair, as if Leigh hadn't spent every second since Lake Placid trying to make up for those two horrible weeks. She'd gotten a job that hadn't required Charlie to work outside the home. She'd never expected him to work, happy to burn the candle at both ends in order to support him and Gus even though people like Cathy Kelliher insinuated that hard work made her a bad mother.

And how did Charlie repay her? By writing about the one failure she wished she could expunge, by planning to expose her as a fraud to everyone in their lives.

Charlie pulled out a kitchen chair. Leigh winced at the scuff it made against the wood floors they'd just refinished. "That's not what that book is about," he said.

"Really? 'Lavinia' is a good person and a dedicated player? A self-starter?" She put air quotes around the name. "What happens to her at the end of the story, Charlie? Once her worth as a player and a person is expired, she what? She just, like, kills herself?" Charlie hadn't written an ending, not that Leigh could tell.

Charlie pushed the hair off his forehead and blew out a breath. "Stop. It's a story. It's fiction."

"Right. About a woman who looks like me and acts like me and lived my life."

Charlie reached an arm toward Leigh, but she stepped back. She could hear the shower running in their second-floor bathroom. "I should have told you," he said.

"Or, you know what you should have done?" The same fury and desperation that she'd felt in the weeks after Lake Placid strained in her chest now. In 2001, she'd thrown every ounce of energy into Charlie, into school, into a future with an MBA, a sterling business reputation, and a big paycheck. And now what? "You shouldn't have written that at all. You should have used some actual imagination. You call yourself a writer? And all you can do is badly retell my past?" She put two fingers against her sternum. "What kind of novelist are you?"

Charlie flinched. "You always go so low. Why can't you be angry without making me feel like shit."

"You make *me* feel like shit. I bought this house. I pay your grad school loans. And your big plan is to strike it rich by airing my dirty laundry? Fuck you, Charlie." She said it quietly and walked up the stairs. She'd put Gus to bed and then close their bedroom door. Her husband could sleep somewhere else.

CHAPTER FORTY-THREE

CHARLIE MACKENZIE

December 2022

Since he'd been twenty-two, Charlie had never refused to sleep in the same bed as Leigh. They'd traversed many a marriage minefield without their fury overcoming them—the horrors of infant sleep training, a massive blowup over visiting Charlie's parents at Christmas one year, and two cross-country moves.

But when Leigh accused him both of cashing in on her history and also of being a complete failure himself, Charlie fought alternating waves of exhaustion and rage. He'd thought about meeting Susy at a brewery, but that would only give Leigh more ammunition. *Real* ammunition. He capriciously flipped channels and magazine pages in the family room. Twice he opened his messaging app with the intention to text Susy. He wanted to talk to one of the few people who knew Leigh well. Susy might be able to understand the carnage Leigh left in the wake of her anger. Finally, he jammed his thumbs against the screen, typing the sentiment he'd drafted in his head: "Isn't it amazing how Leigh can be such a total heartless bitch?"

He pressed the blue arrow and watched her reply ellipsis pop up and disappear as she edited her message back. Finally, it came through: "She's intense. I'm here for you."

Intense. Charlie's former boss Cynthia had described Leigh the same way. "Hyper," Cynthia had said. "Controlling." Charlie had written off her comments as Cynthia's adherence to outdated gender roles, but now? Charlie knew she was right. "You do everything she says," Cynthia had accused when he'd announced the move to Minnesota. In fact, Charlie had done everything Leigh had said, from the very first days they'd been in college, shoved together and sweaty in their dorm room beds. And his adherence to her plans had gotten him here: a night he was determined to spend on the family room couch and a future he wasn't sure of for the first time in twenty years.

It was Leigh's lack of confidence in him as a writer that really made him feel nauseous. She shouldn't be able to both disparage his talent and censor his subject matter. It was Leigh's own fault that she was so insecure about her past that she still viewed her failure to make the Olympic team as the defining moment of her life. He'd tried over and over again to rewrite that assessment: with their wedding, the birth of their child, their trip to Italy. And the danger of that single-mindedness, that's what he'd been trying to show with the fictional Lavinia—that people should consider their full humanity and not ascribe every ounce of self-worth to one particular pursuit. He'd started rewriting the novel just after Gus had been born, when Leigh had seemed more whole than she had since he'd known her.

Charlie nodded off on the couch midway through a long-form

New Yorker article and woke when he heard Leigh close their bedroom door upstairs. Although he had no intention of sleeping there, he'd need to get into their bathroom to brush his teeth. He took the stairs slowly. Leigh had always been about control. But try as she might, she couldn't dictate Charlie's creativity and mandate with whom he shared it. If Leigh wanted to be depicted more favorably in fiction, maybe she should just be a better person.

Charlie stopped by Gus's bedroom door, cracked it open, and listened for his son's deep breathing. He froze for a second when Gus whimpered. Charlie studied his son's features in the shaft of light from the hallway. Gus rolled onto his back and flopped his arm over his head. His mouth gaped. The kid was still so little.

Charlie smiled as he closed the door. And then, as soon as he couldn't see Gus anymore, his anger at Leigh overtook his whole body. He marched, arms straight at his sides and fists engaged, into their bedroom. He saw his wife in his peripheral vision, one of the formulaic detective novels she liked balanced against her bent thighs, but walked past as if she weren't there. In their bathroom, Charlie splashed water on his face and examined his reflection. He ran his hand down his firm-enough torso and took his time brushing his teeth while simultaneously checking his workout app. Susy had done deadlifts the previous afternoon, as well as some exercises called Russian hops and single-leg seated jumps.

Mouth rinsed, Charlie paused in front of the bathroom door. He wondered for a moment if he could just stay in there until Leigh fell asleep, and then dismissed the idea. He'd win this argument on the motherfucking high road. He strode out and thought Leigh might be on the verge of saying something to him as he plucked his Kindle off the nightstand and shoved his pillow under his arm, but she didn't. He closed their door behind him just slightly more firmly than he'd meant to, but not loud enough to prompt a reaction. On the couch with his phone in hand, Charlie searched for videos of Russian hops and single-leg seated jumps. Susy would advise him on strength training if he asked. She'd taken an interest in his writing, encouraged him to spend time on it.

Meanwhile Leigh hadn't offered to read any of his work in progress since Gus had been born. She rarely even made it to Gus's hockey games, which she supposedly loved. She'd missed Thursday's matchup because of a "deadline," but Charlie knew she took time out of the same workday to go for a run. She'd refused a Friday-night date with Charlie last week despite built-in free babysitting. Her priorities were clear, and he and Gus didn't crack the top five.

Charlie dropped his phone on the rug and turned toward the bookshelf he had recently organized. In front of the albums he'd curated, he'd placed his favorite of their wedding photos. Taken on the dance floor, his and Leigh's faces were inches from each other's and their hands clasped. Her hair had fallen loose from her updo. Sweat beaded at her temples. She looked sublime and wild.

Charlie stared back at the ceiling. If he had X-ray vision he'd see Leigh fuming on their bed above him. Or maybe she'd just be calmly reading. Maybe her eyelids had already drooped, and he was the only one reliving their argument. Usually, Charlie liked how Leigh maintained a focus on the future. From the moment she arrived home after the Olympic trials, she'd been swift and sure about leaving the heartbreak behind. She never seemed to rehash old defeats. It was always the next challenge—job, coup, or accolade. But it seemed like after this damaging fight, she could engage in just one tiny moment of reflection. She hadn't wanted to save her hockey career back then, but certainly she would want to save their family right now?

When he rolled onto his side in the morning, a deep pain registered in Charlie's shoulder. He blinked. Leigh stood over him in her work clothes. "Are you going to move off the couch before Gus gets up?"

"Don't worry." Charlie looked at the coffee table behind her legs. "I'll get him to school. See you after work."

He lifted one hand over his head and stretched. He was stalling, waiting to sit up until Leigh gave him some space.

He could feel her stare. "You don't want to say anything else?"

Charlie yawned, unexpectedly sure of himself from his position on the couch. "I think you covered it all last night." He tried to keep his tone neutral, no sarcasm or hostility. He smiled, pleased in the moment that his calm seemed to be contributing to her disquiet.

He grabbed his phone from the table, his hand just grazing the side of Leigh's leg. "Sorry," he said. She didn't move. "Was there something else?" He leaned back and clicked open his email.

She shifted her weight from one foot to the other. "I guess not."

"Okay."

They both heard Gus's door open then, his little feet padding to the bathroom. "You should get up," Leigh urged. "Move the pillow and the blanket."

"I know how to deal with Gus." Charlie shifted his feet to the floor and resisted the urge to nudge her out of the way. He didn't want to give her any satisfaction or provoke another tirade. "Don't worry." He stood. "I'm not going to tell him I slept out here because you infantilized me and made me feel like garbage."

He put a hand on Leigh's shoulder for balance as he reached his full height and grabbed the blanket from the couch behind him. He passed Gus on his way up the stairs. "Hey, buddy," he said warmly, knowing that Leigh was still standing there in the living room. "I'll be back, okay? Mom's here if you need cereal right away."

"Hi, Dad." Gus gripped the handrail and sleepily thudded downward. If he were alert enough to ask questions, a reality Charlie very much doubted, then Leigh would have to field them. She was in charge anyway.

CHAPTER FORTY-FOUR

GUS MACKENZIE

December 2022

December 17, 2022
Game vs. SLP: 5–3, LOSS
Record: 7–2–2 (including scrimmages)
Performance Rating: 0/5
Minutes This Week: 126
Lifetime Hours: 485
Points This Season: 4
Quote from Ashberry: "Get your head out of your ass."

When Uncle Jamie picked him up for a postpractice ice cream cone, he hugged Gus. "I admit I was skeptical about your ability to transform yourself in just a year. But, kid, you did it."

"Skeptical?" Gus asked.

"It means, like, doubtful. Like, you don't think it could be true."

Gus thought about that. He didn't feel that different now from how he'd felt playing in Tampa. If anything, he felt a little worse. He'd been the best on his team by far in Florida, but now he was barely hanging on to the third line. In eleven games so far this season, he'd scored just one goal, a fluky shot from the blue line that the goalie bobbled. He had three assists on the season, which was something. But there had been so many more points in Tampa.

"Things are clicking," Jamie told him. "Double scoop tonight, kid. You're on the precipice."

There was another word he didn't know. "Precipice?"

"The edge!" Jamie shuffled him toward the parking lot. "On the edge of glory, as Gaga would say."

"Okay." Gus wasn't sure what Jamie meant, but he'd already asked too many questions.

On the center line in Saturday's game, he thought about "precipice" again. Maybe this was the night that he became a goal scorer. Coach Ashberry said he would eventually. And even when Owen lost the face-off, Gus didn't panic. It wasn't until he fanned on his pass to Axel and turned it over to a well-positioned Oriole that Gus started to feel sick. The St. Louis Park kid skated it into the Lions' zone and scored with a blocker-side snipe.

"No!" Coach Walker shouted from the bench as the shot went off. "Mackenzie!" She hardly ever yelled anything. It must have been a gigantic mistake. When he got back to the bench at the end of his shift, no one patted his shoulder or knocked his helmet. The next one would have to be a million times better to make up for his disastrous start.

But on the ice a few minutes later, Gus forgot to cover point as a defender battled for the puck, and his failure led to a two-on-one. It was only because Chris McMillan was the best goalie in the league that the Orioles weren't up 2–0 just because of Gus's own mistakes.

At the end of the first period, Gus looked at the wall near the

Orioles' net where his mom usually stood if she made it to the game. She was there, her arms crossed and her face mad. Gus checked his dad and Arnie's spot. His dad had pulled his cap low over his brow, so Gus couldn't see his eyes.

Gus would turn things around. In the second period, he caught the puck in the Lions' zone high in the slot. He thought he saw an opportunity to skate it out himself, but as soon as he started his dangle, an Oriole forward poke-checked it away and scooted around Gus. The kid passed it to a winger who shot. On a tip, the puck leapt over Mac's paddle. Now there really were two goals that were Gus's fault.

When Gus got back to the bench that time, Ashberry shook his head at him. "Get your head out of your ass, Mackenzie," he said. "Sit."

In the locker room after the game, the coaches gave the puck to Chris McMillan for the third time that season. "You kept us in it," Ashberry said, "even when our forwards seemed determined to sabotage you." Gus hadn't been player of the game even once, and he wouldn't ever be if he kept making the dumbest mistakes of anyone on the whole team.

Gus ripped his shin guards off as fast as possible, hoping no one had time to talk to him before he could get out of there. Georgie did find him, though. "It's okay," she said. "It happens to everyone."

Gus shoved his skates in his bag. "Not you." He couldn't remember Georgie ever being the reason the opposing team had scored a goal. Instead, she herself had scored like twenty. She had one that night, unassisted. She'd skated the puck coast to coast.

"No," she said. "But . . ." She pulled her hair out of her ponytail and shook it over her shoulders.

"What?" Gus asked.

"I'm, like, ready for this level, you know?"

"And I'm not." It was the first time anyone had actually said it.

"Well, I'm just saying." Georgie heaved her bag onto her shoulder.

"You're just saying what? That I'm the worst?" Gus whispered it, so the other kids still in the locker room wouldn't overhear.

Georgie shook her head. "It might have been better for you to be on B1 this year. For your own development." It sounded like something a grown-up would say. Gus wondered if that's what Coach Walker had told her.

Georgie walked out, and Gus moved extra slowly through the rest of his cleanup, delaying seeing his parents. They wouldn't be able to say anything different from what Georgie had—that he just wasn't good enough. Finally, even Mac, with all of his equipment, was ready to head out. "Dude," he said. "Live to fight another day, okay?"

"What?" Gus bit his lip as the goalie grabbed his paddle from the rack by the door.

"I don't know." Mac shrugged. "That's just what my parents say to me when I have a bad game. Plus, if not for you, I might not have gotten the game puck. So thanks, man."

When Gus finally walked out, Coach Walker was huddled with Gus's dad next to the drinking fountain. They looked up as he approached. "Where's Mom?" Gus asked.

"She had to run back to work for something." Gus's dad looked mad. It was Saturday night. Gus imagined his mom running out after the final buzzer, avoiding talking to anyone about how much he sucked.

"We'll get back to work, too." Coach Walker reached out for a fist bump. "Sports is a roller coaster, right?"

That game hadn't been anything like Space Mountain or Expedition Everest. "I guess," he said. "Sorry, Coach."

"No sorrys." Coach Walker shook her head. "Just get right back to it. Twenty minutes of stick handling tonight, okay? Your dad will text me when you're done."

Gus would make it thirty. It was the least he could do.

CHAPTER FORTY-FIVE

SUSY WALKER

December 2022

A text from Charlie pinged in an hour after Susy had made it home from the disastrous St. Louis Park game. "Cathy Kelliher sneered at me in the lobby," he wrote. Susy rolled her eyes and put her phone on the dryer as she poured Tide in the washer with her coaching clothes. Ignoring haters should be second nature to all of them by this point in the season. Hockey parents were notoriously mercurial. Charlie should have thicker skin.

"Ignore her," Susy wrote back after she'd pressed start on the load. "Just put her in your novel!" The novel was a sore spot, she knew. Charlie had texted her late in the evening that week, letting her know that his "secret" novel was no longer secret.

"Working on my book," he texted again the next Monday, the last before winter break. "You never said why Leigh didn't make the team."

Susy sat in the PE office as she read the text. The answer to the question was complicated. "Leigh was on the bubble. Could've gone either way on any given day."

"Gus was on the bubble, too," Charlie wrote back. "I guess we got lucky with Squirt As this time." Susy remembered Jeff Carlson in the decision room, the subtle way he'd fed Gus to Ashberry as an alternative to Kelliher. Ashberry had been exasperated with Gus after the loss to St. Louis Park. The traits that usually kept Gus in the mix—a nose for the pass, a sense of how the play would develop—had completely failed him.

"But what are the possible reasons she might not have made it?" Charlie pressed about the Olympic team. "If you had to pick one, what was it? She didn't work hard enough? She wasn't tough? Her shot was off?"

Susy knew the answer: Leigh didn't believe in her skills or trust her training. She turned to Jeff for assurance rather than betting on herself. Susy rubbed her index finger and thumb together, imagining the etching on her silver medal. Her WhatsApp chats had been lively in the past week with speculation from both the '02 and '06 Olympians about the complaint against Jeff. There had been another woman in the player pool in '06 who'd come forward now with a similar story to Sydney's. That woman, Alison Collins, had been on the bubble, too, and Susy hadn't known her well. Jeff had promised her his influence with Coach Miller. And she, too, had been on a flight home hours after the final decision.

"Like I told you on that run: I don't know why she didn't make it," Susy finally texted. "Why don't you ask Leigh? There might have been some dynamics with coaches I didn't totally know about."

"What kind of dynamics?" She pictured Charlie across the table from her in one of the dim breweries they frequented with Arnie, his sleeves rolled up to his elbows and his green eyes alert. He'd learned so much about hockey in the last couple of months, soaking up everything she and Arnie had to offer.

Susy sent back a shrug emoji. She felt guilty about it, but she went a little further: "What do you know about Jeff Carlson? Leigh acts a little weird around him, don't you think?"

"Is there history there?" Susy stood up from her desk and walked into the hallway where the department posted the fitness test records. Georgie would break the shuttle run mark next year, for sure, and maybe the mile, too.

It seemed wrong that Charlie didn't know the facts about Lake Placid, and unfair that Susy was his gatekeeper. Charlie seemed like a good guy—like the best kind of guy. Sure, Susy had her medals, but also a philandering ex who'd never really appreciated her. Meanwhile Leigh Mackenzie had a husband who wrote her poetry and cooked her dinner and drove all their kid's carpools. And those dimples. What had Leigh done to deserve her good fortune? She'd begun her whole marriage with the exact type of lie that had eventually ended Susy's. Still, her experience with Dirk made Susy acutely aware of the complexities of being "the other woman."

"You have to ask Leigh," Susy wrote. "Not my story to tell."

Then, still in the hallway and with at least thirty-six minutes left of her prep period, Susy clicked on the WhatsApp conversation she'd been contemplating for days. One of her Torino teammates was close friends with Alison Collins. "This is awkward," the teammate wrote, "but if anyone has information about similar situations with Jeff, it would help if they came forward now." The message included a contact at US Safe Sport, the organization that ostensibly protected athletes from abuse and harassment. Susy clicked the phone number and felt her heart beat faster. She walked toward the door, the December sunshine high and bright. Susy put her hand against the chilly glass when the woman answered. She heard her voice shake as she glanced around, making sure she was alone.

Then she told the Safe Sport rep what she knew, answered questions about dates and times, and disclosed that Leigh had left hockey entirely after the Olympic selection camp. "It didn't happen to me," Susy said, "but I feel like it's my duty as a woman to report, to support the other women who have come forward."

Even as she said it, Susy wondered if her motive wasn't a little more nuanced. There was something that bothered her about Leigh keeping her secret, not from other women, but from her adoring—and adorable—husband.

CHAPTER FORTY-SIX

LEIGH MACKENZIE

December 2022

As soon as Leigh picked up Jeff's call, she regretted it.

"This was not our fucking deal, Mackenzie!" he yelled.

She held the phone six inches from her ear and played back her interview with Jeff's attorney. She'd insisted that their affair had been consensual, that Jeff hadn't exploited her. "What are you talking about? I said exactly what we planned."

"Then why am I getting calls from an arbiter at Safe Sport?" Leigh heard something crash on the other end of the line and imagined Jeff in his office, slamming things around on his desk.

"Safe Sport?" Leigh hadn't heard of it.

"Don't pretend you don't know. They're talking about a lifetime ban for sexual misconduct. You fucking called them!"

Leigh had done no such thing. If it were up to Leigh, she'd never speak of Lake Placid again, and certainly not with any kind of US sports official. The idea made her nauseous.

"Listen." Leigh closed her office door and leaned against the wall next to her painting, her head even with the pink color block. "I've never heard of Safe Sport, and I didn't call them." She used the same voice she did when she pitched an acquisition to Fred—low, calm, confident.

"Well, someone did!" Jeff's voice was thick with fury. "They have your name. They've scheduled an arbitration. I'm going to need you to testify."

"Testify?" *No way.* Leigh had written the letter Jeff had asked for; she'd answered the attorney's questions. If she kept talking about Lake Placid, Charlie would find out about it. She wasn't sure their marriage could take the additional strain, what with the book and his friendship with Susy. Leigh wasn't going to testify. "I'm done, Jeff. It's over. I was young. I don't want to talk about it anymore."

Jeff's laugh sounded like a grunt. "Well, I think you'd better talk about it. I've already got Ashberry in my ear about Gus's failure to develop. I saw the footage from the St. Louis Park game. You were supposed to make him credible."

Leigh shut the blind on her glass door. She sank to the floor, her silk blouse snagging on the light switch, turning off the overhead on her way down. She thought about Gus's better moments in the season, the passes that had connected. Gus was on par with Owen and Axel and nine games out of ten, he was better than Hank. A slump couldn't erase all of the work he'd put in. It wasn't like a fanned pass in Squirts was akin to not making the Olympic team.

"He's credible and you know it." Leigh's anger spiked. "And I didn't call Safe Sport."

"Well, then, who did? Who knows about us?"

Leigh cringed at "us." "Let me figure out what's happening, and

I'll call you back." She hung up and crossed her legs, channeling the same focus she needed when a negotiation verged on collapse. She ran her hands over her trousers and texted Susy.

"Safe Sport?" That should suffice. She stared at her phone for a while, but no answer came. Instead Leigh startled at a light knock on the door. Nicole cracked it open.

"What are you doing down there?" Nicole stepped in and closed the door behind her. Just as Leigh put a hand on the floor to stand up, Nicole dropped down. Her corduroy trousers inched up to reveal light pink socks with bumblebees on them. Leigh imagined her friend, a senior partner in one of the most prestigious law firms in the city, online shopping for bug socks. She smiled in spite of Safe Sport. "Are you okay?" Nicole asked.

"I don't know." Leigh felt a little woozy, her head heavier than it should be and her shoulders stiff.

"What's happening?"

Leigh thought about it. The fight with Charlie the previous week, Jeff's accusation, the fact that Susy had told some kind of governing body what she knew about Lake Placid, and then there was Gus. He seemed to be falling apart just at the exact second he was supposed to get it together for the big Nova Tournament. After Christmas, they'd go to Fargo. It was supposed to be the highlight of youth hockey, the exact thing they'd moved back for. It wouldn't be worth it if Gus rode the bench.

Leigh flipped her watch over. Nicole had arrived for their run. "Should we go?" Leigh asked. "I'll tell you while we jog." She'd been able to speak full-sentence responses to Nicole's questions in the last week. Leigh had even added a run or two on the weekends, though she hadn't yet downloaded the workout app that Charlie was so obsessed with.

"So today's the day!" Nicole hopped up, veritably jumping when she reached her feet. Her leopard-print ankle boots were clunky and cool. She reached a hand down to pull Leigh up. "There you go." She flicked the light on. "Meet you in ten."

Whan Leigh looked in the mirror on her way out, her cheeks were already flushed in anticipation of telling the story she'd been avoiding for twenty years. She still felt queasy, but at the same time, she wanted an objective outside opinion. Leigh had imagined telling Nicole. She'd even imagined Nicole's face at the end of the story, after she related the part about proposing to Charlie. Nicole would be sympathetic, she thought. She'd say that Leigh had been young, that she deserved absolution after all this time.

And if Nicole didn't say those things? Leigh told herself that she wasn't that close with her yet. The loss of a work friend would be a bummer, but not tragic.

They started running. "Okay." Leigh stared at her feet. "Here it is." Her breath felt short, but she'd completed this loop and longer at least eight times by now. And, as Nicole had promised, she'd gotten back in shape faster than she'd imagined she would. Leigh had been an elite athlete, after all. The potential for basic fitness had to be baked in her DNA someplace. "Don't say anything, okay?" Leigh asked. "Not until I'm all done."

Leigh couldn't help laughing a little. Nicole loved interjecting opinions. Sometimes over lunch, she sucked in a breath and smashed her lips together, as if forcibly preventing the words from spilling out. It was endearing. "Okay." The pom on the top of her hat tipped forward as she nodded.

Leigh launched in: "When I was twenty-one years old, I almost made the Olympic team." She'd rehearsed this part. "I think you already know that. I was willing to do anything." Leigh looked out over the Mississippi River, studied a thin layer of frost-covered ice near the bridge supports. "I told my dad when I was in kindergarten that I was going to play in the Olympics, even though women's hockey wasn't a thing then. I thought I'd have to make the boys' team."

"That's a big dream—" Nicole started, but Leigh held a hand up. She didn't want any commentary, not until she'd finished.

"So, hockey players try out for the Olympics in August." Leigh scrunched her fingers together inside her mittens. "And then they prepare together as a team for the six months before the Games. In July, I got a long letter from one of my assistant coaches. He was the youngest coach and the most attractive. I thought he was cute even though I was already dating Charlie."

She glanced at Nicole's hat and saw the pom bounce as her friend turned toward her, but as she promised, she said nothing.

"Jeff offered me special treatment, he took an interest in me, and don't you dare even look at me right now—" She glanced over to check, and sure enough, her friend looked straight on. Leigh would have watched, policing for side eye, but she worried about slipping on the uneven surface and looked at her shoes instead. "So Jeff and I had a thing at the camp." Leigh squeezed her fists tight. "I slept with him, okay? And it was intense for those two weeks, and then I never told Charlie. He doesn't know." She was almost there. After all these years of secrecy, the story had taken less than two minutes to tell. "Charlie and I got engaged as soon as I got home, and I quit hockey forever." The truth weighed her chest down, and she felt herself leaning forward.

"Did—" Nicole started to ask a question, but Leigh jumped in again.

"And now, there's that complaint you saw with Sydney Kirk-patrick in Denver. Remember you asked me about it? I guess Jeff is kind of a sleaze and took advantage of some other women in subsequent camps. I guess it worked so well for him with me . . ." Leigh trailed off as they passed a drinking fountain, decommissioned for the winter. In a few months, the park board would turn it on again.

Leigh wondered if she would still be running with Nicole when that happened, or if the story of Jeff would change things between them.

"Is it my turn?" Nicole asked.

"No." Leigh looked ahead at the bridge. When they started over it, they'd be at a half mile. The first day they'd run together, Leigh's lungs had already been burning when she'd gotten there. Now she barely noticed the exertion. "I thought the thing with Jeff would be worth it if I made the team. I was willing to sacrifice my integrity and my relationship and my"—she lifted her hand and dropped it again—"I guess my principles. And then, I didn't even make it. Jeff didn't even have the power to do what he said he could. I failed."

She stopped talking. Her nerves dissipated, and she started running faster. Nicole matched her stride. Leigh tried to keep her breath as even as possible until she couldn't anymore and it came in heavy blasts. They made it halfway across the bridge, and Leigh looked over her shoulder back at downtown. Nicole went a few steps farther until she realized Leigh had stopped.

"Okay?" Nicole said, turning around.

Leigh put her hands on her knees and stared at the brown snow between her feet. "You think I'm a horrible person?" she guessed.

"Am I allowed to talk now?" Nicole lightly kicked at Leigh's shoe. "Do you really want to know what I think?"

Leigh stood up and staggered a few steps back. "I want to know." That had been the whole point of this confession.

"You're not going to like it," Nicole warned. She reached out and grabbed Leigh's wrist. "None of this is your fault."

Leigh gasped. That wasn't what she had planned to hear, and the dissonance of it took her breath away. Nicole's response was supposed to be about youthful indiscretion and still wanting to be her friend. Leigh tried to shake her arm free, but Nicole held on, not hard but firm.

"Nope." Nicole stared at Leigh until she stopped moving. "That guy took advantage of you. He thought you were vulnerable, and he used you. And then he did it again in the same way with other women." Nicole's voice was low and calm, the same tone Leigh had used to placate Jeff that day.

Leigh felt her head start to shake "no." "I made a bad choice." The way Nicole was saying it, it seemed like she hadn't been in control. But she had been. Leigh had chosen Jeff despite her relationship with Charlie, and she'd been trying to make up for that choice for twenty years.

Nicole squeezed Leigh's wrist once more and then let go. "You should add your name to that complaint. Those other women, they're making sure this doesn't happen to anyone else. And what are *you* doing?"

"It didn't happen to me." That summer before Lake Placid, Leigh had been the one to pick up the phone and call Jeff. She'd followed him out of the training room. She'd gotten into his car. No one had grabbed her or forced her. She'd made that first call. And now, she was making sure that Gus was getting his shot, too.

"Leigh." Nicole turned her palms up and took a step toward her. Leigh looked away toward the strips of open water on the icy river. "This is classic harassment. A million women have been through it."

But Leigh wasn't a million women. Couldn't Nicole see that? She was gritty. And she couldn't stay on the bridge any longer. She turned around and ran back in the opposite direction. She ran fast enough that it was clear she didn't want to be followed.

CHAPTER FORTY-SEVEN

GUS MACKENZIE

January 2023

January 8, 2023
Practice
Performance Rating: 3/5
Season Record: 12–3–2
Points This Season: 6
Minutes This Week: 135
Lifetime Hours: 514—Low because of a break for Christmas
Time Left to 10,000: Only 16 years, if Ms. Estroff's math is right
Quote from Walker: "Keep your head down."

At practice the night before the bus left for the Nova Tournament—the biggest, most famous Squirt tournament in the state—Coach Ashberry gave an epic speech after the last drill. Gus had taken a knee for long enough that the Zamboni driver had already opened the rink doors and moved the goalie nets. Ashberry ignored him and continued on about "energy in the third period" and "doing the little things, so we can win the big one."

Gus was watching the Zamboni when Coach suddenly called his name.

"What?" Gus blinked.

Ashberry clapped his hands over his whiteboard. "Am I boring you, Mackenzie?"

Gus shook his head and chewed the end of his mouthguard. It was the first time he'd gotten in trouble for not listening. He thought he'd just about recovered from the St. Louis Park game. He'd even had a goal and two assists since then, not good enough to get a game puck, but no "head up his ass," either. In one of those games, Georgie had even caused a turnover. "See?" his mom had said. "No one's perfect."

Now Gus kept his eyes on Coach, but he knew that Nik and Colin were probably snickering at him for getting yelled at. Those two always seemed glad when Gus messed up, even in a game. They never seemed to notice how hard he worked. Gus tried to outhustle Colin in every practice, to "prove that he belonged," as Uncle Jamie advised after the board had added Colin to Squirt A. "Show them there was a reason they picked you in the first place," Jamie had said.

A minute later, when Ashberry was finally forced by the Zamboni to let the team go, William put his gloved hand on the top of Gus's helmet and shook it, a sign he didn't think Gus should have been singled out. William noticed how much better he'd gotten. They'd done sprints side by side just the previous week. William had beaten him all six times but then he'd said, "Not bad, Florida. I used to obliterate you, and now you're just losing by a little." They'd laughed. Getting as good as William was textbook "long game." He'd need at least a thousand hours.

On the way home, Gus's dad asked all of his usual boring questions. "How was practice?" "What did Coach say?" "Are you nervous for the tournament?" "Any information on line changes?" Gus's dad tried to sound easy on that last question, like he didn't care about the answer one way or the other, but that wasn't true. His dad was dying for him to get on the second line, up from the bottom.

"I'm not changing lines this season." Gus tried to say it with confidence. "That's too ambitious," he added, sprinkling in one of his mom's words.

He heard his dad take a breath in through his nose and watched as he sat a little straighter, his head tipping slightly toward his window. "Oh?" he asked.

Gus rolled his eyes. In the dark of the back seat, his dad wouldn't see him. "Dad. The kids on the first two lines have way more points."

Big Gus had shown him a couple photos a week ago when his dad had dropped him at his grandparents' after school. They were blurry action shots of his mom when she was little, her stick pointed at the net, her leg stretched out behind her as she aimed. "We didn't have good cameras back then," Big Gus had said. "That's why there are so many blurry ones." On the backs of some of the pictures, Big Gus had written notes in his pointy handwriting. One of them—a picture of his mom with both arms in the air, her stick dangling—said, "17th goal of the Squirt season."

In contrast, Gus had scored exactly two goals in his season and had four assists. Six points. Last year, he'd had over sixty. Georgie and Nik averaged two points per game. Gus didn't even compare.

"Don't sell yourself short," Gus's dad said for what seemed like the two hundredth time. "You haven't had the same training—"

"I know!" Gus said it louder than he'd meant to.

They were both quiet for a minute, and Gus's stomach started to growl. He'd had a quick microwaved quesadilla before they'd headed over to the ice, but he was ready for round two. Maybe he could have one of those instant Velveeta mac and cheeses before bed. His dad would probably insist on some apple slices on the side.

"Look, buddy." They pulled into the driveway, and Gus watched the garage door lift. "I don't want you to give up on yourself. What is it that Greystone says? 'It's a long game'?"

"You want to know what Coach Ashberry said tonight?" Gus knew Coach Walker would probably tell his dad anyway, since they were friends.

"Sure." His dad cut the engine, but the headlights still shone against the back wall of the garage.

"They said they'll shorten the bench at Nova if we're in close games."

"Do you know what that means?" his dad asked.

Of course Gus knew what it meant. He'd been watching hockey games with his dad and Uncle Jamie for years. "It means I'm going to sit more. The top lines will play if the games are close." Gus pulled his knees up to his chest and rested his cheek against the shiny material of his hockey tights. The car was already getting cold, even though his dad had just turned it off. In Florida, it would have been the opposite—he'd have been sweating.

"Coach Walker tells me all the time that you're a valuable member of the team."

"Whatever." Gus reached over and undid his seat belt. Coach Walker told Gus stuff, too. That night during one of the harder drills, she'd said, "Keep your head down and just keep doing what you're doing. Your time will come."

In the moment, Gus thought she'd been impressed by the goal he'd just scored, but afterward he realized that Coach Ashberry was going to make the announcement about short shifts, and she was trying to prepare him.

In the locker room after practice, Owen and Axel, Gus's line mates who would also have their shifts shortened, had seemed excited about going to Nova even though they'd heard the same news. Owen's brother had been there before and had a whole wall full of pins he'd collected from other teams. Colin's mom had sent a photo of this year's Lions pin in an email. Gus had pulled his fingers apart on his dad's iPhone screen to zoom in on it. It was definitely cool with a fiery lion above the team logo, but pins were not as important as playing. Greystone and Jamie were both clear on how important ice time was. Maybe Georgie had been right. Gus should've joined a lower-level team.

It was too late now, though, with only six weeks left of the season. He'd have to "keep his head down" and try to prove he was good enough, just like he'd been doing since they got to Minnesota. He'd do that same thing now with his dad, act like a short bench was just part of a normal day.

CHAPTER FORTY-EIGHT

EMAIL FROM HEAD MANAGER CATHY KELLIHER

January 2023

It's TIME, Hockey Fam!

We're leaving for Nova in T-minus 48 hours. I'm pleading with you to read this entire message AND to click all the included links. (There will be a quiz on the bus. I'm not kidding. I'll bring prizes.)

For those of you who haven't been to the Great Nova Tournament before, get ready for the hockey experience of a lifetime. This is an iconic, historic event, and I'm guaranteeing you'll never forget it.

Just a reminder from the coaches: the highest-ever finish for a Liston Heights Lions team is fifth place in the year 2000. YEP! THAT'S TWENTY-THREE YEARS AGO! I don't want to jinx anything, but this year's team has huge potential! If you read the Youth Hockey Hub blog, you'll know our ranking has steadily risen this season, and we're currently sitting at eleven. We still have to play hard, but let's BELIEVE! Anything is possible, especially if we dig deep and play our game. We can be inspired by the special recognition they're hosting for Team USA skaters past and present! Lots of former Olympians, including Coach Walker, will be on the ice just before the final game. Let's hope we're also PLAYING in that game!!

GO LIONS!

OK, I'll leave the rest of the pumping up to the coaches. Here are your to-dos:

First, the bus. If you're riding it, I need to know. Fill out the RSVP form linked here IMMEDIATELY. (This is the fourth reminder.)

Second, the taco bar. Click HERE to see your assignments. If you didn't sign up for something, I added you. Everyone does their share.

Third, adult beverages. My favorite is Mango White Claw (a few have asked for my preferences–thank you for thinking of your humble manager!). Bring your own cooler. With ICE. Pro Tip: bring the first bag of ice with you, and then refill from the hallway ice machines when we get there.

Fourth, IMMEDIATELY upon arrival, send your room number to the group chat. There are some special deliveries that I will ferry around, but I can't find you unless you tell me where you are.

Fifth, the tournament has an excellent tradition of sportsmanship and a firm code of ethics. Mistreating the refs, taunting players, or otherwise screaming obscenities, insults, or especially slurs will not be tolerated.

Finally, and this goes without saying, but I've been around the bend a few times, so you can all benefit from my experience: don't overdo it at the "safety" meetings. No one needs more than one White Claw before the games, especially given rule five above.

Click the links, people! Bracket HERE. Rosters HERE. Rules HERE.

GO LIONS!

Cathy

CHAPTER FORTY-NINE

LEIGH MACKENZIE

January 2023

In the week before the big Nova Tournament, Leigh took trips to scout acquisitions in Ohio and Kansas. After a full day of touring, fact-finding, and owner-wooing, and then a quick flight home from Wichita, she collapsed on her bed and looked at her phone.

Nicole had texted. "Hope your meetings went well. Did you give any more thought to the complaint?" Nicole had asked her this at least five times in the three weeks since Leigh had confessed. Leigh deleted the message. She had thought about the complaint plenty. She'd ignored the voice mail from the Safe Sport arbiter and the one from Jeff Carlson's attorney. When the lawyer called a second time, Leigh sent her an email: "I stand by my letter and statements. I didn't call Safe Sport." She'd also texted Susy. "It seems like this request might be hard for you what with your apparent interest in my husband, but please mind your own business."

Susy had written a few hours after that. "I don't want to sleep with your husband. And also, the person I used to know, the Leigh who played in the World Championships in '01, she would want to stand up for other women."

Leigh had deleted that message, too. No one seemed to understand the truth of what had happened between Leigh and Jeff. He hadn't pressured her, rather she'd decided that the Olympic team was worth any sacrifice. Her own ugly ambition had led to the affair. Leigh had doubled down on a losing hand and betrayed her ideals. The age difference between Jeff and the women who came later was more significant. It's possible they had been taken advantage of. But not Leigh. Leigh had just made really shitty choices.

And then, she'd done it again in thinking she could come back to Liston Heights and keep living as if Lake Placid had never happened. In Florida, no one knew or cared that she was an almost-Olympian. In Minnesota, everyone knew about Ms. Hockey and the Gophers and what had come afterward.

Although things had been tense between Leigh and Charlie after their fight, and neither of them had apologized, they seemed to tacitly agree that they'd put things back together for Christmas. They had such a long history—so many natural ups and downs—it wasn't really hard to slip back into normal. Christmas with her parents was fine. For New Year's, they'd invited Amelia and Kevin Matzke over for board games. Leigh brainstormed the idea, hoping to shore up Gus's friendship with William. She'd chugged two glasses of prosecco before the Matzkes had arrived and done a decent job of making some non-hockey-related conversation during dinner and dessert. The only hiccup had been when Amelia reminded Leigh excitedly about the on-ice recognition of Team USA players at Nova. "You have to do that," Amelia said. "Gus will love it!"

And now, even though she was swamped at work and even though she'd initially said she wasn't going to the tournament at all, Leigh had decided to change her flight home and hop on the coach bus. She felt weird about missing it, especially since her parents were driving up themselves and had reserved their own room on the team block. Leigh had even read—well, skimmed—the stream of emails from Cathy Kelliher in preparation. Cathy had mentioned the Lions' previous highest finish. Jamie had been on the team for that fifth place. Never had a Liston Heights team made it to the final game of the Nova Tournament. There were whispers and some full-throated endorsements from people who didn't believe in tempting fate: this could be the year. In terms of the Team USA business, Leigh didn't want Susy or anyone else to think she was staying home because of ancient sour grapes. She'd stand to the side and applaud the elites with everyone else.

"I can't believe you're taking a day off to go to this tournament." Charlie walked in the room as Leigh folded her clothes, including his Headwaters T-shirt, and loaded them into the carry-on she usually used for one-day trips. Halfway into her packing, she realized she needed a bigger bag to accommodate all of her fleece and down.

"I don't want to miss it," she said. "Will I mess up your routine? Keep you from your friends?" She tried to keep any ounce of snark out of her voice, but she did wonder if Charlie might have preferred to have Arnie and Susy to himself.

"Of course not," he said without any trace of subtext as he disappeared into the bathroom.

The next morning, Leigh woke before her five fifteen alarm. She turned it off and shuffled out of the bedroom, anxious for a half hour alone to catch up on emails. She looked at her phone as she flicked on the kitchen light. There was a message from Jeff. "Got the updated RSVP and see you're joining us for Nova. It'll be nice to spend a little time together. I'd been worried you're avoiding me."

Fucking Jeff. "Not avoiding you," she typed back. "Trying to keep things professional especially with the complaint going around."

Leigh deleted the text chain between them and loaded her email. There was a new message from Halden Ashberry titled "Nova Strategy." She scanned it, noted at least four punctuation errors, and frowned at the line, "coach's discretion in critical game situations."

That meant Gus would sit when it mattered. Gus had seemed upset after the Lions' final pretournament practice. The coach must have prepared them for a short bench. Leigh could see why Ashberry kept Gus on the third line. Although Charlie had chastised her for missing games, she'd been at more than half. She saw Gus's tentativeness on breakaways and rushes. He had trouble beating the other team to the puck in defensive situations and sloppier edges than most of the team.

But she could see what Susy noticed, too. Gus had the right instincts. Except for that one disastrous game (and the one semidisastrous one), he was almost always in position, and his work ethic was stellar. Georgie was the only one who hustled back harder, who more tenaciously stayed with the play. Like mother, like daughter.

Just before she closed her computer, an email from Susy came in. It was forwarded from someone affiliated with the tourney. The on-ice recognition, the email said, was meant to include everyone who'd played for Team USA, not just those who'd played in the Olympics. The tournament had matching jerseys for all of them, special ones with a Nova insignia juxtaposed with the Team USA logo. There was a list of people who'd be recognized. "Please alert us of any other USA players who'll be in attendance at Nova!" the email read.

"You should do this," Susy had written at the top. "Gus would love it, and frankly, he needs the boost. His confidence is flagging, and the timing is critical. You know it."

The last thing Leigh wanted to do was remind everyone that she'd been good enough to play for the team, but not quite good enough to represent the country on the biggest stage. But, at the same time, she could imagine Gus's shining eyes watching her. If the Lions made it to the final, she'd do the recognition just for him.

An hour later, Leigh pushed a bleary-eyed Gus ahead of her as they approached the gaggle of Lions players and parents near the bus door in the Braemar parking lot. A dad Leigh hadn't met took Gus's hockey bag from her and slid it into the storage area beneath the bus. "Okay, champ?" he said. "You awake?" Gus nodded.

"Who is that?" Leigh whispered to him. She should know by now, but she'd watched games alone and left all the team pizza parties to Charlie.

"Mom," Gus said at full volume. "That's Colin Kelliher's dad. He works the doors at like every game."

Not only had Charlie certainly heard Gus, but Kelliher probably had, as well. And Susy, whom they'd just approached. "Leigh!" Susy raised a fist for a bump. "I'm so glad you decided to come. Charlie told me you were swamped. But you got my email?"

"I'll think about it." Leigh squeezed Gus against her, but he pulled back, his eyes on the team.

Susy tilted her head and looked at Charlie, who smiled at her. Leigh hadn't been jealous when Charlie had become best friends with his boss, Cynthia, in Tampa. But Cynthia was married to Mark. Susy was single, and she knew about Jeff.

"Excuse me." Leigh stepped around Susy, escaping them. She kept her head down as she boarded the bus. Cathy Kelliher had commandeered the front two seats with coolers and giant canvas totes.

"Late RSVP," Cathy said. "But it's good you could make it."

"Sorry," Leigh mumbled. "Appreciate your flexibility." She kept moving and chose a seat four rows back and scooted in toward the window, leaving room for Charlie. She pulled out her phone and scrolled through investment Twitter while trying not to look out the window at her husband. Once as she glanced at them, she caught Susy looking apprehensively up at her. She'd counted on Susy's leftover loyalty to keep her secret, but when she saw her affinity with Charlie, she realized it had probably transferred. Leigh's stomach felt sour.

"Hey, Leigh." Amelia Matzke smiled from the aisle, and Leigh felt relieved to see a friendly face. "I'm glad you could make it. Charlie had said you were busy with work?"

Leigh's chest tightened. Everyone must think her impossibly disconnected. "Last-minute decision."

Amelia tapped her hand on the back of Leigh's seat. "Well, I'm pretty sure there'll be enough for you at the taco bar." She winked and cocked her head at Cathy Kelliher, who pored over her clipboard. Leigh attempted a laugh as Amelia moved a couple of seats back.

Susy boarded next and pointed at the seat next to Leigh. "I'll sit here, okay? And we'll let Charlie and Arnie huddle over Youth Hockey Hub together." Leigh blinked, frozen. "I mean, unless you want to spend four hours reading the YHH blog."

What could Leigh say? Susy sat, and Leigh thought about pulling out her laptop, claiming that she had to work on the ride up.

"Don't even try to say you're working," Susy said, beating her to it. "I remember that wicked car sickness." She dropped her voice to a whisper and tipped her head close. The familiarity of the gesture took Leigh's breath away. "I know you picked this front seat for more than just the proximity to Cathy Kelliher." Leigh and Susy had spent hours next to each other just like this on buses and airplanes. What had they talked about? Everything, Leigh remembered. The game, their families, Charlie.

For a few minutes as the rest of the parents and players trickled on the bus, Cathy checking each of them off on her clipboard, Leigh and Susy didn't say anything else. Susy fist-bumped the kids and some of the parents who trailed after them down the aisle. Ashberry put a hand on Susy's shoulder on his way past. "Coach," he said.

"We've got this." Susy patted his hand. "It's gonna be good."

"He's nervous?" Leigh asked when he'd lumbered off toward the middle of the bus.

"Carlson has him all hyped up." Susy's ponytail swung as she shook her head. "It's a little silly, right? Either we win or we don't. The kids are nine."

A pain generated in the middle of Leigh's forehead as she thought of Jeff. She remembered his thick forearms, the dip of his waist, the fraying cuffs of his wind pants. She closed her eyes and brought a hand to her temple.

"He's coming, you know," Susy said. "He wouldn't miss our first shot at a Nova victory in program history. Has to be on hand to take credit." She whispered this last part. Another secret just for Leigh.

Leigh brought her heels up to the seat and hugged her knees. In a moment, Arnie and Charlie were there. Leigh caught her husband's eye for a second, but then he broke contact.

"Oh, I see how it is," Arnie said. "You ladies leaving us to it? You've got important national team business to discuss?"

"Not at all." Susy nudged Leigh with her elbow as if they were still nineteen and hadn't had years of weirdness between them. "We just don't want to analyze the prospects of teams from rural North Dakota for four hours."

Arnie threw his head back and laughed. "They're onto us, Charlie," he said. "Fine." He settled in an open row a few back. Charlie followed without saying anything.

Cathy sprang up the bus steps, tapping her clipboard with a blue ballpoint.

"All set?" the driver asked.

"I wish," she said loudly. "Swear to God if Jeff flippin' Carlson doesn't get here in five minutes, we're leaving for Fargo without him."

I wish they'd leave without me. It was Leigh's last chance to bail. If she hustled out and feigned a work emergency, she could just pick up Charlie and Gus after the whole thing was over. But it would be a scene. She'd have to crawl over Susy, ask the driver to retrieve her bag. There would be a conversation with Charlie that the others watched from their windows. She'd already disappointed her husband so thoroughly.

Plus, just as she might have moved, Jeff's Jeep Wrangler pulled in. Seconds later, Jeff himself appeared near its trunk, from which he retrieved a black duffel. Leigh rubbed her temple again.

"You've seen him, right? Charlie said you've had drinks a couple of times?"

Leigh nodded. "You haven't told Charlie—"

Susy shook her head. "Not my business, Leigh. But you should tell him. And you should talk to Safe Sport."

"I can't tell Charlie." Leigh remembered the texts from Nicole. She missed her new friend. They would have exchanged tons of messages in these last weeks if Leigh hadn't spilled her secret. Now, the price she'd paid for sharing was more isolation. Now, Nicole and Susy thought Leigh owed everyone the deepest parts of herself.

"You can." Susy leaned in close. "Can't you see you've been reading this all wrong all these years? You were foolish, sure, but it's *his* fault."

Leigh covered her mouth. "But I did it."

"I feel so frustrated." Susy didn't sound mad. "Being so hard on yourself—so incredibly stubborn—who does it serve?"

Leigh refused to look as Jeff got on the bus to a smattering of applause from the parents who were anxious to leave.

CHAPTER FIFTY

SUSY WALKER

January 2023

Susy hadn't planned to sit down next to Leigh, but then she saw the tension between her and Charlie. Leigh had walked ahead of him toward the bus; he'd nodded tersely when she'd asked something. And Susy did want to talk to Leigh about Safe Sport. The other women who'd come forward—Sydney, Alison, and Sheila—needed Leigh. Leigh was an investment banker with a long and stellar professional reputation. Her voice would be instantly credible. In the moment when Susy picked the seat next to Leigh, she imagined she could rely on their old-time alliance to convince her to do the right thing.

And, if she was being honest with herself, Susy wanted to understand what Charlie saw in Leigh, to connect with her again. Susy had watched Charlie field text requests from Leigh. Could he pick up some milk on the way home? Could he tell her once more how to reheat the pasta bake? What time did the game actually start? Leigh often rushed into rinks, her hands shoved in her parka pockets, at the start of the second period, leaving warm-ups and transportation to her husband.

And Charlie had told Susy that Leigh didn't appreciate his novel. That didn't seem fair. As if Charlie's only purpose should be managing Leigh's whims. Susy knew what it felt like to be taken advantage of in a marriage. She'd been the keeper of the calendar and the default parent for Georgie for years before she'd finally figured out that she was better off without her ex-husband. Charlie might be headed for the same realization.

Still, Susy wasn't angling for him exactly, but if she could meet someone like Charlie? Someone who loved kids and loved hockey and maintained an active creative life? Susy thought of Charlie sometimes as she watched detective shows after Georgie went to bed. She imagined his observations both about the mysteries and the writing of them. She and Charlie could theoretically be happy together. Their kids even got along.

However pleasant, the fantasies made her feel guilty. And that guilt had been part of Susy's snap decision to sit next to Leigh on the bus, too.

Neither of the women said much after Jeff boarded, and they rolled out of the lot. It wasn't until they started seeing exits for St. Cloud, an hour and a half out of the city, that Susy glanced up from her Kindle. Leigh looked pensive and pale. In the old days, Susy had distracted her from her motion sickness.

"What are you thinking about?" Susy asked.

"Nothing." Leigh kept her eyes on the big-box stores next to the highway.

"Sometimes I can't believe you're here after all this time." Susy tried again.

Leigh didn't answer.

"Do you regret moving back?"

Leigh flicked her eyes toward Susy, but didn't turn her head. "Why would you ask that?" She didn't sound angry, exactly.

"I don't know." Susy coughed. "You don't seem happy. All this old stuff popping up. It can't be easy."

Leigh sighed. "Frankly, it would be easier if you hadn't called Safe Sport." She chewed the nail of her index finger. "I had things handled."

"I was just trying to do the right thing," Susy whispered, though the noise of the bus would keep anyone from hearing their conversation.

"You don't know what happened," Leigh said.

Susy raised an eyebrow. She did know what happened. She'd read Sydney's, Alison's, and Sheila's complaints against Jeff, the ones that had been forwarded to the women on the WhatsApp chats. The pattern seemed clear: Jeff targeted a player on the bubble and then made promises he couldn't keep. He used his power as a Team USA coach to coerce young women. It was wrong. And yet, the sympathy Susy had for Leigh had been diminished by her unwillingness to accept that she'd been a victim.

And also, her unwillingness to come clean with Charlie, who was such a nice and interesting person.

"I feel like I do know what happened." Susy swiveled her head back toward where Arnie and Charlie were sitting, bent over their respective iPhones.

"Well, whatever you think it was, you're wrong." The sunlight from the window made a streak over Leigh's cheek, accentuating the hollow there that had developed with age. Leigh hadn't bothered with makeup that morning. The circles beneath her eyes looked almost blue. "I know you think you're doing the right thing, but please stop," Leigh said. "You're just making things tricky between Charlie and me. He's my husband."

Susy didn't like her implication. Although she had imagined

more, Susy hadn't crossed any lines with Charlie. "You should tell him." Susy blurted it this time. She leaned over and grabbed a pack of Trident from her bag. She offered a piece to Leigh, but her friend's hands were frozen in her lap.

"You have no idea." Leigh's voice was stony, harsh. "That time in my life—those weeks before the camp and during it—they're just this tiny piece of my existence. I was twenty-one years old. It's eons ago. I was a different person."

"Charlie said you got engaged the day you got back." Susy wasn't sure what emboldened her, but she felt justified. "You're a different person than the one who proposed to him?"

Leigh looked back out the window. "You think you know what happened, Suse, but you're wrong. It's not your story."

Susy had seen Leigh every day at that Olympic selection camp. She'd been sitting right next to her when she'd been cut. Charlie should know what happened, too. And besides that, as women athletes, they should both be invested in the Safe Sport complaint. "I was there with you," Susy said. "And I know what happened, and Jeff knows, and you know, and meanwhile Charlie doesn't. And we're all here." She gestured at the bus. "It's inappropriate."

"I don't want to talk about it. Let's not talk." Leigh turned her whole body away.

Susy glanced over her shoulder again, and this time caught Charlie's eye. He cocked an eyebrow, and Susy smiled and shrugged. She'd try to make whatever tension he detected seem like nothing. At least for now. His text came in a minute later: "All good over there?"

Susy didn't look at him as she sent back a thumbs-up.

CHAPTER FIFTY-ONE

LEIGH MACKENZIE

January 2023

Cathy Kelliher gave an overlong schedule rundown from the front of the bus when they pulled off the highway in Fargo. Leigh refreshed her work email and scanned something labeled "urgent" from Fred. She forwarded it to her assistant. Just as she went back to her inbox, a text from Jeff buzzed in.

"Doesn't this remind you of the olden days? We could pretend we're back there . . ."

Leigh dismissed the message and tipped her phone toward the window and away from Susy. "That's a no then?" Jeff's next message read. "At least have a drink with me before the first game tonight. I want to update you on a few things, including Ashberry's plans for bench shortening in the final minutes."

No. She'd done enough. She'd answered all of the attorney's questions. She'd kept paying and paying. Surely, they were square now for Gus's placement on the A-team.

Just to verify that she didn't have to placate her old coach, she turned to Susy. "Does Jeff Carlson tell you how many minutes each kid should get?"

"Is he texting you?" Susy leaned over, but Leigh pulled her phone back.

"Can you just tell me whether he has any say?"

"Jeff likes to give his opinions, but Ashberry makes the calls. I do, too, sometimes, but mostly him."

Leigh looked back at her screen and typed, "I'm here to focus on Gus. Let's table the drink." No need to anger Jeff, but no promises, either.

"Fair enough," Jeff wrote back.

She thought she'd handled it, but that night after the first game—with Gus picking up an assist in the 8–2 victory—Jeff cornered Leigh in the community room next to an open box of cheese pizza. "Not bad for the Gus-man today." Leigh bristled. No one called him "Gus-man."

"He's been working hard. I told you he would." Leigh grabbed a handful of M&M's from a dish between the pizza boxes and shoved them all in her mouth at once.

"And you've been working out, too?" Jeff scanned her torso. Leigh looked around the room for Charlie and found him near the door, in a pod with Arnie and Susy.

"I've been running." Leigh thought of Nicole. She'd been avoiding her, too, unable to face Nicole's assertion that she owed it to woman-kind to come forward. She'd sent a few texts back to her, agreeing that the younger women's experiences with Jeff were terrible. Leigh had even teared up once when Nicole wrote again that what had happened with Jeff was criminal. It wasn't that she didn't support the other women; it's just that her experience had been different.

Leigh couldn't think of herself as helpless. Telling her story so many years later would only jeopardize her marriage *and* cloud Gus's future in Liston Heights Hockey. Even if Jeff was a creep now—even if he'd replicated his affair with Leigh in Lake Placid— she'd been the first one. It had been different from what happened to Sydney, Alison, and Sheila. Leigh had been a willing participant. She'd emboldened Jeff, perhaps. Maybe she'd turned him into the slimeball predator he'd become by '06.

"Hobby jogger, eh?" Jeff rubbed his own stomach. "Anyway, you're looking good, Mackenzie."

Leigh caught Amelia Matzke's eye near the White Claw cooler. "I need to ask Amelia something," she mumbled.

Before she left the party, Leigh's phone buzzed again. Jeff. "You look like a twenty-year-old in those jeans." She deleted the text, grabbed a second White Claw, and shoved it in her vest pocket. She grabbed Charlie's elbow and whispered to him that she was headed back to their room. She'd say a quick good night to her parents on the way.

"I'm going to stay," Charlie said. It was fine with Leigh.

At eight the next morning, the Lions took the ice against the number one–ranked team in Minnesota. Leigh stood against the boards in the offensive zone, surprised when Charlie joined her. She looked for Arnie, but he wasn't there.

"You okay?" Charlie asked. She'd gotten up early that morning and put out a few email fires in the hotel lobby. They hadn't really spoken before they hustled Gus, still groggy, out to the bus at seven fifteen.

"I'm fine. This is the number one team everyone's worried about?" Amelia had been buzzing about the matchup the night before, had pulled up rankings on the website Charlie was always refreshing. The score was 0–0 seven minutes into the first, and it seemed like a fairly even match to Leigh, especially with Chris Mc-Millan in the net for the Lions. Amelia had shown Leigh Mac's headshot on the tournament website as a "Goalie to Watch," as if the kids were already college prospects at age nine.

"Yeah. Mahtomedi is undefeated." The bags under Charlie's eyes sagged. The room had been hot overnight, hot and dry, and Leigh had heard her husband get up a couple of times.

"You sleep okay?" she asked.

Charlie shook his head. "I hate hotels." She knew that. "You?"

"It was okay. I worried I wasn't friendly enough at the party." She hadn't actually been worried about that, but she wanted Charlie to think she'd tried.

"You seemed fine." On the ice, Nik took a penalty for slashing. "Damn. We definitely don't need to be down a guy against this team."

"Are you disappointed that I came with you? Am I cramping your style?" Leigh watched the face-off as she asked, but she could feel Charlie's gaze. He reached out to rub the arm of her jacket just as Georgie broke out between two Zephyr defenders. She rocketed the puck to Abe Senko, whose shot skimmed the top of the goalie's glove before sinking into the back of the net.

"A shorty!" Leigh banged the Plexiglas and her heart raced. The elation surprised her. It was just youth hockey, right? But she felt herself catching everyone else's Nova fever. Once again, she wanted to win.

Charlie put his arm around her and pulled her toward him. He didn't seem sorry she'd come to Fargo. The two of them watched the rest of the game together. The Lions went up 2–0, and then held on in the third for a tie. Gus blocked a shot at the end of his last shift, doubling over as he skated to the bench for a quick change as soon as the play left the zone. Charlie took a step toward the bench, anxious to check on him after the hit, but Leigh grabbed his wrist.

"He's fine." Sure enough, he was the first to skate out to congratulate Mac after the game. Susy had likely given him huge props for that blocked shot. If the goalie hadn't had the game puck sewn up with an incredible number of saves, Leigh might have given it to her own son.

"Darn good," Leigh said as they headed to the lobby to meet up with her parents. The senior Mackenzies watched from the top row of the bleachers, and Leigh had heard her dad's cheers on each of Gus's shifts.

When they ran into Arnie in the hallway, he and Charlie did a hilarious, frat boy–style chest bump.

"That's a lot of enthusiasm for a tie," Leigh said.

"Against the number one team in the state?" Arnie raised both fists Rocky-style. "I'll take it!"

Suddenly, Jeff was there. "Good game." He turned to Leigh. "Mind meeting me for that drink when we get back?"

"Mind if these guys come?" Leigh tried to sound casual.

Charlie shook his head. "Can't. I'm on lunch duty in the community room. Arnie is, too. I notice you avoided the volunteer sign-up." Charlie winked. Obviously, Leigh hadn't read that part of the email. "You should go!" He squeezed Leigh's shoulder again and kissed her temple. "It's kind of the last reprieve—we've got another game tonight, one tomorrow, and then the quarterfinals."

"If we win," Jeff said.

"*When* we win!" Charlie and Arnie said together, and then high-fived.

"So, we're on for the drink, then." Jeff didn't wait for an answer before he walked away. Leigh felt lonely again.

Jeff had already had at least one cocktail when Leigh joined him in the poorly lit bar next to the Holiday Inn Express ninety minutes later, never mind that it was barely eleven a.m. "The gin and ginger is mostly ginger," he told her, though she detected a slur.

She left him to put in her order. "Same drink." The bartender pointed at Jeff. "Cute. He's got a tab."

Of course he did. Leigh sipped her drink on the way back to the table. There was plenty of gin in hers. "What's this all about?" she asked Jeff, speeding things along.

"I just wanted to explain about Alison Collins and Sheila Cooper," he said. "I know it looks bad."

Leigh used her thumbs to crack the knuckles on each of her index fingers. "I honestly don't care." She moved on to her middle fingers, but her left one wouldn't crack.

Leigh could see sweat on Jeff's brow despite the frigid outdoor temperature. "You were special to me, Mackenzie. I thought you were going to make it."

Leigh held her thumbs over her ring fingers and glanced down at the platinum band she wore on her left hand. She and Charlie had pooled all of their money to buy a set of rings. The total had been seven hundred dollars, which was probably less than what they were spending for this weekend in Fargo. "Listen," she said, "I'm doing what you asked me to do. I made the statement. I answered the questions. Aren't we even? Gus is holding his own."

"I miss you, Leigh." Jeff looked up at her, and a piece of hair fell over his eyebrow.

"What?" She pushed her drink to the right, the sweetness of the ginger ale suddenly sickening. Their dalliance had been two weeks long. They'd never actually been attached. "Lake Placid was half a lifetime ago," Leigh said. "We haven't seen each other in twenty years."

"Yeah, but you got me." His eyes shone. "I had this bright future in coaching. I had a couple of seasons at Providence under my belt. I thought I had a big future with the national team. Maybe the US men's team. And now?" He looked around the dingy bar, at the clusters of other hockey parents whose kids were likely at the pool or sprinting through the hotel hallways unsupervised.

"You did have a big future with the national team." Leigh

counted Olympic cycles on her fingers. "You were on the staff for like fifteen years."

Jeff pushed his jowl up, so his cheek blended into his crow's-feet. "I thought I'd become head coach. Be a legend. And now I refinance people's suburban mortgages."

Leigh looked at the door, wondering how long she'd have to stay here to satisfy him. "Sports end for everyone." She remembered her stick bouncing off the bottom step of her parents' basement stairs. She could still hear the crack of the fiberglass against the concrete.

"And now these women are accusing me of all of this horrible stuff. After I supported them!"

Leigh put both palms on the edge of the table and pressed her flesh in. She flashed again on Sydney Kirkpatrick's St. Christopher medal as she had so many times before. Sydney hadn't deserved the heartbreak that Jeff had delivered. "I don't think we should talk about it." If Leigh knew details, it only made it more likely she'd have to testify.

"I just cared too much." Jeff sniffed. "I wanted the best for them. I knew they were on the bubble. In the end, it just wasn't enough."

"You didn't have as much influence as you thought you did." It had been obvious when Leigh hadn't made the team.

Jeff shrugged. "And you didn't play as hard as I thought you would." His voice had turned cold, the pleading curtailed.

Leigh remembered the last scrimmages, the taste of bile after her shifts ended, the way Jeff's champagne spilled on her thigh in the car that last night. She dropped her hands into her lap. "I'm gonna go," she said, although she didn't move.

"Everyone leaves me. Why did you leave me?" Begging again, Jeff looked up at her, and a tear gelled in his lower lashes. Leigh nearly gagged.

"I didn't make the team," she said. "I had a boyfriend."

"You're too much for Charlie." Jeff reached a hand across the table, but Leigh kept hers on her jeans. "He doesn't know what you're capable of."

"It's been twenty years, Jeff." It took all her strength, the weight of the old memories holding her back, but Leigh stood up. "*You* don't know what I'm capable of. I'm gonna go."

After she'd taken a couple of steps toward the door, she almost stopped short, overwhelmed by the sudden realization that she knew what she had to do to make this situation better. Leigh would tell Charlie the truth. She had to.

And she let herself think that it might even be okay. Charlie had forgiven her for countless missteps. He'd been the person to bring her back to herself after Lake Placid. Susy was right: Charlie deserved to know. But not in Fargo, not when Jeff would ride the coach bus home with them. When they got back, she'd find the time to tell him what she'd been hiding.

The resolution made her feel simultaneously more free and more nauseous.

The Lions won their afternoon game, but Leigh couldn't focus on the details. Gus had played fine; her dad had hugged him enthusiastically afterward. As she lay in bed that night next to Charlie, whose light snores sounded childlike and whose hair reeked of chlorine despite washing it with the hotel's shampoo, another text from Jeff buzzed in. "I can't get over how hot you are. Your confidence kills me."

She deleted the message and tossed the phone onto the floor before she turned off her light.

CHAPTER FIFTY-TWO

LEIGH MACKENZIE

January 2023

The Lions' parents were raucous and jumpy after the team won against Rochester and headed to their last pool-play game in first place. The kids seemed destined for the best finish ever by a Liston Heights team. When Leigh hugged Gus, she couldn't help but give in to the fervor. Nothing exhilarated her like winning. Her dad hugged them both, too. "This brings back so many happy memories," he said. "Gus, you're doing us proud."

In between games, though, Leigh had to delete six texts from Jeff. He commented on her beautiful skin, Gus's serviceable play, the way her ass looked in her jeans.

When they got back from Fargo, she'd block him. Delete his number. Leigh just had to make it through this weekend without making a scene.

The texts kept coming as the Lions battled Minnetonka. She turned at one point between the first and second periods when the Lions were up 2–1 to see Jeff staring at his phone in the top row of bleachers. He had a direct view of her backside, about which he'd written twice already. Leigh told Charlie she wanted to watch from behind the net and nearly sprinted out of Jeff's sightline. When she got home, she'd call Jeff's lawyer. In the meantime, these last games—they were about Gus. He was the only reason she'd reengaged with Jeff at all.

The game was tight into the third period, with the teams tied at 2. Georgie fanned on a pass in the Lions' zone and Rocco recovered it with a heroic sprint, during which he tangled with a kid from Minnetonka and slammed into the boards. The parents in the stands and Leigh herself collectively gasped.

From her spot behind the net, Leigh could see Rocco's anguish as he skated toward the bench. The medic pulled him immediately, and Rocco's mom sped by Leigh a minute later. "He'll be okay," Leigh called after her. He would be okay, but he might have also broken his collarbone or dislocated his sternoclavicular joint. Jamie had done that once. He'd missed two weeks of games. She hoped Rocco would be cleared for the rest of the tournament.

Leigh watched the bench. Susy shuffled Georgie to defense, a good move, given her superior awareness of the ice, although it would be hard to generate scoring chances without her up front. Leigh hadn't really been nervous during any of Gus's games this season, but she found herself shifting her weight from one foot to the other in the final minutes of this one. With ninety seconds to go, Nik Ashberry skated the puck out of the zone and whipped a quick pass to Simon O'Malley, who was just a microsecond from being off-sides. Simon had already lost his footing when he shot from low in the slot and snuck the puck in between the goalie's skate blade and the pipe. 3–2, Lions. The parents leapt to their feet and roared. Leigh once again pounded the Plexiglas.

In the final minute, Minnetonka pulled their goalie, and Ashberry put the top line on the ice with Georgie still on defense. With ten seconds left, Hank Teeterow poked the puck away from a desperate Minnetonka winger, skated it into the neutral zone, and then slid it easily from the blue line into the Skippers' empty net.

The bench and the parents erupted. Leigh's phone vibrated. "I don't think this would have happened without your energy," Jeff had written. "You're magnetic."

As the final buzzer sounded and the kids piled on top of Mac, Leigh had another message, this time from Jamie. "What time are the quarterfinals? I'm fixing to drive up there."

Leigh laughed. "Don't you have a game tonight?"

"That's right," Jamie wrote. "But my nephew is a Nova finalist!!!!!" Though he couldn't come, he'd definitely check Twitter on the bench.

In between the Minnetonka game and the quarterfinal four hours later, Ashberry and Susy banned the kids from the swimming pool and sent strict orders to the group chat: "Hydrate and leg drain. Mandatory no-screens rest from 1:30–3 when we hit the bus." Gus was overly serious about these orders and mandated that they keep the lights off in their hotel room. Leigh signed in to her work computer, insisting that "no-screens" was a rule only for the kids. When she picked up her phone a few minutes from bus time, she saw two new texts from Jeff. "I'm sorry," he said, "but I need to see you." Obviously, she hadn't answered, but fifteen minutes after that, he'd followed up. "How about now?"

"No," Leigh replied. "You don't need to see me." Something was clearly wrong with him, and Leigh wondered if he'd ever stopped drinking after their meeting at the bar.

The texts didn't stop during the quarterfinal. They ramped up. "I didn't know how lucky I was to have you." And then, "You were an animal, just sexy as hell." Leigh watched the game in the stands with her parents, hoping her proximity to them might deter Jeff's messaging. It didn't. When the fourth one—"I'm dying for you"—came in at the end of the first period, Leigh whipped her Lions beanie off and stuffed it in the pocket of her parka, suddenly hot and panicky.

"Are you okay?" her mom asked.

"I got hot," Leigh said lamely. She unzipped her jacket. "I'm okay." William Matzke distracted them by stealing the puck and zipping back toward the Roseau net. His shot hit the post and Leigh looked at her phone. "Do you still like it from behind? Does Charlie know?" She pitched her body forward, planting her elbows hard on her thighs. Popcorn littered the riser.

"Goodness!" Her mom put her arm around her as William passed the puck back to the blue line. "Let's get you out of here."

"No." Leigh straightened and glanced at the boards where Charlie and Arnie stood. She wanted protection and comfort from Charlie that she didn't deserve. Leigh pictured sitting Charlie down in their living room after the tournament. She'd start at the beginning, like she had with Nicole. Maybe he could understand, especially after experiencing the intensity of Nova.

Gus's line began their shift. Gus dished a pass to Axel, whose parents were on their feet two rows in front of Leigh. Axel's one-timer sailed over the net. Gus raced into the corner, but the Roseau defender beat him. The puck flew past Georgie into the neutral zone, but the crew recovered it, managing two more shots on goal before the change.

Leigh breathed a sigh of relief about Gus's competence despite Jeff's escalation. What the Lions needed now was a hit of Nik Ashberry's fire. A goal at the close of the second would keep the kids in it, despite their slightly slower skating. The momentum could carry them.

As Gus tumbled onto the bench, Leigh made eye contact with Charlie. He raised his eyebrows, waiting for her assessment. She gave a thumbs-up. He'd played well, demonstrating the IQ that Susy always blathered on about. *Please love me at the end of all this*, she thought.

And then just being in the same room as her husband became too much for her, the secret too heavy.

"I'm going to take a bathroom break," Leigh said to her parents as she started up the stairs.

"You want me to come with you?" her mom asked.

"I'm fine." But Leigh felt wobbly. Her feet fell harder against the bleachers than she meant them to. She trained her eyes on the last step, on the verge of a stumble.

She pushed the doors open into the lobby and began a jerky march toward the bathroom. When she was halfway there, she glanced over her shoulder to see Jeff approaching. *God damn it*. She propelled herself faster, almost running, but Jeff caught up and grabbed her arm. "Hey." She looked down at his fingers against the black of her coat, and he let go. When she started to walk around him, he moved to block her.

"Christ," she said. A mom holding a baby at an adjacent table turned to stare. Leigh whispered, "What the fuck is wrong with you? It's been almost twenty years. I don't want to think about you that way." She glanced back at the mom, who held a palmful of Cheerios in front of the baby's chubby fingers.

"I just can't stand seeing you again," Jeff whined. "I think not pursuing you back then was the biggest mistake I ever made. I think you can feel the heat, too." He pointed at her unzipped coat.

Gross. Leigh shoved him to the side and raced into the restroom without looking back. She remembered Jeff's low baseball cap, the way he'd waited for her in his car after the practices at selection camp. She remembered Susy's warning, her assertion that Leigh was good enough to make it on her own.

In the stall, Leigh pulled her cell phone from her pocket and deleted Jeff's most recent texts. Suddenly, she heard the crowd erupt in cheers. She'd missed a goal. Leigh tried to discern whether the jubilation came from the Liston Heights side or the Roseau side, but it was impossible. She'd just opened the team app to check when Jeff's next text came in. "Your boy got the job done," he said. "Just like we always did."

Charlie texted, too. "Where are you!???!? Did you miss it?!?!"

Fuck. Gus had scored three goals all year, and she'd missed the most clutch one, in the quarterfinals at fucking Nova. Her fingers shook with rage. "Seriously, Leigh," Jeff texted again. "I can't stop thinking about the way you wrapped your legs around me after that scrimmage. I've never come so hard in my life."

"Oh my God!" Leigh shouted aloud. "Gross!" Only after the outburst did she think to check beneath the stalls for extra feet. None. Tears collected in her eyes and her hands shook. She fumbled the phone and recovered it.

Charlie texted as Leigh stood in the stall, her head pounding with anger and her breath coming in raspy gasps. "I can't find you! He's so happy! Fist bumps from the whole bench."

Leigh jabbed at the screen, furious with Jeff for ruining this moment. "Jesus, Jeff," she typed. "Sleeping with you was a nightmare, and I regret it every fucking day. STOP FUCKING TEXTING ME."

She hit send and collapsed onto the toilet seat, her whole body trembling with an anger she hadn't experienced since the days after Lake Placid. She leaned forward and let her head rest against the stall door. She palmed tears off her cheeks and opened her eyes. Grime clogged the tile grout. She should get back out there, lest she miss Gus's next shift. Being a mom was more important than whatever she was doing right now.

As she stood, her phone buzzed in her hand. She took a deep breath and glanced at it. It was Charlie. "Are you saying you slept with Jeff Carlson? And you're telling me this now?"

Leigh wailed and then frantically opened the message app. She reread the chain with Charlie, and there was the text she'd meant for Jeff. She held her breath and felt the stall spin, the greasy eggs from the free hotel breakfast buffet lurched in her stomach. She turned and vomited violently as the crowd cheered again outside.

For minutes afterward, Leigh knelt there, her body curled in on itself and rocking, her forehead intermittently grazing the lid of the toilet seat. Everything was gross. The smell of her sick, the stickiness of the floor against the bumpers of her Vans, her own despicable failures, and the worst parts of herself that had burst through the armor even though she'd reinforced it for two decades with her business degree and promotions and perfect deals.

Someone came into the restroom and exited again, probably deterred by the stench. Leigh didn't even care if people knew it was her in there. It seemed right that she'd be on the floor of a filthy ice rink bathroom.

When she could breathe again, she turned around and leaned her head against the stall door. "Charlie," she texted, "I had just decided to tell you the truth, but not like this. And it's not what you think." She pulled the phone to her chest and stared at the ceiling. How could she make him understand after all this time? She kept going. "It happened in Lake Placid. It was all my fault. I thought he could help me get on the Olympic team. I thought it was a means to a medal. I thought—" She sobbed again. It sounded stupid and futile and so selfish. "Anyway. It doesn't matter. All that matters is how much I love you and Gus. And this was so long ago. It meant nothing except that I'm a complete idiot."

She hit send, and then watched as the app told her the message had been delivered. She prayed for a reply, but there was nothing. Only when she heard the buzzer for the end of the second period did it occur to Leigh to leave the stall. She was washing her hands when her mom came in. "I've been looking for you!" she said, but then she caught sight of Leigh in the mirror. "Honey!"

"My breakfast," Leigh said as she dipped her head to splash water on her face. "I was sick, but I'm okay. I'm not missing any more of this."

CHAPTER FIFTY-THREE

CHARLIE MACKENZIE

January 2023

Charlie watched the end of the game with Arnie, unwilling to address the message his wife had sent. When Leigh tried to pull him away from the boards, he'd leaned down and whispered in her ear, "I will not have you further ruin this experience." He kept his eyes on the ice. "Let go of me. Your breath is foul." She hiccupped a little as she walked away, and Charlie didn't care. She deserved to simmer. Charlie had spent their whole relationship making her feel better.

After the buzzer and the high fives with Arnie, the two of them walked toward the door. The parents had taken to forming a tunnel, their hands up and fingers thrumming like college football cheerleaders as the kids strode onto the bus, buffeted by the adults' whoops. It was silly, but fun. After the Rochester game, Leigh had stood next to him, lightly hip-checking him and smiling huge. He'd thought about how happy he was that she'd decided to come on this trip after all. It felt like things were going back to the way they had been before she'd read and totally misunderstood his manuscript.

But now, just hours later, everything had changed. Charlie watched her walk out of the rink with her parents, and even Leigh's face looked different to him, something just slightly off about the way her mouth moved. If she tried to stand next to him in the cheer line, he'd find another spot. This afternoon's reception for the team was more important than all the others. Gus had scored the go-ahead goal in a do-or-die game. And instead of celebrating that remarkable fact with his wife, Charlie felt more disconnected from her than he ever had.

Leigh and Charlie had been together as teenagers. They'd grown up together. Not even her follow-up text, a missive explaining that it had all happened in Lake Placid, lessened his disgust. He'd been there the day she'd gotten home from that selection camp. He still had the twist tie she'd shoved around his finger. They'd told their parents they were engaged the next weekend. The summer after that, he'd handed over 100 percent of his tiny salary for the platinum wedding band she still wore.

And twenty-four hours before they'd set their whole life in motion, she'd been screwing Jeff Carlson.

Charlie tried to act normal as he stood next to Arnie. Arnie clapped him on the shoulder. "Kid's goal was absolutely clutch," he said for the third time. "The momentum swung after that. Highlight reel, man. You gotta be flyin'."

Charlie attempted a smile. "I'm thrilled for him." Despite the crisis, Charlie had resolved to preserve this victory for Gus. There weren't many moments in life like this, though surely Gus didn't realize it yet. Charlie had had just one, at the Headwaters Ultra. He could still see Leigh's face as he passed the 45-mile marker where she'd met him. She had jumped and whooped. "You're doing it," she'd yelled. An hour later, the elation had spread all over his body as he'd crossed the finish line and fallen into Big Gus's and Helen's arms. He'd never felt more whole in his life, and he'd finished in the back of the pack. Gus, on the other hand, was poised to be one of the best hockey players in the actual State of Hockey.

Charlie glanced down the line to where Leigh stood with Amelia, the senior Mackenzies already en route back to the hotel. He cupped his hands over his mouth and blew warm air into them.

"You okay?" Arnie asked.

Before Charlie could decide how to respond, the coaches exited the building. Susy led the line, beaming. She took her hat off and waved it at the parents as she hustled beneath their exuberant tunnel, which ended at the bus door. As she passed him, Charlie sniffed, searching for the rosemary and peppermint of her shampoo. Ashberry followed. "First time in the semifinals in fifty years!" he boomed. "Let's hear it for the Lions!" The parents hollered. Charlie opened his mouth, but no sound came out. Instead, the threat of tears locked his jaw. Fighting them, he lowered his hands and beat them together. *Get a grip*, he told himself. *Get a fucking grip*.

When Gus appeared near the end of the line, his smile was bigger than Charlie could remember. The kid's eyes glistened. Gus was a happy kid in general, but he'd taken on a dry and acerbic humor, too, as he made his way through fourth grade. Glee had become less frequent. Charlie choked out a laugh and reached up to dab his eyes. Gus's glance flitted between Leigh on one side of the parent tunnel and Charlie on the other. He drifted toward Leigh first, who reached out and pulled him into an awkward hug, her arm under the straps of his bag. And then Charlie noticed the puck poking out of the front pocket of his hoodie. Charlie could see Susy's handwriting in silver Sharpie on the top edge. Gus had finally been named the goddamned player of the game.

In spite of himself, Charlie broke ranks and crossed to his family. He grabbed the puck. "Player of the game?" he said. "The whole stinkin' game?"

"That's right!" Arnie cheered from the side. "Well deserved, Gussy!"

Charlie allowed himself one look at Leigh, whose eyes were shining, too.

"Dad." Gus shook free of Leigh and grabbed the puck back. "I've gotta get on the bus."

As Charlie stepped back to his place, he flashed forward to all the other times Gus would walk away from him—at graduations, moving days, out with his friends. He couldn't wait to see a grown-up Gus, and yet he ached for the little one, too, even before he was gone.

Leigh hadn't wanted a second baby. Charlie had made one final plea, just months before they'd left Tampa, but Leigh had curled her lip. "You really want to go back to diapers now that everything is finally getting easier?" she'd said. "I don't think so."

And it was true that Leigh and Gus were enough for Charlie. They'd been a tight unit. Charlie just hadn't realized that Jeff was in their circle, as well, that he'd been there all along. Jeff began his walk down the corridor of parents toward the bus then. Although there was no reason for him to be in the locker room with the kids and coaches, he couldn't seem to help himself.

As he passed, Jeff smiled and Charlie froze. He could see the chewing gum oozing between Jeff's back molars. "Your kid played a hell of a game." Jeff reached out and jabbed Charlie's shoulder, as if they were actually friends. "He's coming along. Tons of potential." Jeff smiled over his shoulder at Leigh. "Naturally."

Charlie kicked the ground in front of him as the parents started to file onto the bus. He twitched, aching for an escape. He scanned the fields beyond the parking lot. Any real exit plan would begin at the hotel.

When Charlie had finished a lap around the building and made it back to their room, Gus had a towel around his waist and stood frozen in front of a Scooby-Doo cartoon.

"Buddy!" Charlie said as he placed his phone and money clip on the laminate dresser. He resolutely avoided eye contact with Leigh, who lay on their bed. "That goal! So flipping clutch! Can you even believe that?"

"I can't believe it!" Gus jumped up and down as Charlie grabbed his shoulders.

"The whole game turned after that, Gus, even Arnie said so. And Arnie knows everything." Gus grinned and punched the air above his head.

"Arnie knows everything, huh?" Leigh laughed. Charlie didn't even turn toward her.

"Mom, he's been in hockey forever," Gus said. "Like, he lives and breathes hockey. He was a professional!"

"Well, I did play on Team USA, remember?"

Charlie looked over Gus's shoulder and glared at his wife. She'd been with Jeff when she'd played on Team USA. He thought of Susy then. She must know about Jeff, too. Susy probably felt sorry for him. She'd dodged all of his questions on their run that time, refusing to clue him in. *Poor, hapless Charlie.*

"I forgot something in the lobby." Charlie had to get out of the room.

"Hang on." Leigh hopped off the bed. "Gus, we'll be right back."

"I got it." Charlie wanted to tell her not to follow, not to provoke him any further, but he also wanted Gus to feel like everything was fine. He was nine. He didn't need to know their lives had changed, at least not quite yet.

Leigh caught up with him next to the ice machine twenty yards down the hall. "Charlie, wait."

"Please don't talk to me." He glanced at the row of Lions door signs. Any loud conversation would be overheard by other parents. Or worse, by Leigh's parents. He was embarrassed that Big Gus had been right all those years ago to doubt their engagement.

"Wait," Leigh said again, full volume. "I should have told you."

He turned around to face her, but pulled his arm away when she reached for his hand. "This isn't the time. You've made a fool of me.

I can't believe you." His anger blurred his vision, and he punched the ice maker with his open palm, letting loose a rumble of cubes, which thudded onto the carpet.

Leigh's eyes took on the same sadness and desperation he'd seen in the hours after she arrived home from Lake Placid, the negativity he'd been able to take away by accepting her cockamamie marriage proposal. They were happy, he'd thought. He thought he made her happy. Instead, he'd just assuaged her guilt.

"I thought it would be worth it when I made the team." Leigh's face paled as she said it. "I never even really liked him, Charlie. I never wanted to leave you. I just thought—once I had a medal in Salt Lake, I could make everyone proud. It would have been worth it."

Charlie blinked at her. "So that's what it would take? You'd trade me for an Olympic medal? A twenty-year marriage, and if you had that one thing instead, it would be worth it?"

"No." Leigh put her back against the wall and slid to the floor, her hands clasped over her knees. "I wanted it all. Both."

She made him sick. "I was never your first choice." As Charlie said it, he knew he was right. "Jeff?" He pointed at her face. "It shouldn't have been worth it for you to fuck Jeff even if you *had* made that stupid team." He looked down the hall, not caring anymore if he attracted attention. "*I* should have been worth it to you." He stooped to pick up the fallen ice cubes and threw them into the drain at the bottom of the machine. "I'm leaving," he told her.

"What?"

He didn't look at her. "I'm leaving," he repeated.

Her voice was a whine: "Leaving the tournament or leaving me?"

He shrugged. "Right now? I'm just leaving." He turned and walked out of the vestibule.

"But what about Gus?"

"You're the hockey expert," Charlie said. "You'll know how to handle it."

CHAPTER FIFTY-FOUR

GUS MACKENZIE

January 2023

January 15, 2023
Game: Nova Semifinal vs. Minnetonka—Best finish in Lions'
   History
Performance Rating: 4/5
Minutes This Week: 327
Lifetime Hours: 519
Points on the Season: 11
Quote from Mom: "Leave it all out there on the ice."

The semifinal was amazing from start to finish. William Matzke scored on his first shift, and after that, everything went the Lions' way. Passes connected, Mac saved two breakaways and a two-on-one, Georgie played defense for Rocco, who had, in fact, broken his collarbone and who stood on the bench with a sling on his arm. Gus didn't have any "egregious" errors. That was another of his mom's words.

She'd tried to pump him up before the game. "Just do what you've been doing, kid," she said. "Nothing crazy, nothing egregious."

"Where's Dad?" Gus had asked.

His mom reached a hand to his cheek, and for a second, he thought she might cry. But instead she said, "He felt sick last night, and he didn't want you to catch whatever he had. He'll be watching the livestream." She'd shown him her phone then, the text message from his dad meant for him: "Champ. You've come so far. So proud of you. Go get 'em! Xo Dad."

When he and his mom had gotten back to their room for mandatory rest time after the semi, there had been another message: "Amazing. Making history. You're a machine." Gus held the phone a little longer than he needed. He tried scrolling up to see what other messages his dad had sent to his mom, but there weren't any. This message started a whole new thread.

Fifteen minutes before the team had to be back on the bus, Gus's mom asked him how he felt. "Nervous?"

Gus thought about it. There seemed to be an energy, a tightness radiating from the middle of his chest down his arms and legs. If he really thought about breathing out, he could make the flow stop for a moment or two. But even then, his body buzzed. It was like he needed to jump or run. It was different from any nerves he'd felt before. "I really want to win," he said.

She sat down on the edge of her bed and grabbed both his arms. She looked him straight in the eyes. He'd tried to imagine what she might say. Something about "ambition," or "accountability." But instead she said something she never had before:

"Listen to me." She stopped, drew in a huge breath, and then let it out. Gus could smell the coffee she'd gotten from the hotel lobby. "There's a lot you're not going to be able to control, right?"

Gus thought about this. He couldn't control how big the kids were on the Woodbury team—huge, he knew, from trading pins with them the day before. And he couldn't really change what happened on other people's shifts. He'd added it up one time, and in a whole forty-five-minute game, he was maybe on the ice for twelve.

"Literally the only thing you can do, kiddo—and this is something I wish so much I had known when I was playing"—his mom tightened her grip on his shoulders and looked more serious than she ever had—"the only thing you can do is everything you can do."

Gus bit his lip. "What?"

"When it's your shift, work your butt off. Skate as hard as you can. Hustle. Make the plays you've practiced. If you screw up, get back."

"Okay." Gus felt a little disappointed. His mom had been so stingy with her stories from Team USA. He thought there'd be something else, some sort of secret.

"There is no secret," his mom said, as if reading his mind. "You've just got to take every bit of energy and training in your whole body and pour it out. Leave it all out there on the ice."

"Leave it all out there on the ice," Gus repeated.

His mom let go and bent over to tighten the laces on the chunky sneakers both she and his dad had. "That's it," she said. "Try as hard as you can, and then win or lose, you'll know you gave everything."

"But I want to win."

"Of course you do," his mom said. "I want that for you, too. Now let's go beat 'em." She grabbed his stick and let him carry the duffel.

"Don't forget your Team USA jersey." Gus had seen Coach Walker give it to her the night before at dinner. He wished she'd had it when they'd posed for that magazine. Big Gus had stuck the cover on his refrigerator with a magnet. Gus's mom had promised she'd go on the ice with the other Team USA players. Between his game puck in the quarterfinal and his mom on the jumbotron, maybe Nik and Colin would finally treat him like he was an important part of the team.

"I've got the jersey." She patted her backpack. "Let's get you on the bus."

CHAPTER FIFTY-FIVE

CHARLIE MACKENZIE

January 2023

I know about Jeff." Charlie texted Susy after the confrontation with Leigh by the ice machine. He was disappointed Susy hadn't told him—they were friends and training partners. And yet, he and Susy had known each other for only a few months. Although Leigh had disappeared after Lake Placid, the women had been a team for years before that.

"I'm sorry," Susy said.

"I'm leaving," he wrote back. Charlie thought of Susy's easy friendliness, the fast runs she logged on Strava, her endearing overuse of emojis. If things fell apart with Leigh, maybe there could be something between them at some point. Maybe when the dust settled.

But as Charlie drove home from Fargo in his rented Kia, all he could think about was Gus. And their home. And Big Gus and Helen. And Jamie. And the fact that Leigh had been his first call in every great and horrible situation for more than half his life.

How could she have kept this secret from him? He might have forgiven her back then. He could have understood. But instead, Leigh built a wall around every aspect of Lake Placid, culling people from their life who could have slipped him the truth.

Leigh had been so pissed off about Charlie's novel. And now he saw he'd gotten too close to those old secrets. She couldn't handle the scrutiny. When he pulled into their garage, Charlie looked at his phone for the first time since he'd stopped at McDonald's three hours before. Leigh had sent him four messages filled with apologies and promises to send updates on the semifinal and final games.

Arnie had sent: "Susy told me you're sick. Bummer, man!! Feel better!"

And then Susy had written, "Before you do anything else, could you please just do me a favor and google Sydney Kirkpatrick? Read every single article. I'm not telling you what to do, obviously, but I do think you should have all the info."

Charlie dropped his bag inside the back door, thumbed through the junk mail and bills, and then headed to his office. It was dark outside and mostly dark in the house. He turned on minimal lighting and padded through the rooms as if sneaking around. Would he still live here next week? Would he insist that Leigh be the one to find an apartment? He made it to his office and turned just the lamp on, the light dispersing in a fuzzy circle over his desk and onto the smooth reclaimed wood floor. He touched the banana-leaf wallpaper, remembering the thrill of seeing John Grisham and Colson Whitehead post author photos with that background behind them at Little Lights. And then he pulled out his manuscript. He hadn't even had the imagination to consider an affair as the reason Lavinia hadn't made it to the Olympics.

And then, Charlie flipped open his computer and googled

Sydney Kirkpatrick. He read the initial hits, as Susy suggested, and not even a handful of Rolaids from his top desk drawer could fully staunch his stomach upset. Jeff had promised Sydney a spot on the Olympic team. He'd written her letters. He'd pulled her away from training. He'd celebrated with her before cutting her from the national team and sending her home. And before and after he pressured Sydney for sex, there were others. Charlie was surprised he hadn't seen the stories before, but then again, Jeff was an "unnamed coach" in all of them. So far, they'd been buried in the local papers and deep on ESPN.com.

When he woke the next morning, Charlie had only fifteen minutes until the livestream from Nova would begin. His stomach ached again, but this time from nerves. There was no doubt Gus had already achieved a great tournament, but he'd forever cement himself in association history if the team managed to hang on. The early semifinal was solid, and Charlie sent texts to Leigh's phone for her to read to Gus. She tried to call, but he sent her to voice mail. In the hours between games, Charlie went for a run. The cold air froze his eyelashes, and when he came home, he had to hold them between his thumb and forefinger to defrost.

Showered and with a fresh cup of coffee, he logged back into the tournament's website, but Charlie nearly sprained his finger as he hit the pause button again when he saw adult players on the ice in their Team USA jerseys. He'd forgotten about the elite recognition, the first public acknowledgment of Leigh's career in more than twenty years. He didn't think he could stand to see her there in that jersey. If she had made the Olympic team, would she have stayed with Jeff?

Susy had told Charlie beforehand that she was making Leigh do the ceremony. "Critical for Gus's confidence right now," Susy had argued. "She just has to."

Charlie wondered if she'd go through with it, especially now. Despite his rage, he hit the play button. The announcer called out,

"From the 2013 bronze medal team at the Helsinki world championships, Ro-gan Reeeeeeid!" The guy shuffled out on the ice in his sneakers, gliding in the way coaches did so they wouldn't bite it during the handshakes.

Rogan waved at the crowd. When the camera closed in on his face, he mouthed, "Hi, Mom!" The announcer had said this guy had played in the Helsinki world championships, not the Olympics. Leigh was like him. Charlie dug a fingernail into the pad of his thumb. Leigh had let him make friends in Minnesota, encouraged him to get involved in the association, to talk to Jeff, without knowing what he was really walking into.

Charlie turned away from the computer and loaded coffee into the espresso maker as the announcer called another name, Eliza Gavic, from the 2018 Games in PyeongChang. Charlie peeked. The young woman gave exaggerated high fives to every other player in line. As the camera panned out from her face, Charlie could see Susy beginning her shuffle from the boards.

The announcer read her bio. "Two-time Olympic medalist and member of the US National Team for six full years, Su-sy Waaaalker!" Susy's smile was exuberant as she followed Eliza's high-five precedent, even pausing to hug a couple of players. The camera zoomed in on her as she took her place in line, and she grinned straight into it. "Go Lions!" she yelled, loudly enough for the feed to pick up the audio even though she didn't have a microphone. She threw both hands in the air, and even though his whole body felt shaky in anticipation of Leigh's intro, he grinned back at her.

And then Charlie's throat caught as he saw Leigh lined up next. She picked at the USA logo across her chest and looked over her shoulder as she walked out onto the rink. She'd pulled her hair back into a ponytail folded over on itself. As the camera began its zoom in on her face, he could see she looked paler than usual. And tired. *Good*, Charlie thought. If he had to feel this awful, her own suffering should be at least double.

The announcer began Leigh's intro: "A former Minnesota Ms. Hockey, a three-time All-American, two-time national champion with the University of Minnesota GOL-den Gophers, and a member of Team USA from 1998 to 2001, Leigh! Mac-KENNNzie!"

Her jeans looked new, Charlie noticed. He didn't remember that particular dark wash from the laundry, which along with the grocery shopping, homework help, and hockey carpooling, was one of his weekly chores. Leigh refreshed her own wardrobe, but never knew when Gus had grown out of a drawerful of shirts or skipped two sizes in skates. Charlie glanced away from the screen to dump a spoonful of sugar into his latte.

When he looked back, Leigh had made it straight to Susy, skipping the line of high fives. Susy put her arm around Leigh and tipped her head in close. Charlie frowned. Susy's loyalty was hers. She said something to Leigh, her lips almost touching his wife's ear, but Charlie couldn't decipher it. As the camera zoomed in on Leigh's face, her arms fell to her sides and her eyes got big.

For a moment, Charlie thought she wasn't going to do anything— she wouldn't say anything or smile or give a thumbs-up. The camera started to turn toward the next player in line, but Charlie could hear Leigh shout, "Wait!"

"What are you—" Charlie said aloud. Leigh pulled on her jersey sleeve and freed one arm. Charlie leaned forward. He could see tears collecting in his wife's eyes. The announcer began his next intro, but Leigh raised her hand to the camera operator. "Just a second." Charlie read her lips.

And then, her jersey was up over her head. Her ponytail caught in the collar, but she shook it free. As the camera finally began its pan away, Charlie hit pause and could see the threadbare cotton of his Headwaters T-shirt, the black of her jacket visible beneath the wearing fabric, a divot in the neckline where the ribbing had finally given way. The USA jersey dangled inside out from her fingers, and Leigh's eyes trained on the camera even as it left her face.

All those years ago when Charlie had earned that T-shirt, he had wondered if he had been hallucinating when he finally saw Leigh for the final time at mile 45. But she was really there through the end of the whole thing. Every three or four steps on the trail, when Charlie hadn't known if he'd make it another quarter mile, Leigh had told him how amazing he was. How inspiring.

In the same time frame, maybe on the same day, she'd been calling Jeff. She'd kept Jeff's letters hidden from Charlie. She'd chosen Jeff even as she'd shown up at the ultra.

Charlie hit play again on the livestream. In the wide camera shot, Charlie could see how out of place Leigh looked in his T-shirt. She'd worn it to sleep forever, donning an alternate only when it was in the wash. Charlie had shoved it into her bag when she'd left for Lake Placid. He'd zipped it into the front pocket with her toothbrush and dental floss.

And now, everyone else on the ice at Nova had USA emblazoned across their chests. The print on the race T-shirt was so faded that if people didn't already know it—weren't familiar with the sticklike font—they wouldn't be able to figure it out. The Nova organizers would undoubtedly be annoyed with Leigh. She ruined the photo op by wearing her pajamas. And she looked so serious, still staring at the camera even as everyone else smiled and waved at the fans.

Leigh wore that shirt for him. That was obvious. Now, Charlie just needed to decide if he believed her.

CHAPTER FIFTY-SIX

GUS MACKENZIE

January 2023

January 15, 2023
Game: Nova Final vs. Woodbury! We made history!
Performance Rating: 4/5
Minutes This Week: 372
Lifetime Hours: 520
Points on the Season: 11
Quote from Ashberry: "Sticks up."

In the third period, Woodbury led the Lions 3–2. Gus had followed his mom's advice about leaving it all out there. Every time he got back to the bench, he felt completely out of breath, his whole body screaming for a break.

He hadn't done anything super wrong so far. He stayed in position. "Good shift," Coach Walker had told him more than once, but Gus knew his main job was to give the top players a break, so they could score goals. Each of the top two lines had points and Georgie had blocked three shots herself already. "Did that hurt?" Gus asked after a puck had slammed into her belly, at a spot below her chest pad.

"I got it," she said. Georgie's dad had driven up to Fargo the night before. He arrived at about the same time Gus's dad had left. Kids from other teams had asked for his autograph. Gus wondered what advice NHL star Dirk Magnussen had given to Georgie. Had he told her to "leave it all out there on the ice"?

With three minutes and six seconds left in the game, William Matzke dished a pass to Hank Teeterow, who buried it on a sick snipe. Gus threw both of his arms up. Even Coach Ashberry was yelling, punching the air over his head. *Momentum*, Gus thought. That was something Coach Walker talked about. It meant the energy was swinging in the Lions' direction.

But right after the goal, the Woodbury center won the face-off, hustled into the offensive zone, and scored on another snipe to the upper-left corner. 4–3. The wave of happiness and hope that everyone felt seconds earlier just crashed. The time-out pep talk during which Coach Walker said they could "get it back," did nothing to lessen the pressure Gus felt building in his chest. He took the ice for what he thought would be his last shift and skated harder and faster and smarter than he remembered ever doing before. Everyone was psyched when he drew a penalty with two minutes and twenty-six seconds remaining. Ashberry pulled Mac, and the first line took the ice.

Though they pummeled the Woodbury goalie, and even when the second line kept the puck in the zone for a full seventy seconds, they couldn't get a shot in. The Woodbury fans shouted, "Three! Two! One!" as the clock ran out.

When the buzzer sounded, the band of energy that Gus had

struggled to control wound out of him, and tears exploded from his eyes. The bench doors opened and Gus skated out. He noticed Georgie, her head rested on the rink, her knees folded beneath her. As he got closer, he could hear her wailing.

He dropped next to Georgie. "It's okay." He took his glove off and rested his hand on her back. It felt warm.

"We lost," she sobbed.

Gus looked up at the scoreboard. 4–3. For sure, they'd lost. The other team had thrown their gloves up and helmets off and now clumped together with their coaches near the bench, shouting and cheering. Gus checked the stands, and all of the Lions' parents were on their feet. His mom and Georgie's dad were sitting next to each other in the front row. They were all clapping and cheering. Most of them were smiling. No one over there looked sad at all. "Georgie," Gus said. "Look."

He reached down and pushed her helmet toward the bench, lifting her eyes so she could see the parents. He heard her sniff, and then she pushed herself up to kneeling. Gus stood next to her and grabbed her hand. "Come on," he said. Ashberry and Walker had already led most of the kids toward the stands. Walker pointed at the ice next to her and the team lined up before the cheering parents. Gus pushed Georgie in front of him.

When they got there, Gus looked right at his mom. Her eyes were shining, and Gus realized she was crying just like he was. But she didn't look disappointed. She was clapping as fast as anyone else, and her smile was the real one, not the one for the Marvel Universe.

"Sticks up!" Ashberry shouted, and everyone raised theirs toward the ceiling. The parents' cheers got louder, and then without anyone telling them when to do it, the team all crashed their sticks down on the ice in one big crack. Big Gus's cheers boomed down from the top of the bleachers.

CHAPTER FIFTY-SEVEN

LEIGH MACKENZIE

January 2023

Twenty minutes after the clock ran out, Georgie stepped out of the cheer line next to Leigh, her eyes still red-rimmed and her nose dripping.

"You okay, kiddo?" Leigh asked. She followed her a step or two away from the group and looked futilely over her shoulder for Susy, but she'd already led the rest of the kids onto the bus. Gus had been in the middle of the pack, all smiles.

Georgie shuddered. "I didn't have a good tournament." She bit her lips and couldn't stop her body from shaking.

Leigh eased her bag off her shoulder and crouched down in front of her. "Are you kidding me? If you weren't on this team, there's no way we would have even made the semis. You've been our absolute star."

Georgie shook her head. "No, that's Nik. Or Abe or William."

"Lady," Leigh said, invoking the same tone she used to take with her own teammates, "you are the only person on the ice who could've taken Rocco's spot. And you blocked at least four shots today." Leigh mentally scrolled back over the Nova games. "And you had the assist on that shorty against Mahtomedi." It might have been the play of the tournament, now that Leigh was thinking about it, a beautiful goal against the top-rated team in a critical moment. She closed her eyes, remembering that she'd missed the other clutch goal, the one scored by her own son.

"But it was my fault Rocco got hurt, and I couldn't get the goal in the end."

Leigh reached up and pushed Georgie's hair off her face. She flashed on the braid she'd done for her mom at the Olympic selection camp. It was true that Rocco got hit after Georgie's only turnover of the tournament, but that was hardly her fault. "Georgie, did you see me on the ice before the final game? With the Team USA players?"

"Yeah?" Georgie sniffed.

"So you believe me when I say I know hockey, right? I used to be pretty good?"

Georgie laughed and wiped her nose with the back of her hand. "I guess."

"You guess?" Leigh fake-punched her arm in mock indignation. "Well, I know enough to tell you something for sure: You are the hands-down leader of this team. You're the one with the most hustle and the most heart, and watching you play just—" Leigh looked up, embarrassed by her sudden emotion. *Get it together,* she told herself. *The kid is nine.* "It just reminds me of everything good in this sport. You're something special."

Leigh smiled, hoping Georgie would return it. She did. "Okay," Georgie said.

"Okay," Leigh repeated.

The girl picked up her bag and walked back toward the bus just as the last of the parents had boarded.

Gus shouted Georgie's name as they shuffled down the aisle, gesturing toward the open seat next to him, and Leigh slid in next to Susy.

"She okay?" Susy asked. "I saw you talking—"

"She's incredible, Suse," Leigh said. "Wow. You must be so proud." She didn't give Susy a chance to answer. "Will this be brutal?" Leigh asked. Georgie hadn't been the only teary-eyed player who'd walked through the tunnel. The loss had hit hard. *Good*, Leigh thought. *Shows you care.*

"Nah, they'll be fine." Susy held out a giant-size bag of Twizzlers to Leigh, who grabbed two. "Cathy gave them a treat bag. They have a trophy." She nodded toward the front, where a giant silver cup took up the seat next to the manager. "They'll be laughing—or sleeping—within ten minutes."

Leigh wasn't sure what to say. "I'm surprised I got so wrapped up in that final. I thought I was immune to hockey nerves after all this time." During the game, she'd felt all of her old emotions, the exuberance of a snipe, the spine-rounding disappointment of getting beaten in the defensive zone. For the first time since Lake Placid, Leigh had actually missed the game. She missed it even more when the kids lined up for their ovation. She couldn't stop the tears from rolling, especially when she thought about Charlie skipping the whole thing because of her.

She'd checked her phone after the on-ice recognition, but Charlie hadn't texted. For all she knew, he hadn't watched her, didn't even know about her effort to show him that Team Charlie was always a million times more important than Team USA. He would probably take the Headwaters shirt with him when he left her, she realized. After the game, Leigh had texted Charlie a photo of the team on the ice with their medals. She'd watched Charlie's reply ellipsis pop up and then disappear.

"Have you heard from Charlie?" Susy whispered.

Leigh shook her head. She was too nervous to ask Susy if she had.

Just seconds before the bus left, Jeff finally boarded, his baseball cap as low as possible over his eyes and sunglasses on.

"Slimeball," Susy said.

"Was Jeff in the locker room with you guys today?"

Susy shook her head. "Too hungover. He passed out next to the pool last night, and Cathy Kelliher had to get security to haul him back to his room. She told me she's putting in an official complaint with the board."

Leigh's eyes bugged. She wondered what the board would do when the "unnamed coach" in the Team USA stories was revealed as Jeff.

"And," Susy added, "I might have sent Cathy a link or two about Sydney Kirkpatrick, Alison Collins, and Sheila Cooper."

"Whoa." Leigh tilted her head up toward the emergency exit and closed her eyes. It wouldn't be long before there'd be links about her, too.

"Enough is enough." Susy touched Leigh's arm with the bag of Twizzlers, and she took two more. "I know you think you're superwoman and all, but really, do you want Jeff Carlson influencing our kids? Other girls? I know you don't."

Leigh didn't. She turned around to check on Gus, who was laughing with Georgie, just as Susy said he would be. He'd had a great tournament, proven himself. He didn't need Jeff Carlson. And now that Charlie knew everything—now that she'd lost everything— she didn't need to keep any secrets.

"I'm going to retract my statement," Leigh said, thinking of Georgie's proximity to Jeff. His behavior at the tournament had crossed so many lines. He became dangerous in a way that she'd never known him to be before. She pictured Sydney's face, too. Those poor girls.

"What statement?" Susy asked.

"I wrote a letter of support for Jeff. I answered some questions. I'm retracting it. I'm not going to help him."

Susy linked her arm with Leigh's and squeezed. "That's a good step." Leigh didn't pull away, but she didn't squeeze back. "Why in the world did you agree to help him in the first place? It's not like you owe him anything. He didn't actually put you on the Olympic team like he said he would."

Leigh stared at Susy. Hadn't she been in the room when Gus was picked? "You don't know why I helped him? You don't know what he did for me?" Susy shook her head. Leigh studied her for any sign of guile. Her friend's face looked open and concerned, her eyes bright. "Don't bullshit me." Leigh pulled her arm away. Susy had to know.

"I swear, I have no idea what you're talking about."

Leigh looked back at the seat in front of her, her heart pounding. "Jeff said Gus wouldn't make the team," she whispered. "He said he could make it happen if I helped him, if I wrote that letter." Out loud, it seemed as awful as their deal in Lake Placid had been. Shady and selfish and just gross. Why had she decided Squirt hockey was worth her integrity all over again?

Susy touched Leigh's forearm. "Leigh," she whispered, "look at me."

Leigh wanted to refuse, but it sounded petulant in her head. Instead, she forced herself to make eye contact. "What?"

"Gus would have made it anyway."

"No." Leigh felt her ponytail swinging as she insisted. "Jeff said—"

"I was in the room," Susy interrupted. "Ashberry wanted him. And I also wanted him. You've seen Gus play. The kid has an incredible sense of position and unbeatable discipline." Susy gestured toward the back where the kids were sitting, and Leigh's mouth gaped. "Jeff wanted him, too," Susy said, "but he doesn't actually decide. Gus was always, from the very first tryout, a kid I'd pick for this team."

Leigh folded over on herself, her arms around her middle and the crown of her head against the seat in front of her. "No," she whimpered. If what Susy said was true, once again she'd sacrificed everything for nothing.

Susy rubbed her back. "Yes. He earned it."

Leigh kept her palms against her eyes. "Are people looking at me?" It occurred to her that she might become a spectacle.

"It looks like all the parents are sleeping." Susy grabbed Leigh's ponytail and tugged it. Leigh sat up.

"I don't know if Charlie is going to be home when I get back," she said. "I'm not sure if he's going to forgive me."

"I don't know, either, Leigh-Leigh," Susy said. "But it's going to be okay."

Leigh's father had said that to her when she'd gotten home from Lake Placid, too. She had been certain it wasn't true. And, in lots of ways, she'd been right. It had been terrible—not really okay ever— but then there had been a new kind of okay.

"I decided something," Susy said.

"Yeah?"

"I love these boys and all, but I'm switching Georgie to girls' hockey."

"Really? Before Peewees?" Everyone said the competition was best with boys through middle school.

"I'm not sure about next winter," Susy said, "but for sure in the summer. This year, I'm going to field an all-girls' team. I've been running that Sunday Skate I told you about. I want to grow the game, you know? I want a sisterhood." She pointed toward Jeff, whom they could see a row up across the aisle, his head collapsed into his hand and a plastic bag in his lap, presumably for vomit. Hardly a great example for the kids.

"Yuck," Leigh agreed.

"I'm going to ask you something, and you're not allowed to answer right away." Leigh recognized the same mischievousness in Susy's eyes she'd seen in Prague that time when they'd gone exploring.

"What?" Leigh asked.

"Come coach some girls with me." Susy gestured at the back of the bus where the team was giggling. "Love the game again, Leigh."

Leigh sucked her breath in and felt tears building like they had in the arena, like they had outside when she'd consoled Georgie. "I don't have time—"

"Nope." Susy held up her hand. "Not yet. I'm not talking to you about this again for a full week. I'll work with your schedule, and you'll be an assistant." Leigh imagined herself in a black jacket and wind pants, she felt the spot on her sternum where her whistle would fall and imagined a breeze in her hair as she skated with the kids. "Let yourself love hockey again." Susy patted her thigh. "You deserve it."

CHAPTER FIFTY-EIGHT

CHARLIE MACKENZIE

January 2023

The text from Susy came as the sun set and Charlie closed the shades in his office. "Home in an hour," she said. "FYI."

Charlie sent back a quick "Thanks" and started to feel the same nervousness he'd staved off as he watched the final game on the livestream. He'd cried as the team lined up in front of the parents at the end. He could see the back of Leigh's head in the front row, her hands beating together as fast and hard as anyone's. Charlie had barely eaten all day. He'd skipped breakfast that morning and choked down a Clif Bar after his run. Susy had given him "kudos" on the workout from the bus.

Finally, Charlie flipped on an East Coast NHL game and ate a couple of handfuls of tortilla chips. When he heard the garage door lift, his heart rate ramped up to run level, and he could feel damp patches in each armpit of his Little Lights T-shirt.

Gus ran in with his medal in his hand. Charlie lifted him and hugged hard.

"Dad!" Gus squealed. "You're crushing me!"

"Crushing you with pride, maybe." Gus's head had that musty hockey helmet smell. "Second place at Nova! Can you even believe that? Highest finish in program history!"

Gus pushed back against Charlie's shoulders and scooted out of his arms. "But we didn't win." He wrinkled his nose. "We almost won, but we didn't."

Leigh was there behind him then. "But your grit and tenacity!" She kept her eyes on Gus. "You showed so much of that this weekend. You'll get 'em next time."

Leigh handed Gus his bag of clothes. "Go shower, okay?" she said. Charlie studied her face, but the only evidence of nerves was a tiny twitch at her eyebrow.

Gus eyed the two of them suspiciously. "You don't look sick," he said to Charlie.

"I feel much better." Charlie ruffled the kid's hair. In some ways, he did feel better. He'd read Sydney Kirkpatrick's account of Jeff's behavior. The other women's stories were the same. None of them had made the teams, and Jeff had made them all promises.

These other stories, though, they didn't change the fact that Leigh had lied to him for their entire life, that their marriage had commenced on the heels of a giant lie. But after reading about Jeff's pattern, Charlie did feel something besides anger.

"I didn't know if you'd be here," Leigh said once Gus had trotted up the stairs. "I thought you might not." She glanced back at the hockey equipment she'd left at the back door. "And, honestly, I'd understand completely if you weren't. I'm awful. I've done terrible things."

Charlie remembered her rounder cheeks, the downy hairs that had framed her forehead in curly wisps that summer before the

Olympic selection camp. She'd hated those curls, but he'd loved them. "When did Jeff first call you?" Charlie turned around and walked to the kitchen.

"He wrote me a letter," she said. "In July that year."

"Before Headwaters?"

She didn't answer, so Charlie looked back at her. "Yeah," she said finally.

Charlie flinched. "And he said what?" He grabbed the open Heineken he'd started sipping as he waited for them.

Leigh sat down across from him at the kitchen table, her face gray. "Do we have to do this? You want to know?"

Charlie nodded. "You owe it to me."

So, she told him. There'd been the letter, the phone cards, the insinuation that he could influence Coach Miller.

About four minutes into her story, Gus came down in his pajamas. "I charged the iPad for you, buddy." Charlie handed it to him. "Go watch Netflix. You earned it."

Once their son had disappeared again, Charlie pointed at Leigh, signaling her to continue. He winced when she told him about the champagne in Jeff's car, his assurance that she'd be on the roster. "I thought it would all be worth it if I made it." She said it again just like she had in Fargo. "But I've thought about what you said. It *wouldn't* have been worth it. Sacrificing my connection with you and Gus, that's not worth anything." She started to cry then and lowered her head into her arms.

Charlie felt sad for her in an abstract way, as if he were watching a television show about someone who'd made a disastrous choice.

"What are you going to do?" Leigh asked.

"You skipped part of the story," Charlie said.

She poked her head up, and her flyaway curls looked just like they'd done when she'd been young. "No," she said, "that's the whole thing. I told you every single part of that two weeks." She looked desperate.

Charlie reached out and smoothed the hair away from her forehead. "I'm talking about Sydney Kirkpatrick," he said. "And Alison Collins." Leigh sat all the way up and shook her head. "And," Charlie continued, "Sheila Cooper."

"No," Leigh said. "Those stories are different. They don't explain any of this away. If you decide to stay, you have to know exactly how horrible I am."

Charlie breathed in. He stared at the calendar he'd written out last week, the list of obligations in green dry-erase marker. He'd indicated the Nova Tournament in big block letters with firecracker lines extending from them. It was supposed to be such a big deal for Gus. He guessed it *had* been a big deal for Gus. Charlie remembered the satisfying crack of the kids' sticks on the ice at the end, the salute to the team and to the parents.

"I read the other women's stories, Leigh. I know you made bad choices. The worst one was never telling me, letting me think everything was different than it actually was."

Leigh lifted her chin and rolled her shoulders back, as if ready to take a punch without defending herself.

"But," he said, "I don't know why you think you're so special. Did you read the article about Sheila? She has the same goddamned story about the champagne. He used you." Charlie bit his lip. "You're self-centered and manipulative," he said, and then softly, "but you're also a victim."

He stood up from the table and knocked the wood next to the Heineken. "I'm going to go read to Gus."

She waited.

"Anything else?" he asked.

"I'm so sorry," Leigh said.

Charlie flicked off the kitchen light, leaving her in the dark. "I think you said that already."

CHAPTER FIFTY-NINE

LEIGH MACKENZIE

January 2023

Do you want me to sleep on the couch?" Leigh asked Charlie after she dumped all of her tournament clothes except for his race shirt in the hamper.

"Are you going to stay on your own side?"

The hint of mirth in the question doubled her over, and she burst into tears. "I'm sorry," she said, and she disappeared into her closet. She wanted to go to him, to kneel beside the bed, grab his hand, and beg him to stay in spite of everything. But his final indictment from the kitchen—"self-centered and manipulative"—kept her from rushing him. She didn't want to manipulate him into forgiveness.

"I'm really mad about this." Charlie didn't look up from his book when she came back out in the ultramarathon T-shirt. He hadn't yet said anything about the on-ice ceremony. "But I'm not sure I want to throw our whole life away over it, either. I need to think."

Leigh cried harder. It could have been worse. He could have left already, but so far Charlie didn't want to trade her for Susy. She might not have to tell her parents and brother—and Gus! *Oh, Gus*—that she'd ruined her marriage before it had even started.

"Okay." She walked toward the bathroom. "I'm really happy to hear you say that." She was crying so hard her voice sounded like a croak.

When she came out, Charlie was still reading. "I don't want to talk to you anymore tonight," he said. "I'm not ready."

She clasped her hands in front of her chest and nodded, eager to do anything he asked just as long as he wouldn't be calling a divorce attorney first thing in the morning.

"Think about those other women," Charlie said as Leigh lay down. "They're younger than you are, right? What are you hoping will happen for them? Do you want everyone to think they're liars and sore losers?"

"But—" Leigh started to say.

"Nope." Charlie turned his light off and rolled away from her. "I don't want to talk anymore tonight. For sure."

Leigh lay awake for at least an hour. Every time she closed her eyes, she saw Sydney Kirkpatrick's St. Christopher medal, or Jeff's stubble and flashing eyes, or Susy's flyaway bangs that she'd braided out of her face in their dorm room. She had the stupid thought that if her brother hadn't given Gus those toddler skates she would've been able to keep him out of hockey, she would have been able to leave every bit of this scandal in the past. Charlie would never have had to know.

But, at the same time, *Leigh* had known. What's more, she had known that Jeff and Susy were here in Liston Heights. She'd chosen their blue house and the best hockey association for Gus, all the while knowing that the advantage for him would require her to dive right back into the fray. Maybe on some level she'd wanted to face it after all this time.

Susy had said she deserved to love the game again. Was that really true? Even after everything?

In the morning, Leigh handed Charlie the latte she'd started making for him when she heard his footsteps above her head. She'd watched a YouTube tutorial about latte art at five thirty, but she'd failed at the tree shape and ended up stirring the whole thing.

"You're right about the women." Charlie took the mug, but he didn't quite meet her eyes as she spoke. "I need to call Safe Sport. Did Susy tell you about Safe Sport?"

Charlie nodded as he took a sip of the coffee. Leigh wondered how much they'd been texting, but quickly pushed her jealousy away. He was still here with her, at least for now.

"But if I call Safe Sport," Leigh said, "and if I speak to reporters like Sydney and Alison and Sheila have"—she studied Charlie, but he looked calm as he sipped her coffee—"then everyone will know."

Charlie raised an eyebrow. "Isn't that the point?"

"I mean, everyone will know that this happened in 2001 when we were dating. They'll know we got engaged right afterward. They'll know I—" Leigh collapsed into one of their kitchen chairs and cracked the knuckles on her left hand. Charlie waited for her. "It's just—it's your privacy, too."

Charlie walked to the refrigerator and grabbed out the implements of Gus's lunch. "I don't need anyone to tell me whether I should still be married to you," he said. "That's between us."

Leigh hoped he still didn't want to throw away their whole lives.

"But this Safe Sport complaint?" Charlie continued. "That's between you and your conscience, right? It's about what life should be like for other women in sport." He spread mayonnaise over the bread and didn't seem to expect her to answer.

Instead of going straight to her office that morning, Leigh texted Nicole in the Starbucks drive-thru line. "Bring you a coffee?"

She walked into Nicole's corner office with a decaf caramel soy latte, and Nicole smiled at her.

"I'm going to report Jeff." Leigh said it as she placed the coffee next to a framed photo of Nicole's daughters. Nicole stood, walked around her desk, and grabbed Leigh in a hug, her arms tight around her rib cage. Leigh patted Nicole's back, surprised by her fervor.

"You got there," Nicole said before she let go. "I bet it was painful, yeah? Come sit down." She grabbed her wrist just as she had on the trail when Leigh had made her confession.

Leigh started to cry again and took a tissue from Nicole's desk. "I can't do this now," she said.

"Okay, no problem." Nicole swiped her hands over her desk, indicating that she wouldn't ask any more questions. "You tell me what you need. I've got nothing until noon. You want me to sit here while you call Safe Sport?"

Leigh nodded, shocked that company and moral support were indeed what she wanted. "And," Leigh said, "you're a lawyer."

"Duh." Nicole smiled. "Somebody made me a senior partner, remember?"

"I think I should go to the media." Leigh put her elbows on the desk and pressed her fingers into her forehead. She couldn't believe she was saying it, but she had to prove to Charlie that she'd changed, and she did owe it to the other women. They were younger, like Charlie had said. Some of them hadn't had time to become senior partners or managing directors yet. She had to publicly voice her complaint to give theirs added credibility.

"Nicole, who's the right media contact, and am I going to get sued?"

Nicole squinted. "Did you sign anything with Jeff's attorney?"

"A letter," Leigh admitted. "And I answered questions in a deposition."

Nicole tipped her chin up. "Did you lie in the letter or in the deposition?"

"No," Leigh said, slowly. "It's just that the facts look different to me now, in context with the others' statements."

"That's fine." Nicole steepled her fingers. "And you're not going to contradict any of the facts you established when you go public?"

Leigh's stomach twisted. *Public.* It had been hard to change out of Charlie's shirt that morning, but she couldn't very well wear it to the office. She fingered the collar of her cashmere sweater instead. "No," she said.

"Then you're good." Nicole smiled. "Go ahead and make your call."

By lunchtime, it was all over. Leigh had given her statement to Safe Sport. Nicole had called a PR specialist she'd used before and asked for a reporter at the *Star Tribune*. Together they pitched the story via email.

"Will she write it?" Leigh asked as they hit send on the message to the paper.

"A Me Too exposé featuring a former Ms. Hockey and a prominent local youth coach? Uh, yeah." Leigh's arms fell to her sides. So many people would know. "So, you know you have to tell your family first, right?" Nicole said. "Anyone who shouldn't find out in the morning paper."

"Oh shit." Leigh pictured her childhood bedroom, the wall of hockey photos, the empty spot in the bookshelf where the Olympic medal was supposed to go. Her dad would be so disappointed. She remembered his shaking hands on the champagne he'd popped when they'd celebrated her engagement all those years ago. He'd been convinced then that she was rushing things. Now he'd know why, know she'd manipulated Charlie and lied to them all forever.

"Here's what you do," Nicole said. Leigh had never been so grateful for someone else's bossiness. "You go home, and you and Charlie decide how you're going to talk to your parents. And"—Nicole grabbed her hand again—"you probably thought of this already, but you're going to have to tell Gus something. Since you reengaged with Jeff last fall because he promised to put Gus on the A-team, Gus will have to know at least part of the story. He'll hear some of those details from other kids and families."

"Oh shit," Leigh said again. How could she tell Gus that she hadn't believed in him? That she'd pulled strings to get him on the team?

"My kids are little, so I don't know how you'd explain it to a nine-year-old, but I know you." Nicole winked at her. "You'll know what to say."

After Charlie dropped Gus at practice that night, Leigh updated her husband on her progress. He still hadn't hugged her, Leigh noted, since she'd arrived home. He hadn't run his hand along her back as he walked past her at the table. But he hadn't packed a bag, either. In fact, he'd unpacked from the trip and done his laundry. Leigh had had twenty years to put the Jeff debacle in its place. Charlie was just finding out that he'd staked his whole life on the aftermath of Leigh's trauma.

"How do you want to tell Gus?" Charlie leaned against their countertop.

Leigh had thought about Gus that afternoon when she was supposed to be reading financial statements for a new prospect. "What if we say, 'You might hear people say you don't belong, but you proved at Nova that you do'?"

Charlie squinted at the chandelier. "We could say that you knew Jeff and Susy from a long time ago, and they agreed Gus deserved a shot even though he was new."

"Yep." Leigh felt eager to affirm Charlie. "That's the way we play it." She took in her husband's flannel, his slouchy jeans. He looked like a writer. He always had. "I'm sorry about your book," Leigh said. "You can write whatever you want." She waited, but he just kicked his shoe against the floor. She went on. "Clearly, you knew how important Lake Placid was for me. It's a good story." Now that she'd be telling her side of it to the press, that she'd be linked with the other women publicly, it hardly mattered if Charlie wanted to write a fictional account of what had happened back then. He'd been right, anyway, about her flawed personality. "Overconfident," Charlie had called her in the book, and "weak." Still, it hurt that he thought of her that way, that he'd forged a friendship with Susy, that they'd had secrets, too.

"You know what's really bothering me?" Charlie asked. His jaw twitched, and before she could even think about it, Leigh was crying again. She sank into a chair at the kitchen table, her body too heavy to support her anymore.

"What?"

"You didn't trust me." Charlie wiped at his eyes with his sleeve. "I was all in on you, and you knew it. We told each other everything. And then, when something really important happened—something that basically ruined your life—you didn't tell me."

Leigh scooted her chair back and rested her forehead on the edge of the table. She stared down at her argyle socks. "I betrayed you. How could I tell you that?"

"I don't know." Charlie was quiet, and Leigh snuck a glance at him, her nose grazing the table as she looked up. "I don't know what would have happened if you'd told me right then. But what about all the time since then?"

"I thought I could make it right by just, like, being great. I thought I could just make our lives great." Leigh remembered the backpack she'd bought for Charlie when he'd defended his MFA, the surprise trip to Puerto Rico after she'd gotten the job at Bonham Royal.

Leigh heard Charlie pull a chair out across from her, and she forced herself to sit all the way up and look at him. "I want a new deal," Charlie said.

Leigh was willing to give him anything at this point. "Okay, done."

Charlie smiled, and Leigh held her breath. Certainly, he wouldn't smile if he didn't still love her. "You don't even know what I want."

"But I'm going to give it to you."

"That's not how this negotiation is going to work." Charlie shook his head. "Do any of your work negotiations happen like that? Like, you immediately agree to mysterious terms?"

"I mean, no." Leigh untucked her camisole and pulled it up to wipe her nose. "Sorry," she said.

"There are tissues on the counter." Charlie pointed at the box he kept next to the potted cactus he'd moved to three houses now. When Leigh sat back down, her first two tissues were already soaked with snot and tears. Charlie continued. "Gus is getting older, and I want to have more of a career."

"What?" This wasn't what she expected.

"I've been the default parent forever, right? Meal planning and summer camps and doctors' visits. And I've loved it! But now I want to use my degree. I want to write, and I want to teach, probably, and so we'll need a new arrangement about how things go."

Leigh nodded. Of course they could reorganize. They lived near her parents now. They could hire a babysitter.

"And you *have* made our lives great," Charlie continued. "Well, mostly great." He sighed. "But everything—all the moves and all of the scheduling and decisions—has been about you."

Leigh's heart sank. He still thought she was selfish.

"You're always proving yourself." Charlie said it like an accusation. "I need you to stop trying to be great. With you, it's always about the next big thing."

Leigh felt her shoulders round and her chin drop.

Charlie went on, "A list of accomplishments isn't a real life."

It wasn't? Leigh wasn't sure how to think about herself if "impressive" wasn't how she'd be described.

"And," Charlie said, "I need you to show up for me and show up for Gus without thinking about how we reflect on you."

Leigh's head felt heavy. Did she do that? Did she calculate Charlie and Gus and their accomplishments as part of her self-worth? She didn't think so, but he clearly did. He wanted her to be different. All of the traits she'd always valued in herself—work ethic, ambition, relentlessness, strategic thinking—they were her. She *was* being real. But maybe Charlie didn't like the real her, at least not anymore.

"I don't know if I understand how to do what you're asking." It came out as a whisper and the soaked tissue Leigh rubbed at her cheek tore in the middle.

"That's okay." Charlie still seemed calm. "It's a big change and a lot of terms, but that's what I need."

If she had any idea how to do what he wanted, she'd get it done right that second.

"If you can't do it," Charlie said, "I might need to make a bigger change."

CHAPTER SIXTY

GUS MACKENZIE

January 2023

January 18, 2023
Practice
Performance Rating: 3/5, back to normal
Minutes This Week: 77
Lifetime Hours: 521
Quote from Coach Walker: "Pressure is a privilege."

Gus had thought that the goal he'd scored at Nova in the quarterfinal might mean that he'd broken through, that he'd keep up with William and Nik and Georgie in practice. But he was still the same kid, still hanging out on the third line. He knew it was still the same because he made the wrong pass in the breakout drill in the first practice after Nova, and the team had to start over. Owen had said, "Come on, man," under his breath, but Coach Ashberry had been loud enough for everyone: "Think, Mackenzie!"

At least his head hadn't been up his ass that time.

When the kids took a knee at the end of practice, Coach Walker gave a talk about how the success at Nova put a big target on their backs. Every other district team would be trying their hardest to beat them, wanting to prove that the Nova result had been a fluke. "But it wasn't a fluke," she said. "You fought tooth and nail for that finish. The pressure you feel is a privilege." Gus remembered Georgie's head on the ice and the tears that had smeared all over his face. He'd tried hard on his shifts, but he hadn't been on the ice at the end. He hadn't ever been on the ice at the end, not for any of the team's important games. Gus knew this meant that he wasn't a player people counted on.

Sure, Gus had gotten the game puck that one time, but if you listed the five most impactful players on the Lions—the Youth Hockey Hub Live Blog had, in fact, done that—Gus wasn't one of them.

Gus could tell something was kind of weird when both of his parents picked him up from practice that night. "We thought we'd get shakes at McDonald's and then go visit Big Gus and Gram," his mom said.

Instead of going through the drive-thru, his dad parked and led Gus inside. Once they'd sat in a booth next to the drink machine, his mom started talking. "Buddy, I have to tell you something."

Gus blinked and imagined what it could be. The last time they'd done something like this, the news had been that they were leaving Tampa, that he would no longer play hockey with Tyler. "Are we moving again?" Gus wrapped his hands around his cup, hanging on. "We just got to Liston Heights."

"No." Gus's dad laughed a little. "We're staying."

"Remember how I grew up here?" his mom said. "In that same house with Big Gus and Gram?"

"Duh." Gus had known that since he was a baby.

"Okay, well, I also knew Coach Walker and Jeff Carlson when I was young." She looked at him with wide eyes, like it was some kind of shock, but Gus already knew that she and Coach Walker had been roommates on Team USA. He and Georgie talked about it all the time. Coach Carlson had told him during Nova warm-ups that Gus reminded him of his mom. "Same fire," Coach Carlson had said.

"I know." Gus sipped his shake so hard that his head hurt. "Hang on," he said. "Brain freeze." He put the cup on the table and rubbed his eyebrows. When it had passed, his mom was still staring at him.

"Okay, well, this part you don't know: I asked Coach Carlson to pay special attention to you in tryouts. He decided to do me that favor because I'd been on Team USA."

Gus thought back to the tryouts, how he'd been beaten in drills by just about everyone in the top pool. He remembered the surprise when his parents had jumped on his bed with the news that he'd made the team. "So, I wasn't good enough." Kids had told him that from the beginning. Even William had said he'd have to get faster.

"No," Gus's dad said. "Your scores were always good enough, and the coaches always wanted you. But Mom also asked for them to pay special attention."

Gus thought about the pictures in his mom's bedroom and the photos Big Gus had shown him, his mom's seventeenth goal of the Squirt season. Gus thought about Nova and Georgie collapsing on the ice when the buzzer sounded. "I get it," Gus said to his parents. "And I have something to tell you, too."

"Okay." Gus's dad looked worried as he shoved three fries into his mouth.

"Next year," Gus said, "I don't want to be on the A-team."

His dad's jaw dropped open, and one of the half-chewed fries fell out. "No, honey, that's not what this is about. It's just that Mom is doing some work with Team USA, and we thought you might hear about some of this from other kids and—"

"I want to be the guy everyone counts on." Gus pictured Nik Ashberry in the face-off circle. "I want to be on the ice at the end, win or lose. I don't want to be third or fourth choice."

"But between now and next year—" his dad started to say, but his mom reached up and grabbed his dad's hand.

"So, what are you saying?" she asked him.

"I'm skipping A-team tryouts next year. My goal is B1." He pictured his journal, the 500 hours of practice he'd racked up. "I don't need to be good right now." He sipped his shake again. "Uncle Jamie said 10,000 hours. I only have 521. I'll be the best later."

It only took a second before his mom said, "Okay." His mom smiled when she said it. His dad was mostly smiling, too.

At his grandparents' house, Gus and his dad went up to his mom's old room while she talked to Big Gus and Gram. "This spot," Gus said, pointing at the middle of the bookshelf. "This was where she thought her Olympic medal was supposed to go."

"Mmm-hmmm," his dad said. He was standing by the bed, looking at the last pictures of his mom on Team USA. "How do you feel about her not getting it?"

Gus shrugged. "It stinks, but did she try her best?"

"Yeah, buddy." His dad smiled. "She did."

"Then it's okay." He took a few steps toward the bed and pulled a little box out from under it. "Gram showed me this one," Gus said. "Do you know about it?"

"I've never seen it before." Gus was pleased that he was the one with the secret.

"It's the stuff she didn't want to put on the wall or in the albums.

But Gram kept it because losing is part of the story, too." Gus opened the box and ran his hand over the old newspaper on top. The article was about the World Championships, the last tournament his mom had played in with Team USA. In the old picture, her head was on the ice just like Georgie's had been at Nova. In the background, the photographer had captured Canadian players hugging and throwing their gloves. The caption read, "The agony of defeat: Leigh Mackenzie of Liston Heights, MN, and her team come up short in World Championship final vs. Canada." "See?" Gus asked his dad. "She was on the ice at the very end. Look how tired she is."

"You're a smart kid," Gus's dad said. And at that moment, his mom and grandparents came in. Gram's eyes looked puffy as if she'd been crying.

"What are you guys doing?" his mom asked.

"We're thinking about you and hockey," Gus said, and he went to her and hugged.

CHAPTER SIXTY-ONE

LEIGH MACKENZIE

January 2023

Leigh's parents were unbelievably gracious when she told them about Jeff. She wasn't sure what she'd been expecting, but it wasn't the bear hug from her dad and her mom's gentle hair-stroking. Leigh felt eighteen again, her high school team losing in the quarter-final of the Minnesota state tournament, the recipient of her parents' soothing condolences.

"What an awful human being," Leigh's mom said.

"Jeff, you mean?" Leigh asked.

"Well, obviously!" Her mom took a break from stroking her hair to whack the crown of Leigh's head. "I don't mean *you*!"

Leigh laughed, but still felt sort of awful. "I don't know what's going to happen with Charlie," Leigh admitted to them. "You might have been right, Dad. We might have rushed things." Leigh looked at her father, whose stony eyes had a few tears in them.

"Rushed things?" he asked.

"Our engagement. I know you thought that was crazy."

Leigh's dad squinted. "Are you talking about twenty years ago? How I was nervous twenty years ago that you were too young to get married?"

"Yeah. Your hands were shaking when we toasted." Leigh realized she'd been trying to prove him wrong all this time, just like she'd been secretly making things up to Charlie. In doing that, she'd kept Charlie from really getting close to her. She thought being lonely was part of her punishment. And she'd done the same thing with her parents. Leigh didn't tell them any of the hard stuff, so they didn't have to worry about her getting married at twenty-two. She'd wanted to make it easy for them to believe in her.

Now, her dad laughed and squeezed Leigh's hand. "Leigh, you've had a happy and successful marriage for twenty years. Clearly, I was wrong to be worried. Charlie is one of us! He's been one of us from the very beginning. And Gus—" He couldn't finish, and put a hand over his mouth.

Leigh kept crying, too. She remembered watching from the sidelines as Charlie stumbled across the finish line at his first ultramarathon all those years ago. She'd fallen back and watched from the side. After Charlie had had his moment under the inflatable arch finish line, she joined the Mackenzie group hug, Charlie right in the middle of all of them.

"You can fix this, sweetheart," Leigh's dad said. Her mom kissed her head. "All the pieces are already there. And don't forget, you're good for Charlie, too. He's lucky in a million ways."

When they joined Gus and Charlie in her old bedroom, Gus was holding a newspaper photo of Leigh losing the World Championship game.

"Why are you crying?" Gus asked. He grabbed her middle.

"I'm just remembering things." Leigh sniffed. She patted Gus's head and glanced at Charlie. His eyes looked curious, not angry. "Hey." Leigh stepped toward Gus and took the newspaper from him. "Look at this!" She held it up for her parents. "I haven't seen this photo in years. That was such a great game. My last game for Team USA."

"But you lost." Gus whispered it.

Leigh shrugged. "It's still pretty cool to be second in the world. Right?" She looked at Charlie again. He sipped in a breath and held it. Leigh eyed the empty Olympic medal spot. It had glared for years, but now it looked small. She stooped to fit the newspaper in there, bending it a little in the middle so it stayed upright against the plaques on either side. "There," she said. "That'll be good at least until you two downsize." She punched her dad in the shoulder. "Condo this spring?"

"Don't rush me." Leigh's dad grabbed Gus in one of his characteristic bear hugs. "How's my Nova finalist?"

"Did my parents tell you?" Gus led the way out of the room. "I'm going to play on the B-team next year. No Nova; that's only for As. But, Big Gus, you can still come to the games. I'll still be in the Lions uniform."

Big Gus looked over his shoulder at Leigh, his eyebrow cocked. "I don't care what level, kid," he said. "I just love watching you play. Same as I felt about your mom."

Leigh's mom shut the door behind them, leaving Leigh and Charlie in the bedroom. "I get it now." Leigh touched the newspaper clipping with her index finger, the photo of her old self.

"What do you mean?"

"Gus wants to play on the B-team. I get it. He wants to be the person everyone counts on, win or lose." She sighed and smiled at the photos over her bed. "I want him to do what he wants."

"Okay." Leigh couldn't read Charlie's expression. His phone pinged, and he grabbed it out of his pocket. "Yes!" Charlie punched the air next to his ear.

"What?" Leigh wanted to peek, but there was a space still between them. She wasn't sure if she was allowed in.

Charlie grinned as he scrolled. "It's the Headwaters lottery. I'm in again."

"After all this time!" Leigh's tears kept flowing. She pictured herself younger, in shape, waiting for Charlie at their prearranged spot on the trail. "I'll crew for you!" Leigh blurted. "The whole thing this time, not just the last stop."

"What?" Charlie looked up. "No, that's okay." He shook his head. "That's too much. You'll have to be able to run like fifteen trail miles to get around the course that day. You don't have time to get ready. I appreciate the idea, though."

"I do have time." Leigh could hit the hotel gyms instead of the bars on her trips. And Nicole would probably be thrilled to train with her. They'd add some weekend runs, get some use out of the trail shoes Leigh's mom had bought her that summer, and she'd get some fitness in if she coached hockey with Susy. "I've got six months, right?" Leigh counted on her fingers. "The race is still in July?"

Charlie stepped toward her and opened his arms. "Six months. Yep. You've got those. But let's just maybe think about one month at a time."

"What do you mean?"

"I mean, I don't want to throw away our life. Can we build something different? Just try some things out? I want you to be my closest friend again. I saw you in that T-shirt."

"Yes." Leigh breathed in his familiar scent, Tide and coffee. "I love you." She sobbed as she said it. "I have always loved you so, so much."

She could feel Charlie's nose in her hair as he squeezed her harder.

CHAPTER SIXTY-TWO

LEIGH MACKENZIE

March 2023

Um," Leigh said to Susy when they sat down with Charlie and Arnie at the Steel Toe Brewery. "I can't believe you said 'summer' hockey when practice starts in March."

"You're in the State of Hockey," Susy said. "Hockey season is twelve months long. Accept it."

Gus had been to baseball tryouts the previous weekend. He'd told Leigh and Charlie he could forgo a few hockey hours to spend some time on the other sport he loved. He'd do a few sessions with Greystone to keep his skills sharp, but third base would occupy most of his headspace that spring and summer.

Susy hadn't liked the idea of Gus skipping the A-team tryouts, but on a run—their first together, though Susy hadn't won the Headwaters lottery—Leigh explained that she and Charlie were leaving the decision to him.

"I guess that's the only way," Susy had said.

"All right," Arnie said at the bar. "Susy, let me see your roster."

"You're familiar with the girls' players, too?" Charlie asked. He put his arm around Leigh, and she reached up and squeezed his fingers.

"A good fan doesn't limit himself to one gender." Arnie whipped his reading glasses from his breast pocket and took the list that Susy had removed from her file folder. "Okay," he said. "Bella is top tier, for sure." Arnie kept reading. "Kaia. Solid." He scanned the rest. "Clara. Yes. Brielle! Awesome, and, of course, Georgie." He looked up, clearly impressed. "Suse, how did you get all of these girls so last minute?"

Susy and Leigh grinned at each other, and Leigh answered. "Arnie, come on. Two former members of Team USA with a Ms. Hockey, two national titles, seven All-America distinctions, and two Olympic medals between them?" Leigh shrugged. "You think we can't pluck a few top dogs from their all-male teams and make something better? We've got a new logo, too, and a new name. The Blue Ox."

"Like Babe the Blue Ox?" Arnie smiled. "Babes, like women?"

"Right!" Leigh offered him a high five. "But also feminist. And our gear is going to be the coolest, too. Abe's gonna be jealous."

"I'm impressed," Arnie said. "And, Leigh, it's nice of you to join us here in our very own Youth Hockey Hub."

"Well, I have to help Charlie with his research." She lifted her IPA and clinked it with her husband's.

"Research?" Susy asked.

"I started a new project." Charlie's cheeks were pink, and he bounced a little on his forefeet, so excited he couldn't contain it.

"Tell us!" Susy said.

"It's offbeat," Charlie warned.

Leigh agreed. His new novel was offbeat. In fact, she'd described it as "delightfully weird" when Nicole had asked her about it on one of last week's runs. He'd written six chapters already, with a goal of finishing by August.

"It's a mystery," Charlie told them. "Set in a brewery." He drew a circle in the air, indicating all of Steel Toe. "The brewmaster is a true-crime enthusiast, and he finds a severed hand in his fermenter."

Leigh broke in. "Think Angela Lansbury infused with Gaston, like from *Beauty and the Beast*. Lots of flannel and blood."

"Does the severed hand belong to Jeff Carlson?" Susy smirked and sipped her stout. Leigh whacked at her upper arm. "Too soon?" Susy asked. They both knew Jeff's case was proceeding through Safe Sport arbitration. Leigh would have to testify that summer, as would Sydney, Alison, and Sheila.

But Leigh had decided not to think too hard about it in the meantime. As arbitration pended, Liston Heights Hockey had suspended Jeff from the board. There had been a lot of pressure after the story ran with his name in it and with new supporting quotes from the other women and from Susy. He'd barraged Leigh with text messages, but she'd blocked his number after writing just one response about seeking a restraining order. His lawyer must have advised him to desist.

"The book sounds genius," Arnie interrupted. "We should probably keep making the brewery rounds, right? Check out a lot of establishments to help you with your setting for your new novel? New series?"

Charlie raised his glass and they all clinked.

The next week, Leigh felt as nervous as she had been in the '01 World Championship final as she packed her bag for her first triple-A practice. She kept checking each piece of gear, including a new helmet, complete with a die-cut Blue Ox sticker, and new skates.

She'd finally asked her parents what had happened to her old stuff, and her mom had admitted that she'd donated it to the Liston Heights youth association years ago.

"I didn't think we needed to hang on," Leigh's mom had said. "Honey, I didn't know you were hanging on." They had hugged, and when they separated, Leigh's mom had put her hands on her cheeks like she had when she was a little girl.

In the end, the Blue Ox practice was easy. All Leigh had to do was follow Susy's directions—lead the Russian circles drill, shoot at the goalies, ref the scrimmage. The girls were friendly and cooperative. At the end, Susy hugged Leigh as the two of them left the locker room.

"That was so flipping fun," Leigh said, surprising herself with her fervor.

"Do you want to get a drink?" Susy asked. "Late dinner?"

"Next week for sure, okay? Tonight, we're having dinner with my parents." The Blue Oxen were scheduled to practice twice a week in the early season, but Leigh would be there for only half of ice time until after Headwaters. She couldn't very well abandon her job in order to pursue fitness full-time.

"Sure thing." Susy gave her a thumbs-up as they headed to their respective cars.

Before Leigh could knock on the door at her parents' house, Gus flung it open. "Were you on time?"

She walked through her parents' front door and helped herself to several green and yellow gumdrops from the dish in the entry. "Yes, Speed Racer," she said.

"You're a role model now," Gus said earnestly.

Leigh lightly flicked his head. "I'm glad I've got you looking out for me."

Charlie rounded the corner and kissed Leigh's forehead. "Gus has been very concerned about your first practice. Worried you've lost a step or two."

Big Gus was there then. "Ice still feel the same? Did you break a hip?"

"Real nice." Leigh rolled her eyes. "Your confidence in me is overwhelming."

"Hey!" Leigh's mom walked in from the kitchen. "Gus has a surprise for you. Come on." She grabbed Leigh's hand and pulled her toward the stairs. When they all got to the bedroom door, Gus was there in front of her, his head nearly level with Leigh's shoulder. He'd shot up that year as a fourth grader. Before too long, he'd outgrow her.

Gus's dimples deepened as he grinned at the bookshelf. "I filled the spot," he said.

"What spot?" Leigh glanced at everyone, not understanding.

Gus lifted his eyebrows and led Leigh over to the bookcase, to the place where her Olympic medal was always supposed to go. Now, in front of the old newspaper clipping she'd put there a couple of months before, there was also Gus's medal from Nova, the red ribbon hanging down in front of an NCAA All-American plaque. And next to that was a thick cut of wood with peeling birch bark still attached. Leigh smiled. It was the Headwaters medal, "finisher" written on it in Sharpie.

Leigh touched both of the medals and smiled back at everyone. Nothing was missing. No hole in the memories.

"It's good, right?" Gus pulled her hand, and Leigh smiled down at him. "We've all got something there, now. Mackenzie Row."

"Yeah." She grabbed Gus in the kind of bear hug her own dad was famous for. "It's perfect."

ACKNOWLEDGMENTS

This book was a total team effort. Let's see how many mixed sports metaphors I can cram into this note.

My editor, Kerry Donovan, quarterbacked the whole thing and called the most brilliant audible as the clock ran down. This sentence right here is the equivalent of me dousing her with Gatorade. Joanna "capital K" MacKenzie coached me through the initial drafts of this novel and retreated with me into my corner when I felt clobbered. I'm lucky to have such a wonderful partner and advocate.

Chadd Johnson, my friend and a brilliant story editor, sank so many clutch threes on this thing. If ever there were a book in which to feature his 5x7, this would be the one. Nicole Kronzer stood at the fifty-yard line with compression wraps, ice packs, oxygen masks, and tough talk. I've never written a real-life pal into a story before, but the Nicole in this book is the same wonderful person I know in real life. Bradeigh Godfrey and Alison Hammer stepped up to pitch hit with precision and efficiency. Nigar Alam and Stacy Swearingen flanked me in the dugout for the duration. Adriana Matzke led the drills, corrected my form, and cheered me along. She and William Matzke (also played by himself) fixed all the hockey in this book and only laughed at me intermittently for making so many silly mistakes.

My other early readers crushed it, as usual. Thanks again to Jordan Cushing, Lee Heffernan, KK Neimann, Dan West, and Miriam Williams. Please keep reading for me forever. And thank you, Ink Tank, for the daily infusion of encouragement and friendship.

I had a lot of extra hockey help from Tricia Dunn-Luoma, Sarah Tueting, Madeline Wethington, and the Bisbee family, especially Alex. Certainly, there are sports inaccuracies in this book, but none of them are the fault of the Matzkes or these other brilliant and passionate experts. Thank you, thank you all for your generosity and patience.

Erin Dady fielded a bunch of my ill-informed questions about business school and government relations (Leigh isn't in that profession anymore, but she used to be!); Rachel Hatten schooled me on Tampa (all those chapters got cut, but now I know a lot about Tampa!); and Doug Neimann, Adam Piatkowski, and Dobby West walked me through the X's and O's of money and private equity over and over again within the span of a few tense weeks right before this book was due. If Leigh is bad at her (new) job, it's not the fault of these savvy professionals.

The Berkley crew went back to the well to make this book happen. Thank you to Mary Baker, Megan Elmore, Randie Lipkin, Jessica Mangicaro, Tara O'Connor, Emily Osborne, Craig Burke, Claire Zion, and Jeanne-Marie Hudson. And thanks to Kathleen Carter, who so skillfully filled out our roster.

Booksellers, you continue to inspire me with your energy and passion. Thanks especially to Pamela Klinger-Horn, Mary O'Malley, and Annie Metcalf for all the high-fives, backslaps, and heartfelt support.

I have loved sports since middle school, and I am delighted to have written a book about how important athletics can be. Thank you to the inspiring women coaches in my life: René Gavic, Jordan Cushing, and Maggie Bowman. I continue to be buoyed by strong women in sport, and my kids and I are mentored by the best.

I also want to thank my family and friends. No one welcomes me into the huddle like they do. Thanks to my parents and siblings and in-laws. And thank you to my hometown team, Mac, Shef, and Dan. I couldn't really do anything without you three, and I wouldn't really want to. Our dogs mostly deterred my efforts here, to be honest, but I do love them a lot.

Okay everybody, hands in! "Novel" on three!